Air & Darkness

by

AK Nevermore

The Dae Diaries, Book Two

Copyright Notice
This is a work of fiction. Names, characters, places, and incidents are either the product of the author's imagination or are used fictitiously, and any resemblance to actual persons living or dead, business establishments, events, or locales, is entirely coincidental.

Air & Darkness

COPYRIGHT © 2024 by AK Nevermore

All rights reserved. No part of this book may be used or reproduced in any manner whatsoever without written permission of the author or The Wild Rose Press, Inc. except in the case of brief quotations embodied in critical articles or reviews.
Contact Information: info@thewildrosepress.com

Cover Art by *Lisa Dawn MacDonald*

The Wild Rose Press, Inc.
PO Box 708
Adams Basin, NY 14410-0708
Visit us at www.thewildrosepress.com

Publishing History
First Edition, 2024
Trade Paperback ISBN 978-1-5092-5647-1
Digital ISBN 978-1-5092-5648-8

The Dae Diaries, Book Two
Published in the United States of America

Dedication

Somewhere between book one and two of the Dae Diaries, my mindset morphed from angsty to amused. I got one hell of a chuckle writing this book, and hope my readers do, too. I mean, without imagining you guys snickering inappropriately in some doctor's office, coming up with batshit scenarios isn't even half as much fun.

Now I need to thank a bunch of people. In particular, my editor, Eilidh MacKenzie, for putting up with my crap and heinous use of commas, and my family for putting up with me in general. Your sufferance is noted and much appreciated. To the cast of ne'er-do-wells lurking about my life—except for Kristine—thank you for keeping me on my toes with the non-writing stuff and reminding me that life's more fun with a cocktail on the porch.

And finally, this book, dear reader, is for you, with a very special hat tip to my first reader, my harshest critic, and my biggest fan. I'm here because you were always there.

Thanks, Mom.

Character List

Envy Starr—A half daemon. The ember anathema was hidden in her chest by Silas, and after becoming on Midsummer's eve, Envy now shares consciousness with Lilith, the Mother of Daemons, Primordial of Fire.

Lilith—First wife of Adam in the Garden of Eden and Primordial fae of Fire trapped in the ember anathema by the Dowager.

Calista Starr—(Deceased) A human and Envy's mother, former Vegas showgirl, and ranking member of Our Lady of the Blessed Inferno. Long time paramour of Silas.

Silas—Envy's father and Calista's lover. Responsible for hiding the anathema in Envy's chest.

Kyle—A half sylph and Envy's former love interest. Consumed the feather anathema and now shares a consciousness with Samael, the All Father, Primordial of Air.

Berk—A half gnome and Envy's bestie. Consumed the pebble anathema and now shares a consciousness with Gaia, Mother Earth, Primordial of Earth.

Morgana —A half undine and Envy's formal rival for Kyle's affections. Consumed the droplet anathema and now shares a consciousness with Aegaeus, Father of Storms and Primordial of Water.

Brennan—A daemon contracted to prepare Envy to become fully fae and her eventual love interest. Suffered under a geas held by Amelda.

Karen—The imp in charge of Envy's affairs, married to Peter.

Peter—The imp in charge of Brennan's affairs and his

confidant, married to Karen.
Jonas—Brennan's bestie and one of the Riders of the Apocalypse (Conquest).
Amelda—(Deceased) Brennan's mother, married to Horatio, former queen of Clan Malten.
Horatio—(Deceased) Brennan's stepfather, married to Amelda. The Dowager's youngest son.
Mica—(Deceased) Brennan's evil older half brother via Amelda and Horatio.
Dowager—(Deceased) The reclusive, all-powerful matriarch of the Malten clan and the one responsible for trapping the Primordial elementals in the anathemas when she was known as Eris.
Serena—(Deceased) Brennan's evil ex-girlfriend, and Mica's long-time partner.

Groups

Riders of the Apocalypse—A band of fiends led by Brennan (Death) and consisting of Jonas (Conquest), Dan (War), Frank (Pestilence) and Stewie (Interim Death while Brennan was under his geas).
Our Lady of the Blessed Inferno—The cult responsible for most of the tensions between humans and Fae. They espouse that the Mother of Daemons will destroy the planet for the sin of humans copulating with fae.
Clan Malten—One of the five great dae families which Envy and Brennan relate to. Malten is also used as their sire name, though they are not related by blood.
The Imps—Imps serve as lackeys for Daemons. On paper, their loyalty was to the Dowager; in reality,

Brennan is their boss.

Places

Priory—The home base of Our Lady of the Blessed Inferno, currently lying in ruins.

Vel City—The hometown of Envy and the other halflings, located in the American Southwest.

Neither—The veil between planes of existence, aka the icky onion skin that's between Earth and Fae made of grey mist.

Fae—The plane where the fae live, broken into four realms, one for Earth, Fire, Water, and Air.

Mesa—The caldera of a large volcano at the center of the Fae realms where the Midsummer's eve festivities take place.

Terms

Normal—A human.

Halfling—A child of a human and a fae, forced to choose between becoming one with their element and fully fae or giving it up e ntirely to become fully human on the Midsummer's eve of their twentieth birthday.

Fae—Being made of elemental spirit falling into one of four categories, Air, Fire, Water, or Earth.

Fae-band—A piece of jewelry spelled to garner the total compliance of its wearer.

Elemental Lord or Lady—The most powerful category of elemental being, able to present themselves as human.

Lesser elemental—The most common elemental, lacking the ability to present themselves as humanoid.

Becoming—When a halfling gives into their elemental nature on the Midsummer's eve of their twentieth birthday, becoming one with their element and ceases to exist on the mortal plane.

Fading—When a halfling refuses to give into their elemental nature on the Midsummer's eve of their twentieth birthday, losing their spark and fading into a human existence.

Geas—A compulsion cast upon an individual.

Primordial fae—The original beings from which all four elements sprang; Samael, the All-Father, Primordial of Air; Gaia, Mother Earth, Primordial of Earth; Aegaeus, Father of Storms, Primordial of Water; and Lilith, Mother of Daemons, Primordial of Fire.

Speaking a Name—Knowledge of a person's true name gives the speaker complete control over them. When spoken in tandem, it allows the viewing of each other's souls and is considered a binding ceremony for the fae, equivalent to marriage.

Cleansing—The human practice of killing halflings on a semi-annual basis.

Anathema—The physical embodiments of the curse that entrapped the Primordial fae. Fire's was an ember, Water's a droplet, Air's a feather, and Earth's a pebble. Used to manipulate the power structure of Fae.

Elemental form—What a fae turns into when not presenting as a human.

Succubus—A rare daemon form that gives the ability to draw off the life essence of its victims and then use what it's taken as its own.

Fiend—An incredibly powerful and unstable daemon form prone to violence and destruction.

Before

When we last saw Adam...

Adam stood in prayer before his Creator: "Sovereign of the universe!" he said. "The woman you gave me has run away."

At once, the Holy One, blessed be He, sent three angels to bring her back.

Said the Holy One to Adam, "If she agrees to come back, what is made is good. If not, she must permit one hundred of her children to die every day."

The angels left God and pursued Lilith, whom they overtook in the midst of the sea, in the mighty waters wherein the Egyptians were destined to drown. They told her God's word, but she did not wish to return.

—Excerpt from Ben Sira's *Alphabet*

But I mean, come on...Would you?

17 Days, 6 Hours, 32 Minutes

Right, so quick recap if your night was anything like mine, and why, yes, alcohol was involved. Sobriety and I aren't really on speaking terms right now, but that's a common theme around here lately. Especially the not-speaking-to-me part.

Nope. Not bitter about it.

Anywho, the last time you and I chatted, I told you all about how I was set to die on Midsummer's Eve and uncovered an insidious plot to subjugate fae and normals alike. Yep. That whole clusterfuck of doom revolving around Lilith, the elemental goddess of fire, who'd been imprisoned in an anathema, then secreted away in my chest when I was a kid. Yeah, that sucked. I appreciate the condolences.

But spoiler, I didn't die. I did end up becoming fully fae and melding consciousnesses with her. Yup. For all intents and purposes, we're pretty much the same person now, insofar as her memories feel exactly like mine, and I have to deal with whatever messes she still has lying around.

Trust me, there's more than you'd think, and sharing my brain with a primordial deity sounds way cooler than it is. I mean, I guess we're making it work—well, I'm making it work. She's data dumping crap about my inherited past on a need-to-know basis. It's irritating as fuck, but a hell of a lot better than what my erstwhile friends have got going on. Not that Morgana was ever my friend, but—

Why, yes, suckering her, Berk, and Kyle into letting elemental gods wear them like meat suits was entirely my fault. Thanks for reminding me about that little tidbit. Guess I don't have to go into my why-they're-not-speaking-to-me spiel.

Ugh. Wise it. We're not here to talk about that. I mean, not yet anyways.

You wanted to know about the kid.

So, I know it's gonna be a shocker after how smoothly Midsummer's Eve and assimilating with Lilith had gone, but things took a nose dive prior to the blessed event. I mean, all Hell didn't break loose for another seventeen days, but whatever.

It all started with a goddamned raven.

Yeah, a raven. Fae are stupid about technology, and what happened totally wasn't my fault. I mean, Socks wouldn't have tried to eat a text. Hmm? Oh, sorry. Socks is my snake. You know, the one from the Garden of Eden. What? No, it's not his actual name, it's—look, you had to be there. We're talking about him eating the messenger. Well, attempting it.

Anyways, when Brennan, my dae-licious baby daddy and I—Yep, he was still putting up with my shit, and yep, it surprised me, too—had gotten back to our cliff-top flat after the whole Midsummer's debacle, it was seagull central. The miserable winged rats had taken over the place. Like, crap literally everywhere. Socks put the fear of God into them and developed a serious taste for birds in the process. Any stupid enough to land on the balcony had become a treat. So when the raven showed up, things got real, fast.

And let me tell you, it was pretty freaking funny seeing the imps go ape-shit trying to make him regurgitate the thing. Peter, Brennan's head house imp, has pics of it somewhere, along with one of everything else. Talk about Christmas gift turned obsession, imps are so—

Oh, the bird was fine, I mean, it was bedraggled as all hell, but it took off quickly enough. Brennan wasn't amused. Like, with anything aside from me since his fiend had been released. And after he read the snake-slobbered note that'd been tied to the raven's leg, his mood got even blacker.

"What's wrong?" I'd watched the entire fiasco from bed. It was either there or the couch these days. No lie, I was freaking huge.

Brennan mussed his hair. It wasn't slicked back anymore and was all messy, falling over his eyepatch. We were still negotiating his chin scruff. He was such a wimp about it being itchy. Still, half a sexy pirate was better than no sexy pirate.

Anyways, Brennan came over to lie against the pillows, lighting a cigarette. It flared.

Crap. That was never good.

"My father's asking to meet you."

Like I said, crap. Meeting the rest of his family had gone so well.

Not.

I didn't exactly glare at him, but the whole anathema-in-my-chest, people-wanting-me-dead thing was still a little raw. I'd gone nine solid months racking up days without incident and wasn't interested in breaking my streak.

He smiled like he knew what I was thinking and

exhaled a fitful stream of smoke. "It won't be anything like that, Lovely. Kennet has every reason to be as protective of you as I." He gave me that crooked smile of his, caressing the massive tumor I'd been toting around on his behalf.

I thought about taking his hand off at the wrist. What? Pirates have hooks.

And newsflash, in case you've never had the pleasure, being pregnant straight-up fucking sucks.

Don't look at me like that, I'm serious. The first few months are all about the vomit, followed by maybe three seconds where you're rockin' a cute bump. From there, it's a quick slide into the bloated, sluggy shape of a certain George Lucas-inspired space-gangster. Then the damn kid drops down, and you're straddling a bowling ball, waddling around like a constipated duck. Ironically, it's mainly to the bathroom.

Ugh. I hated it. I'm supposed to be the gold bikini chick!

I know, I know, first fae born of fae in like, I don't know, a couple millennia. Blah, blah, blah. Apparently, it was a huge deal. I didn't care. I mean, I didn't wish the little bastard any ill will—Yeah, all right, that wasn't totally true. I was four days past my due date, and the longer it hung out in there, the more I thought about selling it to the circus.

Oh my God, please. Like Brennan would let me. You should see the nursery he'd set up.

He was watching my face while all of this went through my head, and I could tell he was just freaking tickled. I hated him, too. Well, maybe not totally. It was hard to hate someone who spoiled the crap out of you. Karen, my version of Peter, might give foot massages to die for, but Brennan could work my hips like nobody's business.

Yeah, I meant that the way it sounded.

I rolled onto my side, and he started rubbing one of them like I'd rung Pavlov's bell. I wiggled a little hoping Brennan would ring mine. I'd read somewhere that sex can trigger labor, and that was a hell of a lot more palatable than shooting back castor oil. I swear they made shit up just to see how desperate pregnant women were.

Of course I tried it. And the match-by-the-toe crap.
Shut up.

Brennan laughed and kissed my temple. "Karen says any moment—"

"She's been saying that for a week." And yes, an imp was my obstetrician. We'd bridged that gap between Brazilian and baby. Brennan's thumbs hit something just right, and I gave a little moan, tipping my rear.

"If you keep arching like that, this is going to digress rather quickly." He kissed under my jaw. I arched more, and he chuckled low in his throat. "But you'd like that, wouldn't you?"

Duh.

Being pregnant also kicked your libido into high gear. Well, mine anyways. He wasn't complaining, and the situation did digress. Progress. Mmm. Like I said, man could work my hips. He was no slouch working his, either.

Anywho, the only response it triggered was my eyes rolling back into my head and a brief conversation with the Almighty. Not that that was anything to sneeze at. Guess we'd have to try that whole stimulating-labor deal again later. Aw, shucks.

So there I was, staring at the ceiling with a smile on my face. I should've just kept my mouth shut, but we all know that's not one of my fortes.

"I thought you were tight with your dad before Amelda banded you."

Hmm? Oh. Long story. Brennan's mother used a fae-band to put a geas on him, locking away the fiend, aka his elemental nature. Needless to say, he has—well had, considering she's dead too—mommy issues.

"Why are you upset your dad wants to meet me?"

"We were close"—Brennan reached for another cigarette—"but it's the way he asked. He's not coming as my father; he's coming as the Gwinth's representative."

I still didn't see the problem. The Gwinth leads the wild hunt, which is basically all the unredeemable nasties of Fae. Think of it as a prison work-release program, and he's the warden, with a really stupid title. I mean, who the heck wants to be known as the Gwinth? You'd think—

Hmm? No, you're not missing anything. I totally sealed off the Fae realms from Earth by filling the Neither with crazy bug-zapper spray foam after I became. What? The Neither? It's a veil between Earth and Fae. Kinda like that gross, super-thin onion-skin slime that's not a part of the layers and only exists to mess with your tacos. Same deal with the Neither, but now everyone's proverbial taco is safe, because ain't nothin' getting through what I flung in there.

Not that there's a ton of fae left in the realms to request visas.

Brennan had once made a comment about elemental lords being assholes and lesser fae preferring to chill out on Earth. Little did I know at the time that the imps had put the word out, and ninety percent of Fae's populace jumped ship when they heard what was going down. The wild hunt came along for the ride.

Yep. Fae had basically invaded.

Normals freaked. I suspect I couldn't blame them. I mean, waking up to find a boggart in the kitchen would definitely ruin my day, but most of that had been sorted. Brennan ran a tight ship and laid down the law pretty early on; normals were not food, and using them as entertainment was frowned upon. The lethal kind, at least.

And to make sure no one "forgot" the rules, Brennan had struck a deal with the hunt to terrify the lesser fae into compliance and to put a stop to normals snuffing out halflings. See, Our Lady of the Blessed Inferno had gained a ridiculous amount of popularity after I'd been blamed for frying their base of operations, and piety of the genocidal kind was at an all-time high. Normals actually made freaking pilgrimages out to that stupid divot in the desert where the Priory had been. Seriously, and I'm talking bus tours. They'd declared it a holy site, which made no freaking sense. Ugh. You'd think they'd listen after their professed deity told them to fuck off. And I had, verbatim. CNN was still airing the interview, and the sound bite was all over the internet. Trust me, I didn't stutter.

No wonder God was all absentee, and He'd only burned a bush.

Whatever. I'd taken a page from His book, and so had Berk, Kyle, and Morgana. They had their own worshippers, too. Kyle was the only one who got off on it. Last I'd heard, he was set up with a harem of honeys in a Himalayan shrine, but that'd been months ago. He and Brennan had gotten into it after Kyle, who was the closest thing I'd ever gotten to a boyfriend, had accidentally-on-purpose poofed in on me in the shower.

Yeah, that didn't go over well.

God, how the hell did we get here? Whoever tells you baby brain isn't a real thing is full of crap. This stupid kid was literally sucking everything out of me but my will to live, and that was a fine line some days. It needed to freaking go. Like, get a job already.

What? Did I know if it was a boy or girl? Really? We were talking about Brennan's father coming as the Gwinth's representative. Stop distracting me.

"Is him visiting a bad thing?"

"Potentially. Though it will be good to see him. It's been a long time." He smiled and his eye laughed at me. Hmm? Oh. His half brother gouged the other one out in a mega-dick move that ended up with him dead. It'd grown back, but Brennan still couldn't see out of it. Trying gave him a headache. "You'll need to dress for dinner. Jonas, Stewie, and the other Riders will be here, too. If it's a state visit, we need to show our strength."

I groaned. Not because Brennan's besties would be here. I just didn't want to get dressed. And judging by the sky outside, I didn't have a lot of time to do it.

Look, I'd never been big on clothes, until I was too big for my clothes, and I didn't care if I had a super imp who could whip me up whatever. Maternity anything was ugly. Christ, even the word maternity is horrible. It sounds like some kind of an institution that comes with bars, just like marriage.

Whatever. I lugged my stupid stomach into the bathroom and let Karen do her magic.

So, as much as I've bitched about being massive, I gotta give credit where credit is due. Karen really was a super imp. By the time she'd finished with me, I looked like some kind of fertility goddess...which I guess I technically am, but it's hard to remember that when you're picking sour cream and onion chips out of your cleavage.

That had become even more impressive than usual, I might add. My boobs, not the chips.

Anyways, I wasn't kidding about the goddess thing. Karen had swept my hair up and put me in some mauve, drape-y Grecian whatnot. Yeah, the color sucked, but after becoming, I'd lost the monochrome look and my seasonal skin tone had gone from a winter to a fall. She kept trying to expand my closet color-wise and knew she was pushing her luck with anything remotely pink. I glared at her, and she didn't even try to get me into shoes. Smart lady.

So, if you don't remember, the flat is pretty much this big terrarium on a cliff in the middle of the ocean. All the walls are glass, and as soon as I hit the hall, five sets of eyes plus one followed my progress to the dining room. They all stood, rapt. Don't ask me why, but apparently a pregnant fae is a serious turn-on. Brennan's expression made me want to grab him by the lapels and drag him right back into bed. Jonas looked like he wanted to eat me, but he always looked like that. Him and the rest of the Riders. Well, not Stewie, but he was way into dudes and making some serious eyes at Brennan's dad.

I couldn't fault him there. Kennet was a smokin' hot older guy. Kind of a Sean Connery meets Robert Downey Junior. Brennan had said he'd been a Welsh chieftain before the hunt had picked him up. I could totally imagine him in a kilt instead of his khaki trousers and crisp polo. He definitely had this whole pagan badger vibe going on with his mullet and grey-streaked goatee. Is it weird that a mullet was sexy? On him it was. He intercepted me on my way to Brennan with the same crooked grin.

"And ye can be none other than Envy." Yeah, he totally had that panty-dropping brogue. He took my hands in his, kissing my cheek. I blushed, and he gave a deep-throated laugh. "Gah, she's a beaut. How the hell did a shite like ye land this one?"

"It was entirely her idea." Brennan came to stand at my side, putting an arm around my waist.

I shifted my weight to lean against him, and he kissed my temple. The flash and wind of Peter's camera sounded in the hall, and I tried not to roll my eyes.

Brennan caught my struggle and smiled. "Let's find your seat, shall we, Lovely?" He escorted me over to the long ebony and chrome table and pulled out my chair. The Riders sat down as I did. Kennet took the seat across from me, and Brennan the one at the end, between us.

"No accounting for taste then." Kennet smiled and gave me a wink.

I smiled back, and so did Brennan.

"None whatsoever, though I'm not about to correct her. We've a very satisfying arrangement."

His father picked up the glass of scotch Peter had just poured him. "And what is that, exactly?"

"I think we've settled on intended."

"Intentions are for shite. Ye need to snap her up before someone else does, laddie buck."

"That's entirely her choice." Brennan's voice had an

edge to it that made me look up. He still had the fiend under wraps, but that became touch and go where I was concerned, and Kennet grunting like he didn't agree wasn't setting a great course for how this evening was gonna play out.

I think his dad knew. He tried to recover with a brilliant smile. "I'm starved! What've ye got t'eat? Nothing green, I hope."

I looked over the dishes the imps were setting out, surprised. It was not our usual fare. Brennan's tastes ran by way of French gourmet. This was pretty much Cracker Bucket take out. There were beans that might've once qualified as green, but they sure didn't now.

Jonas winked at me from just past them, already loading his plate with meatloaf. I'd say out of all the Riders of the Apocalypse, he was probably the most intimidating with his piranha teeth, tusks, and scar-pocked hide, but after catching Brennan's bestie and the other guys crocheting granny squares? Not so much. In their defense, the resulting blanket had a skull on it, but still. You can't unsee that.

"Lookin' real good, Miss Kitty," he noted midmouthful. "When you gonna pop that kitten?"

I glowered at him, and he laughed.

"Any time now," Brennan said, filling his plate along with the others.

God, I was tired of hearing that. Peter put a salad in front of me, and I blessed him, though I was planning on snagging some of that mac-n-cheese, constipation be damned. Kennet moved the entire platter of country ham in front of himself. No one but me batted an eye.

"How's huntin'?" Jonas asked him.

Kennet gave a little shrug, ignoring the fork and

taking his own knife out from God knows where. He sliced and stabbed a chunk of meat, then nibbled on it as neat as you please. "Routed more of them fanatics. It's like playin' whack-a-mole, but the host enjoys it."

I frowned as I chewed. Stupid cult. How the hell do you get people to unfollow you? I wished it was as easy as being banned from social media.

Don't ask.

"Ye've done well with the lesser dae. Can't say we've had much call t'keep them in line. Them damn naiads is another story. It's like nobody's runnin' the bloody show for Water."

"The holder of that anathema hasn't transitioned well," Brennan said, saving me from answering. He knew I felt like shit about the whole Morgana thing. Hmm? Yeah, seriously. It was bad. "Your note said you had the Gwinth's business to discuss."

Kennet finished chewing, then glanced over at him with a sigh. "Well, I suspect now's as good a time as any. He's sent me t'open up negotiations with Envy for her next consort."

Crap.

The temperature in the room instantly dropped about thirty degrees and filled with murk and shadows. Brennan's eye glimmered like ice. "Envy is mine."

"Then ye better put a ring on it."

I laughed. Come on, Sean Connery quoting Beyoncé? That's freaking classic.

Oh, I guess I should explain. Fae queens are required to have a consort. Yet another stupid fae rule and part of the whole power-being-tied-to-fertility thing. Although I was about as graceful as a humpback in the Sahara right now, I could also command more power than I knew what to do with, and that filtered down to every other Fire elemental. While I carried Brennan's child, he was my consort by default, but because I hadn't made it official, as soon as I gave birth, I had a year and a day to choose my next consort. Conversely, if some wily fae managed to get me pregnant again before that, they would gain the title. Good fucking luck there. Fool me once, and all that.

Brennan wasn't as amused. Like, at all. He pushed his plate away and lit a cigarette. It didn't quite incinerate. "I did, and he's a bit premature, don't you think?"

"Banding isn't the same, and ye damned well know it. In case ye hadn't noticed, with the veil sealed up, there's a dearth of fae ladies."

He was right about that. Just me and Berk. Well, kind of Berk. He had the right equipment after merging with Mother Earth and the inclination for dudes had always been there, but wrapping his head around the mechanics of being in a female form was a whole 'nother story. I mean, he was pretty zen about the anathema turning him into a woman, all things considered, but definitely not up for dating.

Morgana? I don't want to talk about her.

Brennan's teeth gritted together at the "dearth of fae ladies" comment. "What's your point?"

"S'what I told you, man. Normals ain't gettin' knocked up by us no more." Jonas winked at me from around his mouthful of potatoes. "We've been tryin' our damndest to do our civic duty and all, but no dice."

Brennan stared daggers at him, and Jonas shrugged, going back to his plate.

I tried to chew real quiet.

Kennet turned to Brennan. "The Gwinth needs an heir, and he's running out of time." The temperature dipped again, like, enough for me to see my breath. "Mind yerself, laddie. Ye know better. It's politics, same as me and yer stepma. Don't mean what's between ye has t'change, save for whose babe she's carryin'." Kennet took another bite of ham like he was totally at ease, but a bead of sweat was tracking down his temple, despite the chill.

With good reason. The shadows had thickened into a sentient darkness and begun threading across the table. Oh, trust me, it was aware. With his fiend released, Brennan acted as a kind of doorway for it, letting it in from wherever it hung out. I was pretty sure that wasn't someplace you'd want to go on vacation. It listened to him, but the damned stuff took liberties when it thought it could get away with it. I mean, it always gave me a wide berth, but the rest of them weren't so lucky. Case in point, a tendril flicked against Stewie's forearm, and he flinched, making the gin fizz in his glass jump as he went to take a sip. It was totally messing with him, independent of Brennan's will.

He wasn't having it. Brennan stood, slamming his hands down onto the table, scattering it back to the corners of the room. He yelled at Kennet in some rough, guttural language. His father's face spiked red, and he answered in kind. The Riders all subtly shifted in their seats.

Me? I sat there, feeling sick.

Look, I told you, the Gwinth is like the warden for the wild hunt. He's under some geas that allows him to hold them together, you know, keep them focused on whatever their chosen prey might be. It's a tough job. So tough that he gets serious burnout, and every couple hundred years the geas needs to be passed on, along with the ridiculous title, to an heir of his body. That's another of those stupid fae rules. Pretty sure Water came up with that one; they're big on nepotism.

So what did this have to do with me? If the Gwinth couldn't pass on the geas, it would kill him. That would give all those fae nasties a get out-of-jail-free card. That was bad. Like, releasing a couple hundred bloodthirsty psycho fae on unsuspecting normals bad, and according to those same stupid fae rules—

"Och! Ye damned well know once she has yer babe, she's back on the table!"

My head snapped around to glare at Kennet. I might've hissed. Everyone at the table looked at me like I did. "You can stop talking about me like I'm not here, and I'm not some freaking broodmare. I don't see how any of this is my problem. I might be the only female fae this side of the veil, but he's not the only male I could choose as consort."

Okay, so I totally could see how it was my problem, I mean, potentially. Having all those degenerate fae running amok would be bad for everyone, but I'm not exactly a take-one-for-the-team kind of gal.

Kennet glared at Brennan, running a hand through his hair as he sat back down. "The Gwinth disagrees. He's setting this as his wergild for ye trapping the hunt here."

I laughed. Guess who didn't.

"You expect us to believe he's just thinking of the succession now?" Brennan seethed, dropping into his chair. His glass of cognac had a rime of ice coating it. I couldn't remember ever seeing him so pissed. It was almost scarier than hot.

"Nay, but ye damn well know the Cleansing wiped out nearly every halfling this side of the veil, and his other get are back in Fae. As long as he's trapped here, none can assume his mantle."

My pulse was very loud in my ears. Being reminded of the halfling genocide that'd been kicked off courtesy of my mother didn't help. Neither did knowing that the handful of halflings still breathing were on lockdown with the lesser fae. Yeah. "For their safety." True though it might be, it was still a raw fucking deal.

What the hell was it with me and unintended consequences? Literally, all I'd wanted to do was leave all that fae bullshit behind me. Well, that and screw a bunch of people over in the process, but it wasn't supposed to screw me back even figuratively, never mind in the biblical sense. My stigmata crackled across my skin. Kennet's gaze jumped to me, and I locked it down with mine.

"The Gwinth can go fuck himself. He should've been in the Fae realms with them. It's not my job to bail out his dumb ass."

The look of sorrow that crossed Kennet's face was a surprise. So was the ultimatum he slapped down. "He thought ye might feel that way. I'm t'tell ye that he'll allow ye time t'have the babe, then he'll release one of the huntsmen every night until ye agree to let him pay ye court."

Allow me? My blood pressure went through the—

Every glass in the room exploded, and Kennet landed on his back, still in his chair. Brennan had gone over the table and held the man's own knife to his throat.

Yeah…like I said, Brennan's control over his fiend

had gotten dicey. His dad was a hell of a lot calmer than he had any right to be.

"Ye really want it t'go this way, lad?"

"There's not a fucking chance that son of a bitch is getting anywhere near Envy. I don't care who or how many he releases. He'll not be blackmailing her into his bed." Brennan spat to the side and pushed off him. The knife clattered to the ground.

He moved to my side and put a hand on my shoulder, watching his father pick himself up. Brennan's breath came fast, and his touch was so cold it burned. The Riders circled behind Kennet, all of them grim. He shook glass out of his hair and laughed, regardless of the cuts peppering his skin.

"As ye said, that's entirely her choice." His eyes met mine. "He's giving ye till the first sunset after the babe comes t'decide. He'll send a raven for yer answer; try t'keep the serpent from the next one." Then that brilliant smile crossed his face, and his cheek dimpled at Brennan. "Well done gettin' the drop on me, laddie. Next time ye won't find it so easy."

"Next time you'll be dead."

His father's eyes freaking sparkled. "There's a good lad."

And poof, he was gone.

17 Days, 2 Hours, 8 Minutes

"Bro, you got problems," Jonas said, sucking in his bottom lip. Brennan glared at him, but didn't disagree. "Any of the host gets loose and it's gonna be a shit storm I ain't keen on cleanin' up."

The other Riders grunted, shuffling the shattered glass beneath their feet. They'd all been hit with the stuff, but most of the superficial wounds were already closed. None of them would meet Brennan's eye.

"So you'd have me stand aside—"

"Whoa, whoa, I ain't sayin' that. Man just wants to court her. Miss Kitty ain't obligated to do nothin' but let him waste his breath." The temperature in the room increased marginally. "And he ain't totally wrong…Yeah, you got yours, but all the rest of us got is needs. You know normals is like snackin' on chips. After a while, man wants a steak."

They were all looking at me, hungry. I took a deep breath, waiting for it.

Brennan crouched down beside my chair. "Can you open the Neither again, Lovely?"

And boom, there it was.

Look, when I sealed the goddamned thing off, I'd done it with the intention of buying myself, Kyle, Berk, and Morgana time to get a handle on assimilating the primordials the anathemas had contained. Since I'd had a head start at being a blessed vessel, I wasn't particularly worried about smacking down any uppity fae, but the others? Berk was struggling, I hadn't seen Kyle in months, and Morgana—

I didn't even want to think about that, but I couldn't clear the Neither without all of them.

"Not alone."

He reached out and turned the fae-band on my finger, looking up at me. My stomach flipped, knowing what he wanted, but I couldn't say yes, never mind "I do."

"It's too late in the game for that, bro," Jonas said softly behind him, sounding real sorry about it. Brennan hung his head.

Ugh, this was all my fault. "I'll talk to them. Maybe…"

It wasn't a maybe. Berk would probably agree, but the other two were gonna tell me to go piss up a rope. I'm sure Kyle would find that hysterical in my present condition.

Jonas clapped Brennan on the shoulder. "Call if you need us."

He nodded, and they were gone. Sighing, he rested his forehead against my belly, then laughed, sitting back on his heels and rubbing at his brow. "Little bastard kicked me."

What? Didn't all expectant couples use terms of endearment for their spawn? Little bastard was a hell of a lot more palatable than "peanut" or "bean." Gag me.

The imps had come in and started cleaning. Brennan scooped me up and carried me through the mess. He'd deflected the shrapnel from me with his aura, but walking over the stuff was a whole 'nother thing. Been there, done that, and it sucks. He took me out onto the balcony and got me situated, drawing my feet into his lap.

I closed my eyes as he started rubbing. I told you he spoiled me. There was a whisper against my ear as Socks slid around my neck. I laughed, answering him. What a wise-ass.

Hmm? Oh, no, we didn't like *talk* talk. It was more like telepathy, I guess. I didn't spend too much time thinking about it. I just did it, and it only worked with him.

"I hope he's telling you he's sworn off white meat."

"I'll tell if you do. What language was that?" I'd picked up Impese again pretty quickly, but whatever Brennan had been yelling at his father was gibberish. That wasn't a surprise. Most of my languages were dead. Like, since Mesopotamia dead.

"Cymric." Brennan sat back and pulled out his cigarette case. He tapped one of the nasty things on his knee. "I was reminding Kennet that his relationship with my stepmother wasn't something I'd wish to emulate. She poisoned the woman he loved and then sent men to murder me whilst I slept. I think I was twelve. That's when my stigmata came in. Shadow destroyed half of his castle and almost took me with it. He gutted the vile bitch and put her head on what was left of the outer bailey's walls. Her clan retaliated, and we had to wipe them out to see it finished."

He lit his cigarette and exhaled a long stream of smoke. "I've never seen anyone mow down men like he did. It's what got him taken up by the hunt. The earth ran red, and I helped him do it. For him to compare our relationship to his with my stepmother..." He chewed on his lip. "It's the absolute worst argument he could've made for me to allow this to proceed."

That word again. Uh, excuse me? You caught it right? Socks did. His head snapped around to flick his tongue at him.

"*Allow* this to proceed? Since when do you, or anyone else, *allow* me to do anything? Last I checked, I was the one who had to agree to the Gwinth's terms. You're not the one he wants to bang!"

"I…No, of course not, Lovely. I didn't mean it like that, but you can't expect me to just step aside and—"

"That's exactly what I expect! The last time you made a decision for me, I ended up saddled with this!" I pushed up from my chair, then fell back into it, a cramp ripping up through my gut. I gasped, and Brennan was at my side. Stupid Braxton Hicks. I bit the inside of my cheek, tasting blood. Ugh, I wanted this damn kid out!

And as soon as it was, the Gwinth would be all over me. Damn it.

"Shhh, calm yourself, Lovely," Brendan crooned. "Getting upset isn't good for you or the baby. Of course this is your decision. I didn't mean to suggest otherwise, only that—My God, Envy, I feel so helpless. My father is right, intentions are for shit. I want you as my wife. and the thought of you having to pander to that son of a bitch—"

"You know how I feel about that." I sat back in my chair, struggling to breathe normally. The cramping had stopped, but it'd been bad enough that I wasn't real keen on moving anytime soon.

Look, I loved Brennan, but Adam—as in the original douche and my first husband—had pretty much ruined marriage for me, and the idea of anyone having a "claim" on me rankled. I was with Brennan because I wanted to be…most days. I didn't care what fae society said or didn't say about it. If Elizabeth could rule freaking England without a husband, I sure as hell could do the same for a bunch of shithead dae.

If—damn it, when—we went back to the Fae realms.

Ugh. It was the last thing I wanted to do. The lesser dae were enough work, which is why I'd shopped it out to Brennan. I mean, I got it, he was doing all the work without the title or the bump in pay, and ironically, you would've thought I'd learned my lesson with that. Way back when, Lilith's lax leadership skills were what had ultimately gotten her trapped in that stupid anathema. Socks bumped against my cheek, and I scritched him. At least I had one stalwart companion.

Brennan sighed. "I know you're not keen on labeling our relationship, and I haven't pushed the issue, but I'm not Adam."

He was so sad when he said it, tears pricked at my eyes. Boy, did I feel guilty…probably because I was. I mean, not about the marriage stuff, but I was guilty of getting us into this whole stupid mess…

Look, we've already established that I've got some less-than-stellar character traits. One of them might've led me to extend the original infertility curse Lilith had cast right before I sealed the Neither, basically giving every male fae an enchanted vasectomy. What? Like they didn't freaking deserve it after leaving all their kids to die on the other side of the veil? Fuck them. And it's not like I couldn't reverse it…except that the thing with curses is you kind of had to be in the same place it was sent out from to call it back, which meant I had to be above the mesa, at the center of the Fae realms.

And we were back to clearing the Neither.

Oh come on, don't look at me like that. Fae are practically immortal. What's a century or two? I figured that'd be plenty long for us to get a handle on our powers and for the fae to learn their lesson. It would've worked out fine if the stupid Gwinth hadn't screwed it up.

Whatever. I felt bad, all right? All of it roiled up and made a gooey lump in my throat, then came out in a rush before I could stuff it back down. "I know you're not him, and I'm sorry, I don't mean to pick a fight, I just…" I squeezed my eyes shut and one of those stupid tears rolled down my cheek. "It's my fault. Before I sealed the Neither, I included male fae in my curse."

His face went very still as he wrapped his head around the steaming pile I'd just dropped.

"Because of what I did?"

He was talking about knocking me up without my consent. Yep. Total dick move, but I was over it. Most days. "No…well, maybe, I don't know. I-I did it so there wouldn't be any more halflings. No one should have to go through that." God, why did that hurt so much to say? I covered my face with my hands, sobbing. Yeah, I was totally being hormonal, but when you're in it, you're in it.

His arms were around me, carrying me back inside. He put me on the bed and pulled the pins from my hair, running it through his fingers as I wept against his chest. God, I was a pathetic mess.

"I'm pretty sure I know the answer but have to ask. Am I included in your curse?" I gave a little nod, and he chuckled, kissing the top of my head. "My God, Lovely, you don't do things by half, do you? Though, I suspect I deserve it."

I sniffled, sitting up. "You're not mad?"

"No more than you when I told you I'd intentionally gotten you pregnant. But that complicates the Gwinth's plans, now doesn't it? Unfortunately, I can't imagine he'll be very understanding. I know the man. Instead of wanting to court you, he'll demand the block on the Neither be lifted immediately." Brennan grabbed a cigarette from his case and lit it.

"We're going to have to buy enough time for you to convince the other primordials. Jonas is right about the huntsmen. Even one on the loose would be a nightmare." He drummed his fingers on his knee, like he was coming to a decision. "Stay still."

The temperature dipped enough for me to see my breath, and I shivered. Darkness rose up from the floor, covering me like a body stocking. I started to freak as it moved up my throat, coating my chin—

Brennan hushed me. "Easy, Lovely. The shadows will prevent anyone from getting a clear sense of you. I don't trust the Gwinth not to poof into your bed." He sat back and the chill dissipated.

I rubbed at my arms. Man, that was freaky. "He can't expect me to hop right back on that horse after the kid's here." Karen had already given me a stern talking to about the dangers of post-natal conjugal relations, and apparently Brennan had gotten his marching orders from Peter as well. I mean, I'd totally planned on ignoring them, but those six weeks of downtime suddenly seemed like pretty sound advice.

And not for nothing, men were super squeamish about vaginas outside of fondling them. I could probably plead "issues" and buy more time.

The chill in the air that had surrounded us since the

dining room wavered, Brennan following the same train of thought. He scrubbed at his face, then looked away, his mouth screwing up. I would've kissed him, but the logistics of getting around my stomach were too complicated.

"Then Jonas was right about that, too. What's the harm in letting him waste his breath?" Brennan took a drag, and the balmy night air rushed in around us as he banished the last pall of darkness.

I sighed, rubbing at my arms. "What are they? Your shadows?"

"They're not really mine. I only borrow them. What did Socks say?"

"That if you needed cheering, he could hack up a feather to tickle your ass with. Borrow them from who?"

Brennan snorted and his cigarette crackled. "My fiend taps into the Underworld."

"Wait, you're telling me—"

"I'm not telling you anything."

My eyebrow arched. Oh no, I knew that freaking look. That asshole had made a bargain. I laughed. "For real?"

He just shrugged and wouldn't meet my eyes. Whatever. If he'd kept it under wraps this long, it would wait until after the rest of this bullshit was sorted. I snagged my phone from the bedside table and texted Berk an invite for coffee.

I was fresh out of ravens.

16 Days, 14 Hours, 14 Minutes

The next morning was one of those bright blue spring days that screams summer is coming.

Well, in Vel City, anyways. It'd been overcast at the flat all week. I met Berk by the corner of Eighth and Willis, at the cafe with the outdoor patio that backed up to Landsing Park. What? I hadn't had a caramel frap in way too long, and yes, I got a second shot of espresso, extra drizzle, whip cream, and then I had them sprinkle it with those crunchies. Berk got a green tea chai. Blech.

We sat down, ignoring the people pretending not to stare. You gotta know that was gonna happen. I mean, I was still gorgeous even with my freakish belly, and Berk was seven and a half feet of kaftan-clad luscious earthiness.

We drew attention.

Jonas and Stewie didn't, which was kind of the point. They were both in their normal guises at a table mid-patio. Stewie looked like a total nerd with his mousey thinning hair and rimless glasses. Jonas had lost the tusks, but was still a scary biker dude. They made a cute couple.

I'll spare you all the baby banter. Yes, I was still pregnant.

"How have you been?" I asked.

"She teaches, I learn. We become closer to a single being within."

Ugh, I know. Berk had gotten way into the hippy-dippy ohm after becoming. I mean, he was always a zen dude, but assimilating Mother Earth, aka Gaia, had pushed him over the edge. I bet he was living in a carpeted van that smelled like a headshop. Before he could go into his existential spiel about form and spirit, I jumped in and laid down everything that had happened from the raven on. He got real quiet. Probably communing with his inner goddess. I crunched on my drink.

Finally, he sighed. "Do you know why Earth was so set against you becoming?"

I paused mid-chew. He had my attention. "Uh, no?"

"One of our oculuses had a vision—"

I groaned. Here we go again. "What, like the planet going up in flames?"

"There's still time."

I rolled my eyes, and he cracked a smile. It made him radiant, and the bush behind him set out new growth. That was new...or really old depending on how you looked at it, I guess.

"No, this has come to pass. They feared the Mother of Daemons being reborn, stealing the lesser fae away, and sealing the rest of Earth's children in a barren tomb to wither."

Hmm? Oh. Yeah, he was talking about me. Mother of Daemons was one of my more complimentary titles. And I guess my little snip-snip cursing side action didn't get past Gaia's hinky seers. They must've sensed a disturbance in the force while balancing their chi. Whatever. I slurped my coffee.

Okay, fine, he had me dead to rights with that, but they'd totally deserved it. The lesser fae, on the other hand, had bailed all on their own. No way was I taking the blame for that and said so.

Berk raised an eyebrow at my scowl. "All of which is immaterial at this point. Will you bargain for our help?"

My scowl deepened. "Bargain? When the hell did you go all fae on me?"

"Mother Earth won't allow me access to her power without certain conditions being met."

Goddamn it. "What does she desire?"

A subtle ripple passed over Berk's countenance, and any remaining vestiges of masculinity melted away. It was freaking creepy. Hello, Mother Earth. I got hit with a quick montage of Lilith's memories being pinned by the alien intelligence looking out from his mossy green eyes. To call her a frenemy was way oversimplifying our relationship. Let's just say it was rocky. Hah.

"Gaia."

"Lilith. I see you've managed to drag us all through the mud with you, yet again."

"It's Envy, and dirt's kind of your thing; I wouldn't think you'd mind."

"You're very flippant for someone who needs my help."

I shrugged, more memories filtering into place. I kind of did have a penchant for stirring shit up back in the day. Whatever. Most of it wouldn't have happened if I hadn't been provoked. "The more things change, the more they stay the same. I asked what you desired."

Her mouth twisted in a decidedly un-Berk-like manner for all she was wearing his body. "In exchange for my help, you will restore fertility to all as soon as the Neither is passable and swear not to tamper with it again.

I loathe it when you meddle with the natural cycle of the realms."

Psh. More like she was all pissy because she felt like I was stepping on her toes. Hmm? You too? Nope, fertility was my schtick…Well, the absence of it. We were supposed to balance each other, hence her whole weakening of the Neither when I originally cursed Fae, letting them get it on with normals. She was always harping on that natural cycle bullshit. Who the hell gets to decide what that even is? It's my natural cycle to screw over anyone who locks me in a goddamned anathema for a couple—Look, I have strong feelings on the subject and hate being bent over a barrel. If I had to do it, she sure as hell was gonna throw in some lube.

"Fine, but you've gotta talk to Morgana for me."

Gaia's fingers tapped down the side of her chai, considering. For way too freaking long. Like, I almost went up for another frap. I'd forgotten how slow Earth moved. God, it was painful.

"Answer me this, without evasion. Why did you give Berk, Kyle, and Morgana the anathemas?"

I should probably mention that primordials can't lie. Kind of like we're bargaining all the time, and as such, can, and do, try to misdirect the shit out of everybody. Regular fae, on the other hand can lie, unless they're bargaining. It makes for some interesting dynamics.

Whatever. I'd said it before, so I said it again. "Proximity. I didn't remember anything about the other primordials until after we'd become, and even then it was sketchy, like, I didn't remember you were such a bitch until five minutes ago."

She laughed, and it was like the air had filled with honey the way bees and butterflies began flitting about us. I expected a couple of rabbits and a deer to wander up for her to pet. "Then the survival of our hosts was ancillary."

"Uh…kind of—no! I mean, I didn't want you guys to die…it just wasn't the thing I thought of first." That would've been screwing over my father, which given her expression, she'd totally figured out already. Whatever. "Think of it like nailing two birds with one stone." Well, to be totally accurate the anathemas were actually one stone, a droplet, an ember, and a feather, I guess. How was any of this important? Jeez, water under the bridge, move on. I sighed, knowing I couldn't rush her, and until I answered her stupid questions, she wouldn't commit to helping me. My hand grazed across my stomach, a part of me wishing I'd go into labor just to escape her cross-examination.

"No small part of you knew?" she pressed.

I threw my hands up, then winced, rubbing at my side. Her eyes followed the motion. "Maybe, but it didn't say anything to me."

"Do you want to know what you're having?"

"Do I—no!"

"Why not?"

I didn't quite growl, or chuck my cup at her. I did crush, then incinerate it. What? Jonas had scared just about everyone off the patio, and I was pretty sure the dumpy trio left was Earth's goon squad. I mean, there was a bunch of people recording us on their cell phones from inside the cafe, but fuck them. "None of your goddamned business. Are you gonna talk to Morgana or not?"

She sat back, smug. "No, I don't think I will."

Ouch. My jaw dropped and then snapped back up as

she smirked around her cup at me. Bitch. "Are you serious?"

"If you agree to my terms, I'll help you with the Neither, but you'll have to dig yourself out of that whole Morgana mess."

"Fine. Agreed." Her wording had sucked, and her terms weren't gonna stick. I hefted myself up out of the chair, and Jonas was there, steadying my elbow.

"Envy—" Berk was back in charge of his body, for all the good it did me. "I'm sorry."

"Yeah, me too."

I poofed.

My eyes were hot when I got back to the flat, and the guys made themselves scarce. I sat down on the bed, wincing. Ever since last night, my tumor-induced sciatica had been killing me.

"Ugh, whatever you're sitting on in there, get off it," I muttered, trying to find a comfortable position. Spoiler, there wasn't one. Brennan's footsteps came down the hall a moment later, and then his thumbs were pressing into my hips. I whimpered in relief.

"That miserable?"

"Those stupid cafe chairs suck, Berk wasn't Berk, and Gaia won't talk to Morgana."

"And the Neither?"

"She'll help with that."

"Not so bad then, one down, two to go. I'm assuming you'll see *him* next?"

That chill was in the air again. "Yeah."

"I don't trust him."

I snorted. Trust him? Brennan hated Kyle. "Do you trust me?"

"Not even a little, especially if dark chocolate

truffles are involved."

He had a point, but come on, they were freaking delicious. My mouth watered just thinking about them. I grabbed my purse and took my phone out, rocking its edge on my belly. From beneath my shirt, a ripple crested beside it like a circling shark. Brennan put his hand over it, smiling. I couldn't stop my own. God, he got so sappy...but I'd be lying if I said it wasn't kind of adorable. He kissed behind my ear, growling as I pulled up the last text I'd had from Kyle, not quite six months ago.

—*What r u wearing?*—

I hadn't responded. Maybe that's why he'd poofed over. My thumb hovered. What do you say to someone after your live-in boyfriend pitches them through a six-inch glass wall into an eight-story drop over sharp cliffs and sea?

Brennan pushed up. "I'll leave you to it—"

"No, stay." I didn't feel like hanging out in a meat locker for the next couple of hours. He resettled himself against my back, and I could tell he was pleased. I sighed. Men are so needy.

—*Hey, u around 2 talk?*— Yeah, lame, but whatever.

Kyle hit me right back. —*About?*—

—*It's complicated. Can we meet?*—

—*Tomorrow @ 6.*— A pic came through of a rustic room with a sunken hot tub and a fireplace. Well, that'd been easier than I'd thought. I gave it a thumbs-up, and Brennan frowned against my shoulder.

"Please. You know there's no way I'd fit into the stupid tub, and if he tries anything I can't handle, Jonas and Stewie will be there."

He tossed my phone onto the bedside table and rolled me onto my back. "You may find this hard to believe, but you're nowhere near as large as you insist, and far more attractive than you feel. There's not a man alive who would object to watching you soak, Jonas and Stewie included."

"And yet, they're not flying through a wall…"

Brennan laughed, unbuttoning my blouse. "We've known each other a long time, Lovely. I don't touch their toys, and they don't touch mine. Appreciating is an entirely different matter."

"Oh, so I'm your toy now, am I?"

He kissed along the tops of my breasts, his hand skating up my inner thigh. "Let's see…you're very expensive, fun to play with, and I enjoy showing you off."

"I feel like I should take offense to that." But totally didn't. He nipped at me, and I moaned, running my fingers through his hair and pressing him close. When I let him up for air, he pulled his shirt over his head, and I wriggled out of mine. My skirt was already on the floor, and his trousers joined it. Then he was behind me, his lips on my throat, my shoulder…

That led to another conversation with the Almighty. The kid still wasn't budging. I took a nap, and Brennan went to go do paperwork.

Yeah, paperwork. You'd be surprised how much there was. After the whole invasion thing, normals had demanded some kind of accountability from us, else they were gonna shoot first and ask questions later. A sharp uptick in armor-piercing ammo manufacturing added incentive. I mean, no one likes to get shot, but most bullets are lead, and it takes a lot to kill a fae. It takes a lot less to piss one off. Armor-piercing ammo on the other hand, has a steel core. Steel's an iron alloy…you get where I'm going with this. I'm pretty sure a .22 would drop Jonas. It might even kill him if he wasn't able to dig the damn thing out.

Anyways, Brennan had somehow gotten a heads-up on the normals stockpiling the stuff, and we'd instituted a registration system to blow sunshine up the asses of their powers-that-be. It was actually easier than you'd think. Hmm? Oh, the sunshine and the system. Every fae is part of a clan, and bloodlines are tracked obsessively. We'd basically just asked all the lesser queens for a list of who's who and then to verify they were on this side of the veil, done deal.

Where it became messy was when normals got greedy. Clan names and numbers weren't enough. They wanted photo IDs, birth dates, biometric freaking data—

Yeah. It wasn't happening, and aside from the Riders and the stupid Gwinth, Brennan was the only fae lord on this side of the veil. The job really should've fallen to us primordials, but well, you're getting an idea of how that was progressing. He'd ended up as Fae's spokesman, and the imps ran his legal department. He poofed to Washington at least three times a week to stroke the normals' egos and convince them we weren't a threat. For someone who'd once told me he didn't give a rat's ass about politics, Brennan had been born for the job.

I mean, he was seriously slick, and the man could schmooze. Peter had pics of him with the President and like a dozen other world leaders. Hmm? I guess it was impressive, if you were into that kind of stuff. I was more impressed with the Thai take-out Brennan brought back from DC.

Whatever. When I woke up, Karen was waiting for me, snapping on a blue latex glove. I sighed. It was her day to give me a once-over. You know, just in case the kid was falling out of me and I hadn't noticed. Shocker, it wasn't, but I was assured it would be any day now.

Fuck my life.

I got dressed, then went out onto the balcony. Everything was still wet from this morning, and the sky was a steely grey. Aside from Brennan's temper, it never got really chilly here, but today it was close. Socks was coiled up amidst the potted plants looking miserable. I leaned against the railing and watched the surf roll in against the rocks on our little beach. There was a rustle of wings behind me, and when I turned, the blackest man I'd ever seen sat at the table.

Don't get it twisted; I'm not talking person of color. This wasn't a skin tone, it—like he was made of something else. Like alien, even for a fae. Onyx skin, inky close-cropped hair, and his eyes were the most startling gold. He wasn't old or young, he just was. I'd never seen anything like him in either of my incarnations.

"A penny for your thoughts."

"You're the Gwinth."

"Were you thinking about me, then?" He grinned, and his teeth were very white. There was a gap between the front two I could've deposited that penny through.

"I thought I had until after the kid's born."

He shrugged, sitting back. His skinny jeans and motocross jacket were an earthy grey over a white tee, and his ankle boots were a very fine dark leather. The sole of the one crossed over his knee didn't look like it'd ever touched the ground. "You have till then to answer, but I thought perhaps we should speak in person prior to the deadline. I realize I've put you on the spot and thought that being able to put a face to He Who Would Court You would help."

Yep, he totally said it in capitals.

"It's not love at first sight, if that's what you were hoping."

That smile again. "It would've made this easier, now wouldn't it? Still, if your past incarnation is anything to go by, I can't imagine the idea of becoming intimate displeases you, and I certainly don't have any objections."

If my—another montage downloaded. You know, it'd be nice if my subconscious was a little more proactive with this whole "remembering things as-needed" bullshit. All right, fine, I can see how I'd been all about free love back in the day, but recently I'd been considerably less orgy-inclined. Several millennia of distance from the original sin and a body swap will do that.

"Actually, I've acquired quite the taste for monogamy, and as long as I carry his child, Brennan is my consort."

The Gwinth waved his hand. "A technicality. His time grows short, as does mine. Nothing prevents me from making my intentions known."

"Other than decency, you're right."

He pursed his lips around a smile. "Do you find me indecent?"

"I find you irritating and presumptuous."

His laughter boomed off the stuccoed walls, and my back pressed to the railing. His eyes had gained a predatory glint I didn't much like. He pushed out of his seat and prowled toward me. The Gwinth was tall, easily Berk's height, but lean and moved like a panther. He stopped at arm's length. I glared up at him, barely coming to the center of his chest.

"You're just a little thing, aren't you? Tiny, lovely, and fierce, like a black-footed cat." His long fingers traced through the air between us, following the lines of my upturned face. He wet his full lips, and I had zero desire to kiss them. Don't get me wrong, he was super attractive as only a fae can be, but he was a dick, and I didn't like him. "As Kennet has explained, withdrawing my suit is impossible. I will have an heir. What will it take for you to come to me willingly?"

Translation: because either way I'm banging you. Fuck him.

"Oh, I don't know, an act of God, hell freezing over, something along those lines."

He smiled, but that golden gaze of his was ice. Brennan was right, the Gwinth was exactly the type of asshole that would blow shit up until he got his way. He took a step closer.

"Don't think me incapable of inciting either."

I lowered my eyes like he'd intimidated me, knowing his type. They thought defiant was cute, up to a point. I was pretty sure I'd reached that. I didn't want to, but his threat of releasing huntsmen wasn't a joke. I needed to buy time. My hands came up to rest on my belly.

"I'm sorry, I didn't—this is just so sudden…" Yeah, I said it all breathless, in a little-lost-lamb kind of way, and you better believe the big bad wolf ate it up. He'd pressed close, his hand covering mine, then trailing up my arm to sweep a lock of hair from my cheek. It was unnerving. He had no scent. I know that sounds weird, but seriously, shampoo, fabric softener, sweat—everybody smells like something. He didn't.

The snick of Brennan's Zippo came from behind him. "You're here early, Connell."

That coin-slot smile sliced across the Gwinth's face. It would have made him charming if he'd never opened his stupid mouth. "Can you blame me for wanting to introduce myself? Your father didn't do her justice. I'd figured he'd downplay her allure, but you would've killed anyone else I sent. I thought opening negotiations with a blood feud poor form. This is just business. You can have her back when I've finished. We're not going to have any unpleasantness between us, are we?"

Oh, yeah. You know that didn't go over well, but it didn't go as expected, either.

My temper and Brennan's snapped at pretty much the exact same moment. He called forth a spate of darkness to eat the man, and I was keen on incinerating the douche-bag that'd equated me to a rental car. The two forces hit, and everything kind of shimmered for a split second, then left the Gwinth standing there, covered in weird goo.

Yeah, goo. I don't know what it was, ectoplasm or some crap. The Gwinth wiped a handful from his face and flicked it to the ground.

"Gesundheit." Then his form blurred, and he was standing there all pristine like he hadn't been covered in snot two-seconds prior. By his chuckle, he must've thought my expression was just freaking adorable, and I was abruptly very glad for my bump between us. He reached down to caress it, and I slapped his hand away.

God, why did people feel entitled to do that?

Brennan moved to my side. The appearance of the goo had cut through the worst of his anger, but he was still pissed, especially seeing the man try to touch me. "You'd best believe it's going to be unpleasant. Now's not the time to press your suit. You've no cause, nor invitation to be here. I'd be well within my rights to react badly."

"Not the time? If you had your way, it would never be." The Gwinth's eyes flicked to him. "And say you did react badly. You'd either be dead, or too busy dealing with the huntsmen to enjoy your victory." He looked me up and down and wet his lips again. "It's been ages for them, and she's the only game in town worth having. Not even you and your Riders could stave them all off." The cold increased exponentially, and the Gwinth grinned.

"I think you underestimate what she's capable of herself."

"Not in the least. I'm rather looking forward to that bit, especially after speaking to her. So much can be learned from observing one's target in their natural habitat. The sound bites available on the internet are rather one-dimensional. I was curious as to the true nature of the mother of my heir, and she did not disappoint."

Huh, and yet, those sound bites were oddly appropriate. He should've listened closer, 'cause I wanted to say the same thing to him. I didn't. We were trying to buy time, remember?

"I'll be in touch." His eyes slid down to my belly, and I clamped down on a full body shudder. "Soon I think."

He grinned again, and then he was past me, his foot

pushing up from the railing and his form blurring into that of a great raven. Its wings made powerful strokes until it hit an updraft, and then it was gone.

I looked over at Brennan, sucking down another cigarette. "What the hell was that?"

"Connell's part pooka and a mongrel born of all four elements. It allows him to shift forms between them. He's also an incredibly arrogant asshole."

Like I hadn't figured that last part out. "No, I meant the goo."

"The—I've not a clue." He scuffed a shoe at what the Gwinth had flicked to the ground. It'd dried into opalescent cement. If the asshole hadn't done that shifty thing so fast, he would've gotten an insta-freeze plastic dip. "But as much as I wanted to smear him across the balcony in that moment, it was probably fortuitous. Damn the man, but he's right about what would happen if one of us had killed him. Odd stuff though, isn't it? I've never seen the like…"

I shrugged, leaning into him. Odd was pretty much my norm. "How did you know he was out here?"

"I didn't. Karen had just finished giving me the rundown on you. I still can't keep effaced and dilated straight, but she makes it sound like the little bastard should be falling out by now. I know you're sick of hearing it and thought you could use some chocolates."

I perked up at that. He'd left the box on the bed, and I made a beeline for them.

Brennan laughed, watching me waggle my fingers over the drizzled and powdered confections, trying to decide which one to pounce on first. He snagged a chocolate-covered cherry and popped it into his mouth.

"Hey! I thought you got these for me."

"Good excuse, isn't it? It's not like I can go buying boxes of chocolates for myself; it would ruin my image."

I laughed. "Oh really, and what image might that be?"

"Why, I'm a horribly terrifying fiend now that you've set my daemon form loose. We're all psychotic, you know. Never can be sure what might trigger me to rampage." Brennan smirked at my eye roll. "How else do you think I keep everyone in line?" He picked up another and inspected it between his thumb and a forefinger. "You do realize how dangerous that breathless bit was, don't you?"

"Huh? I was trying to buy time—"

"You presented yourself as prey. The Gwinth hunts the huntsman, Lovely. The way you shivered as he touched your cheek…"

"It was creepy. Why doesn't he have any scent?"

"I'm surprised you noticed. My father doesn't either. None of the huntsmen do. Better to stalk their quarry."

Great. I'd gotten my fill of being hunted the last time I'd been in Fae. No freaking thank you.

"Did you mean what you said about monogamy?"

"How long were you standing there?"

Brennan shrugged. "Not long, but I can hear through shadow if I know where to listen and am able to step through. He would've sensed me materialize, and I thought it best to remind him what I'm capable of."

My jaw dropped. "That's how you knew the normals were stockpiling ammo last fall."

He smirked and would've looked way too smug if it weren't for the cocoa powder on his chin. I wiped it off with my thumb.

"I've some feelers out that have paid dividends, yes," he said.

I ate another truffle. "The monogamy stuff was true. I wouldn't have done anything with Kyle—I mean, even if you hadn't thrown him through the wall—and the Gwinth is a dick."

"I was under the impression you rather liked that."

He had me there. I snorted. "Yes, but no. He's the wrong kind."

"And if someone came along that was the right kind?"

"Someone already did." I pulled him to me and kissed him stupid.

The kid still wasn't budging.

I resigned myself to the fact that it was probably a good thing now. Brennan curled against my back, his skin hot on mine, both of us muzzy post-coitus. I closed my eyes, a smile tipping up my lips as he kissed the nape of my neck, happy.

I know, weird, right?

"If I was your wife, would that have really made a difference to him?"

"Yes and no. He could still try and woo you away from me, but he'd not be able to threaten you with the hunt."

Brennan said that, but I wasn't buying it. Something told me that prick had a tendency to do whatever he wanted.

Shut up.

Brennan propped himself up on an elbow. "Lovely…your meeting with Kyle. You do realize there's a time difference? Six tomorrow night in the Himalayas is five tomorrow morning for us."

I blinked at him, and then my temper spiked. God, Kyle was an asshole! He knew I didn't do mornings. Saying he'd meet and then making it for some ungodly hour was just the kind of payback after the shower incident that he'd think was freaking hysterical—

I wish I could say I threw on some clothes and poofed there to kick his ass, but the only thing I was capable of throwing was a hissy fit. I did while Karen got me dressed, and you better believe I had her go full-blown goddess. If that son of a bitch wanted to play, oh, I was gonna play.

Brennan's mouth twisted around his cigarette watching me, but having been on the receiving end of my present mood more than once, he wisely kept whatever comments he had to himself. So did Jonas and Stewie.

I went to grab my phone, and Brennan put a hand on my arm.

"Lovely, please remember you're going there to ask for his help clearing the veil."

I glared at him, not wanting to hear it.

"Chocolate?" He tipped the box toward me, and I snagged one. Okay, two. He kissed my cheek. "You look divine. Come home soon so I can worship you."

I might have smiled as I poofed. That's why I kept him around.

16 Days, 7 Hours, 26 Minutes

I don't know what I was expecting, but it wasn't Kyle sitting alone in front of the fire with a glass of wine. Everything was dead quiet except for its crackle, and freezing despite the blaze. If you're ever in the market for a refurbished temple, keep in mind they have seriously crappy RF values.

Whatever. I wished I'd brought a jacket. Short of that, I called flame to warm things up. I'd become somewhat of an expert on that after living with someone who could literally give you the cold shoulder.

Kyle looked over when I did, a sad smile on his face. "Hey."

The way he said it broke my heart. I made a motion for my boyfriend-mandated bodyguards to stay back and went over, sitting in the armchair beside Kyle's. He was wearing ripped jeans and a cream, cable-knit sweater. His feet were bare, and his golden curls just kissed his jaw. I'd totally forgotten how gorgeous he was, and his mood was stirring some weird part of me that just wanted to make it better. Stupid nesting mode.

"Hey…you okay?"

He shrugged. "I didn't expect you until later today."

His vibe was totally throwing me off. "That whole time zone thing—"

"Ah." His lips quirked. "Kyle failed to take into account the sanctity of your mornings."

Whoa—wait, Kyle failed to take it into account? I started sweating.

"Or perhaps that's exactly why that time was set." He stared into his glass, then took a sip. "You wanted to talk?"

Not anymore. "I-I need your help. To clear the Neither."

"Yes, you do."

That blinking thing again. "Are you really okay?"

He turned to me, his eyes steely. "Not in the fucking slightest, but I'm assuming that was the idea, so why bother asking?"

Uh-oh.

I should explain. Kyle's always been a seriously chill guy, like, you can insult him to his face, dump his books in the mud, and give him a wedgie, no big. He's pretty much gonna laugh it off, one-up you with some shit that makes you look like a complete ass, then buy you a beer. But get mad? Never.

The All Father, who was the primordial he was sharing a body with, was an entirely different story, and whatever vestiges of Kyle I'd stumbled on when I came in had left the building.

It was a solid plan, and I went to leave. "I'll come back—"

"Sit." The sky outside the window flickered.

I sat.

"Wednesdays are for remembrance."

A sprite drifted in through the door with a bottle and another glass. Hm? Oh, think air-ghosts with boobs. The All Father poured me a drink, then topped off his own. I could smell the honeyed herbs as he handed it to me.

Mead, not wine.

"Drink with me."

I did, his eyes lingering on my belly. His irises were churning instead of placid blue. Another bad sign. I wished to hell I'd waited to come.

"To new forms and new rules, eh?" He toasted.

That one time, at band camp…

My cheeks were not the only part of my anatomy that got hot. Crap. I was in deep shit.

I should explain. The All Father, aka Samael, and Lilith had history. Like, *history*, and the majority of it had been spent buck naked doing dirty, nasty things to each other.

Sooo dirty.

Mmm. Sorry. Anywho, the rest of it had been spent pissing each other off, usually by playing with some fae to make the other one jealous. Why? Because make-up sex is freaking hot, duh.

But that came with a caveat. We'd had an understanding how far we could push each other. Having favorites never went well. Especially for the favorite. Brennan being my baby-daddy crossed a line we'd established somewhere pre-Jericho. Up until this incarnation, it'd been pretty easy to keep. I told you I wasn't real big on kids, and that was true in both my lives, but for whatever reason, it didn't feel like the whole truth. There was like this void where I knew something should be, and my subconscious wasn't going into details.

Which was fine, because I was going into a full-blown panic attack.

The All Father's irises stopped churning as I started hyperventilating. "You didn't remember."

I shook my head, wanting to kick my subconscious's

ass. Lilith's stupid words from before we became were coming back to bite me....*Brennan is your love. I know better. So would he...pretty quickly I'd imagine. If you check out, first thing I'm doing is some backtracking with that sylph...*

Yeah, that sylph. I'd thought Lilith had meant sylph as in Kyle, not Samael, the All Father of sylphs and every other Air elemental, whom, by the way, she'd been leading around by the dick for like a bajillion years. Mead sloshed sticky all over my hand, and I laughed when no more memories were forthcoming. Yep. My subconscious was suspiciously silent after mind-fucking me. God, I couldn't even trust myself, and there was still something she wasn't—

What? All right, fine. If I was being completely honest, me screwing myself wasn't much of a revelation, but the rest of it…

Samael.

He came over and kneeled in front of me, taking my glass. Somewhere behind us I could hear Jonas and Stewie trying to get through the curtain of air that'd gone up. I'd forgotten he could do that, too.

Samael gently tucked a lock of my hair behind my ear, and I shivered.

"I didn't either until that boy toy of yours forcibly evicted me. I've spent the last several months assimilating under the assumption you already had…but you're not quite you yet, are you?"

My hand drifted to my abdomen. I wasn't ever going to be me again. "No."

He sighed, his fingers entwining with mine over my belly. Little bastard was curiously still. "I heard about the Gwinth's proposal—"

"He's a dick."

"I thought you enjoyed those."

What? So I have a type. He laughed at my expression, his eyes going a clear sky blue. Yeah, they were like a mood ring. You ever see them go green, run like hell.

He brought my mead-sticky hand to his lips, gaze locked on mine as he laved it clean with his tongue. The fire in the hearth jumped along with my libido, and his lips quirked. "I'll help you clear the Neither," he said, nipping at me, "but after the child is born, our game begins anew."

Something in my abdomen tightened, and the air tinged with brine.

He looked down, smiling. "I'll take that as a yes."

My freaking water had broken.

Right, so I'll spare you most of what went on after. Jonas and Stewie poofed me back to the flat, and Karen snapped on a pair of those blue gloves.

It was awful.

Like, I'm not a huge fan of pain in general, and she wasn't licensed to give an epidural. All that bullshit about breathing? Yeah, fuck that. Those women mid-twentieth century didn't know how good they had it. Knock my ass out and then just hand me the kid. What? Bonding? Like having graphic memories of a squalling dwarf ripping my vagina in two is gonna make me more inclined to fall in love with it.

Little bastard.

I mean, I guess he was kind of cute. In a red, wrinkly, helpless-lump kind of way. Karen handed him to me, and I just stared at him, wondering what the hell I was supposed to do, and terrified I was gonna break him.

Brennan spooned against my side, and proud papa didn't even come close.

Yes, it was a boy. Shot Brennan's aspirations of a hold on the clan throne to shit, but he didn't seem particularly upset. He kissed my sweaty brow, letting the baby wrap its teeny tiny fingers around his.

"He's beautiful, Lovely. What will you call him?"

Believe it or not, I had thought about it. Shut up. I wasn't completely devoid of maternal instinct. The kid nuzzled up to my boob and latched on like a striking cobra. I took a sharp breath, and Brennan chuckled.

"There's a good lad."

I would have glared at him, but weird things were going on in my insides while the kid fed. On what, other than my soul, I wasn't sure. My stupid eyes welled up, and my chest got all tight.

"I want to call him Rhys."

Brennan kissed my brow again. "Then Rhys it is."

After that, things are pretty fuzzy. Karen got me cleaned up, and I basically passed out.

I woke up to Brennan singing softly in Cymric. My throat got tight, and I concentrated on the room. At some point, it'd been filled with flowers, and he was by the windows, playing daddy. It was a good look on him. What is it about guys doting on kids that's so freaking hot? My itchy stitches were an unwelcome reminder I couldn't do anything about it for way longer than convenient. I watched him totally enamored with the little bundle in his arms, his face alive with pure joy. I didn't know how I felt about that. Sharing him. Them. My stomach cramped at the concept of an "us." He looked up at me and smiled. I smiled back. I couldn't help it. Maybe I could do an us.

"Good morning, Lovely. You've woken just in time. I think he's missing you."

Missing me? Oh. I rubbed my eyes and bared a boob. Brennan got a silly smile on his face. "What?"

"I never would have pegged you for the maternal type, but you're a natural."

My cheeks got hot. "You think so?"

"I do."

Of course that made me cry. Everything else did. Ugh. I was getting really tired of being a pathetic mess, but it was nice to do it wrapped up in his arms.

"How do you feel?"

"Like a sore deflated sack," I muttered, wincing as the little piranha clamped down, trying to figure this nursing thing out as much as I was. Brennan's hand drifted over my abdomen and warmth spread from it, easing the ache. "You find a florist that was liquidating stock?"

His face got tight. "No, that's from your suitors."

Suitors. Plural. Crap.

"Brennan, I—"

"Do you love him?"

I felt like he'd slapped me, and I must've looked at him like he had, because his brow crumpled. He leaned over to kiss my cheek. "I'm sorry. Now's not the time. Forget I asked. Let's try to enjoy what little time we have as a family, shall we?"

A lump instantly materialized in my throat. "What little time—What the hell are you taking about?"

He pulled a cigarette from his case. "They both sent envoys this morning. I was able to negotiate a week before they begin pressing their suits, at which point I'm being forced to find alternate lodging until you've chosen a consort. The Gwinth has no issue with me returning after his 'business' is concluded, whereas the All Father prefers me to disappear. He made it very clear that was not a euphemism, though I'd like to see the son of a bitch try—"

"What? No!" My nipple tugged out of the kid's mouth, and he started wailing. I wasn't far off. "Why would you leave me with—I can't—"

Yeah, I lost it.

So did the kid.

The room erupted in black flame. I tried to jam my boob back in his mouth, and he wouldn't latch on to the damn thing. Why do they do that? Like, just take it and shut up already. Brennan threw his aura over us and between the combination of the two, Rhys settled and the flames snuffed out.

The flat was trashed. I mean, you thought flaming textiles were bad? Whatever the kid had called up had vaporized the greenery, eaten through the floor, and left huge corroded holes in the glass walls. Not destroyed. Ate. Brennan and I just kind of looked at each other, and I started laughing.

I mean, come on.

Seriously, how much worse could things be? Forget about the huge mess I'd made with my curse. My babydaddy was leaving me, I was about to embark in some fucked up version of *The Bachelorette*, and my day-old son was dissolving matter with black hell-flame.

Sorry, I'm laughing again. Every damn time I say something like that…

"Is he supposed to do that?" I asked after I'd calmed down enough to form words. Well, as calm as I could get suckling the anti-Christ.

Brennan was peering down one of the holes in the floor. A flash flared up through it, and he sat back on his heels, blinking. Peter had some weird ideas of what needed photo documenting. Maybe it was for insurance purposes, though I was pretty sure Spawn of Satan fell into the same category as an Act of God.

"Little bastard melted right through to the billiard room…And I've no idea what he's supposed to do."

My mouth just kind of hung open. "No id—What d'you mean you have no idea?" How could he have no idea? He researched the crap out of everything else, what the hell had he been doing for the past nine months?

I mean, other than being in charge of normal/fae relations and catering to my every whim. Shut up, totally not an excuse.

He traced the edge of a mangled panel and shook his head. "What little experience I have with children is based on the human ones from my father's keep. Rhys is the first fae born of fae in ages, Lovely." A grin split his stupid face, his dimple as deep as the damned hole in the floor. "But after that, he's definitely a fiend."

A fiend. I laughed. Forget about a doctor or a lawyer, my baby was a future psychopath. I wonder if they made a bumper sticker for that, like, "My child dismembered your honor roll student."

My eyes narrowed at Brennan strutting over, all Cheshire Cat, like he'd done something other than take a minute forty-five to deposit genetic material.

Okay, fine. It'd been longer than that, but this was still all his fault.

"You're not leaving, and I am not doing this by myself." I hadn't even wanted the kid, and now he was just gonna up and split? My temper spiked. How dare he!

He sat next to me, running a hand down the boy's back. The dark, tattooed wings of his stigmata already flowed from his shoulder blades to the back of his chunky thighs. "I don't want to go, but you won't be alone. Jonas will stay as my representative to make sure all the forms are followed. You'll have the imps, and Gladys—"

I hissed, holding Rhys closer. He was mine, and I'd be damned before—

Look. You know me pretty well by now, and I'm sure it will come as no surprise that I'd absolutely planned on dumping this kid on someone else to deal with. Gladys was a normal in stout, sensible shoes that Brennan had lined up for me to do just that. Karen had pitched a fit when she found out, and trust me, having an imp pissed off at you is no joke. She was still burning my waffles.

Whatever. All of that was pre-episiotomy. I didn't get it either, but I'd developed an undeniable possessiveness over the burgeoning little serial killer nestled against my breast. I've said that dae are territorial, but I didn't realize that extended to our spawn—

Well, fae spawn. It had to be different for halflings.

Yeah, I wasn't gonna go there, and I was busy being mad at my douche-bag boyfriend for pimping me out and abandoning me with his kid.

"Jonas and the imps didn't saddle me with this!" My voice was shrill, and he winced around his cigarette. I wanted to make him eat the fucking thing.

"The Proscriptions are very clear. Your time must be spent amongst your suitors equally…We've agreed to a rota."

"Oh, you've agreed, have you? Do tell. Who gets first dibs? You pull sloppy seconds, or you end up on clean-up crew?"

His brow furrowed, and he gave me a look, like I was being unreasonable or some shit. "Please, Envy, don't make this any more difficult—"

Yep. He actually said that. I couldn't believe it'd come out of his mouth either. I didn't stick around to hear what else might.

I poofed to Berk.

Yeah, I know that never ends well, but I wasn't particularly rational, and the worst thing I could imagine walking in on was illicit drug use or him taking a dump. After just having my bits splayed for the world to see, I wasn't real sympathetic to anyone else's need for privacy.

Whatever. He'd been expecting me. Or rather, Gaia had. Maybe she'd had a vision or a transcendental awakening that gave her a heads-up. I didn't ask. What I did do, was burst into tears again at her smirk. What? Yeah, I had the kid. He was kind of attached.

So, I know I called her a bitch before, but our relationship has always been way complicated, and if she showed up on my doorstep in my condition, I'd be out for blood.

Gaia didn't do blood. She did food.

Hmm? Oh, hah. No van. We were in what had been Berk's lair before Martha Stewart had thrown up all over it in earth tones, but I'd totally called it smelling like a headshop.

Anyways, she got us curled up on a too-soft designer couch and brought over a tray with a plate of brownies and a bowl of nachos. I'm not complaining about the combo, it was delicious. She even made cocoa. Like, the real stuff from a chocolate pot. I sat there gorging myself with Rhys zonked out, drooling against my shoulder. Gaia plopped into a beanbag chair with her own mug, waiting for me to start. I licked my finger, blotting up the last crumbs and sighed.

"I don't wanna do this anymore."

She snorted. "Which part?"

"All of it." It should tell you something that I was looking back on my impending death sentence pre-becoming as the good ol' days.

She grunted, not disagreeing. "You talk with Kyle?"

"You mean the All Father? Yeah. Thanks for the heads-up."

Gaia shrugged, not sorry in the least. "If your memories are integrating the way I suspect, would it have done any good?"

My mouth curdled, but she had a point. "He'll help, but I have to date him for the privilege." Just saying it flushed me with heat. God, that was annoying. I gave her the skinny on the rest of what'd gone down.

"So how do you plan on juggling the three of them?"

"They've decided on a rota."

Gaia snickered. "Bit presumptuous."

"Right?" God, even she thought so, and she was like the queen of pedantic. I bet she had a spreadsheet for her socks. I put down my empty mug and sighed, head dipping to breathe Rhys in. I don't know if you've ever experienced that new-baby smell, but it's way better than the car version.

"What are you calling him?"

"Rhys."

A smile curved over her lips. "Adored, enthusiasm,

and rashness. All will be fitting, I'm sure." She paused at my expression. "What is it?"

"Do fae get their abilities as soon as they're born?"

"Yes and no. If he feels threatened, he'll be able to protect himself, but it's more of a reflex than an ability." Her eyes narrowed. "Why, what did you do?"

"I didn't try to drown him in the bathtub, if that's what you're asking. When Brennan dumped all that on me, I lost it and so did the kid." No, I wasn't gonna tell her about the black hell-flame. I didn't even want to think about it.

"All children read their parents' moods. Sounds like he was vibing off your energy and reacted to your upset, and probably Brennan's to some degree. For whatever reason, the man's devoted to you. This can't be easy for him, either. Especially given your past with the All Father."

"I didn't tell Brennan about that." Hell, I hadn't remembered it, and then, well, baby. God, I couldn't stop looking at him. I stroked the fine black down on the back of Rhys's head and followed the bow of his parted lips with my eyes. He was beautiful, and I'm not just saying that because he was mine. Some kids are little trolls from the get. Oh, shut up, you know I'm right.

"Are you going to?"

It was like a fist tightened in my chest. "I think he already knows."

"Pity neither of them will share."

A visual of myself sandwiched between a sexy pirate and a golden god put one hell of a smile on my face, but it was short-lived. She was right. I might be able to convince the All Father, but Brennan wouldn't...

Right. Who am I kidding? Challenge accepted.

Gaia rolled her eyes at me as I extracted myself from her couch. "Will you hold him? I have to pee." Stupid cocoa. Her eyes lit up, and I narrowed mine. "I want him back when I come out."

She laughed. "So this you want to do?"

Maybe. I stuck my tongue out at her, handed the kid over, and then waddled to the loo.

In case you've never had the pleasure, peeing on stitches sucks—hmm? Why didn't I heal myself? Wow. That'd never occurred to me. Boy, do I feel stupid.

Shut up. You don't think that was the first thing I asked Karen when she went on that whole stugots for sex spiel? Look, I told you when I was pregnant I had more power than I knew what to do with, right? Well, let's just say I was at a deficit now, and poofing was the extent of it. I was basically back to halfling status.

Timing's not really my thing.

Whatever. It was supposed to come back as I healed, and that would happen way faster than if I was a normal. I just had to stay out of any intense fuckery until then.

Stop laughing.

I came out of that bathroom a hell of a lot sorer than I'd gone in. Gaia was all snuggled up, crooning something at the kid.

"That better not be a curse."

"I'd say having you as his mother is enough of one."

I shrugged, rummaging around in her fridge. She had a point, and short of a sitz bath, I needed a beer.

"I'm assuming you didn't have the foresight to bring any diapers."

"You would be right." I cracked a bottle and took a long pull. Oh, stop. We went over this. Drinking isn't the same for fae. "Why, does he stink?"

"No, but he's wet."

"How can you tell?"

She shifted him so I could see the dark streak across her kaftan.

I didn't quite spit out my beer. Whoops. Gaia rolled her eyes at me and stood. She passed me back the little bastard in all his sodden glory, muttering to herself as she left the room. When she came back, it was with an ugly yellow-and-white-striped bag.

"Your baby shower gift," she said, plonking it down with a raised eyebrow.

What? It's not like I didn't invite her—I'd never had one. I hate those stupid things. Why would I want to inflict that kind of pain and suffering on anyone else? God, even I'm not that much of a bitch. Anyways, it was full of kid crap, and she gave me an impromptu lesson on how to change a diaper. He peed again, this time on me. It wasn't nearly as funny being on the receiving end and strangely awkward dealing with boy parts when I wasn't, um, dealing with boy parts.

Whatever, half of what was in the bag I had no idea what to do with. Okay, more than half. Gaia took pity on me and expanded her tutorial. By the time she'd finished, Rhys had fed again, was dry, sleeping soundly, and securely strapped to my chest in some bizarre halter. At least that was grey. I wasn't particularly fond of the rest of the gender-neutral palette. Yellow makes me look all pasty.

We said our goodbyes, and I poofed back to the minibar at the flat. Brennan walked in as I was making a drink and came up short.

"What did you do with him?"

You can see my face, right? I kept my back to him

and made it a double. "Who?"

"Don't fuck around with me, Envy. Where's Rhys?"

I'd read that, statistically, couples are more likely to break up within the first six months after the birth of a child than at any other time. That sounded spot on right about now. His Zippo snicked, and his exhale was a half an octave shy of full-on fiend.

Good.

"You're leaving me. I didn't think you'd care what I did with him."

The room dropped the typical thirty degrees, and his steps behind me were heavier than they should've been. "Where's my boy, Envy?"

Not *sorry I was a dick.* Not *I was worried about you*...I bit at my lip, hating the tears streaming down my cheeks. God, I thought after I'd popped the kid out I'd be off the hormone crazy train, and here I was sitting in first class. Rhys started to fuss, and I put a hand on his back.

"Why? Did you want to take him from me when you go?"

"You never wanted him."

That was a yes. A sob escaped. When I turned, the way he was looking at me—

He saw Rhys, and his expression became stricken.

"Since when have I ever known what I wanted?"

I left him standing there and stormed out onto the balcony. The sun was about three fingers from the horizon, and I wasn't surprised to see a raven circling overhead. Goddamn it. I wiped at my face, holding the baby close.

The Gwinth was standing beside me a moment later. He scented the air, drawing it in through that gap in his teeth.

"You've been up and about too much today; you're bleeding heavier than you should be."

Eww. "Intrusive much?" Asshole.

He smiled, tipping up my chin, his gold eyes cold. "You're very fetching when you cry."

I didn't answer, or pull away. His thumb swept over my cheek, then down to the hollow of my throat, lingering on my pulse. His other hand slid down my back, pulling me to him. "Will you cry for me?" He flashed those too-white teeth, and I looked away.

"Brennan said I have a week…" It came out as a warble, I couldn't deal with this right now, that sucking void inside me surged upward, everything becoming oddly disassociated. He dipped his head, inhaling along the side of my face, his lips grazing my temple. I trembled, trying to keep myself together, and a rumble started in his chest—

Rhys's cries jolted me from the abyss. If I checked out, what would happen to him? The last thing I needed was for the Gwinth to see me fall apart.

Yeah, I know, the thought shocked the shit out of me too. I wasn't even sure it was mine. I swatted the creep's hand off my rear and glared at him, trying to shush the baby.

He chuckled like it was a game and stepped back, looking decidedly vulpine. "Pity forms must be followed, else I would take you now. I've brought a gift." He held out a small velvet bag from inside his jacket, and I eyed it like a snake. What? I'm cool with Socks, but I don't trust the rest of them. That and the whole taking-gifts-from-fae-being-dicey thing.

"Come now, it's traditional to bestow a gift upon the one whom you would court. It's free from obligation, other than affording me the opportunity to press my suit, which you've already agreed to."

He was right, but I still didn't want it. I took it anyways, avoiding his fingers. His smile widened. It was a vial of milky vapor. I went to open it, and he stopped me.

"Ah, ah…you'll want to save that for when you plan on using it."

"What is it?"

God, I hated his smile. "Bacchanal fog. I'm told succubi have an affinity for it, and I'm eager to experience the results of that for myself."

My hand tightened around the vial, the memory of acrid sweetness on my tongue. He wasn't wrong, and I glared at him. Asshole wanted me to roofie myself so he could get off? "You're a dick."

"I've heard you're fond of those."

For the love of—I crossed my arms over Rhys's fussing. "You heard wrong."

He laughed. "Somehow, I very much doubt that. Now why don't you thank me with a kiss?" His head tipped toward mine—

"That's enough, Connell." Brennan leaned against the bistro table and lit a cigarette with his Zippo. "As you said, forms must be followed. She's free of you for a week, and after that time, she must initiate any intimacy." Socks slithered up to coil around his shoulders. Huh. He'd never done that before.

The Gwinth grinned. "Of course. I was just allowing her the opportunity, but there will be others. Congratulations on your son. He looks like a bonny lad. Shame he doesn't give you a claim on the throne…not Malten's at least." His eyes found mine again. "I can assure you, whatever you whelp, I will find adequate."

What a fucking pri—He was at the rail, then winging through the dusk.

I sagged, and Brennan was at my side. I wanted to push him away, but—

Since when have I ever known what I wanted?

He caught me up and carried us inside, his apologies a steady stream twining with Rhys's cries. My chest ached at them.

Like seriously, my milk had come in, and I was soaking wet on top of everything else.

He set me on the bed and helped me peel everything off. I settled in to nurse. This time Rhys's sharp bite was nothing but relief. Brennan sat at the foot of the bed watching us, his face drawn and hollow. His cigarette trembled as he chain-smoked.

We sat like that for a long time. Long enough for Rhys to finish and fall back into baby-catatonia. I held him against my shoulder, rubbing his back. Feeling like everything I wanted to say wasn't enough.

Brennan broke the silence.

"I-I don't know why I—I never would've taken him from you." He hung his head, raking a hand through his hair. "When you left, I thought you went to *him*. The thought of that man having the both of you—" Brennan scrubbed at his face. God, he looked broken.

If you haven't figured it out by now, every time Brennan says *he/him* it's referring to the All Father/Kyle, and he always says it with this sour look on his face, which would kind of be adorable if he didn't actually want to murder him. Historically, that's exactly the thing that Lilith would've eaten up, but now, not so much. I wasn't certain who would win in that throw-down and had no desire to find out.

Yeah, for real. Our forms were mortal this time around, albeit the fae version of mortal. The All Father was a crazy powerful Air deity, but Brennan's shadows…I didn't understand them, and the whole "borrowing them from the Underworld" thing bothered me. I know, I know, I said I wasn't gonna worry about that, but by now you know I'm full of shit ninety percent of the time. Not to mention I have a proven track record of things I've ignored biting me in the ass at the worst possible moment.

Whatever. I kept ignoring it.

"Do you want to hold him?"

Brennan's voice was thick. "I want to hold both of you."

I handed Rhys off and went to take a shower. Stop. I didn't do it to be a bitch, the little bastard had spit up in my hair. I was gross and sore.

And I still didn't know what to say.

When I came back, Brennan was lying skin to skin with the baby on his chest. I stopped in the doorway, watching them drowse. My heart ached. Karen was tidying up the room. She gave me a look and jerked her head toward them. I sighed. She was probably right.

Don't tell her. I hate it when she gets all smug.

I climbed in, and after a moment, he reached out like he was afraid to touch me. His lips brushed the top of my head when I snuggled close.

"I didn't see Kyle. I went to see Berk, but it was Gaia. He wasn't there at all. The others aren't assimilating the same as me; it's like their consciousnesses are being overwritten." I wiped at my stupid eyes. "Kyle and Berk both remember more of the primordials' history than I do, and for them, it's like nothing's changed."

His fingers twined through my damp hair. "Have things changed for you?"

God. I knew he wasn't gonna give me a pass on this, but how could I explain to him what I didn't really understand myself? "You know my true name, and it's not Lilith. I have her memories and emotions, but they're like carpaccio."

"Carpaccio?"

"Remember the last time Peter made it and I tried some?"

"That's not a visual I can erase, no matter how much I may want to." He smirked.

I frowned against his chest, but I'd brought it up for a reason. Pun intended. I'd been violently ill afterward. I'm not a fan of meat, and bloody meat makes me sick just thinking about it.

"A lot of what I get from her is like that. A weird craving or feeling I know isn't mine. They aren't me, not who I am now. I can keep them separate."

He didn't seem convinced. "Then why did you try a bite?"

"It took me a while to figure out what was happening." And had totally been able to pass on the pot roast.

"You've romantic ties to Kyle and the All Father from both your incarnations, and I'd wager either is more tempting than carpaccio." Brennan wasn't wrong and knew it. He sighed and kissed my forehead when I didn't say anything, his hand slipping down to my abdomen and warmth suffusing me. I closed my eyes, feeling the depth of his emotions as he healed me. Sayonara, stitches.

I was in a sleepy haze when he called for Karen to take Rhys. I bit at my lip, not wanting him out of my sight. Yeah, I was as surprised as you, but just go with me on this. For whatever reason, I wanted the little bastard near me for all I had wanted him out of me. Maybe there was something to that bonding through pain crap.

Whatever. Karen took the kid, and I stretched out, feeling bereft without his little weight. "What did the Gwinth mean about Rhys giving you a claim to some throne?"

"He was referring to Kennet's clan, and it was said in very poor taste."

Ouch. Yeah, the whole fae-ruling-over-normals thing had gone the way of Rome. Not for nothing, but most of them considered it way beneath them, and I was sure the Gwinth had meant it as an insult. Brennan looked down at me like he was memorizing my face, and my brow crumpled.

"Why won't you kiss me?"

A sad smile ghosted across his lips. "You need to get used to initiating intimacy from here on out, Lovely. None of us will be able to touch you without your explicit permission."

I pushed up so I could nip at him. "You have permission."

It became explicit.

Yeah, yeah, that sentence of stugots.

We both didn't need to suffer. I told you, I'm not that much of a bitch.

15 Days, 22 Hours, 45 Minutes

Rhys was squalling when I woke, and the bed beside me was empty. My anxiety jumped. It was a little past two a.m., and my shirt was soaked again. I scrambled up, rushing into what had been the walk-in closet. Brennan had blown out a wall and sacrificed half of it to make room for the nursery. Hmm? Yeah, it'd been huge, and still wasn't anything to sneeze at.

The nursery had all the expected stuff, I guess. Cutesy crap on the walls. Rocking chair in the corner. Crib and a changing table.

Brennan was standing in front of it with his back to me, presumably on diaper duty. His stigmata was dark against his bronzed skin, pj bottoms hanging low on his hips, hair all mussed.

Dae-licious.

I pressed against him with a sigh and kissed his shoulder. "I thought you'd left me."

"Is my punishment being slathered in breast milk? You're positively soaked."

"You didn't mind earlier."

"No, I can't say that I did, then or now, but it's the lad's turn." He turned with Rhys, red-faced and screaming. I took him and settled into the rocker, lamenting my fate as a milk dispenser for the foreseeable future.

Yep, still big on lamenting.

Brennan leaned against the crib, and Socks slithered up to wrap around his shoulders again. His tongue flicked against his earlobe. My eyebrow cocked. The two of them didn't have anything against each other, but they'd kept their interactions to a minimum. I was pretty sure that was on Socks. He wasn't big on people, but then most people weren't big on snakes. Especially not emerald green vipers as long as said people were tall.

"Does he speak to you?" I asked Brennan, not entirely thrilled with the possibility.

"You'd have to ask him, but he's become notably more friendly since Rhys's arrival."

Socks dropped to the ground and came to coil across my lap. His vertically slit eyes met mine for a long moment. I looked away first, blinking. Stupid hormones.

"He was in the crib when I came in." Brennan lit a cigarette. "What did he say?"

"Did you find someone to repair the baby-pocolypse in the other room?"

"The glass is on order, and a duergar will be here tomorrow to regrow the floor. Well, today, I suppose. What did he say?"

Socks flicked his tongue at me. Great. Now my snake was conspiring against me. I shot him a look and swapped Rhys to the other side. Gaia had warned me that if I didn't, my boobs would get all uneven and weird, but there was all that stuff about hind milk, and I wasn't sure if I was letting him—

"Envy."

I pouted up at him. "I think you know and just want me to say it."

Brennan's eye smoldered from behind that messy fall of hair, and my stomach flipped. "What I want you to say is yes."

"You said you wouldn't—" I bit my lip, blinking back tears. God, men were needy! I knew what he wanted, I just—

He came to kneel at my side. "I did. I know you have strong feelings on the subject of marriage, but I do too, and now…" He traced Rhys's stigmata. "I want you as my wife so bad it hurts. It won't stop with Connell and *him*. Once the veil opens, it will be all of them. My mother, sisters, they were hounded until they wed, and should you choose another, the first thing they'll do is come after Rhys. Why do you think I spent so much time with Kennet? My stepfather would've gladly killed me."

I held the baby tighter, feeling sick. I knew Brennan was only telling me the truth, but it wasn't that simple…

Oh, all right, it was.

Socks had even said as much, calling me an idiot, but my stupid emotions were a mess, and despite what I'd said about carpaccio, I was having trouble weeding out my feelings from Lilith's. "And say we did. The Gwinth will release the huntsmen as soon as he finds out."

"If the Neither is cleared, you're not beholden to him."

I bit at my lip, but he was right.

"You need to speak to Morgana."

I winced. That wasn't gonna go well. Crap. I had to try. "Get my phone. I'll text her." He retrieved it from the bedroom, and I took it from him, thumb hovering over her name. God, I didn't want to do this—

I didn't want to do the Gwinth more.

—Hey, Morgana, it's Envy. Can we talk?—

Those three stupid dots in a bubble sprang right up.

Went away. Came back.

Nothing.

I was sweating.

What if she wouldn't talk to me at all? If she knew about the whole Gwinth mess, or the curse, she'd gladly let me hang just to be spiteful. Hell, I would if I was in her position.

Ugh. I tossed my phone down and burped the baby.

He spit up down my back.

Brennan chuckled and took him from me. Today already sucked.

I went back to bed after another shower, and when I woke, it was Groundhog Day all over again. I was gaining a lot of sympathy for Sisyphus's never-ending rock-rolling gig, and it felt like the damned boulder had plowed me over on its way back down the hill. Don't get me wrong, Brennan was steadily chipping away at healing my exit wounds, but having a kid is like a whole body experience. Every part of me wanted to crawl into a hole and die.

Whatever. I left Rhys zonked out with Uncle Socks. He'd volunteered to babysit, and for whatever reason, I felt a lot better knowing the kid had a guard-snake instead of some biddy in prescription sneakers watching him.

Karen had a heaping plate of charred waffles for me, and I tore through them. They'd become my breakfast of choice ever since blueberry crepes had almost killed me. I was still mad about that. Not the attempted murder part, but that bit of deliciousness being ruined for me was freaking criminal.

Beside my plate was the aforementioned rota. I scanned it, frowning. The Gwinth had first dibs. Because of course he did. It failed to mention his plans for wooing me, but then it also failed to take into account I was freaking exhausted, felt like I'd been hit by a truck, and had a newborn to take care of.

Oh, and that I hated him.

I finished up and padded to Brennan's office. It sounded like he was taking another stupid meeting, and by the chill in the air, it wasn't going well.

"...don't care what Ms. Morte has requested. I've already—"

An imp murmured something I couldn't catch, and Brennan's Zippo snicked.

"Damn her." That murmur came again. "Yes, yes, I know what will happen if she leaks it to the press. Fine. Set it up—"

I pushed the door open. Brennan was at his desk, surrounded by a bevy of imps in business suits. The chill left like he'd flipped a switch. He grinned up at me, way too chipper. God, I hated him sometimes.

"What was that all about?"

"Politics," he said around his cigarette. "You're just in time. Quinton heads up our publicity department." An imp with a blue tie stood and gave me a formal bow. "We've been going over the details for Rhys's Presentment. Given our limited window of opportunity, we've scheduled it for Friday."

If he was trying to distract me, it worked. My eye twitched. Two days. What the hell ever happened to a lying-in period? Didn't I rate one of those? "Have fun with that." I turned to leave.

"Envy..."

Oooh! I might've stamped my feet. Asshole smiled like I did.

"It won't take long, and you can recline upon your throne throughout the entire thing."

Throne? I peeked over my shoulder at him.

He grinned wider. "Would you like to see?"

"Maybe."

Brennan rounded his desk with a folio. It was more like an ebony fainting couch with smokey scarlet cushions. I leaned back against him, warming up to the idea. Those were my colors…

"When I commissioned it, I was envisioning you lying there with your wings extended," he murmured in my ear.

"What was I wearing?"

He chuckled, his hands sliding around my hips. "Karen has something more appropriate in mind. As is traditional, it will be a closed event for the lesser queens and their consorts; however, I've had to make concessions and agree to have it televised for the normals. I'm afraid the little bastard's arrival coincided with a great deal of volcanic activity."

Huh. Well, I guess that explained how Gaia had known I was coming. Funny she hadn't mentioned it though. She usually gets real pissy when I blow up stuff. Maybe she got a nice archipelago out of it—

Hmm? No, lava's me. It's one of those nebulous boundaries we kind of share. There's more than you would think, but that's a big one. The line between Earth and Fire gets real blurry around volcanic eruptions. Same deal with lightning. That's Air's gig, but it wouldn't happen without Fire. I don't share anything with Water. We're opposing forces, duh. Same with Earth and Air. You fall off a mountain the only fuzzy boundary you're hitting are clouds.

Good luck with that.

Anywho, Brennan blabbed at me for a while longer about publicity stuff and politics I didn't care about, and then my lord and master beckoned from the other room.

Rinse and repeat.

Well, more like repeat and rinse. Babies are filthy little things, and despite my aversion to smelling like sour milk and poo, I came away from every interaction in just that condition.

He was lucky he was so cute. Whatever. Shut up.

This time when His Majesty was sated, he stayed awake, checking things out. He didn't seem real impressed, and yeah, I was on that list.

It was awkward.

I did what I always do when I'm nervous. I called a trickle of flame to thread around my fingers. What? Why was I nervous? Oh, no reason. I mean, I'd had such a stellar upbringing myself, there was no way I could possibly screw this up.

Look, I had pretty low aspirations as far as motherhood was concerned, but one of the milestones I'd set for myself was not putting the kid in therapy before he hit training pants.

Anyways, he seemed to dig flame. I mean, he basically had two settings, tyrant or potato, and he was definitely in spud mode. It was actually kind of fun watching his eyes follow it. Even though fae kids developed way faster than normals, he hadn't figured out fingers yet. After a while Karen came in to remove his barrel of toxic waste. She kept giving me the side-eye while she was changing the crib sheet.

I finally snapped at her. "What?"

She shrugged. "No thing. Just think-ing is time to

call Glad-ass."

What the hell was it about everyone wanting me to fess up to crap lately? She was lucky I had the kid, otherwise I might've been tempted to smack the smug off her. I mean, I'd probably lose a hand doing it, but since when have consequences stopped me?

"Forget about Gladys," I muttered.

"What this? I no hear you…" Yes, she actually put a hand to her ear and batted her eyelashes. I liked her better when she just grunted. Being subjected to her sarcasm was definitely one of the downsides to getting too familiar with the help.

I rolled my eyes. "Fine. I was wrong and you were right. I don't want a stupid nanny."

"Ah! That what I thought you say." She picked up her laundry basket and sashayed from the room with way too many teeth showing.

Stupid imps. Hmm? Yeah, I could speak Impese, but she liked to practice her English. She'd enrolled in community college and there were some language accessibility issues…Oh, ah, culinary. Peter was taking photography.

Anyways, in case you were wondering, Morgana hadn't gotten back to me, and I was pretty positive she wasn't going to. That didn't leave me with a lot of options. Like, just the one.

I had to ask the All Father for help.

Look, it wasn't a decision I came to lightly. I stared at his name long enough for my home screen to lock—twice—before I pulled up our last text and started typing.

—*Can I ask u 4 a huge favor? I need u 2 talk 2 M 4 me. She won't answer my texts.*—

—*Sure. What do u want me 2 say?*—

Well, that'd been easier than I'd thought...What the hell did I want him to say? I wanted him to get her to agree to help so I didn't have to talk to her at all—

—*I'll be over w/ lunch in 10. Tty then. Leash ur toy or I'll break him.*—

Shit! I moved faster than I'd thought possible, clean shirt, brushed my teeth, hair—What? Oh, please. Trying to look good in my present condition was flat out impossible. I'd be lucky to pull off zombie-apocalypse survivor.

Brennan was less than thrilled when I told him about our impending visitor, and the why of it didn't do much to raise the temperature of the room. All the imps had gotten real quiet, and his cigarette crackled in the silence.

"*He* stays on the balcony."

I nodded and poofed out before he could say anything else.

The All Father had just raised his hand to knock at the glass slider. Becoming had bulked up Kyle's form. I mean, he'd never been scrawny or anything, but turning fae had given him that defined muscularity that a T-shirt couldn't hide. Especially one a size too small. That I associated with Kyle. Maybe he was still kicking around in there. I hoped so. I'd wanted to save them, not have their consciousnesses snuffed. Whoever was driving the bus out there shot me a dazzling smile, and my stomach twisted.

I cursed my stupid pulse and held up a finger.

No, not that one, I wanted him to wait while I strapped on Rhys. Oh yeah, you better believe I was gonna hide behind him. Socks gave me a look I ignored as I was heading out.

A checkered blanket I thought I recognized from

Vel City was spread out on the patio, and the All Father waggled a grease-stained take-out bag and a frap with all the fixings.

"Hey, babe, got your fave."

Some of the tension went out of me hearing Kyle's inflection. I was a lot more comfortable dealing with—He pulled his shirt up over his head and tipped his face to the sun.

Okay, scratch that. What? Yeah, he was gorgeous. Curly blond hair all tousled by the light breeze, his stigmata like a cobalt tattoo against the bronze of his skin. His muscles rippling as he leaned onto an elbow—

You know what? Shut up. You're not helping. I snagged the bag.

"You went to JD's to get me chipotle waffle fries?"

"Yeah, with that sauce you like."

I already had a mouthful and nipped a drip off my lip. Their garlic aioli is to die for.

He laughed, unwrapping the sloppiest bacon-chili cheeseburger I've ever seen. That settled it, Kyle was definitely in control. He moaned around a bite. "Mmm. Been craving one of these. You should see all the organic crap they've been feeding me."

I laughed. Prior to all this, he'd never eaten a meal that didn't come with a free toy. I dredged another fry in sauce, and we ate for a while, just soaking up the sun. After the past few days of volcano-induced grey skies, that wasn't a coincidence, and I wasn't complaining.

Rhys was. He'd started that meeping noise that I'd begun equating to a countdown on a bomb. I pulled him out of the halter and laid him in the sun. He blinked a lot but settled back into spud mode, gurgling and stretching out, his little toes spreading like fingers.

"Damn, Snow."

I glanced up, and the smile slid off my face. Kyle's eyes were slate as they trained on the kid. Crap. ...*Should you choose another, the first thing they'll do is come after Rhys*...No. Kyle wouldn't...But the All Father might. I swallowed, ignoring the brewing storm like someone had farted in church, and nabbed my frap. The motion broke his mood and he blinked it away, but the mash-up of emotions on his face...And they say women are confusing. He jammed the last of the burger into his mouth and wouldn't look at me.

Ugh—men. "What?"

He grabbed his orange soda, cheeks sucking in around the straw. "Nah, it's just, you're a mom and shit. S'gotta be weird. You like it?" Yep, he said it totally incredulous.

I was playing with the kid's toes again and shrugged. "Too soon to tell."

Voices came from inside, and Brennan walked into the bedroom with the duergar—oh, sorry. Think three-foot-tall craggy dude with crazy white hair and massive ears. They cultivate rocks like Midwesterners grow corn. Anyways, Brennan spotted the two of us, and I felt the chill through six inches of plate glass.

"Kid looks like him."

"Yeah? You think so?"

Kyle cocked his head. "Yeah, same wrinkled head, knobby knees—"

I chucked a fry at him and laughed. "Asshole!"

He rolled onto his stomach, kicking his feet into the air behind him as he rested on his forearms, frowning in Brennan's direction, then at Rhys. "So, what's it like?" Kyle's voice was flat, and so was the look on his face.

I shrugged again. "A lot of work."

"Didn't think that was your thing."

It wasn't but…I squirmed, there was something, I don't know. Familiar about it. Whatever, I crunched my frap. Kyle was chewing his lip like he was having deep thoughts or something. It was a bizarre look on him. Like, I wasn't used to him thinking much past pizza toppings. After a moment, he sighed and riffled his hair.

"So what do you want me to ask Morgana? I mean, I'll try, but I haven't spoken to her in months. Her and Aegaeus—the All Father kind of ghosted them. He's been pretty hot on the whole assimilation thing." He ran his eyes over me. "Dude's got it bad for your other half."

I didn't want to hear it. "How was she the last time you saw her?"

"Lilith? Smokin'. Think we were in Corinth."

My eyes got real big at that info dump. Say what you will, but the Greeks knew how to bathe…and do a bunch of other stuff. He tongued a canine, and I flushed. How much had Samael been telling him? God, he was a jerk.

"I—No, Morgana."

"Shitty. Aegaeus's still a major dick, but it should be her time of the month." I raised an eyebrow, and Kyle snorted. "They hashed out some kind of a schedule where once a month one of them gets to be ascendent, but both are pissy about it."

Gee, that was hard to believe. I rolled my eyes. Being stuck in a body with either of them would make me want to slit my wrists after five seconds. "Do you think she'd talk to you?" Believe it or not, of the two, Morgana was more reasonable. Hah. I know, right?

He shrugged. "Maybe, but even if she did, I don't know that'd she'd help, and Aegaeus still fucking hates you. They're gonna be ripped when I start pleading your case."

That was also true. My relationship with Water had always been contentious, and I can't say I'd gone out of my way to improve relations at any point. Quite the opposite, in fact.

"But it's not just my case." I mean, aside from having to bang the Gwinth and save the few remaining halflings waiting to become, I couldn't care less if the Fae realms stayed sealed or not.

Kyle rolled to sit, chucking his wrapper into the to-go bag. "Look, I'll see what I can do, but I can't promise anything."

My head jerked up from playing with Rhys's toes. Yeah, I was obsessed. "You will?"

"Sure, if you bargain for it."

Crap. He grinned, and the sun seemed that much brighter.

"What do you desire?"

"One kiss." He tapped his cheek. "Right here."

"That's all?"

"That's all."

I bit at a cuticle. Brennan and the duergar had long since left the bedroom, and it's not like—What? No, I— All right, fine. He was a lot more tempting than carpaccio, but a part of me knew I'd be sick to my stomach if anything happened between us.

The other part of me was thinking about reenacting Corinth.

I shook my head, and his grin stretched to his ears. "Can't blame a man for trying. Tell you what, I'll talk to them anyways. For old time's sake."

My brow knit. Why would he—Kyle leaned closer

and tickled Rhys's belly. The baby just squirmed, starting to fuss. I was glad for the distraction. "Karen says he's too little to laugh or smile."

"Mmm. Samael remembers. Do you?"

I picked Rhys up, my hands shaking. "No."

His brow knit. "I don't understand how you can pick and choose—"

"I don't. Lilith does."

Kyle snorted, and it definitely had tones of the All Father in it. "It's like you're going in reverse. Instead of you becoming her, she's becoming you."

"Is that a bad thing? I like Kyle."

He searched my gaze. "I like you too, Snow."

Goddamn men. "Are you okay? I didn't mean—" Ugh, yeah, I was crying again.

He scooted over and put an arm around me. "Nah, babe, we're cool. Shhh. Hey, I'm fine. Most of the time he lets me drive, but I told you, he's got it bad for Lilith."

I sniffled, trying not to lean into him. Rhys started squalling, and Kyle moved away.

"Kid looks hungry. You should feed him."

I'd half pulled out my boob before I gave him a dirty look.

He laughed, wetting his lips. "What? It's hot—"

"Kyle."

Crap. Brennan had stepped through the shadows beneath the greenery. Had he been listening? Ugh! Of course he had. My irritation warred with relief, and that ticked me off. I didn't need a freaking chaperone—Okay, maybe I did.

Shut up.

Kyle grinned at Brennan. "Hey, man. S'up? I'd have grabbed you a burger but didn't know what you wanted on it. You dig chili?"

Brennan's cigarette crackled, and I shot him a pleading look. "It's not my favorite."

"Fair enough. Double bacon cheeseburger cool? Right on. I'll hook you up next time." He stood, tossing his shirt over his shoulder and grinned at me with a weird mix of the All Father's intensity and Kyle's nonchalance. What the heck was that like in his head? The external results were way too appealing, and a flush of heat went through me. "Until then. Later, babe."

Poof.

Brennan snagged the last of my fries and pulled out a chair. "I don't like him." He grumbled, chomping a fry. "Is this garlic aioli?"

I laughed, getting the little guy settled to nurse. "Good, right?"

He grunted, finishing them. "Will he talk to the fish?"

"Yeah, but he doesn't think it will do much good."

"Well, it's something at least. Why didn't you kiss him?"

See, I knew he'd been listening. I batted my lashes. "Did you want me to?"

"You would've if it didn't mean anything to you."

Ouch. "Maybe I didn't want to upset you."

He raised an eyebrow with that sour look and pulled out a cigarette, pausing to tap it on his knee. Cue him saying something I wasn't going to like. "I've arranged to stay with the Riders during this…whatever this is."

And there it was.

"In Vegas?" My hackles rose at his nod, and Rhys started fussing. I shushed him, pissed. Entertainment aside, that whole city held too many memories—Yeah, I know. Like my head didn't, but that wasn't the point. I'd grown up in Vegas, and I damned well knew what went on there.

He blew out a long stream of smoke. "The tables will be a much needed distraction, and it's a good base for any politics that arise. I'm going to have to start wining and dining the way things are going."

Mm-hmm. Not to mention all the rest of it. I fumed, and the kid started squalling. Not for nothing, but the Riders were basically frat boys, and with his fiend unleashed…Brennan's stupid smile didn't help. I switched the kid to the other side, certain the distraction wasn't going to stop at the tables. As to the wining and dining, you gotta know that was a euphemism for him flipping dollar bills at some—Ugh! My stigmata flared, and Rhys pitched a fit, hell-flame licking down the railing.

Goddamn it!

I stormed into the nursery and slammed the door. Flames crackled across my skin and my eyes burned. I get stuck here, and he was going to be off in party central having a grand old time with a bunch of whores. I slid down the wall, that hollowness eating at me again and my heart rate jumping. How could he do this?

How could any of this be happening?

I was well into hyperventilating when he knocked at the door. "Lovely?"

Rhys wailing was the only response he got. That anxiety attack I'd been flirting with for the past few days? Yeah, time to pay the piper. The kid's cries ticked up, the room telescoping out. I couldn't breathe—

Brennan burst in and swore, dropping down beside us. "Shh…Oh God, I didn't mean…" His face buried in my hair as he rocked me in his arms, and I lost my shit. What else was there to do? He couldn't glamor me out of it, and we were fresh out of hypodermics.

I don't know how long it lasted, but it felt like forever. This time, there was no place of flame and shadow to escape to, and being locked in my head with my crazy and a screaming baby was sooo much worse. Socks slithered in and roped around my shoulders, hissing in Rhys's ear. Whatever he said worked, and the baby settled. I wished he could do the same for me.

No dice.

I had to ride it out, and a horrible exhausted numbness stole over me when my panic ebbed. I pressed close to Brennan, shivering. The walls were thick with hoarfrost, and shadows writhed at the corners of the room. He stroked my hair, and beneath my ear his heart thumped slow and deliberate.

Fiendish.

"I'm going to kill them for putting you in this position."

I whimpered. It wasn't them. It was me. All of this was my fault, just like the last time in the Eden, and now he was going to leave. He was going to leave and some bimbo—tears leaked out my eyes, feeling round two getting ready to roll over me.

"Shh…" Brennan pressed my head against his chest, his lips on my brow. "It's all right."

It wasn't. Memories assailed me. Things I knew, but didn't. Didn't want to.

Adam.

I could see him standing there with *her* in my mind's eye, that stupid whore that'd supplanted me, and the way he looked at her…had looked at me…My hands balled into fists, and I pressed them to my temples. "Stop it! I don't need to know any of this—"

You do.

Brennan's arms tightened around me. "Lovely—"

"Don't touch me!"

I skittered away, and flames erupted between us. Brennan flinched back, the glass wall splintering into fractals from the abrupt change in temperature. I screamed, more memories playing out. Everything from the garden, from after. He was abandoning me, and I was back in that desolate wilderness, alone—

"Envy!"

Brennan lunged for me, but I was already gone.

Poof.

15 Days, 12 Hours, 57 Minutes

Well, not entirely alone. But Rhys, Socks, and I were in the middle of a wasteland.

Think valley of dry, red rock, a handful of stunted trees, scraggly bushes, and a whole lot of nothing. Socks's head weaved at me, flicking his tongue. Yeah, he was pissed, and Rhys started meeping. The combination shocked me out of my crazy.

Time to make the donuts.

I wiped at my face and settled onto a rock under the nearest tree to feed him. It was better than dwelling on the data dump I'd just gotten.

...All that's really left for you to assimilate are my memories, and I won't thrust them upon you unless you need them...

Why the hell would I need to be reminded of the intimate details of what a piece of shit my ex-husband was, and why now? Socks dropped to the ground and slithered away. I kicked a rock.

Adam. Man, he'd been a prick, and yeah, I'd gotten off on it, at first anyways, but submission had never really been my thing. Might have been a different story if he'd been all yes ma'am once in a while, but nooo…Ugh. I ran a hand over my face. Our relationship had devolved from some kinky-as-all-get-out BSDM to a textbook case of domestic abuse, and the Almighty hadn't said boo about it.

I mean, granted, there hadn't been a label for it then, and the whole first-man-and-woman schtick couldn't have been easy. Free will and all that. I didn't hold any grudges against the Big Guy. Creation had to have had a pretty steep learning curve; He was bound to make mistakes.

What? God doesn't make mistakes? You've seen platypuses, right? Please. Tell me that's not a Frankenstein fuck-up with a straight face. The entire continent of Australia is like the land of misfit toys. Whatever. My point is, we were all trying to figure it out. Some more successfully than others, and I drew the short straw.

I sat there beneath that stupid tree, lamenting the whole cosmic clusterfuck while Rhys nursed, wishing I'd been smart enough to grab his diaper bag and a bottle for myself.

Yeah, 'cause I was a big baby. Shut up.

Damn it.

I was going to have to go back, and I didn't want to. It felt like that was admitting to something, and I'd had my fill of that lately. Socks coiled around my feet and popped his head up on my knee, pretty much telling me to get over myself. I managed to burp Rhys without him ejecting everything he'd just downed, but his diaper was soaked and super mushy.

Everything was conspiring against me.

I sighed, looking around the barren valley. Why I'd come here on autopilot…It didn't matter. I was leaving.

I poofed back to the flat.

I laid Rhys on the changing table. Everything was creepy quiet—

I shrieked, totally unprepared for what was in that

damned diaper, or the little bastard peeing as soon as I peeled it back. I dodged. Socks was not so lucky. Kid had one hell of an arc.

Gaia had said something about poo yesterday, but she'd failed to mention that it would stick to him like gooey asphalt. What the hell did he eat that would make him shit tar? God, it was disgusting, all up in his…

Whatever. I changed his diaper, reconciled to my new gig as a waste-removal technician. That set, I poked my head into the bedroom. The balcony was pretty much gone, and the remaining glass between me and the cliffs below was Swiss cheese. No one was around. I crawled into bed and offered Rhys a boob, initiating the vicious cycle again.

He was more interested in sleep, and with him zonked out, the flat was quiet. Too quiet. I was used to Brennan and the imps moving about. Murmured phone conversations from the office, him plinking away at the piano…Was this what it was going to be like? I dashed a hand across my eyes. Stupid hormones.

I looked down at the little bastard and caught myself smiling despite the shit-show my life had turned into. My finger trailed down his cheek, his face smooshed against me as he drooled, perfect.

Had my mother ever looked at me like this?

The thought slapped the cynic back into me, and I snorted. Fat fucking chance. I teared up and then my eyes got heavy. I must've passed out, because when I blinked again, the sun was dropping past the horizon and Rhys was fussing. Strains of *Moonlight Sonata*'s first movement drifted into the room. Crap. Brennan only played Beethoven when he was dealing with serious shit. His phone chirped, and the music cut off mid-chord.

He started arguing with someone. Like, loud.

"What—No. We've been over this. I have it handled. She's not the issue, it's…Damn it, you will leave this alone! Yes, I'll be there—"

His office door slammed.

Yeah, my anxiety had ticked up. Trust me, I was getting pretty sick of it, too. Being all spun up is exhausting, as is trying to figure out how you're going to explain your crazy. Once again, I had no idea what I was going to say to him.

I buried myself in baby bullshit. Repeat everything that'd just happened, minus the evil poo and peeing on the snake. I was onto Rhys's game and way too proud of that fact. Ugh, what my life had digressed into—

Brennan was leaning against the door frame when I turned. He didn't say anything, just opened his arms.

I went to him.

Yeah. I lost it. I told you, I was a pathetic mess.

After a while, he put Rhys in his crib and led me into the bathroom. The water in the shower was already running and steaming hot. It's a big spa-type deal with a built-in bench and a ton of nozzles. You know, river rocks on the floor, the whole shebang. He'd put in one of those lemon-eucalyptus urinal-cake-looking thingies I liked, and the air bit into my lungs. Our clothes ended up in a pile on the floor, and we got in.

He had me sit and started washing my hair.

God, how much can a person cry? I mean seriously, I was gonna get an electrolyte imbalance or something if this kept up. I didn't even know why I was crying, which kind of makes it hard to be cathartic. I just felt wrung out. And no, I didn't ask him about the phone call. I was pretty sure it had been about me and had no desire to find out what I'd screwed up now.

Brennan cleaned me up, wrapped me in a soft robe, and then just held me.

I don't understand how he does it. Well, yeah, dealing with me on a daily basis is pretty amazing in and of itself, but I meant how he always knows how to make me feel better. Right then, that was exactly what I needed. The only thing missing—

Peter came in with a tray and set it on the bedside table. The smell of udon soup wafted through the air, and beside the bowl was one of those big Japanese beers and box of truffles.

God, I loved him.

I sat up and dashed a hand across my eyes, cracking the beer first, followed by a truffle, and then started slurping noodles. Brennan lit a cigarette, watching me with a pensive look on his face I didn't much like. I liked it less when he tapped his third cigarette on his knee.

Oh yeah, you better believe that was one of his tells.

"I've come up with an alternate lodging arrangement for your consideration." My eyebrow quirked. His delivery was better this time. "How would you feel about me staying here, and you rooming with Mother Earth?"

My lips froze mid-slurp, and I coughed. "What, like, in her hole in the ground?"

"No." He relaxed when I didn't reject it out of hand. "I was going to wait, but…there's a small estate available in the hills just outside of Vel City. I've put a deposit down to hold it."

A small estate. I snorted. All the digs in the hills were multi-million-dollar McMansions, built by the last wave of tech entrepreneurs that'd blown out of Silicon

Valley. I snagged another mess of noodles with my chopsticks.

"You would stay here?"

"I would. Karen and the Riders will go with you."

"And Gaia."

"And Gaia." He blew a long stream of smoke to the side.

My eyes narrowed. "What did she desire?"

"You know that's not how it works, but it's nothing you need to concern yourself with."

Somehow I very much doubted that, and he already owed Morgana twice for saving my ass and Rhys's after the whole poisoned-crepe incident. "Why her?"

"You went to Gaia when you were upset, and she's a neutral party." His mouth turned down, and I knew he was thinking about the All Father. She wasn't that neutral. The two of them got on about as well as I did with Aegaeus, but as far as Brennan was concerned, that would be a point in her favor.

"The Gwinth and All Father are fine with it?"

"Given your reaction to my previous proposal, they've agreed it's in your best interest, on the condition that they also have an envoy present."

Great. So they all knew I was a basket case. "Who're they sticking me with?"

"Kennet and some sprite I've yet to meet."

Whatever. I sighed and finished my noodles. "Is that gonna work, or are you going to try to kill your dad at dinner again?"

"Not without just cause." He was totally serious, and I rolled my eyes.

"Fine." I was tired of fighting, and at least I wouldn't be rattling around here by myself.

He look beyond relieved. "Wonderful. I'll push the paperwork and have the imps get everything ready. We'll have to have a dinner with everyone either Thursday or Friday—"

"Wait—what? Everyone?"

"Yes." He hissed out the word with another stream of smoke. Guess I wasn't going to just have to worry about him killing his dad. Fun times. "Tradition—"

"Whatever. Do it Thursday. We already have that stupid pronouncing thing Friday."

He smirked. "Presentment."

I rolled my eyes, not caring what it was called, there was no way was I putting on real pants more than once in twenty-four hours. I sat back against him with the box of chocolates and another beer.

Brennan played with my hair, threading it through his fingers. "Where did you go this time?"

"You can't find me through the shadows?"

"Enough to listen. Location gets lost in translation. I was only able to sense a faint direction and get an impression of your emotions. I knew you were safe, just needed time."

My brow furrowed. "I don't know where I was," I said, busy hollowing out a truffle with my tongue. "It was pretty much the middle of nowhere. I'm not sure why I poofed there." And I didn't want to explore the possibilities. I'd had enough of thinking about my ex, for like, ever, thank you very little.

He took a long drag of his cigarette. "I'm not Adam, Lovely."

"Why do you think it had anything to do with him?"

Brennan snorted. "The look on your face. If I didn't know any better, I'd think you were an undine." He chuckled when I smacked him. "Have you heard from her?"

I grabbed my phone from the bedside table. "Nope, but Kyle texted me. Morgana agreed to meet with him, but not when." God. I chucked the phone down. As much as I felt bad about her current predicament, I was starting to get pissed. I mean, what kind of a selfish bitch would screw everyone over just because she was having an identity crisis?

Shut up.

"Mmm. Well, I'm sure it won't be long before he pins her down so he can sniff around here again."

My eyebrow arched. "Sniff around?"

"I don't know what else you'd call him panting after you and trying to shove his snout up your skirts."

I snorted at the visual. "Planning on smacking him with a rolled-up newspaper?"

"I was thinking more along the lines of a minibus. You know, despite your fears to the contrary, I'm not planning on going anywhere, and as soon as this blasted veil is cleared, I'm throwing you over my shoulder and making it official."

I ate another truffle. "How neolithic of you."

"I'll only club you if I have to." Jerk. He kissed my brow, and I couldn't help but smile. "Is that a yes?"

I sighed. Maybe it was because I was so worn down by everything, but…"It's not a no."

His face lit up and when he kissed me—

Rhys started screaming.

Goddamn it.

Brennan chuckled again. "I'll get him."

I let him. If the kid's diaper was packin' anything like last time, no freaking way was I volunteering for that. Unfortunately, as much as I would've like to continue lying there, my body was having a decided response to his shrieking, and my damned shirt was soaked again. God, motherhood was a raw deal.

I padded into the nursery.

Brennan was glowering over round two of whatever that evil mess was coming out of the kid. It was seriously gross. I laughed. At that and what was dripping off Brennan's chin. He flicked it off, swearing.

"Little bastard tagged me," he muttered, handing him off. "What the hell have you been feeding him?"

"Radioactive bananas." I settled into the rocker and presented a boob. Rhys latched on, and I winced. "You wanted to change him."

"I wouldn't have if I'd known what was in there."

I laughed again, and he shot me a look over his shoulder, leaving to clean himself up. After I while, I caught myself smiling as I rocked. Maybe I could do this. Be an us. The thought had begun to make my insides warm instead of wanting to piss myself…Which made me want to piss myself for an entirely different reason.

Look, good things didn't happen to me. And when they did, they sure as hell didn't last. I broke out in a cold sweat, gripping Rhys a little tighter, filled with the worst feeling that something was about to rip it all away.

14 Days, 16 Hours, 3 Minutes

The small estate Brennan had found wasn't small.

It was a huge gated affair set way back from the McMansions on a hillside of old oaks and locust trees. He said it'd been built by some railroad baron way back when, and I totally believed it. The grounds were parklike and immaculate. Something like seventy-five acres of them. I had zero doubt Gaia had already had her way with the place; it was way too lush otherwise. I wasn't complaining. It was straight-up gorgeous.

And huge. Did I say it was huge? Because it was huge. Three stories, gabled, and there was a freaking turret on one end. I stood in the drive of weedless, pink crushed gravel gawking up at it like I had a nose bleed.

Brennan kissed my temple. "Do you like it?"

Was he stupid? "You rented this for me?"

"No. I bought it for you. If you decide to keep it, you'll need to sign the paperwork."

I just stared at him, and his smile widened.

"Jaw, Lovely."

"You—really?"

"It's traditional for a suitor to—"

"This is your freaking courting gift?" He was insane.

"Yes and no." He shrugged, his gaze moving over the massive ivy-covered edifice.

"But it had to cost like a bajillion dollars. How—"

"My finances are more than adequate. We needed a

home reflective of your status, and somewhere for Rhys to grow up, like I had with Kennet. A boy needs woods to play in. There's no place to ramble at the flat." He smiled softly at me. "And no room to run. I know you miss it."

He couldn't be real. My heart was in my throat, and I melted against him, his mouth on mine—

Rhys squalling between us. Baby wearing definitely had its drawbacks.

"Little bastard's quite the cock blocker, isn't he?" Brennan murmured against my lips.

I scowled. He was at that. Not that I could technically do anything about it, even though I was feeling way better. Maybe waiting had just been a guideline. Like that hour after eating before you swim. No one did that, and I'd never seen bodies floating after a picnic…

Brennan grinned at me. "Do you want to see the inside?"

Did I want to see the inside.

It didn't disappoint. Fully furnished, massive airy rooms, a master bath with a tub I could swim in if I got bored with the other two pools—what? Yeah, they were heated, indoors and out, servants' quarters for the imps and the Riders, an entire nursery with a loaded playroom, and a section of the first floor was all done up like offices. Brennan could deal with whatever political crap he had to do. I leaned against a moiré-silk-papered wall, my breath coming fast.

This was a life.

Like, a real one. Not a tricked-out Vegas hotel paid for by some sugar daddy's largess. Not a cell in a convent. Not even a sweet bachelor pad overlooking the ocean.

A home.

Yeah, I was crying again.

Brennan gathered me up in his arms, kissing my tears away. How was any of this real? "The paperwork's in the desk drawer with that album Peter made of us and Rhys. I've had everything put in your name. Even if—" His voice caught. "It's yours. No matter what you decide. I want you and Rhys to have it."

I stared at him. No matter what I decided? It was too much. "No, why would you—" Crap. It was because he said he wouldn't pressure me. This was him putting this money where his mouth was. "It's a bribe, isn't it."

He raised an eyebrow with that grin of his. "Is it working?"

God, he was a dick sometimes.

And yeah, it was the kind I liked. Long story short, I signed the papers. I was a blubbering mess about it, but that had been my default lately, and how could I not? I mean, come on, the man was all golden ticket about buying me a freaking estate. No way was I pissing on his parade…but I was curious how he'd ponied up so much cash for damned thing. The place was mint.

"You really can afford this?" We were walking through a ballroom—yeah, it had a ballroom!—to the gardens in the back. It opened up to a big portico with a terrace and then the grounds—freaking grounds!—rolled out into the hills.

Brennan shrugged, lighting a cigarette. "Kennet was a lord back in the day. I inherited his lands. They've done well over the centuries, and I've had very little to spend my income on. The imps have made some wise investments for me. Liquidity isn't something I worry about."

Translation: "So you're saying you're loaded."

He smirked. "I suppose that's one way of putting it."

"What about all that crap about your stipend not covering the damage I did to your flat?"

"It didn't. Your father is a cheap bastard, but I got quite a chunk of change out of him in exchange for making him warlord. The balance was applied to the accounts you gained as Clan Malten's heir. Peter can show you, if you're interested. You're a wealthy woman in your own right, Lovely."

I stopped, having been under the impression I had maybe seven fifty to my name, like as in dollars and cents, and half of that was in subway tokens. The only account ever associated with my name began with "of no." I mean, the library wouldn't even give me a card.

"I have accounts? Like real ones? At a bank?"

"Banks." He corrected, laughing. "Yes. Were you not paying attention when we filled out the paperwork?"

I shot him a look. He knew I hadn't been. We had an arrangement, he showed me a line, I signed. My literary tastes ran by way of manga. If it didn't have somebody getting their ass kicked throughout framed-out boxes, I wasn't interested.

My chest got tight. Maybe I should be…or at least make an effort to be.

I started walking again in a daze, a hand on Rhys's back as he slept. I had a baby, bank accounts, and a house—no, a freaking estate. Christ, I was a homeowner—Did I have to worry about taxes and shit now? Agencies with three letter acronyms that wanted accountability? I couldn't keep my manicure up, how was I supposed to—

Brennan kissed my brow. "The imps will continue to take care of everything. Just enjoy it, Lovely."

Enjoy it. How the hell could I enjoy it when I felt like I was going to wake up any second? All of this was too good. Too adult. Something was gonna fuck it up.

And let's be honest, that something was probably me.

We went out onto the terrace, below the portico. Wisteria hung down shading the expanse, and I could hear the whirr of Peter's camera from somewhere in the garden. It stretched before us into green hills sloping to the horizon. Gaia was out past the lush hedgerow, amidst a cloud of butterflies.

Yeah, for real.

"She wanted to see you. I'll be in the office finalizing the paperwork for the sale and the details for tomorrow's Presentment. Think you can find your way back?" Brennan's brow crumpled like he wanted to ask if I'd be all right and wasn't sure if that would set me off again.

I nodded and forced a smile, overcome. He kissed my cheek and smiled for real, running a hand over Rhys's downy head, then went inside. I wandered through the garden, trying to wrap my brain around all of it. How was this mine? I couldn't even keep track of my shoes half the time. How was I gonna get a handle on all this?

I still hadn't figured it out when I got to the clearing where Gaia was grubbing around. I sat on an ornate affair of twisted iron that served as a bench, watching her rear end sway. It was oddly soothing. The rest of her was hidden by a bunch of ornamental grasses. By the time she pushed back, I was kind of numb again, wishing I had a bottle. There had been at least three minibars scattered around the rooms for entertaining, but trying to find them again was gonna be a—

"Hey, Vy."

"Berk?" Cue waterworks. He came over and sat at the ground by my feet. It took about half a second for me to end up in his lap. He smelled like freshly turned soil and weed. No, not weeds, weed. Gaia was big on herbal medicinals. And yes, I'm using that term broadly. Pot, shrooms, peyote, she was like the original Deadhead. Whatever. I breathed it in, half tempted to ask for hit or seventeen.

"It is good that you have come to this place. Your chi is imbalanced. The gardens will help ground and dispel the negative energy which surrounds you."

I sniffled against him, too happy to see him to tell him what he could do with my imbalanced chi. He'd probably take it negatively. Hah. "Is that why Gaia agreed to babysit me?"

His brow furrowed. "Not entirely. When your dae came looking for you, he needed help, Envy. As do you. Your mood affects the lesser fire elementals, and they have been…erratic."

"What do you mean erratic?" I pushed back, wiping at my eyes.

"It is as foreseen. The planet burns, and the normals rise up against us."

"I thought Brennan had a handle—"

"No." His features shifted, and I scrambled out of his—her, lap. God, that was creepy. Gaia was back in charge and, from her expression, had a serious stick up her ass. Her tone confirmed it was pointy. "This is *not* something he's equipped to deal with. You need to get a grip on your postpartum depression."

My postpartum—the fuck?! My temper jumped, and Rhys started meeping. "I'm not fucking depressed! I'm pissed! Lilith's dumping memories on me, Brennan's hell bent on dragging me to the altar, the Gwinth's set on breeding me, and the All Father's a complication I don't need! Oh, yeah, and the whole baby thing." His little face was red and squalling, and that just pissed me off more. "I'd like to see you in the same goddamned position and keep your shit together!"

Gaia threw up her hands. "Regardless, all the normals see is the destruction left by the wildfires and an uptick in volcanic activity, which Earth is getting blamed for." She glared at me all "you had to go there, didn't you?" Told you it was a sore subject. "Washington is having hearings about it, and I'm getting called on the carpet. It's Pompeii all over again."

Oh ho…we were going there. My teeth clenched together, jaw popping. "Pompeii wasn't my fault. If Aegaeus hadn't—"

"Mm-hmm." She started rolling a joint all zen, and I wanted to punch her. I incinerated a bush instead. Her eyebrow rose. "I've agreed to help ease your transition into motherhood and provide what calming influence I can."

I snorted. "Yeah? And what did you desire for the privilege?"

"That is between Brennan and I."

"You're gonna spill it, now, or you're gonna get the hell off my lawn."

Gaia sighed, licking the spliff closed. "I swear that no harm will come to you and yours from my half of the bargain. Indeed, it is in your best interest that it goes forward. Your dae is shrewd, although admittedly he suffers from tunnel vision where you're concerned. What he's been dealing with on your behalf…I honestly don't understand why that man tolerates you." She shook her head and toked up.

It wasn't like I hadn't been baffled by the same phenomenon, but I wasn't in the mood to meditate on it, and calming Rhys was fraying my last nerve. I shoved my boob in his mouth and he shut up. "That's not good enough."

"It's all I can offer. He was firm on that point."

Wait—Brennan was the one going all hush-hush on me? Bastard. I snagged the spliff when she offered it. Oh, shut up. She wouldn't give me anything that would hurt the kid, and I told you, fae are different from normals like that. Still, it tasted weird, like it wasn't pot.

"What's in this?"

Her eyes were all slitty, and she smiled. "Herbs."

Mine rolled, taking another hit. No shit.

Whatever it was, I gotta tell you, it leveled me right the hell out. Don't get me wrong, I didn't go all kumbaya, but my desire to immolate things went poof. Kind of like a bottle without the buzz, but I did get a wicked case of cotton mouth. I smacked my felty tongue against my teeth. Yuck.

"You need to drink more water to keep your milk supply up."

Right. That wasn't happening. "I'll make sure to add some to my whiskey."

"Try pairing it with a self-affirming mantra. Be the person who feels like sunshine…"

I snorted, and she gave me a look, then went back to gardening. I went back to the house to look for a bottle.

Be the person who feels like sunshine. What the hell did that even mean? Like Sahara sunshine or South Pole sunshine—or that shit on the back of cats' eyes? Wait, no, that was eyeshine—

You know what, no. This is what she did. Got me all fucked-up and then planted some dirty hippy gunga gunga lunga in my brain for me to trip out over.

It took a while to find a minibar—for absolutely no other reason than the place was huge and I had to dodge like a bazillion imps—in a long room with thick brocade drapes.

What were the imps doing? I dunno, imp stuff. Moving crap around, cleaning. I figured we were moving right in. When Brennan set his mind to something, shit gets done, and they made it happen. Like, if I ever agreed to marry him, I was pretty sure a rose-covered bower and priest would appear in five minutes flat.

Crap. Don't remind me about that.

I snagged a bottle and sat on one of the wide leather sofas facing away from the floor to ceiling windows, smoothing Rhys's fluff as he slept. That, poop, and eat…must be nice to just have three things to occupy your time. Well, four, if you counted cock blocking.

The room was all done up in teals and blues with silver accents. An undine probably would've thought it was classy. Maybe it was. I wasn't real fluent in interior design. The last thing I'd decorated with had been band posters, and Calista had made me take them down.

On that note—bottoms up.

Look, we can discuss my fitness as a parent later. I'll add it to my to-do list, along with finding that therapist you recommended the last time my crazy was showing.

Anyways, once I'd gotten the funk out of my mouth,

I just felt sleepy. I must've dozed, because the next thing I knew, Karen was waking me up to get dressed for dinner. Crap, I'd forgotten about that. Rhys wasn't excited about it either. Like super fussy and all anti-boob. I took it personally. I mean, what the hell? Aside from being wicked uncomfortable, no one had ever turned down a chance to get at my rack.

"You pump," Karen said, laying out something strapless, red, and slinky. Because that's what every woman wants to wear three days after giving birth.

"A pump? For what?" I asked in Impese, pretty sure there was a language-barrier whatsis going on.

"You milk. He no take, you pump. I give him later." She left the room, then came back with something that looked like a cross between a medieval torture device and an airhorn. She plugged it in and traded me for the baby. "It make better. Try, else hurt, and you leak."

I snapped my jaw shut. Fuck my life.

So I'm just gonna lay it out. Being milked was definitely one of the most humiliating experiences in all my existences. In case you've never had the pleasure, that little mechanical wonder she foisted off on me simulates the suck-and-swallow of an infant. Pull-stop. Pull-stop. That in itself isn't so bad, I mean, it's way weird and kinda gross to watch yourself squirt, but whatever. What got me was the sound every time it cycled.

Moo. Moo.

Okay, maybe it didn't actually moo, but it was close enough that I made the association and then I couldn't un-hear it.

Moo. Moo.

Seriously. Fuck my life.

So there I was, filling up bottle number two, lamenting my fate as a Guernsey. Whatever Gaia had given me was still chilling me out, and I was feeling a deep kinship with dairy cows everywhere when Brennan walked in. I screamed, throwing the damned thing.

Yeah, milk-tastrophy.

Him laughing when he figured out what'd happened didn't help. He picked up the gurgling contraption, salvaging half my slave labor, and grinned as I fixed my shirt. My face burned, like hot, even for me.

"What's this?"

"Karen made me do it," I muttered, horrified he was touching it. Christ, it was like a pastor had found my vibrator.

"Look at you all embarrassed." He chuckled.

I glared, but I could kind of understand why he was so tickled. Not that it made it any better. I wasn't exactly what you'd call shy when it came to bodily functions, but this definitely ranked right up there with taking a crap in front of him.

Not happening, no way. If there was one thing my mother had instilled upon me that I wholeheartedly endorsed, it was that women didn't poop. I mean, we did, but men weren't supposed to know that. I was pretty sure they weren't supposed to see us mechanically milking ourselves, either.

Brennan set the wretched device on the table. "I'll try to remember to knock next time I hear mysterious mooing from the bedroom."

See?! I freaking knew—Oh God, he'd heard it. I buried my face in my hands, and the asshole laughed. He came over and kissed the top of my head. "Just when I think you can't possibly surprise me—"

I grabbed the front of his shirt, balling it up in my fist. "If you tell anyone, I'll kill you."

"That's more like it." He failed to swallow a smile. "And I wouldn't dream of it."

Liar. I glared at him again for good measure and went to take a shower.

When I came out wrapped in a towel, both he and the moo machine were gone. I stared down at Karen's fashion pick, hating my life more than usual.

Yeah, that again.

Look, the stupid dress was strapless and one side of the floor-length skirt was slit so high you'd be able to see my garter. It sounds dumb, but I had to psych myself up to try the damned thing on. Fuck diamonds. I'll argue to the death that sweatpants are in fact a girl's best friend. They sure as hell had been mine for the past few months. My figure wasn't totally blown out, but it was a lot curvier than it'd been and jigglier than I was cool with. The prospect of clambering into this getup had zero appeal. Don't laugh, but I locked the door to change, wondering if I could snag one of Gaia's kaftans when this went horribly awry.

Surprisingly, it didn't.

I'm sure that could be entirely attributed to the super-structure of support hose that Karen had smuggled in with it, but I wasn't complaining. The results of being encased in a push-up compression body stocking weren't anything to sneeze at. I've said before I'm pretty much pin-up perfect—well, I was—but thanks to the assist, now I was voluptuous on top of smokin' hot. Like Pam Anderson in her prime had zip on me. For real, don't hate.

There was a knock on the door, and I let Karen in to

do my hair. She piled it up high and gave me a fierce, smokey cat-eye. My lips were stained crimson, and she fastened a collar of black diamonds around my throat. She's been right about the scars from the last one I'd had snapped around my neck—you could hardly see them anymore. I sighed at the shoes, but honestly, the ensemble demanded four-inch heels. I slipped them on and started buckling their crisscross ankle straps.

Oh yeah. She'd tricked me out all femme fatal for this shindig. Couldn't wait to see how that went over with the boys. And speaking of which...

"Where's Rhys?"

"I feed. He sleep. Snake and Becky with him."

Becky was Karen and Peter's granddaughter. Yeah. I hadn't known they were a thing either. Imps are weird about their personal relationships. Everything was on the DL, but they'd been married basically forever and had like six kids and a couple dozen grandkids. Becky was the youngest of those. She'd just gotten her babysitting certificate, and I trusted her almost as much as Karen, but still stopped in to check on the little bastard before I went downstairs.

He was zonked out in his crib with Socks coiled around him. The snake flicked his tongue at me, snickering. Jerk. And yes. As a matter of fact, I did need to make sure the kid was still breathing and was probably gonna stop after dinner to check again.

Shut up.

The dining room was this massive formal affair with a table that sat like twenty. All dark wood and crystal chandeliers. Yep, it was totally a bit much, but hey, so was I.

The shouting coming from the room as I came down

the hall seemed way out of place.

So, despite being a fiend, Brennan was super chill most of the time. Like, I'd pitched a fit a couple of months ago and blew a hole in the side of the infinity pool, draining the damn thing. He'd lit a cigarette, run a hand through his hair, and muttered something about it being bloody inconvenient.

Right now, he was swearing a blue streak that made *me* blush. Yeah, I know. I'm not exactly a shrinking violet when it comes to colorful vernacular. Curiosity piqued, I edged closer. I felt the chill rolling out of the room a good ten feet down the hall, and it was noticeably darker. Shadows shambled from my path, edging away as I approached the doorway.

"There's not a fucking chance this is happening! Are you trying to make her completely lose her shit? My God, your head has to be farther up your ass than that dumb cunt's G-string! And you, how can you sign off on his bullshit? What the hell happened to all your fucking concern about her delicate state of mind? I hope the lesser dae fry every single fucking—"

He broke off as I came in, and yes, I was totally smug at the way tongues lolled.

I may have pulled my shoulders back and paused for effect.

Yeah, all right, I did, but it was short-lived.

Eleven of the seats were filled, their occupants all tux or gown-clad. Only one of them held my attention.

Hah. You'd be wrong.

Aegaeus was sitting at the table, his eyes on mine as he bit into a piece of honeyed bread.

I swallowed a groan along with my surprise, very grateful for whatever I'd toked up in the garden. I could feel my anxiety, but it was remote. Totally not the shitstorm that would've engulfed me if they'd sprung this on me unmedicated. No wonder Brennan was so worked up. He came over, banishing the shadows and returning the room to a reasonable temperature. His hands smoothed over my hips, all composed and totally full of shit.

Told you he was born to be a politician.

"You look divine," he murmured, his lips grazing my ear to nip at my lobe.

Okay, maybe he wasn't totally full of shit.

"You're not so bad yourself." I smoldered up at him through my lashes, and his chest rumbled. "Trying to distract me from our dinner guest?" Guests. More than one of them sucked, but I'd be lying if I said he wasn't. Distracting that is. Man could fill out a tux. Mmm. Daelicious. And focusing on him was a hell of a lot more appealing than the alternative.

"I had nothing to do with Aegaeus being here. You can thank the All Father for bringing him." His lips teased mine. "Do you think they'd take it amiss if I threw you over my shoulder and carried you right back upstairs?"

Funny, I'd been wondering the same thing—

"Get your fill of her while you can. After tomorrow, you're relegated to the back of the bus," the Gwinth said, taking a sip of his cocktail with that damned gap-toothed grin.

God, I hated him, and I wasn't the only one.

Brennan growled and offered me his arm. I took it, and he escorted me to the table. All of the Riders were in attendance and looking dapper. I honestly didn't know they made tuxedos that big, and surprisingly, the guys didn't look like trained gorillas in them. Stewie definitely had shades of Gomez Adams going on, and the other two were all mafia-tough. Jonas fell into that category, too, but kept pulling at his collar. I was pretty sure it wasn't just the fit that was making him uncomfortable.

The room was hella tense, and the table broken out by factions. Anyone associated with Fire was at one end, then Gaia. She had on a cloth-of-gold kaftan that made her skin literally glow, and her hair was in intricate braids. She exuded vitality and beauty, everything that the title of Mother Earth evoked. She also looked stoned off her gourd.

Aegaeus was across from her.

Cue the data dump.

All right, so look. The All Father wasn't the only one I had history with. Oh please, like that's a huge shock, but this wasn't like that one time at band camp. This had been very specifically, that one time after a bris in Canaan. The wine hadn't watered been nearly enough, not that I'd complained, and for whatever reason, Aegaeus had decided to let loose, and I'd totally taken advantage. You know, that whole opposites attracting— Okay, maybe it was more seeing how far I could push him, and then he totally called my bluff. What? There was no way I was backing down, and let's just say that our sexual game of chicken went further than either of us intended.

Anywho—I think I mentioned make-up sex was freaking hot. Well, let's just say hate sex with Aegaeus had been steamy.

Literally.

Yeah. So I know I said after he first merged with Morgana he was all skinny with a shrunken chest, but that's not how he looked way back when, or now. Whatever body sharing set-up he'd worked out with her had let him fully assume his form, which was basically the little mermaid's daddy on steroids. His grey hair flowed across his shoulders all Fabio, and his beard was close cut. He was in an inky black tux, and the buttons on his shirt were pearls. Anyways, I smiled at him, and he scowled.

Yup, still hated me. Moving on.

Kyle—no, the All Father—was farther down. He was Baywatch meets GQ amazing with some svelte blonde chippy at his side, the sprite Brennan had mentioned if I had to guess, and most likely the dumb cunt he'd been referring to, though I doubted she was wearing a G-string or anything else resembling panties. Not under that dress. Remember that air ghost with boobs back at the temple? Sprites can turn corporeal if the mood strikes them, but she probably wouldn't be able to maintain it through dinner without frequent reminders. They weren't known for their mental prowess. They were known for being wide-eyed, brainless gutter sluts. Figures the All Father would bring one. He knew they made my teeth grind. God, I hated bimbos.

Whatever. They both ignored me, too busy eye-fucking each other.

I ground my teeth.

At the end of the table was the Gwinth. He looked good, but so had crypto when it first came out. His eyes burned gold as they ran over me, and he licked his lips. It made me want to bathe in bleach. Kennet sat at his right hand in a formal kilt. No lie, it was the ugliest plaid I'd ever seen. Mustard yellow, periwinkle, and a weird shade of red that couldn't make up its mind to go orange or purple. His calves made up for it. They were super impressive in those tight fringed socks.

Brennan pulled out the chair at the end of the table, and I sat, all eyes less two pairs on me.

Well, wasn't this nice.

I smiled so I wouldn't scream, and Brennan tapped the side of his glass with a butter knife to get Joanie and Chachi's attention. Everyone else was already rapt. Some of them disturbingly so.

"I appreciate all of you bringing your candidates for representation." Brennan glared at the All Father, and he didn't seem to notice, still intent on that sprite. Was he trying to make me jealous? What? No, it wasn't working; it was just rude.

The imps came in with salads. It was one of my favorites. Hearts of palm with supremes of citrus and sliced fennel bulb. I munched as Brennan continued.

"As of midnight tomorrow, none but those formally approved by all parties shall have access to Envy. We're in agreement that the rota will run from sunrise to sunset—"

"I'm not getting up at sunrise."

"—until a consort is chosen. The proscribed hours are traditional, Lovely."

"I don't care." I batted my lashes at him. If I had to play along with this crap, I sure as hell wasn't doing it at the ass-crack of dawn. "Ten to ten."

"That cuts into my hunting time," the Gwinth said.

I rolled my eyes. "Boo-freaking-hoo. Being dead will cut into it more. Have fun with that. I agreed to let you court me, not rearrange my schedule to suit yours. Take it or leave it."

His eyes glinted. "Oh, I firmly intend to take it."

Asshole.

"Right." Brennan looked between us, his "T" way crisp. "Ten to ten. Gaia will be acting as my representative and remain with Envy during her interactions to ensure all the proper forms are followed during—"

"And the Riders?" the All Father asked, feeding the chippy from his plate.

"The Riders have been included tonight as a courtesy to all of you. They will be maintaining the security of the grounds, but I don't anticipate them having much, if any, interaction with her. As you're all aware, normal/fae relations have been strained of late, and I'll not put her or our son at risk. Do you all find that satisfactory?" Didn't sound like the others were real keen, but they let it slide, grunting their agreement and Brennan sat.

I shot him a look. He hadn't mentioned anything to me about security issues. Were things really that bad? Calista's words chose that moment to come back to me. *...God, crawl out of a bottle once in a while, maybe pick up a newspaper...* Son of a—like I needed my bitch mother's voice rattling around in my head. I pushed the last of my salad away along with the memory of her and motioned for another glass of wine.

The Gwinth did the same. "Kennet will be acting as my representative and is more than capable of protecting Envy should the need arise. I'm assuming there's no objections?"

There weren't any from me. Honestly, I was kind of looking forward to pumping him for information about Brennan. Specifically that little tidbit he'd dropped about almost being taken by shadow.

Kennet pushed his plate away, untouched. "Och, there's objection if this rabbit food's the norm. Ye best have somewhat in that kitchen fit t'eat. Where the hell's the meat?"

"You'll have to take that up with Envy," Brennan said dabbing his lips with a napkin. "I'm afraid she's not a big fan, and this is her table, not mine."

My eyebrow rose. Passive aggressive much? Guess he was still pissed at him, and that meat comment wasn't totally true. Unfortunately for Kennet, I had a feeling seafood and chicken didn't qualify as such.

He looked aghast. "Jesus, Mary, and Joseph, tell me ye haven't gone and shacked up with a bloody vegetarian…"

"Not quite." Brennan's eye glimmered, thoroughly enjoying his father's distress. "She's quite fond of fish." From the look on Kennet's face, I'd hit the nail on the head about that not qualifying. The imps brought in the next course. Salmon on a bed of wilted spinach and cherry tomatoes with pilaf.

"Oh, for the love of—" Kennet poked it with his knife. "What the hell is this shite? How are ye even supposed t'eat it…?"

"Try a fork," the All Father said, picking up his. "Bunny will remain as my representative."

"Bunny?" My lips curdled, I couldn't help it.

He grinned; his features softened to Kyle's. "Yeah, babe. She's cool."

I snorted. She was most definitely not cool. The sprite smiled shyly at me, and I rolled my eyes, very aware of my support hose and the fact that she wasn't wearing a bra and didn't need one. Great. A live-action wet dream was just what I needed hanging around the pool. And speaking of which, I turned to the sea-elephant in the room. "And you, Aegaeus? To what do we owe the pleasure?"

He took his time before looking up from his plate, his azure eyes trapping mine. "I found it remiss that every element would be represented tonight, save Water. If your toy can request Gaia's addlepated attendance, I didn't see any reason why I couldn't tag along. You wanted to speak to me, and I felt it opportune."

"Gaia is here for a very specific reason," Brennan said, icing the air. "Your presence has the potential to negate any benefit of hers."

Aegaeus's grin made me want to vomit. So did the All Father canoodling with Bunny like he wasn't responsible for the asshole being here. I'd asked for his help with Morgana, not…Ugh! This was just something he would do to piss me off. Bastard.

"All things unfold as they should," Gaia said, her voice thick. She waved her fork like she was catching trails off it and smiled. What the hell was she on? A better question was did she have more—

Aegaeus snorted. He on the other hand, was a total teetotaler. Like, painfully sober. Probably had to do with that slipup in Canaan.

Sorry, not sorry.

"Why didn't Morgana come?" I asked, stabbing at my fish and hoping he'd read into it. "I was under the impression it was her time of the month."

By the way his lips pursed up like an asshole, he did. "You were mistaken. Besides, she has nothing to say to you, whereas I have plenty."

I smiled at him, hoping spinach wasn't stuck in my teeth. "Oh? Do tell."

He grabbed the salt shaker and upended it into his water goblet, making me wait for it as he showed off, forming a little whirlpool to stir it. Wasted talent, man. He could've been a killer bartender.

"Samael tells me you're in a bit of a bind, and its resolution is contingent upon my cooperation." He took a sip of the nasty stuff and set it aside.

I shrugged, stabbing a tomato. There wasn't any point in denying I needed his help, and the asshole knew it. He also knew I'd be damned before I begged.

Which meant he was absolutely gonna twist the screws.

Where was the Gwinth during all this? Funny you should ask. He'd gone so still it was hard to remember he was even there, which I'm pretty sure was the point, and he was laser-focused on the conversation. I blotted my lips and took a sip of wine. If he thought I was trying to weasel out of the whole courting thing, it was gonna be hello huntsman.

"We have limited time before Midsummer's and the last of the halflings have to choose to become or sputter. Given our own histories, I'd think you'd like to see them become fae as much as I would." I popped another tomato into my mouth and raised an eyebrow at Aegaeus.

What? All of that was true. Elementals can't lie, remember? It just maybe wasn't the most pertinent reason. Yeah, that whole misdirection deal, and you better believe that he was doing the same damned thing. I just didn't know what point he was trying to screw me on.

Aegaeus laughed. "You expect me to believe that you actually give a damn about someone other than yourself? Since when?"

Okay, point taken, but…"Maybe motherhood's changed me."

He went to say something, and the All Father swore, his wine sloshing across the table.

My eyes narrowed. That seemed awfully convenient. "What were you—"

"I was going to call you on your bullshit." Aegaeus glared at the All Father, his lips tight, then flicked his eyes to me. "You've never thought of the consequences of your actions. You just bulldoze through everything with zero consideration for the implications. Opening the veil is case in point. Regardless of your professed motives, what's going to happen when it opens up and all those pissed off lords of Fae come pouring through? Do you think they've just been sitting over there for the past several months twiddling their thumbs and lamenting the error of their ways?"

Ouch. I flushed, taking a sip of wine.

"Haven't thought that bit through, have you?" Aegaeus sneered. "They declared war before you closed the veil, and I'll guarantee you that they're waiting to finish what they started, if you don't fry the planet first."

"You don't know that—"

"No," he said, tossing his napkin onto the table. "And you don't know they're not."

He was right, but—

"Envy's been under a considerable amount of strain, and Gaia's here to help her get a handle on it. As for the rest, the Riders and I are fully capable of holding the veil, should it come down to it," Brennan said. "I'd assume that the four of you, with your not inconsiderable powers, would be as well, and should Connell contract the hunt…Well, I don't see an issue."

"Yet he does bring up a salient point," the Gwinth said, twisting the stem of his wine glass between his fingers. "What's the harm in waiting a century or two?"

"You don't wanna see Stewie pent up that long," Jonas growled.

I was pretty sure I didn't want to see any of the Riders after a century or two of snacking on chips. The way War and Pestilence had been eyeing me since I came into the room made me seriously question Karen's fashion selection for the evening.

"Even if they're prepared to invade, my father's the warlord of Fae's army. I can get them to stand down." Probably. I was Clan Malten's queen. They had to listen to me, right?

"My father's the warlord," Aegaeus mocked. The little shimmy he did in his chair was totally a Morgana move. God, I hated them both. "It's always about you. Your father, your consort, your stupid kid—"

I might have hissed at the last. Yeah. I definitely hissed.

He laughed, and it was super creepy, like two voices came out of his mouth. I would've shuddered if I wasn't so busy being pissed. "Bit of a nerve there, hmm? I can't wait to meet the little dickens. With the veil sealed, there will be plenty of opportunity for us to become acquainted. Mind his bath—so many accidents happen in the home."

Did that motherfucker just threaten my kid?

The blast of plasma I sent at him was most definitely not an accident.

Taking out the entire north wall of the room kind of was. Guess my powers were coming back. Whoops. Unfortunately, Aegaeus didn't get incinerated with it.

Chickenshit tucked tail and poofed back to whatever swamp he'd crawled out of.

I stood there with my palms on the table, seething at the smoldering hole overlooking the front drive, everyone else at the table very, very still.

Brennan's Zippo snicked, and he exhaled a long plume of smoke into the frigid air. Shadows shambled behind him. "Well, that's going to be hell on our insurance premiums."

The Gwinth snorted. "Indeed. Can I get another glass of wine?" Out of the corner of my eye an imp trotted over with a bottle. My gaze went from the hole to Kyle. Aegaeus wasn't the only primordial to tuck tail. The All Father had left his other half to take the fallout. With good reason. My rage built, like, I could feel the pressure increasing in my skull. The sprite edged away from him, smarter than she looked.

This was all his fault.

Kyle's throat bobbed. "Shit, Snow, you gotta—I didn't—"

"You brought him here. While under your surety, he threatened my son. In my fucking house, sitting at my table, having partaken of bread and salt..." Behind the scenes, I was getting a data dump of exactly how many guest rights Aegaeus had just shit all over and was fucking livid. I mean, this went way beyond any modern day breach of propriety. He'd met my goddamned eye and bit into the honeyed bread, made a show of taking salt—the ancient part of me wanted to hunt him down and rend him limb from limb.

And was entitled to. Words spoken in the first language of man seared across my tongue.

"Aegaeus of the storm, father of the seas, I name

thee oath breaker and claim redress."

...break my peace at your peril...

My form began to fall away—

Socks poofed into the center of the table with Rhys. It and everything on it erupted in black hell-flame. My body reformed, and I lost my grip on my anger. It sped off into the night, unfocused. Crap, that was never good…

"Shit!" Brennan dove for Rhys and Socks, throwing out his aura. The table collapsed into cinders as he grabbed Rhys up, and I snatched the squalling baby from him, Brennan's arms wrapping around us both. The flames cut out, and Rhys whimpered against my breast.

I knew how he felt.

Everyone had scattered, and poor Socks…He was a mess. His beautiful emerald-green scales were charred black and chunks of him were missing. I didn't even think that was possible. Gaia toed through the wreckage to his side and laid a hand on him, healing the damage.

Hmm? Oh, undines may corner the market on healing humanoids, but Gaia one-upped them when it came to everything else. Seriously. Flesh reformed, and his scales shimmered beneath the filth in under a minute flat. His head rose, shooting me a venomous glare, and he poofed from the room.

Crap.

Yeah, he could poof. The telepathy thing didn't clue you in that he wasn't your average garden serpent? I've got a bridge for sale if you're interested.

Gaia stood, her kaftan ruined. She frowned at it, then at me. Not like she was pissed, more like I was a problem that needed solving, which was just as bad. The last thing I needed was to be one of her projects. She made her way past us to the door.

"I'll be in the garden."

Great. She didn't need to say she expected me out there for me to know it. Brennan's hand stroked my back, murmuring against my hair. It didn't register. I was numb again, sooty tears dried into tight lines down my cheeks. Across the room, the Gwinth had found a chair. He lounged back, ankle across his knee, a sly smile playing about his lips as he sipped his wine. His gold eyes were very bright in the gloom, and they were locked on me.

14 Days 3 Hours, 18 Minutes

I went upstairs.

Look, I'd had enough. Brennan could see our stupid guests out. My head was pounding, and for the life of me, I couldn't understand why the hell Aegaeus had thrown down like that. Remember all that crap about getting drawn and quartered for leaving the table to pee? Spoiler, dining etiquette is a huge deal to the fae, and not threatening host or guest was kind of the gold standard. Him breaking the peace was the ultimate slap in the face, and on top of which, it was his goddamned rule.

You thought it was Gaia's? Oh, hell no. I mean, she was all about natural order and stuff being done a certain way, but you heard her—"All things unfold as they should." Letting that happen organically gave everything a certain leeway. How many times have you heard someone complain about a late spring or an early winter? I mean, she gets around to it, but punctuality isn't her thing.

Aegaeus, on the other hand, was the most hidebound prick I'd ever met. He didn't care a lot about the how of things, but the when was another story. That whole changeability of the seas? He wasn't wishywashy, that was him keeping the tide schedule and everything else be damned.

Seriously? The gravitational pull of the moon? You honestly believe some floating space rock yanks the oceans around? Suure…how about we revisit that after I write up the contract for that bridge?

My point is, Aegaeus breaking his own rules didn't happen, or at least it hadn't ever happened before. I chewed on my lip. He'd looked like himself, but becoming had changed all of us to various degrees. How much of Morgana was still in there, and what the hell was she doing to him?

You know what? I didn't care. As far as I was concerned, they were both culpable. And who the hell threatens a baby? Assholes. I pushed open the door to the nursery, surprised to see it still standing. The crib was a sooty smear, but aside from some wicked scorch marks, the room didn't look nearly as bad as it smelled. Becky and Karen were directing the clean-up crew.

"You're okay?"

Becky nodded. "OMG, ya! I was doing homework, and like, all of a sudden he started screaming and there was this, like, dark flash out of the corner of my eye. The crib totally went whoosh, and Socks bounced with Rhys, and then it was all game over." She took a huge breath and a glanced between me and Karen. "I'm still gonna get paid for tonight, right?"

Hmm? Oh, she went to public school with a bunch of normals. And if all that that sounded baffling, envision it coming out of imp with braces, clad in the latest juicy pink whatever romper jammies and pigtails.

"We discuss later," Karen said, reaching for Rhys. "Give to me, I clean up."

My arms tightened around him. "No, I-I'll do it." What? It's not like I didn't trust Karen, I just…I didn't want him out of my sight.

She grunted, oddly smug, and shooed me toward our

suite. "Packed and played in you room."

Packed and played? Oh. One of those portable crib things. Shut up. I peeled myself out of the support hose, gaining a better appreciation for why Socks was so crabby when he molted, then headed into the bathroom with the kid.

It wasn't ideal, but I got us cleaned up in record time. For once I wasn't real keen to linger in the water. God, as if having blueberry crepes ruined for me wasn't bad enough, now showers were on the list, and there wasn't a chance in hell I was going swimming.

Brennan was sitting on the commode when I came out. Eww, no he wasn't—He was waiting for me. I handed him Rhys to dry off.

"They gone?"

"Two of them." He grabbed a diaper with his free hand, cigarette dangling from his lips. Man could do anything with one of those damned things in his mouth. It was almost more impressive than gross. Whatever. Like I didn't have a ton of bad habits he put up with. "Kennet and Bunny have been given rooms on the first floor, in the east wing. The imps are assessing the structural integrity of the west."

Bunny. I rolled my eyes, then bit at my lip. Brennan had bought me this beautiful estate and I'd gone through it like a wrecking ball within the first twelve hours. I knew I was gonna screw this up. "I'm sorry. About the wall, the normals…I didn't mean…"

He got that sour look on his face that meant he was thinking about the All Father/Kyle and for once I agreed. I was way pissed at them, too. "It wasn't your fault, Lovely. As soon as I saw that fishy bastard—It's nothing that can't be fixed. Normals included." He snapped up

Rhys's jammies and cradled him against his shoulder. God, he was so good with him. "With that wall blown out, what do you think about putting in a conservatory? It's the only thing the estate's lacking."

My anxiety heaved. "I don't want to do this anymore."

"You don't—" He paled. "What do you mean?"

"I want things to go back to how they were." My eyes got all glassy, and my throat felt thick. "Aegaeus isn't going to help clear the Neither. The Gwinth, Kyle…When they find out about the curse—"

"Shh…let me see what I can do. I'm not without resources." He drew me close and ran his thumb over my cheek. "I don't know what you said at the end of dinner, but I can guess, and promise you, if not by your hand, the seas will run red at mine."

The cold vengeance in his voice—He always knew how to make me feel better. Rhys didn't make a peep when Brennan kissed me this time, but I was too spun up to enjoy it. Whatever calm I'd found this afternoon had left the building.

Brennan must've known it and pulled away with a sigh. "Go see Gaia. I've got the little bastard for a bit." He did, and I had to smile. Rhys was drooling against his shoulder, comatose. I couldn't understand how I deserved either of them.

I didn't. I hadn't even wanted Rhys.

I threw on some sweats and trainers, lamenting what a piece of crap I was, then found a bottle and my way down to the garden. There was more activity around the estate than I would've figured for this time of night, and War's dogs were flitting in and out of the trees. I froze when one began baying at the moon, the rest of the pack answering from the surrounding grounds. A chill stole up my spine, the sound was nothing like what mortal dogs made, and every other creature went still.

Well, almost all of them.

"How you doin', Miss Kitty?" Jonas asked, resolving from the shadows in full camo like it was no big.

All righty then. "I'm okay. War's dogs are out?"

"Yeah. Boss man's got us on lockdown. He's takin' this shit serious, callin' in some of the lesser dae. They're fuckin' pissed."

"Wait, they know already?"

"You blowing the South Seas to shit when all that at dinner went down tipped 'em off."

I winced. Guess I knew where that rogue burst of power had ended up. Crap. That wasn't gonna go over well. "How bad?"

"Bad, but I ain't blamin' ya." Jonas cracked his knuckles. "Aegaeus's a dead man—he just don't know it yet. S'already shapin' up to be one hell of a fish fry."

I ran a hand over my face, not having considered what the lesser dae were going to think about all this, but it made sense. If their leaders were at war, they were too, and as much as I didn't want the job or the title, I was stuck with both.

Fuck my life and Aegaeus. What the hell had he been thinking?

"Is Gaia around?"

Jonas jerked his head toward the clearing I'd found her in earlier, the moon glinting off his tusks. "She's got a tent or some shit set up in the back. I'll keep you company."

I had the distinct impression the offer wasn't

optional.

We made our way through the shadowed grounds, the night coming back to life in the wake of the dog's howl. Fragrant night blooms perfumed the air, and wisps glowed around them. It was beautiful, but a weird tension threaded through all of it. A kind of waiting. I could feel the other shoe about to drop, and that space between my shoulder blades prickled.

Gaia was sitting by a campfire, some big hide-covered igloo-looking thing at her back. She was smoking a long, thin pipe, and Socks was coiled in her lap. He wouldn't look at me.

Traitor. Jonas left me at the edge of the circle of light, melting back into the darkness. I sat against a conveniently placed hillock directly across from her. Her slitty eyes trained on me, and I rolled mine. Yeah, it was kind of my go-to.

"You wanted to see me?"

"I did. I thought I told you to leave my volcanos alone." She threw a baggie of capsules filled with dusty green shit at me. "You owe me a rather large island."

"Yeah, sorry about that." I cracked the bag and jerked back at the stench. Shit was definitely a part of the mix. "Ugh, what are these? And if you say herbs, it's gonna be ash."

Smoke wreathed around her face. "Borage, valerian, rosemary. St. John's wort. Hibiscus—"

"Forget I asked." I cracked the top of my bottle and threw back three or four.

She smirked. "I'd suggest no more than two."

"Yes, Mom." I took another swig to get rid of the aftertaste. Damned things were already repeating on me. "So what the hell is up with Aegaeus and Morgana?"

"I don't know. It's of concern."

I snorted. "Ya think?"

"I do. Morgana is capricious, but I wouldn't have thought she'd be able to sway his personality so severely, and to insinuate the child's life is at risk—I can't say that I blame you for your reaction." Her eyes blazed; kids were historically her schtick, and she didn't play where their safety was concerned.

"Jonas said the lesser elementals are already going at it."

"They are. I've told my people to stay out of it, but they're not pleased, nor am I. The All Father's involvement in the whole sordid affair has my hackles up, and it won't take much to tip my hand against either of them."

Great. A primordial free-for-all was just what we needed. I took another pull off my bottle, then worried at the label. The All Father's part in kicking shit up bothered me. Like, a lot. After what Brennan had said about my suitors coming after Rhys…but Kyle had played with him…I mean when the All Father wasn't glaring at him…

God, this sucked. I didn't know where I stood with Kyle or the All Father anymore, which was kind of because I wasn't in the same place either. Yeah, Lilith had a shit ton of baggage with the All Father, but all of it was basically sexcapades and brinksmanship. I couldn't remember any real—I mean, not for me, ugh, Lilith! It wasn't like she loved him—did she?

I got crickets.

Whatever. The All Father knew how much Aegaeus hated me, which is why I'd specifically asked him to talk to Morgana. He should've known Aegaeus would pull some shit and was probably cool with it to get me back for the whole baby-daddy thing, but I'm pretty sure he didn't expect Aegaeus to lose his damned mind. And Kyle…He wouldn't hurt me on purpose, but he was dumb enough to let it happen.

"I don't think Kyle had any part in it."

Gaia blew smoke rings, then a long plume through them. "Not intentionally, no, but he was stupid enough to go along with it and stand in surety for Aegaeus's good behavior. As far as I'm concerned, he shares the blame."

She was right, and that couldn't be going over well with the All Father or Kyle. Air elementals had this honorable streak they took wicked serious. Yeah, even Kyle. It was kind of bizarre.

"I don't get it," I said, all muddled. There was no way straight-up herbs were the only thing that was in those capsules. I wasn't complaining. I would, however, stick to two next time. "I mean, it was like Aegaeus was purposely trying to piss off us and the normals in one fell swoop, not to mention screwing me over with the Neither. There's no way we can clear the veil without him."

"I need to meditate on it, but I'm tempted to agree with you. Though, why he would want to incite a war of that magnitude…" She shrugged, chewing on her pipestem. "What are you going to do about the Gwinth?"

Crap. Back to that.

"Let him court me, I guess. Brennan thinks he can do something, but short of killing Aegaeus—" Her face went very still, and I blanched. "Do you think he could kill Aegaeus?"

"I don't put anything past that dae where you're

concerned, but I've no idea if it would do any good. Yes, these forms are mortal, but as to what will happen when they expire?" She shrugged, her cheeks sucking in around her pipe.

It was a valid question and not one particularly comfortable to contemplate. I mean, fae returned to their element when they die, but we were primordials, the embodiments of the elements. What would happen to our consciousnesses?

I abruptly felt like even after all that angsty shit I'd been through, I'd only prolonged the whole sputtering as a normal vs. becoming a fae hoopla.

It was time to go. Talking too long with Gaia always devolved into weird existential territory I wasn't keen on exploring. I stumbled as I stood, and Jonas was right there steadying my elbow. Where the hell had he—You know what? Never mind. I leaned against him and let him shepherd me back to the house. The night air felt amazing on my skin.

So did Jonas's hands. That was a problem.

I laughed, finding my balance with a stupid smile on my face, and bolted from him. He swore and I didn't care. God, running felt good. I didn't have any direction in mind, and the garden paths were wide and expansive. Pink gravel crunched under my trainers, and my stride ate up the distance.

At some point, War's dogs began to keep pace with me. I'd veered off the gravel and onto an overgrown trail through the woods. It opened into a clearing with a ramshackle building at its far edge, like an old barn or something. I stopped, bathing my face in moonlight.

The sky was clear, and I don't know if you've ever seen the stars in the southwestern sky, but they're something else. My breath slowed, and I plonked down in the grass. Just being. It was kind of nice.

One of the dogs ambled over and laid at my side, tongue lolling with that smile all canines get. I smiled back and scritched behind its ears where its brindled fur was soft.

Its head jerked up a second before I heard the Gwinth's voice.

"You shouldn't be out here alone."

Christ. "Apparently I'm not. I thought you left."

He chuckled and sat too close beside me. His arm brushed my back, and I shivered. The jerk noticed, and the fingers of his other hand rose to trace my jawline. I made myself pull away, ignoring his smile. It was a lot harder than it should've been. Stupid pills.

"I did but felt it wise to set my own perimeter. The escalation of tensions in the past hour has not gone unnoticed by the normal powers that be, nor has a certain natural disaster in the South Seas, and I have an invested interest in your well-being, now, don't I?"

"I can take care of myself." What the hell was wrong with me? My voice was husky, and he slid closer, his thigh pressing against mine, arm at my back, hand curling to find my hip bone. His thumb stroked its contours through my sweats. The rhythm…I can't explain it. I didn't know if it was whatever I was on or him, but I couldn't focus enough to poof my ass out of there.

"Perhaps if you weren't higher than Apollo's chariot. I could have slit your pretty little throat before you or that beast had gotten to your feet." The dog growled at him like it'd understood. The Gwinth growled back, and it whimpered, showing its belly. Well, wasn't that just tits. I didn't have anything to say, so I didn't. His nose skated beneath my ear, inhaling. "Mmm. You're not bleeding anymore."

Ugh! Whatever spell I was under fizzled and popped. I jerked away, slapping his hand off my hip. He chuckled again, his breath warm on my cheek as I scooched farther from him.

"Do you have any idea how skeevy you are?"

"It was a simple statement of fact." He wet his lips and stood. "And it means my timetable can be moved up. You should go to bed. It's late, and you have a big day tomorrow."

A big day—crap. That Presentment thing.

"Tonight has been edifying on a number of levels. I can understand Brennan's reluctance to share. He might not get you back."

I snorted. As if.

The Gwinth's grin widened. "I look forward to our day together. Dress pretty." He swept up my hand, and before I could snatch it back, his lips grazed over my knuckles. "Until Saturday."

Poof.

My lips curdled. Go to bed, you have a big day tomorrow. Dress pretty. Like that was happening. Sugar Daddy used to say the same stupid things before trotting Calista and me out for his associates to ogle. Burning the midnight oil and finding a burlap sack rose to the top of my to-do list. I flopped back in the grass, the night closing in on me.

The dog whimpered again, resting its head on my thigh. I scritched behind its ear. "Some help you were." Psh. Some help I was. How the hell did I get myself into this mess? Okay, rhetorical question, but what'd just gone down burned my ass. There, there, little lady, now don't you worry your empty little head—God, I hated him.

Ugh. I hated myself for not punching him in his stupid face. Him and Kyle. The All Father. Fuck them. I didn't care who the Gwinth released. I wasn't going to entertain this shit show anymore.

That settled, I sat up, dusted myself off, and poofed back to the house.

Estate. Whatever.

Brennan was pacing the room in his pj bottoms, crooning to Rhys and texting furiously one-handed. The baby was red-faced and wailing in his arms. "Shh, there, there, see, Mommy's here. She'll make it better."

Mommy. I put a hand to my cheek, the memory of a slap burning over my skin.

...My name is Calista. Use it...

I took Rhys to the rocker, trying to keep my shit together as I settled him to nurse. "Why didn't you come get me?"

Brennan threw his phone onto the bed, frowning. "You needed time to yourself."

Okay. For whatever reason, that ripped me open. What the hell was wrong with me? Here I had Daddy dae-licious not only willing to put up with my shit twenty-four seven, but our kid's to boot. Brennan was the total freaking package. Gorgeous, loaded, an amazing father, killer between the sheets, and despite whatever delusion was responsible for it, he loved me.

Like for real. This wasn't a game to him. Socks was right; I needed to get over myself.

I peeked up at Brennan, my pulse going gangbusters. "Did you know there's a barn in the woods?"

He snapped his Zippo shut. Yeah, he hadn't even been attempting to light his cigarettes himself. That, Beethoven, those calls I'd overheard…God, I'd been too wrapped up in my own drama to appreciate the stress he had to be under. Boy, I felt like a sack of shit. All of this must be killing him, and I kept jerking him around.

"I did. I believe the former occupant fancied himself a potter. He used it as a workshop."

My fingers trembled, tracing Rhys's cheek. His eyes were a muddy grey. I'd heard the color changed after a couple months and wondered what they—Okay, fine, maybe that's not what I was wondering, but in case you haven't figured it out, commitment is on top of the Envy-has-issues pyramid, and right below it is admitting when someone else is right.

Shut up. That doesn't mean I'm wrong.

Was I really gonna do this? That little voice inside me was screaming: *Abort! Abort! Abort!* But the look on Brennan's face, the ache in my chest…I couldn't keep doing this to him. He, Rhys, they deserved—well, let's be honest, they deserved better than me, but for whatever reason, I was who they wanted.

No one had ever wanted me. Not like for me, I mean. An epic lay way back when and ticket sales in this incarnation didn't count. I took a deep breath, the words tumbling out before I could think too much about them.

"It would make a good studio…you know, for all your music stuff." He hated being interrupted when he was composing, and as big as this place was, it was bound to happen. Especially if I kept blowing holes in the wall and setting off my mini-me.

"The thought had crossed my mind." He caught my

expression, and his lips parted, breath catching between them. His gaze pinned me through those messy locks. God, it got me when he did that. "Are you saying what I think you're saying?"

I didn't answer until Rhys had fallen back asleep and was in that crib thing. Brennan's eye never left me, alight with—all of it. Everything I was scared shitless of. I wiped my sweaty palms on my pants and went to him, making myself meet that silvery grey depth.

Terrified. *Abort! Abort! Abort!*

His hands settled on my hips. The longing on his face…I shoved that stupid voice down. It wasn't me, it was Lilith, and I needed to stop buying into her carpaccio.

"I'm saying yes."

"To marriage. To me. You want this? For true?" I nodded, and his cheek dimpled a mile deep. He kissed my forehead. "Then it will keep."

What the—keep? I didn't want it to keep. I wanted to release him, to say his true name as he said mine and bare my stupid soul to him, to—my brow crumpled even as my knees went weak with relief. "But I thought you…" I choked on the lump in my throat.

Why didn't he want me?

"I do. God, Lovely, you've no idea how badly. When this mess is all sorted—"

"What do you mean when this mess is sorted? I say your name and it's done!"

He riffled his hair, frustration marring his face. "It can't be, not yet. Bloody politics…normal/fae relations aren't going well. Our refusal to provide those damned biometrics—If the Gwinth makes good on his threat to release huntsmen, they'll view it as provocation, and things will get very ugly, very quickly. Tonight's fallout between Fire and Water has them dangerously on edge, and I'm running out of options. I need more time, and only you can give that to me."

"But I thought…No! I want this to be over—"

He gripped my shoulders. "I swear it will be. Give me three days from tomorrow. I need you to trust me."

Trust him. I went limp at that timbre in his voice. Three days. What the hell could he do in three days that would get the Gwinth off my case and keep the normals—

Oh, hell no.

"You made a bargain." My mouth twisted. Goddamn it. Look, I'll admit he was good at it, but his penchant for side deals drove me nuts. I didn't care if it was a fae thing; even I was smart enough to figure out it was bad practice. "With who? What—"

"You know how this works." He pulled me against his chest, hand buried in my hair. "When it's over, I'll tell you everything."

Which meant that the damned bargain was already in effect. Tears pricked at my eyes, and he raised up my chin.

"It's nothing I can't deliver on." That look in his eye…He believed he could do this; whatever it was, how could I not? Three days. I'd only have to spend one each with Kyle and the stupid Gwinth, and it wasn't like Brennan could renege on whatever dumb deal he'd made. Asshole would get himself flayed again.

Motherf—That crooked grin spread across his face at my sigh. I glowered back at him. "All right, fine. Three days, but you owe me."

"Brilliant. What do you say to a big, traditional fae

wedding afterward?"

I rolled my eyes, burned out on the T word. Stupid freaking tradition. I didn't get it. I mean, we were different, why did all the dumb rules have to stay the same? "I thought you wanted me to agree to this."

"We can have a chocolate fountain…"

"It better be big enough to swim in," I muttered. Whatever, his dumb bargain had backed me into a corner, and I won't lie, a big part of me felt like I'd narrowly escaped making a huge mistake saying yes to him. Stupid pills.

"Done. I'll take care of everything, save the formal wear. Karen can help you with that." His brow furrowed at my giggle. "What?"

"Just imagining her and Gaia as bridesmaids." It was dumb, but if there was a silver lining to this latest tangle, it was the prospect of picking out the ugliest, most expensive dresses I could find, then gushing about how they could totally wear them again. Oooh…in that hideous tartan Kennet had been wearing. Wool. June wedding—"Do you think Jonas would wear a kilt?"

"The better question is will I," Brennan grumbled.

"But I thought you said you wanted this to be traditional?" You have no idea how hard it was to keep a straight face. Like, I was literally having trouble not rubbing my hands together, way too excited at the prospect.

He glowered at me. "Don't for one moment think I don't know what you're doing."

I batted my lashes. "Celebrating your heritage?"

Brennan grunted, nuzzling at my neck. "I'd prefer to celebrate your change of heart. Tell me you want this. Us. I need to hear it, to know you're very sure. Tell me you want to be my wife."

God, when he put it like that…I swallowed the lump in my throat. When have I ever known—

Right then, I did. I mean, I was pretty sure I did.

Crap.

"I'm sure. I want to be your w-www…" My lips puckered, and I couldn't get the word out. It flitted around my skull, a flock of angry memories trying to peck it to death.

Lilith's memories. Not mine, damn it! Ugh! I pulled his face down and put my pursed lips to better use. Stupid word.

"Close enough." Brennan chuckled, poofing us to the bed, his hands busy finding my skin. Then my sweats were on the floor, entangled with his pj bottoms. The long length of him pressing against me, silken steel in my hand. God, I wanted him…his lips played over my body, between my thighs…I arched against him, his hair so soft beneath my palms.

He kissed along the cleft of my legs, tongue darting to make me gasp. His eye met mine. "Yes?" he asked, his voice hitching. Fingers questing, hovering—I answered by rocking them into me, slick, and a rumble rose from his chest. "Mmm…"

"Oh God, yes…please…" I've never wanted anything more than I did in that moment.

He moved above me, teasing, his lips at my throat, and I burned for him. My hands slid down his back, gripping his rear—

"Shh…softly now."

We came together slow and gentle. He took himself away and then filled me again, over and over. I was drowning in him, sensation. Smokey aftershave, toothpaste, and cognac. His breath speeding with mine. I clutched at him, my passion rising, and the whisper of my name on his lips…

Let's just say I bypassed the Almighty and had a conversation with whatever had birthed the Big Guy. Like, those existential conversations with Gaia almost made sense.

Ohm…M. G.

13 Days, 15 Hours, 42 Minutes

Anywho, now that that was out of the way, I have to admit I slept a lot better and woke up feeling like a million bucks.

Hmm? Stugots? Okay, Karen. Psh. In case blowing up an island halfway across the globe hadn't tipped you off, my powers were back up to snuff, and between Brennan healing me and me going all elemental at dinner, physically I was feeling the high side of fine. Like seriously, and for the first time in basically forever, I hadn't had any weird dreams, just sweet oblivion. Mind-blowing sex and Gaia's funky pills must be a winning combo, and Brennan's smile—God, it radiated from him, filling up the room and melting all over me, totally contagious.

Yeah, too bad I was genetically resistant and only caught a mild case of bliss. I was still a basket case on about a zillion levels.

Why? I'd agreed to marry him, and that was terrifying. Yeah, it was stupid, I mean, it's just a label right? A dumb piece of paper. He already knew my name, and aside from getting dibs on his insurance, nothing would really change.

Okay, everything would change.

What the hell had I been thinking? I scrubbed at my face and chalked it up to Gaia's pills and the Gwinth pushing my buttons. Wouldn't be the first rash decision

I'd made under the influence or for spite, and I could guarantee it wouldn't be the last. I didn't need to psychoanalyze it, even if Brennan's whole "it will keep" crap gave me way too much time to do exactly that.

Whatever. I'd made my choice, right?

Moving on. So there I was snuggling in bed with him and Rhys, and the faces he was making at the little bastard were giving me a serious case of the giggles. The kid wasn't amused, like at all, which just made it funnier. It was nice having them both there. Brennan was usually in meetings by the time I got up. His phone having seizures was reflective of that, but for once he ignored it. Today he'd cleared his schedule since the stupid present thing was this afternoon, and it was our last day before this speed-dating clusterfuck began.

I smiled, tweaking Rhys's toes. Yeah. I was happy, despite my angst and not knowing what Brennan was up to. I know, right? It freaked me out, too. I went to take a shower. A long one. Screw Aegaeus.

When I came back into the bedroom, Brennan had gotten Rhys into a clean onesie, and he was all business casual dae-licious. God, what is it about men holding babies? I licked my lips and glanced at the kid, wondering if he'd morph from potato to tyrant if we parked him in that crib thing for a quickie. I swear he shot me the stink-eye, daring me to try it. Really? How the hell did he think he got here in the first place?

Whatever. I pulled on a set of sweats and trainers, then settled the kid in his halter with a kiss. Stupid little cock-blocker.

We went downstairs to breakfast. The dining room was cordoned off with plastic, and workmen were already all over the place. Something with a serious engine was running outside, metal clanking. I peeked behind the sheeting. It was a full-blown construction zone. Like hardhats and safety vests had thrown up on everybody, and a monstrous digger-thing was ripping up the front lawn.

"They're excavating the foundation and re-routing some plumbing that was damaged," Brennan explained. "Should take two weeks, as long as the monsoons hold off."

I dropped the plastic, not surprised at his timetable. I told you. He doesn't mess around when it comes to getting things done. Knowing him, he'd probably had the plans drawn up before I'd blown out the stupid wall.

Breakfast was being served in some swanky room at the back of the house overlooking the gardens. I think he called it a solar, which made sense since the sun was coming in like, boom, right there. The walls were glass, which I thought made it a conservatory, but I guess it didn't meet the square footage requirements or something.

Anyways, the floor was flagstone, and Kennet and Bunny were sitting at a linen-draped table in the middle of it. My steps faltered at the livid pink scars her tube top wasn't hiding. They hadn't been there at dinner. The marks raked across her left shoulder like something nasty had tried to get ahold of her. I glanced at Brennan; had the estate been breached last night?

He didn't seem to notice them, and neither did she, all wide-eyed as Kennet speared a sausage from the pile in front of him and waved it about like he was reenacting storming the Bastille. For all I knew, he was.

"Kennet, Bunny," Brennan said all suave, pulling out my chair. I sat, and he took the one beside me. Karen brought over my waffles, unburned. Guess she'd forgiven me for the whole Gladys thing. Two of those pills were beside my orange juice. I ignored them. Kennet snorted at the poached eggs and asparagus she set in front of Brennan and chomped on his sausage like he was trying to make it sorry.

Brennan didn't seem to notice that either, flicking open his newspaper. Front page was that volcano that had erupted. My stomach dropped. It had taken out an estimated twenty-seven million people. Holy crap…

"I hope you both slept well?" Brennan asked.

"Aye," Kennet said around his bite. "Room's a far cry from where the hunt's bivouacking, and I can't say as I miss Rodrigo's sawing. Man could wake the dead. How's the wee fiend this morn? Lemme look at him…" I pushed my hair back so Rhys's little face peeped out of the halter, and Kennet grinned across the table at us. "Och, he's a bonny lad."

A lump formed in my throat at the pride in his voice. You gotta understand, it'd always just been Calista and me. I'd never met my grandparents, and she'd never said boo about them. For the longest time, I'd thought she'd sprung fully formed from a cake mid-stage. The closest I'd ever come to seeing anything like the emotion on Kennet's face was from Sugar Daddy after my reviews had come in.

I wiped at my cheeks. God, I was fucked up. How was I even remotely qualified for this? My angst beat loud in my ears, and I closed my eyes, trying to keep my breathing even. I didn't need to add to the death toll.

Kennet chuckled. "Mark my words, he'll be as green-eyed as his mother and have all the lasses after him. He's gonna give us both a run for our money, and it's about damned time."

I looked up at the edge in Kennet's voice.

A muscle in Brennan's jaw jumped. "Can you blame me for waiting?"

"Aye, I can. Man wants t'be surrounded by his grans and then some at my age. Half the clan thought ye'd gone gay, and the rest was convinced ye were sterile. I'll admit t'being on the fence myself."

The comment snapped me out of my funk, and I snickered. Brennan shot me a look. Kennet didn't notice, gorging himself on sausage. Was he really going to eat that entire platter? Bunny was giving him some serious side-eye, probably wondering the same thing as she nibbled on her melon. Man those scars were nasty. Had to have been something with claws.

Brennan stabbed his egg. "The geas chaining my fiend precluded any relations—"

"Figures that bloody harpy had somewhat t'do with it. Made no sense otherwise. Some of it still don't." He looked at me, waggling his dagger. "Before that last hussy, he went through women faster than pints durin' playoffs, and none of them the wiser of the others, fallin' for his every word. By deed alone, I should be able t'claim the entire British Isles as kin."

Brennan's Zippo snicked, his eggs forgotten. "That was a very long time ago."

"Ye knew yer duty."

"And now I've done it."

"I'd expect ye t'continue."

"I'd planned on it, but the Gwinth pressing his suit complicates that, now, doesn't it?"

The temperature in the room was dipping, and I shivered.

"She ain't the only lass t'come calling of late. Suggest ye pick up the phone instead of smackin' it down."

Wait—what? My head snapped up to look at Brennan, glaring at his father. He said something in Cymric, and Kennet replied in kind. I was seriously gonna have to learn—

Bunny had turned a pretty, pretty pink and was very purposefully keeping her eyes on her plate. Oh, hell no—

Yeah, I hissed, and she poofed. Definitely smarter than she looked. The men went silent. Across the table Kennet concentrated on his sausages, but it didn't look like they tasted very good anymore. Brennan just looked guilty.

"Bunny?" God, he was an asshole! "The fiend did that, didn't it? When, last night when I 'needed time to myself'?" What a crock of shit. Was that why he didn't want me to speak his name? Had he been afraid I'd see whatever he'd been up to staining his soul?

Brennan riffled a hand through his hair. "It wasn't like that. The fiend…I almost killed her, Vy. The All Father left her here solely to put me in a compromising position. They're trying to make you doubt my intentions, and if they can't find anything to suit their purposes, they'll manufacture it." He glared at his father. "Isn't that right?"

Kennet shrugged and stabbed another sausage. "Nothin' personal, lad."

"Like hell it isn't."

"I'm just statin' the facts. Envy'll do with them what she will."

What I was doing was seething, but I was rational enough to know Brennan was right. Ha. Yeah, it surprised me, too, but I'd gotten hit with another round of memories, and this was exactly the way the All Father played ball. It didn't do a damned thing to raise my current estimation of him. Rhys's meeping erupted into a full blown caterwaul, and I tried to calm myself. Wasn't working for either of us. Damn it, he'd just eaten, and I had no idea how else to diffuse the little bastard.

"I want her gone." I gritted out over his squalling.

Brennan stubbed out his cigarette, scowling at his father like he felt the same about him, then reached for Rhys. "Give him here." I passed the kid over, and he stood, patting his back. Like that was gonna work. "I'll see what I can do. Have you taken your supplements?"

My eyes narrowed. He knew damned well I hadn't, they were right there on the—

Brennan started singing softly to Rhys, and it was like a switch flipped. The kid went silent. Whatever I was gonna snap out died on my tongue. How was he so good at this? Like, he just knew what to do while I floundered...I snagged the stupid pills and downed them.

"Apple don't fall far from the tree, do it, lad?" Kennet's eyes sparkled watching them, and then he turned to me. "Bit of song always curbed his temper. And ye should've seen what a rabid little monster he was."

My stomach turned. Singing, huh? Great. The one frickin' thing that gave me blinding panic attacks was the little bastard's reset button.

Nope. Wasn't jealous or feeling totally inadequate, why do you ask?

Brennan's expression softened to irritation, and I got the distinct impression his father regaling me with stories of his childhood was the equivalent of flashing naked baby pictures. I shoved down my prepubescent-starlet-induced trauma à la Vegas and snickered. Brennan flushed crimson.

Kennet missed it, lost in the past. "Ye were just as much of handful when yer harpy of a mother dropped ye in my lap. Had not a bit of use for ye till ye were out of nappies." He grinned at me. "S'why I let him mess himself for so long. Must've been seven before—"

"Yes, yes, I was a little savage. Would you like to hold him?"

His father's face lit up, and Brennan rounded the table.

I choked on the last of my waffles. What the hell? "I—watch his—"

Kennet laughed, taking Rhys far more gently than I would've believed him capable of. "Ye think this is the first baby I've held? Nine of me own, but I don't recall one as bonny as this, and what a temper! Does me proud."

Brennan sighed, running a hand over his jaw as his father took off on another spiel.

"When his stigmata came in, half the keep was devoured by shadow. Waves of the stuff meltin' stone like hot toffee. Was a fit companion t'my own heart. Would that I could've sent it out and wiped every one of that vile clan from the Earth, but we didn't do such a bad job with our swords, hey?"

"The end result was the same, just took a bit longer." Brennan's lips quirked around another cigarette, pulling out the seat next to him.

I snagged a cup of coffee. Kennett holding Rhys was making me twitch, and I couldn't figure out why. I mean, people did that with their kids, right? Passed them around? I'd seen women at the coffee shop oohing and ahhing over babies that weren't theirs, the proud mama looking all smug and superior. Like having a kid was some big achievement.

I mean, I guess keeping them alive was, but even Calista had managed that. A flash bulb went off, and Peter waved a pic in the doorway. I don't know why he bothered, wasn't supposed to make it show up any faster. He put it down by my seat and cleared the dishes. I picked it up, watching the image resolve.

Three generations. It was a good picture.

There hadn't been anything like this of me, generational, good, or otherwise. At least, not that I knew of. Maybe Calista had an album somewhere before the Priory was torched, but if she did, I'd never seen it. I had seen plenty of her press photos and news clippings, all carefully trimmed and bedazzled onto fancy scrapbook paper.

But that's what was important to her.

I didn't realize I was crying until a big fat tear landed on the photo. I brushed it away, hoping no one had noticed. They hadn't, both of them enamored with Rhys.

I got up and left.

The air was still early morning dewy, and I started running without really deciding that's what I was going to do. My feet took the same track as the night before, and I ended up in that clearing. It was choked with wildflowers and tall grass, and the barn didn't look as ramshackle as it had in the moonlight. It was only one story and stained russet.

The door was open.

Brennan had been right about the pottery. Stacked piles of nebulous-looking pots were everywhere and a beehive-y-looking kiln sat in one corner. A bench was against one wall, and a shelf with dried-up glazes tilted above it. One of those big wheel thingies was in a rectangle of light streaming in from the windows. Motes of dust floated above it and strains of "Unchained Melody" flitted through my mind. I sat on the floor against one of the exposed pillars holding up the place, and my head dropped into my hands.

What was I doing?

Yeah, it was kind of a recurring theme with me, but not knowing the answer was becoming a serious problem. Nothing in my past incarnation gave me any clues on how to be a mother, never mind a wife, and this one? Please. Calista wasn't exactly a role model I wanted to emulate, and up until ten months ago I was positive I was checking out at twenty.

What was I supposed to do with myself? Brennan had all these skills, and the other primordials had, I don't know, interests at the very least…What did I have?

Fantastic tits and a chippy manicure.

Oh, and a penchant for genocide. Yeah, I totally felt like shit about that island.

Whatever. It wasn't like I'd meant to do it. See, this is what happened. If people would just leave me the hell alone—ugh! It was all Aegaeus's fault. He'd threatened my kid! I whipped a handful of plasma into the kiln and tried to calm down. Maybe I shouldn't stick with two of those pills.

I watched the flames re-blacken the brick, my mind circling back. The boobs and nails, sans chips, had been enough for Calista, but the thought that I was anything like that vapid, grasping bitch in sequins made me ill. I wasn't, was I? Had it been enough for Lilith? Crickets again on that front, and when I tried to will the answer out of my brain, all I got was the beginnings of a migraine.

I sighed, my head falling back against the pillar. I didn't think I was supposed to have an identity crisis until midlife. Scratch that—I didn't think I was supposed to have a life.

I probably wasn't supposed make Hitler look like a boy scout either.

That rectangle of light had moved halfway across the wheel thingy when Brennan stepped through shadow into the room. I have to admit, it was pretty impressive. The darkness just kind of took on his form, and then he was there with Rhys. Little bastard looked curiously sated, but I didn't trust him. I started unzipping my hoodie.

"There's no need, Lovely. Gaia has a goat. She said you can pump when we get back, for next time."

My eyebrow cocked. "A goat?"

"Apparently its milk is a suitable substitute." He leaned against the bench, eyes sweeping the room, already flipping through mental paint swatches and *Architectural Digest*.

"Oh." I dragged the zipper back up to the lump in my throat. Great. I'd been replaced by crotchety livestock, though in fairness, tin cans and bracken probably had the same nutritional impact on goat's milk that whiskey and chips had on mine. Brennan settled Rhys against me, groggy with his clandestine meal, and something in me eased once he was drooling on my shoulder.

"I'm sorry about all that in there. I've arranged for Bunny's replacement. A jinn will be arriving later tonight. He'll remain in an agreed-upon form until a consort has been chosen."

Yeah, that eyebrow thing again. Jinn were sketchy. Remember I told you there's some boundaries elements share? Jinn were fuzzy like that. Technically, they were born of smokeless fire, but they're totally undetectable unless they want to be, which got their card stamped for Air, too. When they do go corporeal, they can look like pretty much anything. They were supposed to pick a team and stick with it, but keeping tabs on them was basically impossible.

The wishes thing? Totally legit, but trying to use them would be even stupider than bargaining with a fae. Like, "I wish I was rich," and all of a sudden you're some dopey IT guy or a cup of pudding. I wasn't worried about that, but the lack of a body was throwing me for a loop.

"And what form would that be?"

"That dumpy little man from *Seinfeld*. I can't recall his name."

"The bald one with the glasses?"

"Mmm. Yes." Brennan shuffled a cigarette out of his case. "Apparently he's a big fan."

Not gonna lie, I was not expecting that. I mean, I wasn't complaining, about that at least. Bunny might've been booted, but her stank was still all up in here. "Why didn't you tell me she hit on you?"

"To what end? It would've only upset you, and the fiend guaranteed she'd keep her distance. Besides, after tonight I wouldn't have had any further dealings with her."

My eyes narrowed, hating how he rationalized so freaking rationally. "What did she do?"

He blew out a long stream of smoke. "It was a repeat

of Kyle's performance."

"She poofed in on you in the shower?"

"For all of three seconds before I damaged her."

Not as much as I would've—or would if I ever saw her again. I put my nose to Rhys's head, breathing him in and trying to keep calm. New-baby smell, new-baby smell…What? It was a mantra. Gaia said I needed one of those.

"The All Father wasn't pleased. I told him you were less so."

"I plan on telling him myself the next time I see him," I said all saccharine sweet. "I'd rather you had told me about that bimbo."

Brennan ran a hand over his jaw. "Duly noted. I am sorry, Lovely. This—A committed relationship isn't something I have a great deal of experience with."

I laughed. Like, a lot. "And I do? I'm drowning over here, and you're—you."

He came over to sit next to me. "Can I ask what you think that is?"

"Will you bargain for it?" Jerk did for everything else.

He swallowed a grin, looking away, then back all coy. God, he was hot. "What do you desire?"

"I want to know what you promised Gaia to get her to help me."

Brennan flicked his ash. "That's worth a bit more than an opinion. I want a promise from you. Whatever happens over the next few days, whatever they tell you, I want the opportunity to refute. This morning was only the beginning of it. They'll keep trying to twist your emotions along with the truth to gain an advantage over your affections."

I snorted. Like I'd believe anything that came out of the Gwinth's mouth, and the All Father was on my shit list. Brennan frowned.

"I'm serious, Lovely. I told you about my sister. She killed one of her suitors because of a vile lie, then the culprit when she found out the truth. Both of them were friends of mine, and good men. I never would have thought they'd turn on one another to win her favor, or that she'd react so violently. Courting brings out the worst in fae."

My brow furrowed. Then why hadn't he let me release him last night? I mean, it's not like a neon sign appears over your shoulder after you speak someone's name…Ugh. He didn't need anyone to make me doubt his intentions. He was doing a bang-up job of that himself, but I'd be damned before I begged him to clarify rejecting me.

No, that wasn't fair. Aside from the past twenty-four hours, he'd never given me reason to doubt him, which ironically was why I didn't trust him. Like, he was fattening me up before the slaughter or something.

Look, my entire life had been a series of dangling carrots being ripped away and replaced with a big-ass stick. Maybe my mantra should be "wait for it."

Fine, last night bothered me, okay? It bothered me that he thought I was gonna jump Kyle/the All Father's bones after the shit he'd pulled, too. Like, enough to think about it just to spite him. Oh, please. Thinking about it and doing it are totally different. God, this entire situation was pissing me off. I was definitely gonna up my pill intake.

"I thought you said this would be over in three days."

"If it was only Connell…" Brennan's face went All Father sour, and I bit back a smile despite my shitty mood. Seeing him sulk was freaking adorable. "You're angry now, but you love *him*, and he has an entire day to remind you of that fact."

I squirmed against the pillar. "The All Father loved Lilith, but she wasn't…I told you, she's not me, and Kyle and I were never serious." I threw up my hands, not wanting to get into it with him. God, I didn't even want to get into it with myself. "This wouldn't even be an issue if you'd—"

"You know why I love you, Vy? You've not a bit of artifice. That's unheard of in Fae, and so utterly tiresome trying to figure out where you stand at any given moment. Always questioning every little glance and comment, wondering if things are real. I've never felt that way with you unless *he's* in the room. If what we have is real, three days or three weeks won't matter." His eye closed and he looked pained. "I need you to be sure. I'd prefer not to see 'what if' on your face every time you looked at him."

"I do not—"

"You do." His mouth twisted around a sour drag. "When you don't want to kill him."

Okay, fine. Maybe. And no, my jaw was clenched way too hard to dangle at what he'd just dropped. I set aside my indignation at the fucked-up loyalty test he was administering to clarify.

"So what, you're giving me a free pass?" Oh, come on, it wasn't like I was going to use it, but I had to admit, the prospect was intriguing…

"No, but when you speak my name, I want it to be without regret." Brennan's face had darkened watching mine, and a chill swept through the room. He stubbed out his cigarette on the concrete. "Are we agreed?"

Agreed? Oh. The bargain. "Fine. I'll let you refute anything they say before I go postal in exchange for you telling me what you promised Gaia to get her to help me."

Brennan's eye gleamed, and I knew my wording was off before he even opened his mouth. Damn it. "Agreed. I didn't promise her anything to help you."

I smacked him, and he laughed. Jerk. "Are you serious? How the hell is that worth more than an opinion? You bargained for something else?"

"Is that another question? You still haven't answered mine."

"What do I think you are? You don't wanna know right now." I scowled.

Brennan's cheek dimpled with that crooked smile of his. "I bet I can guess."

Good, then I didn't have to answer. I cuddled Rhys's warm little body. Yeah, I was totally pouting. I hated it when Brennan went all fae on me.

He kissed my temple and stood, offering me his hand. "We should get ready for the Presentment. This is important, Vy. Especially after last night. Officially, we've disavowed any involvement in the disaster, but the normals are having difficulty swallowing it. I need you to be dazzling. Karen has something a bit extra for you."

See, carrot.

I took his hand anyways, and we poofed.

I'll spare you the flurry we materialized into. There was mooing involved.

And a bit extra didn't cover it. Like holy guacamole. Karen didn't trick me out as a femme fatale this time, I was straight up Queen of the Damned Dae. Scarlet gown, dripping diamonds, and I had a crown.

A freaking crown!

Oh yeah, I was super impressive. Brennan thought so, too. Tux clad, he came back into the bedroom, and the gleam in his eye left no question as to what he desired.

Take that, Bunny.

Karen handed me Rhys, and Peter started snapping pictures. You'd think he was a tourist or something. They'd put the kid in some starched white communion-looking getup with a frilly bonnet. He wasn't a fan. I couldn't blame him and told him it wasn't my idea. Totally got the stink-eye again. God, how could an infant be so judgmental?

Brennan chuckled, catching it, too. "Taking after you already with that glare."

I blinked. Taking after me? My mouth went dry. Yeah, I know it made sense, he was half my kid and everything, but I hadn't—

"Ready? They'll need time to stage us."

I nodded, feeling numb again—

Poof.

—and then total panic when we literally end up in the wings of a stage. The throne Brennan had commissioned was stark in the footlights, a pattern of dancing shadows splayed over a backdrop of smokey curtains. A spot snapped on for a lighting check, and I flinched, no longer seeing what was there.

The memory of a little girl belting out "Castle on a Cloud" ripped through my guts. I think I'd been five…Sugar Daddy's eyes alight, standing where I was now, and me out there, so happy I could make him proud—Until Calista had fed the roses he'd sent to our suite into the garbage disposal, one by one.

Then all I'd felt was dirty.

My head went light, fingers biting into Rhys, and he meeped. Brennan turned at the sound and did a double take. I took a step backward, my throat closing up.

"Lovely?"

"I'm not going out there—He's not going out there. Not now, not ever."

Poof.

Yeah, I bailed, and autopilot was on.

We were back in that desolate valley, the late afternoon sun blurry through my tears. I stumbled past the trees, my skirts snagging on the hoary bushes. Rhys whimpered, and I took off that stupid bonnet, kissing his head. "I'm sorry…"

God, I was so sorry.

I walked for a long time, stopping to nurse twice. Rhys's diaper became a disgusting mess, and I tore strips of my gown to swaddle him. My hands went through the motions with a familiarity that hurt to think about. I'd ditched the crown and heels after the first few steps, and my feet were cracked and bleeding from treading over jagged stones. For whatever reason, that felt right. Like I needed to punish myself.

Why? Oh, I don't know, maybe for being an epic failure at life?

I stumbled across a cave just as the sun was slipping below the horizon. It wasn't much to look at, but people had been here at one point. A circle of carbon was close to the cave's mouth and a smoothed-out shelf was at the back. My vision doubled, and I saw it heaped with furs and the walls painted with figures before blinking it away.

I called flame, the barest shadow of pigment visible in the flickering light.

I'd been here before, but I bet you'd already figured that out.

Why hadn't I?

It bothered me, but I didn't think about it too hard. After last night, and everything today, I was exhausted, and my body ached from the impromptu hike across Purgatory. I curled up on the rough slab of stone around Rhys, cushioning him on what was left of my skirts, and slept.

Whatever dreams I'd opted out of last night decided to gang up on me with another installment of *This Was Your Life.*

Yeah, that again.

I was here, like in this cave, but it was as it had been, not as it was. Instead of scraggly trees and brambles outside, it was verdant, and before it extended a sparkling vista of blue. The cave was on its shores, and I gotta say, prime Red Sea real estate. It was beautiful, and everything I go for, sand, salt water—

And just me.

Until the angels came. Yeah, the real deal, heavenly bodies of light given form. I know, my jaw dropped, too. Well, until they told me why they were there.

Apparently, after my exodus from the garden there'd been a period of time, albeit brief, when Adam professed to miss me. I'm not sure if God took pity on him or just wanted to shut him up, but regardless, in His infinite wisdom, He sent those angels to bring me back.

Cue free will.

I told them Adam could piss off. I mean, come on,

get off your lazy ass and make an effort instead of whining to Daddy. Him sending His goons after me was like having your friends go talk to that girl and tell her you're really sorry for pushing her in the mud, but you only did it because you like her.

Grow the fuck up.

Whatever. They did their best to convince me to go back. Wasn't happening, but I'll be honest, I was lonely and hello—angels. Three totally dreamy beings trying to be all "there, there, now little lady, don't you worry…"

Yeah, it pissed me off then too, but surprise, surprise, I totally took advantage of the situation, and it wasn't long before I was knocked up. God wasn't real pleased. I mean, He'd meant for me to procreate with Adam, and here I was pumping out semi-celestial beings.

Yep. You guessed it. That was the beginning of fae, though I didn't know it at the time.

Keep in mind that in anticipation of birthing the entire human race, my fertility had been seriously jacked, and pregnancy? I'm not going to get into it, but it was nothing like what I'd just gone through. Wham, bam, thank you, ma'am, springing from me totally self-sufficient.

So much for bonding.

The Big Guy? Yeah, He was pretty much pulling His hair out after I highjacked His creation and slapped down an ultimatum. I get my ass back to the garden, or He was gonna start snuffing my kids. I might've laughed. What? It was a long time ago and before I figured out that God doesn't play.

Trust me, whatever checks His mouth is writing, His ass can cash.

12 Days, 4 Hours, 6 Minutes

I'm not sure if it was Rhys nuzzling my breast that woke me, or the shifting shadows at the cave's entrance. Someone stood there, startling me. I blinked the sleep from my eyes, trying to reconcile then and now.

It was Brennan, with Socks wound about his shoulders. Guess that answered my question about the two of them talking. I sat up, wincing as my feet hit the ground. FYI, I don't recommend grabbing a nap on a stone slab. It's hell on your back.

"Are you all right?"

I wasn't but nodded, settling Rhys to nurse. What had happened to my other children? That void on my memories had slammed down again, and I was abruptly certain I didn't want it to lift.

Brennan let out a huge sigh, his shoulders drooping as he ran a hand over his jaw.

I peeked up at him. "Sorry I ruined the present thing. You mad?"

"No, it's my fault. I should've anticipated—I smoothed everything over by spinning it as a cancellation out of respect for the disaster victims. God, I'm a fool, Lovely." He came in and crouched by my feet, then took them in his hands, suffusing them with warmth. "I've had so much on my mind lately, I didn't think…Forgive me?"

I did. I mean, it was hard enough for me to keep

track of my crazy. How could I expect anyone else to? Socks slid from his shoulders to my lap, then butted his head up under my chin. I snorted. Yeah, we were cool again. Jerk.

"Then let's get you home." Brennan stood, gathered me into his arms, and poofed.

Things were kind of disjointed after that. I showered, turned down dinner, and ended up in bed with Rhys. That void in my memories drew me. I didn't want to know but had to at the same time.

Brennan's brow had set into a permanent wrinkle of concern. He climbed in next to us, his arms a welcome weight as I pressed my back to his chest.

"Are things really that bad? I mean, before I made them worse."

"With the normals?" he asked. "They're not good, and that damned cult spewing about Judgment Day being at hand doesn't help. It's given rise to several powerful factions pushing for more fae oversight that comes far too close to what they wanted before they started collaring us, and there are plenty of lesser fae that remember those days."

I put a hand to my throat. They weren't the only ones.

Brennan lit a cigarette. "If the legislation goes forward as is, fae will riot, and if it doesn't, the normals will."

My eyes were hot. I was just like Calista. She'd brought the Cleansing to a boil, but my dumb ass had snapped the lid on by sealing up the Neither, then jacked the temperature with my infertility curse. I brushed away a tear that had fallen onto Rhys's cheek. Sooner or later, the normals were going to come for me, and by the look on Brennan's face, he knew it too.

His arms tightened around me, and he kissed my temple. "It'll be over my dead body, Lovely."

I wasn't gonna go there.

"Why don't you have any other children?"

"Aside from not wanting to emulate my parents' arrangement?" His fingers teased through my hair, and my eyes closed. "For all the same reasons you were so angry when I told you that you'd been chosen to become. I had halfling siblings, Vy…going through that—how could I do it to a child of my own? You made it very clear that you felt the same. I look at Rhys now—I don't regret my decision. This is how it should be, and I would do it all over again."

"Minus the courting, genocide, and worldwide destruction."

A smile tipped up his lips, and he stubbed out his cigarette. "Yes, those I could do without."

"And the other night…if you weren't included in my curse now, would you have gotten me pregnant again?"

"I don't know, would I have?" He smiled at my expression. "Female fae used to be just as capable of controlling their fertility as the males. We'd both have to want it. If you did, then yes. I'm more than agreeable to expanding our family, but the ball is entirely in your court."

You'd think I would've remembered that. My eyebrow quirked. "You mean the Gwinth not only expects me to bang him, but to want his kid?"

"I'm afraid so." Brennan frowned, glancing at the clock. It was well past eleven. My stomach churned. "Promise me something?" His cheek dimpled at my glower. No way was he getting a blank check without an itemized receipt, and the jerk knew it.

"Try not to antagonize Aegaeus. We'll deal with him after all this is settled. Our people are standing down. I've several meetings scheduled and have contracted the hunt to quell any uprisings, but it's a fragile peace at best."

I snorted. For once it wasn't me he had to worry about. Until I heard what cosmic wisdom Gaia's meditation had dug up on Aegaeus's motives, I wasn't doing a damned thing other than fantasizing about giving the asshole a lobotomy. And trust me, that was pretty much what was going to have to happen to get him to cooperate.

Whatever. I promised and Brennan kissed me. Rhys went into the crib thing, and I didn't spend too much time thinking about anything after that. Brennan's lips moved on to other parts of my body, and he was hell bent on giving me something to remember him by.

I'd be lying if I said I wasn't trying to do the same. I was still pissed about Bunny, and knowing I couldn't have any contact with him for the next two days made my chest hurt. Like, not even texting. I know, right? Maybe I'd sneak him out a raven, but I was gonna train it to crap on the Gwinth first. What? They were supposed to be super smart.

Anywho, Brennan and I definitely made good use of what little time remained to us. Man, that sounds fatalistic, doesn't it? It felt like it, too. My satisfaction definitely suffered, and as much as I didn't want his last image of me to be bawling, shit happens.

Especially to me.

And at the stroke of midnight, he was gone.

Poof.

I laid there huddled in sheets, inhaling his scent from the pillows, miserable. Rhys didn't let me wallow for too long. Kid ate like a hummingbird. Karen had said that was because fae kids grew so fast, meeting their milestones sooner than normal kids, whatever that meant. I didn't have anything to compare it to—well, nothing I remembered at least—but I didn't doubt it was true. His dark hair had grown long enough to curl over my fingers, and when he pulled his head back to look at me, I wasn't surprised.

But I did laugh. It wobbled like Socks's when he was annoyed. Maybe having a snake as a nanny wasn't the wisest—

Rhys smiled. It was crooked, and his cheek dimpled.

Yeah, I can't even tell you what that gummy, drool-filled expanse did to me. I kissed him and held him close, wishing—God, wishes were for shit. The moon cast long shadows through the windows, and I tried to take comfort from them. Maybe Brennan was watching, knew that his son had his smile. I dashed the tears from my eyes, convincing myself that he did.

Meanwhile, the little bastard was way smug about his newfound skills and had zero intention of going back to sleep. That was okay. As wrung out as I was, I wasn't particularly eager to find out what was waiting for me when I closed my eyes. Hanging out with the kid was definitely preferable, and I wanted to see that gummy smile again.

Shut up.

We passed out sometime before dawn, and not nearly enough time had passed before I heard footsteps. I knew before I'd opened my eyes that they belonged to the Gwinth.

Let me be very clear that he'd let me hear his footsteps, and I was pretty positive the perv had been watching me sleep. Jonas was going to get a serious talking to about his lackluster security.

"You're not ready." He was all country club chic in chinos and a sports jacket.

I glared at him, tugging the sheets over what skin I could. Time to invest in some jammies. "And you're not invited into my bedroom."

He scented the air. God, that freaked me out. It was probably why the prick did it.

"Another has been. One last fling with Brennan? Wise of you not to quicken his seed."

Man, he was a creep. I didn't answer. Socks slithered onto the bed and coiled up between us, his head weaving. He didn't like him either. The Gwinth smirked like he thought he was cute, then checked his watch.

"It's ten thirty, and we've a schedule to keep. I suggest you get ready and meet me downstairs. Wear something complimentary. I like you in heels." He flashed that gap-toothed smile at me and poofed.

My head felt like it was going to explode I was so pissed. Heels? Fuck him.

I threw on the dumpiest pair of sweats I could find and pulled my hair up into a messy bun. Rhys went into his halter. No way I was letting him out of my sight with that perv prowling around.

The Gwinth was in the sitting room just off the main foyer, stretched out on the sofa like he owned the place, and sipping a gin and tonic. I hoped the quinine gave him diarrhea. He didn't look pleased to see me. The feeling was mutual.

"You look—"

"Like I just had a baby? Perceptive of you. I agreed to let you court me, not to let you dictate what I wear, when I leave the house, or any other minutiae of my life. By definition, in courting me, you're attempting to seek my favor, not piss me off."

His lips pursed. "Touché. Well then, what would you like to do?"

Not hang out with you. "I'm having breakfast."

He was at my side before I'd gotten into the hall like I wanted him there, and I got the faintest whiff of something floral from him. What was that, lilac? Dude needed to work on his choice of cologne as much as his social cues. I don't care if he hung out with convicts on the reg, his people skills sucked. Yeah, and that was coming from me.

Whatever, I found the solar, and Karen brought me my waffles. He asked for some, too. I hoped she spit in them. I hid behind the paper and kept waiting for Gaia, Kennet, or that jinn to show up. Weren't they supposed to be chaperoning this shit show? I probably should've paid more attention to the job description segment, but I'm pretty sure I'd been too busy clipping my toenails or something equally riveting.

Today's top stories? Mounting death toll, unchecked wild fires, and senate hearings. Oh, and the present thing being canceled. Sounded like the normals had bought Brennan's spin there, but they weren't having any of the volcano disaster being a coincidence.

The Gwinth's conversation was only slightly more palatable. He was blathering about some leviathan he'd singlehandedly brought to heel. He must've thought it was a good story, or just liked the sound of his own voice. Both, if I had to guess. I sure as hell wasn't encouraging it, despite him leaving me plenty of opportunity to ooh and ahh throughout it.

Yeah, like that was gonna happen.

So the imps had put him across the table from me, which I figured was the lesser of two evils. I mean, I had to look at him, but he was basically as far away from me as possible. I was absurdly grateful for that, especially with the way he was eyeing Rhys. Think unaffiliated lion scoping out another's cubs.

"You do know wet nurses are a thing." He cocked his eyebrow like he was expecting an answer.

He could wait for it. I took another bite of my waffles, and yes, you better believe I'd downed the happy pills waiting for me. I needed all the help I could get to deal with this crap.

"Why would I need a wet nurse?" I asked when I'd finished.

Apparently two could play the wait-for-it game. He pretty much ignored me, finishing his own. What a dick. Forget about a little spit, I hoped Karen had slipped in something like, oh, I don't know, drain cleaner would've been cool.

Either she hadn't, or it wasn't as toxic as those Mr. Yuck stickers had led me to believe. He pushed his empty plate away looking like he'd enjoyed it. She was gonna get a talking to, too.

"A wet nurse would allow you your freedom. Traditionally…"

Blah, blah, blah, blah, blah. I spent his monologue rolling my eyes. Yep, the back of my skull was still there.

"…had never taken you to a Broadway play and thought to remedy the situation this afternoon. I've front row seats for *Phantom of the Opera.*"

Wait, what? I stared at him. Holy shit, he was serious. Yeah, I just about died laughing. For an inappropriately long time. Ugh! Can you imagine?

It was not the reaction he'd been anticipating. Nor did he appreciate it. I dabbed at my eyes, still chuckling. God, my life sucked.

My hand rose to stroke Rhys's downy head. Well, not all of it.

"Sorry." Yeah, totally not sorry. "I'm not a big fan of the arts."

"Lose your taste for it after your own stint?"

Crap, did he know about how that last show in Vegas went down? I wouldn't put it past the asshole to know all about my bodyguard-turned-murderous-molester PTSD. I grabbed my coffee, not wanting to have this discussion, or any other, with him. "Who can say?"

"I'd imagine you could and find it quite interesting that you don't." He leaned back in his chair, those gold eyes of his luminescent even in the daylight. I wondered if he could see in the dark. Ugh, probably.

"What kind of fae are you?"

His mouth quirked. "Whatever kind I want to be. I'm pleased you're well enough to resume having intercourse. Perhaps spending the day in bed is more to your tastes? I'd still like to see you in heels." His eyes skated over me. "Those red ones from dinner were marvelous."

And just when I'd thought he'd gotten as skeevy as he could.

I called for some whiskey to add to the dregs of my coffee. Oh, okay, fine. Fuck the coffee, I just wanted the bottle, but I mean, come on! "You know how totally inappropriate that comment was, right? Like, between that and poofing into my bedroom, I'm pretty sure a judge would sign off on a restraining order."

"I'm afraid delicacy isn't my forte." He wet his lips like he was weighing his words. "After spending the entirety of my life with the wild hunt—"

"And I was raised in a convent. Do I look like a nun?"

That won a smile, not that I wanted one. I did, however, want the bottle Karen delivered. She started bussing the table, not even trying to pretend she wasn't listening.

"I begin to see how you gained the loyalty of a viper. Your tongue is certainly as deadly."

Yeah, I just about barfed. I took a swig off the bottle, and he smirked.

"Disarmament is a tactic I find useful in profiling those that interest me. I find it highly pleasurable studying your reactions and anticipating them in turn."

I checked the label. Were we drinking chianti? If he called me Clarice, I was gone. There was not a doubt in my mind he was as bat-shit dangerous as the fae he babysat.

"Well, since the theater is off the table, and you're not in the mood for heels, I suggest you find alternate child care, lest something unfortunate happen to the wee lad." Karen stiffened beside him, her eyes as narrow as my own. "We're going hunting, and the host isn't fit company for a child." He clarified, getting one of those reactions from me that he found oh so pleasurable. I wondered how he'd react to my foot in his ass.

"But they are for a lady?" I batted my lashes at him, wanting to put my fist through his stupid teeth.

"Not in the slightest. You, on the other hand, should fit right in."

Asshole. He laughed and sipped his coffee. Karen and I exchanged a glance. If she hadn't been spitting in his food before, she would be now. "I thought I told you, I'm not—"

"Don't!"

Both our heads snapped to the door.

Enter the jinn.

Holy crap. Brennan hadn't been kidding. It was like that dumpy little dude in a plaid shirt and chinos had stepped straight off the sitcom. What the fuck was his name? I blinked. A lot. I mean, if you could look like anything, literally anything—just, why?

"Refusing to abide by the terms of the agreement thrice results in a forfeiture of said rights, defaulting settlement of the consort-ship, referenced in Appendices A through C, to the slighted party, in this case, a Mr. Gwinth."

My jaw dropped. And he was a lawyer?

"It's an office, jinn, not a title." The Gwinth growled, and I swear I saw actual hackles rise.

The jinn grinned back, his teeth a titch too pointed. "And that's a species, not a moniker. Call me Monica."

"Jinn."

"Mr. Gwinth."

I choked on my whiskey. "Monica?" What the ever-loving fuck was that about?

"Lost a bargain." The jinn shrugged.

Oh, okay, well, that made total—I slammed the bottle down and glared at the Gwinth. "Hold up—You've been pissing me off on purpose!" Asshole wasn't stupid. He knew there was no way I was gonna bang him willingly, so he'd found a loophole. Goddamn it! And I'd almost walked right into it. I needed to get a copy of that stupid contract and do something with it other than even out my table legs. You know, like read it.

Shut up, I can read, it's just more fun to look at pictures.

The Gwinth's glare flicked from the jinn to me, and I returned it. "Have I been?"

"You're a dick." I turned to the jinn. He'd sat beside me, one arm over the back of his chair, that grin still on his face. God, that was weird. "What the hell is your deal?"

"No deal." He shrugged, then waggled a finger at our plates. "Pancakes?"

"Waffles."

"Gluten-free? I sent over my dietary restrictions last night." He tucked a napkin into the neck of his shirt, rubbing this hands together as Karen deposited a plate in front of him. They looked sad enough to be gluten-free. He stabbed into them like they were actual food. "You have any tomato juice? Caffeine makes me antsy. Thanks. Now, where were we? Ah, yes. Subsection 42a of your agreement stipulates outings, designed to showcase one's suitability as a consort. They're at your suitor's discretion, and attendance on your part is mandatory, else the previously mentioned forfeiture clause goes into effect."

Yeah, my head hurt, too. "What do you mean, suitability as a consort? I thought he just wanted me to incubate his demon seed."

The Gwinth's lips pursed. "You already have familiarity with Brennan and the All Father. The outings are intended to provide an opportunity for us to become better acquainted, unless you'd like to skip them and get right to it?"

Eww, no, and yeah, he was trying to baffle me with bullshit. "If that was true, you'd have gotten tickets for Comic Con instead of *Phantom*. Cut the fae-speak. What's in this for you, aside from that whole geas-passing thing?" Yep, I'd totally just asked a fae what his motives were, and he looked smug as hell that I had. Crap.

"Would you bargain for the answer?"

You had to know that was coming. I laughed. "Nope, I bet Monica here will give me the skinny for free."

The jinn's head bobbed in the affirmative, chewing. "You've allowed Brennan unprecedented control over your affairs and shown zero desire or initiative to assume them, rendering him King-in-Absentia. Granted, the man is a gifted administrator, but the jury's out as to if you're being clever utilizing in his skills, or if your intellect renders you unable. Mr. Gwinth is no doubt betting on the latter, and you requiring your next consort do the same. His unique heritage gives him a plausible claim to the daemon throne. For the record, the All Father has no interest in gaining any purview over Fire. However, should you choose him as consort, a cease and desist encompassing any and all relations with Mr. Malten will be stridently upheld. Addendum A requires you to personally take charge of your affairs or appoint an alternate administrator of your choice. If you are incapable of doing either, one will be assigned to you by the courts."

Great. Everyone thought I was an idiot. I pinched a hand across my temples. God, this just kept getting better and better. I mean, it made sense—the Gwinth wanting to be consort, not the potential of a court-ordered babysitter. With the geas passed on, he'd be looking for something to do, and traditionally—ugh, I know, that word—war was dae business, and killing shit totally fell into his wheelhouse.

"I have no choice about going with him?"

Monica grinned, and I didn't much like it. He took his tomato juice from Karen and toasted me with it. "There's always a choice."

Check that—I didn't like him.

"Enough," the Gwinth said, throwing his napkin on the table and getting to his feet. "Hand the urchin off. It's time to go." His eyes glinted and all that crap about choices? Yeah, not so much.

I gritted my teeth. "Isn't Gaia supposed to go with me?"

It was a total stab in the dark, but it drew blood. The Gwinth's knuckles went from midnight to charcoal. "Where is she?"

I shrugged. "You know how new routines are. Bound to be hiccups along the way. I don't see Kennet either."

The Gwinth sat back down and drummed those long fingers of his against the table like he was mulling something over. "He's minding the host in my absence."

My eyebrow rose at that. Brennan had said he was a bloodthirsty bastard, but a human, second-in-command to the Gwinth? How the hell did he keep them all in line? I mean, not for nothing, but even a lesser fae could stomp the crap out of a normal.

Whatever. Rhys was fussing. I stood. "Let me know when she gets here. Apparently I need to make alternate childcare arrangements."

You know I didn't want to, but I didn't want to sit there more, and as much as I hated to admit it, bringing Rhys around the hunt was definitely not a good idea. Me being around the hunt probably wasn't either. That crack about being the only game in town worth having wasn't giving me the warm fuzzies. Maybe I'd luck out and Gaia would forget she was on the clock.

Karen had beat me upstairs and laid out clothes on the bed. She hustled me over to the vanity and started brushing and braiding while I nursed Rhys.

"Do you know where Gaia is?"

"Test-timony."

I winced, planning on avoiding her for the next century or two. "What about Jonas?"

"Boss call. Back soon." She was making these twisty little ridges of hair down my scalp that fed into different sized plaits. It looked way goth. I was digging it.

I buzzed my lips. Stewie would probably be up for a hunt and said so.

"No, all go."

My eyes narrowed. Brennan had taken all the Riders? What could possibly require five fiends to take care of? I mean, short of annexing the globe. "What for?"

Karen shrugged. "I no ask."

Et tu, Brutus? I scowled at her in the mirror. "That doesn't mean you don't know."

The back of my head must've developed some kind of stylistic emergency, because she totally ducked behind me to tend to it. Great. My imp was holding out on me. I eyed Socks, chillin' in the porto-crib.

"You know, too, don't you?" Crickets. My stomach

plummeted. "He went to kill Aegaeus, didn't he?"

Karen popped up like she was spring-loaded. "No. Deep-lomatic emergency."

I swapped Rhys to the other side, chewing on my lip. Crap. It had to be major if Brennan was taking all his muscle…which meant it was probably my fault.

Damn it.

"Close eyes." I sighed and let her attempt to make me look well-rested.

I've said it before and I'll say it again, she really is a super imp. Mission accomplished, though the whole goth vibe totally helped. The outfit was less successful. Like, in theory low-rider leather pants and the matching motocross jacket would've worked, but a muffin top only looks good on a muffin. It's totally not bad-ass, I don't care who you are.

"I'm not wearing these." I couldn't even zip them up after laying down and doing that wiggle and pump move with my hips. Oh shut up, like you've never been there.

Karen looked at me like I was an idiot. Man, her too? "Burn off. No, not pants. You fat."

Did she just call me—

Data dump.

Oh…duh. I laughed. Why? Remember that whole becoming the element and my form falling away gig? Yeah, the becoming-actual-fire schtick. When I reassumed my humanoid form, it was based on my concept of self. Like, all I had to do was rewind the tape to pre-pregnancy me and hello hip bones.

Hmm? You better believe I was keeping the boobs.

Flame on. Take that muffin top.

The results were smokin'. Hah. I was like heavy

metal Emma Peel. Brennan was gonna freak—I slumped on the bed.

Goddamn it. Karen came over burping Rhys.

"No weak in front of host. They eat you."

I snorted. Yeah, so I've been told…and I was back to Brennan. Man, how bad had I screwed things up for him this time? Socks slithered over and draped himself around my shoulders, tongue tickling my ear. I stood, giving Rhys a quick kiss.

Socks was right.

Since when have I waited for anyone to do anything? If Brennan needed me to buy time, I was gonna buy time.

And you better believe I was gonna kick ass while I did it.

11 Days, 13 hours, 17 Minutes

Socks and I went downstairs. Yep, he was my plus one.

The Gwinth was in the foyer, smirking at his cell phone. That prick did have a—what the hell was with the raven? He shoved the cell into his pocket, glancing up the stairs at me, then did a double take, those creepy gold eyes popping out of his head.

Vy-1, Gwinth-0.

Yeah, I posed. Peter took a pic.

"If we're gonna do this, let's do this."

The Gwinth wet his lips, giving me the up and down. "What about Brennan's representative?" Socks hissed at him. "You're joking."

"If you'd rather stay here—"

"I didn't say that." He looked over his shoulder at Monica gawking at me. "You ready, jinn?" He shook himself like a dog and joined us.

Poof.

We arrived in a massive clearing. Based on the surrounding trees and the dank heat blanketing everything, we were somewhere subtropical, and no lie, there were easily a hundred psycho fae milling around.

They all turned to stare.

I might've wiped my sweaty palms down my pants, but then I totally owned it.

New-baby smell, new-baby smell—

Beside me the Gwinth, like, morphed. You ever see that superhero movie where the blue chick shingles into different people when those scale-things ripple out from her? Yeah, like that but without the sound. One minute he was ready for the country club and the next he was all decked out in military ballistic gear with a cape.

You heard me, a freaking cape. Hmm, oh, it was a dark purple-y grey. Oh yeah, totally like the super villain magnet guy, but without the sexy chess-playing vibe.

"Mount up!"

A tremor went through the entire host, and fae steeds began to appear. Hmm? Oh, they look like regular horses until you get close. Their hooves were cloven, and their teeth were pretty much what the imps were rockin'. Yeah, maybe don't get too close. Kennet resolved from the clamoring mass of fae and led three mounts over.

Two of them, as Brennan would say, were a bit extra.

Their hides were onyx, and bony carapaces the color of soot covered their bellies and chests, then ridged out over their eyes. They glowed the same ethereal gold as the Gwinth's and looked about as personable. Their dark manes entwined with spines as long as my hand, running down their necks and over their haunches. The ones in the center must've been sawed off so they could be tricked out with what equated to a polo saddle.

For those of you not vested in equestrian do-hickeys, think barely padded flap of leather with zip to hold onto. That thing made a sudden stop, I was gonna be an Envy-kabob. What the heck was it with things trying to impale me?

Whatever. I'd rather spines than the Gwinth. What about the last horse? The third was a birthday party reject. Seriously, it was the oldest, fattest pony I'd ever seen, and I wouldn't be surprised if they were dropping it off at the glue factory after this. Monica had gone over to make friends and was feeding it a carrot. Hmm? God only knows where he'd gotten it from. I told you, jinn are sketchy. I shook my head and started for one of the others.

The Gwinth's hand was on my arm. "Not so fast." He grinned. "You're riding Mab."

Wait, he expected me to—He jerked his head toward the pony, then laughed, mounting one of the others. Monica poofed onto the one beside him before I could even form the words to argue. When had that asshole gotten in on the joke? God, I hated men. They looked down at me, and the Gwinth made a shooing motion with his hand. Asshole.

Whatever. I stomped over to the stupid pony, because you know what? They were more than welcome to leave me in the lurch and go do boy things with the host. Maybe me and ol' Mab here would mosey on down to the nearest petting zoo and see what we could rake in while they peed on stuff to claim it.

I threw my leg over her back, and Socks wrapped around my waist like a really expensive belt. My toes would've totally scraped the ground if it wasn't like straddling a wine cask. The pony turned to look at me like it was just as offended. Its gums pulled back exposing a mouthful of razor-sharp teeth.

"Lilith."

"Uh, Mab." Yeah, the pony was totally talking to me.

"It's been a while."

Cue the memories…and then the massive groan.

Crap.

I should explain. So Mab, yeah, that—and please envision me using air quotes and heavy sarcasm here—Queen of the Fairies Mab. But even Jane Austen got that little tidbit wrong. Mab was no queen. I mean, in Ms. Austen's defense, the stupid pixie had been billing herself like that to normals for aeons. Everyone in the Fae realms just kind of rolled their eyes and snickered. Shakespeare was on the money. Mab was Fae's midwife and had a penchant for messing with dreams.

Anyways, way back, when those shitheads back in Fae decided to trap Lilith and the other three primordial elementals in the anathemas, it kicked off a classic case of shit rolls down the hill. Or maybe it was you fuck me, I'll fuck you harder? Whatever. That's why Lilith cursed them with sterility, so I guess none of that fucking mattered, because they didn't have any more babies, and Mab became obsolete.

Whoops, but whatever.

The stupid pixie flipped out and had zero qualms about letting Lilith know it every time she closed her eyes. It became an issue. Like, there wasn't a hell of a lot to do in exile, and Mab was screwing with what little escapism there was.

Unfortunately for her, all that flitting around making a royal pain in the ass out of herself while Lilith was trying to get her beauty sleep created an opportunity to figure out how she was influencing dreams. Lilith couldn't physically leave the ember, but she did gain some mad skills messing with people while they slept.

Like, eventually enough to poison the well against Mab back in Fae and get her shipped off to the wild hunt, but God, that had been ages ago. She had to be over it by now, and besides, neither of my incarnations had anything to do with turning her into a geriatric pony. Seriously, her current predicament was her own damned fault.

Not that I was gonna tell her that while I was humping along on her back.

"You look…good."

She snorted, spattering my pants with snot. Ugh, that was gross. "Lies. I don't want that viper touching me."

Socks hissed. He wasn't a fan either.

The Gwinth made a kind of whooping noise, and the host formed up. Beside him, Monica had pretty much forgotten me, holding the reins with a feral grin. I couldn't fault him. Riding with the hunt was one of those bucket-list things for fae. Plodding after it on a decrepit mare was not.

I frowned, taking up the reins. "So what happened?"

"You mean after you ruined my life the second time?"

Guess she wasn't over it. "Uh…yes?"

She ambled to the end of the column, behind Monica and the Gwinth's mounts. One of them was kind enough to crap out a steaming pile just as we arrived. Mab tossed her head, dancing back.

"You see many female fae here?"

I hadn't seen any, actually, which kind of didn't make sense, I mean women were just as capable of being psychopaths as men—

"As soon as one comes in, the host passes them around and they're torn apart."

My stomach dropped along with my opinion of the Gwinth. Yeah, I hadn't thought that was possible either. My eyes roamed over the host, horrified, but confused at the logistics where Mab was involved. "But you were like two inches tall—"

"You think all of them are big hulking brutes? Look closer."

I squinted, and she was right. More than one of the mounted fae had something smaller flitting around them. I swallowed the lump in my throat, feeling sick.

"There's no way I would've—If I'd known that's what was going to happen—"

She looked back at me and snorted again. "Don't you think I know that? No one in Fae knows what goes on here. And it didn't happen. Not to me at least. The Gwinth knew I got exiled on trumped-up charges and gave me a way out. I took it."

Huh. That didn't sound like his MO…

A polished ivory horn materialized in his hand. He held to his lips and blew, the host surging forward. Mab trotted after them, her spine jarring against my tailbone. God, that sucked. I leaned over her neck, not that it did much good.

"Any reason he couldn't have sprung for a better model?"

"I didn't start out like this, you twit. His power is fading, and every time the host sees me they're reminded of it. You need to take me with you when you leave."

Was she kidding? "What like just ride off into the sunset?"

Mab's head tossed, her eyes rolling back in her head to flash the whites. "No. Ask for me as a gift. The host thinks you're riding me to humble you, but it was so we could come to an agreement. He's promised me my freedom but can't grant it outright."

I glared at the Gwinth's back disappearing over the

rise and pulled back on the reins. Mab stopped, pawing at the ground, her sides heaving.

"No way. He's gonna want something in return."

"You're giving him a portion of his power back. Don't you get it? He's losing control of them. If Kennet wasn't so feared, they'd already have turned against him. He needs every smidgen of his power, and you owe me—"

"Like hell I do. If you hadn't been such a pain in the ass—"

"You made me obsolete!"

"Fae weren't the only thing having babies!"

"Normals? That's insulting!"

"This is better?"

She tossed her head, teeth gnashing. "Fine! What do you desire?"

I blinked. What did I desire from her? A better question was what the hell could a disenfranchised pixie do for me? Crap. When in doubt, indentured servitude was always the best option. "Your service, for a year and a day."

She went super still. "Seriously? That's it?"

"No, I also want you to stay the hell out of my dreams and those of my kin in perpetuity."

"Agreed," Mab grumbled and started trotting again. We stopped at the top of the rise. Below, the host stood on the shores of a pristine lake. Well, it would've been pristine if the center wasn't exploding in gouts of red-tinged—had that been a head?

The body followed, clearing that up.

Eww…The majority of the host ringed the shore, cutting off any escape while the Gwinth's Water fae were having their way with an enclave of nixies. The fishes' war song faded into screams, setting my teeth on edge. Crap. I hoped me being here wouldn't be seen as provocation.

Mab ambled to the Gwinth's side.

"There you are." He grinned down at me and I scowled back. "Enjoying your ride?"

"Not especially, but the conversation was enlightening. I want her."

His eyebrow raised. "Enough to bargain?"

"You can tack her onto that lousy courting gift, you cheapskate." He looked insulted. I didn't care.

"I'd hardly call Bacchanal Fog cheap."

I batted my eyelashes. "It doesn't rate with an estate."

"Perhaps not..." He got off his steed and took Mab's reins from me. "I'll agree on one condition. I want to kiss you."

The host around us stilled, their attention drawn from the lake. Monica moved closer to listen, a frown marring his brow. He wasn't happy, but I guess it was legal.

I might've thrown up in my mouth a little. "Where?"

He laughed. "On those lush crimson lips of yours."

"If I agree"—and yeah, it was a big if—"it doesn't constitute me initiating any form of intimacy. Like, one time deal, no tongue, no touching me anywhere else, and it can't last more than ten seconds." Behind him, Monica gave me a thumbs-up.

The Gwinth laughed. "What kind of a kiss is that?"

"The only kind you're getting." Now or ever. Ugh, I was seriously going to be sick.

"Five seconds, but I get to kiss you properly, and you have to let me."

How long was five seconds exactly? One Mississippi, two Mississippi…Christ, I couldn't believe I was actually considering this. I slid off Mab's back, bow-legged and saddle sore for all of the hot minute I'd been on her. Socks wriggled up around my shoulders, his tongue flicking in my ear. Good point. "I want her changed back, now."

"Then we are agreed?" The Gwinth stepped close, a smile on his stupid face.

Monica shrugged.

My face screwed up like a prune. God, I was gonna make that pixie scrub toilets with her toothbrush for this—"Fine, agreed."

The Gwinth's hands skated over my hips, pulling me against him, and his stature shrank to fit against me. Ugh, full body shiver, and he got off on it. Trust me, I could tell.

"Agreed." There was a shimmer behind me, and Mab zipped around us, trailing dust. Yeah, pop culture got that right.

His nose brushed mine. "Put your arms around my neck, and act like you want it."

"Fuck off."

He chuckled, and then his lips were against mine, his hands cupping my rear, then one reaching up to fondle my breast, tongue darting—

Okay, look, if I hadn't hated him so much, I might have enjoyed it. But I did, so I didn't.

At five Mississippis, I pulled back and slugged him.

It didn't lay him out, but it sent him back a step since he wasn't expecting it. Probably because he was standing there in those tight pants with a semi. I mean, for his sake I hoped it was a semi. You'd think a shape-shifter could—eww. Never mind. He was too creepy for that thought to go any further.

Moving on.

The host just about died laughing. I spat, trying to get the feel of him off my mouth. He didn't taste like anything.

Apparently I did.

"Delicious." He dabbed a spec of blood from the corner of his mouth and smiled. "You'll be a fit mother for my heir. The others were decidedly lackluster in comparison."

Well, la-de-freaking-da. There's a metal I wanted to pin on my chest. Socks hissed in my ear, and I snickered. Having to chloroform your dates probably did put a damper on things. The Gwinth's eyes narrowed, and I rolled mine. It was kind of a reflex. The barest weight flitted against my ear, and Socks went for it.

"Aeeek!"

Motherf—Something so small should not be able to emit a shriek that loud.

"Tell him not to eat me!"

"Don't eat her. Not for a year, at least," I muttered, fingering my ear. Socks wasn't impressed, but snakes rarely are. They're kind of like cats in that way. "Oh, hush. I'll have Karen find you a gopher or something when we get back."

While all this was going on, the nixies hadn't made out well. A big fae with gills and a purple crest was directing the rest to haul the bodies onto shore. Like, dozens of them. The Gwinth ordered them counted, and when his numbers matched, he blew his horn again.

Then it was party time.

Seriously.

Two long semi-trailers poofed in behind us. They were decked out as food trucks, and the front side of each popped open to make shaded bar areas. Some of the host started setting out tables, and Bob Marley's "One Love" came over the speakers. For real?

"Join me." The Gwinth held out his hand for mine. That stupid gap-toothed smile spread over his face when it became apparent I wasn't taking it, but I did follow him over to one of the trailers. Stools were attached below the bar, and I snagged one. He took another, and Monica joined us.

A troll with a towel thrown over his shoulder asked me what I wanted to drink while he eye-fucked me. He wasn't the only one. The rest of the host was doing this synchronized crotch-shifting sequence that made the hair on the back of my neck prickle. No wonder Mab had gone equine. The worst of them was that crested fae. He caught my eye and pumped his hips with a this-is-happening look. Eww, gross…no way in hell was that prediction coming true, Crest-kin.

I turned back to the troll. "Jäger." Yep, it'd been that kind of a day.

"Make it three and bring the bottle, Rodrigo." The troll grunted and went to find it. I flicked my hand at Mab, her flitting against my ear was making me nuts. The Gwinth smiled. "She's making a nest in your hair."

Fuck my life.

Yeah…let me explain. I probably should have thought the whole indentured-servant thing through a little more. Shut up. Pixies imprint on things and have a tendency to become a wee bit obsessive. Hence Mab freaking out about being furloughed way back when. By taking her service now, I'd just become the recipient of all that pent up OCD. Like, her new job was me, and she was literally moving right in. Oh, and FYI, pixie nests aren't like bird's nests. I was going to have what equated to a hairy ball sack dangling by my ear.

Go on, get it out of your system. I'll wait.

No, there wasn't any use in stopping her. Once a pixie was set on a project, forget it. I was just gonna have to let her finish, then chop the mess out and tack it up on a wall somewhere. Karen was going to have words to say about that. Imps and pixies didn't exactly get on to begin with, for all they were Fire and Earth.

Whatever. I ignored the Gwinth's amusement and downed my shot. He followed suit and poured us both another. Monica didn't seem to be a fan. Probably wasn't keto approved or some shit. I grabbed mine and put my back to the bar, watching the host. The Gwinth was doing the same. Specifically, he was watching Crest-kin, and it didn't take much to figure out why. The others in the host deferred to him, and if what Mab had been saying about the Gwinth losing his power was true, that right there was trouble waiting to happen. Trust me, I was kind of an expert in impending fuckery.

Whatever, not my problem. Back to those nixies. They'd stripped them down and piled their corpses beside a big tanker-looking thing belching smoke. Hickory was in the wind.

Then the meat hooks came out.

My stomach lurched. Christ, this was a BBQ.

"Waste not, want not," the Gwinth said beside me.

"That's disgusting."

He picked the side of a tooth with his pinky nail. "It's a lot like alligator, actually."

Like that made it any better. I threw back another

shot, wincing at the tightness of my jacket. I needed to feed Rhys, if Gaia hadn't broken out the goat already. Hell, even if she had, a date with the moo machine was preferable to this.

"Are we done here? Reggae's not my thing." Neither was hanging out with cannibals or creepy perverted shitheads like him.

The Gwinth shrugged, rolling around a mouthful of liquor. "We could be."

I took that as a yes, grabbed the bottle, and poofed.

Rhys was squalling, and the goat was in transit. Socks took his leave, and I highjacked the kid from Karen. Let me tell you, his little bite was sweet, sweet relief.

Which made it all that more shocking when Karen bared her teeth at me. Like all eighty-seven razor-sharp points. Yep, they're multi-rowed like a shark's.

"Is peek-see in you hair. Stay steel, I crush."

Oh yeah…that. I edged away from her. You'd think it would be hard for someone three feet tall to loom, but she did a bang-up job. "No, she's part of a bargain—"

"*In. You. Hair!*"

Okay, so imps have a thing about hair. A pixie in mine was probably pretty close to worst-case scenario as far as Karen was concerned.

Said pixie poked her head out. "Suck it, razor-face."

Yeah, not helping.

"A baby! I heard you'd had one, but didn't—" Mab zipped down and snuffed at Rhys's cheek. It dimpled, and he waved his pudgy hands at her. Mab flitted out of his reach, clasping hers below her chin. "A true fae! I never thought I'd see—"

Snick.

Karen held a plastic container to her breast with a malevolent grin.

Christ, Mab hadn't even had time to scream. She pounded at the sides and no lie, the most diabolical laugh I've ever heard rumbled out of Karen's throat when she burped the lid.

"You can't keep her in there."

"What? Is flay-vor say-vor."

I gave her a look.

"Ten minute. I let out then."

"I'd prefer her still breathing. I didn't kiss the stupid Gwinth for you to asphyxiate her. Look, she's my servant for the next year and can't clean out the dryer vents if she's dead. Trust me, it wasn't my idea, and Socks gets first dibs. Can you find him a gopher?"

Karen's lips pursed, tapping the container against her palm way harder than contemplation required. Mab wasn't amused. She wasn't looking so good either. "No in you hair."

"No. Chop the nest out and tack it up on the wall over—let her go first."

Karen shot me one hell of a side-eye, but tipped up a corner of the lid enough for air to get in, just not enough for Mab to get out. I fought a shiver of revulsion as Karen approached with the shears and decided the stupid pixie deserved it. Especially after the nest was removed. Forget about a ball sack, how the hell had she had time to macramé half my damned head?

Karen started to regrow it, and I screwed my eyes shut. New-baby smell, new-baby smell…"Are Gaia and the Riders back yet?"

Her fingers slowed. "Downstairs."

"What happened?"

She shrugged.

"Karen…"

"Is fine."

In my experience, that pretty much meant the opposite. "Is Brennan okay?"

"No worry about Boss. He beeg strong fiend."

Well, that didn't make me feel any better. God, I hated not being able to talk to him, and yeah, I pouted, swapping Rhys to my other boob. You know, multi-tasking.

"Done. Keep peek-see out." She picked up the mess of hair and stuck it on a hook in the walk-in closet, accidentally-on-purpose knocking the container Mab was in onto the floor as she passed. That relationship was getting off to a banner start. Can't wait for the next 365 days.

I finished nursing Rhys and let Mab out. She bitched for a while, but the kid distracted the hell out of her. I put him in his porto-crib and went to brush my teeth, like thirty-seven times, then killed the mouthwash trying to do the same to any vestiges of the Gwinth. I traded the leather duds for sweats and threw my pixie-free hair up into a messy bun. Feeling better in my mom-iform, I collected my son. Mab had somehow already torn a hole in one of the padded halter straps and came along for the ride. Whatever. We went downstairs.

The Gwinth was waiting for me, because of course he was.

"So, what would you like to do for the rest of the day?"

My eyes went to the clock. It was five after one. I still had eight plus hours to suffer through with this asshole.

Shut up. I didn't cry.

We watched *The Godfather*. Well, he watched *The Godfather*. I passed out on the other end of the couch. Karen came in with snacks at some point. I know because there were the remains of them on the coffee table when Rhys started fussing again. The sun wasn't nearly far enough across the sky, and the Gwinth had switched on a football game. Monica and the Riders were on the other couches with beers debating draft picks. None of them even glanced in my direction when I stood. Weird. I didn't know they were that into football. Gaia was still MIA. Mab zipped out of the chip bowl to follow me when I left them to take care of the kid.

Which, according to her, I did totally wrong.

As affirming as my verbal flogging was, it didn't take long enough. I dicked around trying to kill more time, but in the end, went back because I was positive if I didn't, the Gwinth would come looking for me.

When I got downstairs, a table for two had been set up, and he was waiting for me by candlelight. Mab snickered from inside the halter strap, and I slapped it.

Crap.

I plopped down across from him, and he shot me that gap-toothed grin of his like I'd performed some clever trick. More like I was starving. Karen came in with drinks. She'd made mine a double, bless her heart.

"You do know how to push a man's limits, don't you? I was just about to fetch you back."

See? I knew it. "Gender has nothing to do with it."

"Equal opportunity irritant, eh?"

I didn't rise to the bait. Asshole was getting off on it. Yep, he did that a lot. Karen brought in a salad, and I chomped on it, trying to ignore his creepy gold eyes drilling into me. He dandled a fork above his plate.

"I've been giving some thought to our next interlude."

"Is that what we're calling this?" I would have gone with one of Dante's circles, but tomato, toma-toe. "What did you have in mind, mini-golf?"

"Not quite. I thought we'd spend the day in New York."

No way would I admit it, but my interest was piqued. By the New York part, the rest of it sucked. "Whatever."

He grinned like I'd said I'd be just freaking tickled, his gaze lingering on my lips, then dropping to the rest of me and fixing on Rhys. "I'm not opposed to you bringing *that* with you, should you feel it necessary, though you won't find a more capable nanny than the one I've just gifted you with."

Damn it, I knew there'd been a catch, but he wasn't wrong. That stupid dust Mab spilled had been flagged by normals as a mood-enhancing narcotic, which is probably where all that flying crap had come from. If it didn't have a shelf life of point three seconds, they'd be rioting for the stuff. Anyways, she could totally use it to soothe the little bastard and keep him in spud mode. What? Oh, please. I keep telling you fae are different, and trust me, if your kid was a massive pain in the ass and you ran across a pixie, you can't tell me you wouldn't be smackin' the damned thing like Emeril kickin' up his Creole.

"How magnanimous of you." I pushed my empty plate away.

"It serves my interests. In either case, you'll have no cause to leave."

Asshole.

Karen took away his untouched salad, and Peter came in with the next course. To the uninitiated, it probably looked like meatloaf. The Gwinth certainly picked up his fork with enough enthusiasm for me to think that was the case.

Yeah, it wasn't. His mouth pruned around the massive bite he'd taken, and I had to make a concerted effort not to laugh. Karen had been trying out vegetarian recipes, and lentil casserole was one of the hard-core fails. Like I said, you don't want to piss off an imp, and that crack earlier about something unfortunate happening to Rhys had done the trick. Oh yeah, way better than spit.

The Gwinth pushed his plate away and drained the wine in his glass, calling for more. "Your preferred cuisine?"

I took a bite to spite him. "To nixie? Yes."

He grunted and grabbed the bottle from Peter to pour. I wished this day would freaking end so I could grill Jonas and get the imps to make me a pizza. This was gross really. Like, who bakes lentils with cottage cheese and shredded carrots? The sesame seed crust was just insult to injury.

"Your reluctance to have an open mind about our relationship becomes tiresome," the Gwinth said, frowning at me.

My eyebrow cocked. Did they have classes on social cues? If they did, he needed to enroll, like, stat, if that's all he'd gotten out of today. Seriously, what about "fuck off" hadn't registered?

He sat back in his chair, scraping his tongue against his teeth. "I can only imagine it's the result of some ill-founded loyalty to Brennan based on his assistance in your becoming."

I snorted. Right. The Gwinth being despicable had nothing to do with it. God, where did this guy—

He slid a manila envelope across the table. "I can assure you he has no such qualms, and is not the man you think he is."

I'd say my bite went ashy, but it was already there. "What's that?"

The Gwinth inspected his nails. "Photos of the last twenty-two hours. He's been very busy."

I sipped my wine, torn between ripping open the envelope and not giving him the satisfaction of watching me rip open the envelope.

...Whatever they tell you, I want the opportunity to refute. They will try and twist your emotions along with the truth...

"How do I know whatever's in there hasn't been doctored?"

"I suppose you don't." The Gwinth finished his wine. "Save for me swearing by the Midsummer's moon that they haven't been."

I had trouble swallowing. That ranked way beyond a Bible and raising your right hand.

"And if that still won't suffice, by all means, ask that big dae of yours. He was there, too. Isn't that right, Jonas?" The Gwinth flashed that smile over my shoulder, then glanced at his watch. "On that note, I believe my time is about up. I hope to find you in a more open frame of mind the next time we meet." He pushed back his chair and stood, giving me a little half bow, then poofed.

That fucking envelope stayed right where it was.

"Jonas?"

Several seconds passed before he sighed from behind me and moved to take the chair the Gwinth had left. His eyes went to the envelope, and he scratched at his jaw, stubble bristling beneath his fingers.

"You wanna tell me anything before I open that up?"

"I can't, even if I did."

My stomach plummeted at the way his voice cracked. I sat there for maybe half a second more before snatching it and going to the bedroom.

I didn't open it.

The awful feeling that whatever was in there was going to mess with me hard churned in my gut. Mab stayed the hell out of my way, and the envelope sat on the table between the two chairs by the window, malignant. I should just immolate it. Somehow, it would be a lie. The Gwinth had given it to me with the sole intention of driving a wedge between Brennan and me...

But he'd sworn by the Midsummer's moon. Whatever was in there, had happened. Maybe was happening...

And Jonas wouldn't tell me, though there wasn't a doubt in my mind he knew what it was. I fed and changed Rhys, put him in his crib. He and Mab watched me like they could feel the blackness seeping from the envelope as much as I did, filling the room with an awful tension, their silence adding to it.

I picked it up. Sat. Unwound the string and lifted the flap.

It was a stack of photos taken with one of those telescopic lenses.

The first was of Brennan in a tux with a wide smile on his face, arms open to welcome someone. His eyepatch dated the photos within the last year, even if it hadn't been the past twenty-whatever hours. The Riders stood behind him, looking less than enthusiastic, surrounded by the frescoed walls of the Venetian.

Yep. As in the fucking casino. He'd been in Vegas, after he said...

My hands trembled sliding the photo aside to the next one.

A woman, tall, with waves of wheaten hair was in his arms, hers around his neck. Her cream satin gown clinging to her curves. His lips on her cheek.

She was beautiful and loved to laugh. God, every photo...they looked like they belonged together. Had that kind of ease. His hand never strayed from her waist, and hers were all over him. At the tables. A restaurant booth. Poolside. The balcony of a suite.

Then the one of her gripping his lapels and him jamming his tongue down her throat as he pulled the curtains closed.

The last one was of his bare ass pumping at her through a gap in them.

...He's not what you think. Everything he told you was a lie. Sweet words to make you do what he wanted...

I shoved them back into the envelope. Numb.

...You've allowed Brennan unprecedented control over your affairs and shown zero desire or initiative to assume them, rendering him King-in-Abstentia....

...So dedicated to your master. He's done his job well...

Brennan's brother, Mica. Stupid Monica. Amelda. They'd laid it out from the beginning. Told me what he was before any of this. I was so goddamned stupid. He hadn't even tried to deny what Kennet said at breakfast.

...went through women faster than pints durin'

playoffs, and none of them the wiser of the others, fallin' for his every word...

This was why he hadn't wanted me to speak his name. He didn't want me to see into his soul and find out what he'd been up to since the fiend had been released.

And the Riders knew.

Who else did?

Socks slithered into my lap. I stroked his scales for a long time. Karen's evasions eating at me. I'd thought she was my—

My eyes burned, chest hollow and raw. I got a pen and wrote Brennan's name on the outside of the envelope. It didn't take much elemental Fire to remove my fae-band, less than the collar had, anyways. I dropped it in and sealed it.

Jonas was still at the table. Stewie had joined him, and they were working through a bottle of vodka. Neither one of them met my eyes when I walked in. I tossed the envelope down between them, and they flinched when it landed.

"Pack your shit and take this with you. I want you to deliver it to him, personally."

Jonas looked up at me, broken. "You promised to let him refute—"

"No one told me anything."

He flinched again, and I didn't care. I'd seen the evidence myself.

11 Days, 0 Hours, 53 Minutes

I didn't stay at the estate, and I didn't cry.

I grabbed some clothes, Rhys, and a box of diapers, then went downstairs to the office. All my financials were in the desk nestled next to the sham that was our family photos, right where Brennan had said they would be. I grabbed what cash was there and left the rest.

Then I poofed to a shitty little town in the middle of nowhere.

Kenzakee, New Mexico. It was in the mountains. Calista and I had driven through when we'd left Vegas. The motel was still there. I slapped down cash, and the clerk slapped down a key. The room's stained paisley bedspread was exactly the same as it had been.

I curled up in the middle of it with Rhys and didn't sleep.

A slice of sun eventually tracked across the room through the slit in the black-out shades. Mab had hitched a ride in the diaper bag and slunk out at some point to entertain him. We didn't talk, other than her prodding me to change his diaper or nurse. Otherwise, I pretty much checked out. Then the sun went away, and it was dark. I don't know how many days passed like that. At some point I did sleep, and then it was basically all I did. My dreams were filled with every single scenario of what could've happened in that hotel room, in painfully graphic detail.

Then Rhys's diapers ran out.

I sat on the edge of the bed with him in my lap, eyes hot.

I didn't want to go out to get more.

I didn't want to go back.

Rhys reached up to touch my face, gurgling with that crooked smile and dimple in his cheek.

I cried.

Yeah. A lot.

I curled back up around him, weak and exhausted. I couldn't remember the last time I'd eaten or drunk, and I didn't really care.

I slept again.

Pounding on the door woke me up. My name. A key fumbled in the lock. Muffled voices. Dogs. I curled around Rhys tighter.

Kyle came into the room with War. He shut the door on the clerk stammering apologies behind them and turned on a lamp. I blinked at the harsh light, hiding my face.

"Damn, stinks like pixie and baby shit in here." War grimaced, waving at the air.

"What do you expect, dog boy?" Mab zipped over to Kyle.

He crouched down by the side of the bed. Pushed my hair back. "How long she been like this?"

"Since we left. She hasn't eaten—"

"For ten days? Damn, Snow. What the hell happened?"

I couldn't even look at him.

"We can't stay here," War said, peering through the crack in the curtains.

"She's not going anywhere like this." Kyle frowned.

"I'm gonna fucking kill him."

War grunted, not disagreeing. "I gotta keep tabs on the dogs. Call me when you're ready." The door slammed behind him.

Kyle scrubbed at his curls, then gathered me against him, his features subtly shifting into the All Father's. "Never did I think to see you like this again," he murmured, his breath warm in my hair. "Bastard has no idea what he's squandered, and it should've been mine…" His fingers brushed Rhys's cheek, and the baby hid his face against my shoulder.

Me? I tuned out. I'd heard it all before and didn't need to pay attention to the recap. Always a bridesmaid, never a bride. It gave him a complex. Well, Lilith had given him a complex after Adam had torn out her heart and stomped on it. Classic shit rolls down the hill, and true to form, Samael was here to pick up the pieces. Hope he'd bought stock in Bond-o.

"…cannot stand. Take of me, Lilith. I offer mine self willingly. Come back, for me, for your boy."

Yeah, the All Father was big on dramatic monologues. He'd hung out with way too many poets back in the day. The wordier he gets, the more upset he is. This rated a seven and a half out of ten. Oh yeah, it got worse. I searched his clear blue eyes. Remembering and not wanting to. He'd said the same to me so long ago. I hadn't been able to give him what he wanted then, either.

But I had taken what he'd offered.

I traced his lip with a finger, and he went still. My hand dropped, and I put my nose to Rhys's head, inhaling stinky baby. God, I must be ripe, and I'd wallowed for far too long. Damn it, I hated feeling like this. A trickle of anger cut through my pity party, and I latched onto it.

"For Rhys…and revenge." There was nothing but the burning desire to make Brennan hurt as badly as I did.

"For now, that's enough." The All Father tipped up my chin and kissed me.

I drank him in succubus style. His being, the memories between us, all that had been—it filled me, pure and true. Revived my spirit and nourished my flesh. Made me whole, and I kind of hated him for it.

Samael.

Goddamn it. I wasn't going there with him.

"Will you be mine as you once were?" His lips teased mine.

I pulled away. "I've never been anyone's but my own."

He stood with a sigh, muttering something about his everlasting sorrow. "Let's get you home."

I scowled at the word, hugging Rhys to my breast. The All Father gathered up my things and called for War to follow.

Poof.

We were in his temple. I went to shower and clean up my kid. A bitter rage boiled within me. At Brennan. At that woman. At my own stupidity.

Look, don't you think there was some desperate part of me that was screaming this whole thing was a big mistake? I'd just spent the better part of two weeks hashing and rehashing every angle of this stinking pile, and it came down to three things.

He'd been in Vegas, knowing how I felt about that, and was there with another woman. Any way you sliced it, those pictures had shown a level of intimacy between them that did not suggest casual acquaintance. And you know, that whole banging thing.

Worse, I had a sneaking suspicion she was fae. I mean, sometimes it's hard to tell, but there was something about her bearing, and he hadn't said a goddamned thing about her when the Gwinth came calling.

But the most damning in my eyes was that he hadn't been the one to come get me. I might have fried the fae-band he'd given me, but his shadows were still slicked all over me, which meant he knew exactly how messed-up I'd been. If he'd wanted to plead his case, he'd had ample opportunity. He hadn't come.

He didn't care.

I was done.

I lay down beside the All Father that night, not wanting to be alone. He didn't touch me, but then he'd visited this rodeo before and knew I would've slugged him. I didn't have the capacity for anything other than survival mode. Not yet. Maybe this time, not ever.

That was probably why it was Kyle who pulled me into a hug when I started to shake. Don't ask me why, but I let him. Kyle was, I don't know…my friend, I guess. Someone who knew me before I was supposed to be Lilith. Before all this fae crap screwed with me. With us.

"Shhh, hey, I'm here, I gotcha. You're safe."

I burrowed under his chin, trying not to blubber and failing miserably. He held me, stroking my back until I was cried out and numb.

"You wanna hear something stupid?"

I nodded, and he kissed my brow, chaste. "The whole time we were looking for you, all I could think about was the night you kneed that bouncer at Bliss in the nads. The look on his face had to've been—"

Kyle had to be the only person on the planet capable of getting me to smile right then.

"He tried to bang me!"

"Don't blame him." He laughed. "Man, all I wanted to do was finish my set so I could meet you. I'm glad the cops took their sweet-ass time so I could."

"Is that why you skipped the second chorus?"

"Yeah. The guys were pissed. Manager took an extra twenty off what we made at the door, but it was totally worth it." I smiled at that, too. The band wasn't the only one that was pissed. He'd ditched Morgana to buy me a beer and then shown up at the station to bail me out. She'd been ripped.

His arms tightened around me. "You've always been worth it, Snow. Get some sleep. I got you."

He did and had from the beginning.

My eyes closed, and for the first time since I'd opened that damned envelope, I didn't end up in a hotel room with Brennan and that bimbo.

Instead I dreamed I stood on the shores of a crimson-stained sea, the waves frothing sticky at my feet. Behind me was that cave, empty. I put a hand to my flaccid abdomen, blood staining my thighs. My face was tight with dried tears. I wiped at them, the wind whipping long strands of hair across my face, sky churning grey.

I looked up and hated.

God had made good on His promise. In the wake of my defiance of Him and not returning to Adam, He'd begun killing my children. Those who had stayed at my side were all gone. The ones who had fled…I prayed He took pity on them, because He had none for me, and I had nothing left.

The tide had just taken the last little body away.

I turned my back on the waves and walked through the desolate countryside to the garden, my feet cracked and bleeding, hair a wild nest of briars. The land slowly changed from stone and scree to a verdant paradise. I stopped to bathe and work the tangles from my hair, not knowing what to say when I saw him.

Yeah, Adam.

Turns out, I hadn't needed to say anything.

I heard his laugh before I saw him and picked my way close. He was in the glade with the stone table, a picnic of plenty before him, and a woman draped at his side.

She was like me inasmuch as she was female, but her curves were curvier, her hair lusher, and when her laugh trilled out to meet his—

It was very obvious she didn't have a brain in her head.

I closed my eyes and swallowed the lump in my throat. Working up the nerve to step into the clearing—

He laughed again and put her on the ground, mounting her.

Yeah, I watched. I shouldn't have, but whatever. He looked up, his eyes meeting mine, and he smiled.

It wasn't a "hey you're back, sorry I was a dick" smile.

I fell back against a tree. All that I'd suffered, my children…and for what? To get me to come back here and find out I'd been replaced with Big Jugs the Bimbo and that Adam couldn't give two shits about me? No scratch that—was fucking glad he'd just been able to shit all over the last remaining vestiges of my self-worth.

The way she just lies there, you'd think he was into necrophilia...

I wiped my eyes and glanced around. Where had that voice come from?

...But when you're packing that, I suppose a moving target is counterproductive.

I snickered despite myself, and a creature resolved from the undergrowth. It was long and slender, not quite as big around as my arm, and a brilliant green. Its tongue flicked out, the tip split down the center. I'd never seen anything like it.

"What are you?"

It coiled up, its head weaving. *Serpent, viper, snake—*

Adam's groans came from the clearing, and the slap of flesh on flesh.

You know he's doing that to make you jealous. Trust me, she's not all that. It's a good thing God built in involuntary reflexes. She's too stupid to remember to breathe.

"That's probably what he gets off on," I muttered.

If only there was a way to spoil that for him...perhaps she needs an education?

Oh yeah. You know how the rest went.

When I awoke, it was with a smile on my face, and Socks coiled up next to me. Kyle was giving Rhys a bottle in front of the fire, and Mab flitted about telling him he was doing it wrong. This time her criticism was on point; kid was gonna be hella gassy.

How could I tell it was him and not Samael? Kyle had a lightness to him. Samael brooded, and there was this don't-fuck-with-me set to his jaw, which was probably why I liked to fuck with him. Anyways, Kyle must've felt my eyes on him, because he looked up and smiled.

"Hey. There you are. How you feel?"

Surprisingly, more like myself. Envy, I mean. Something about that dream…Yeah, it had sucked on like a billion different levels, but losing my kids aside, in the end I'd screwed over the two of them way harder than Adam had screwed me. Literally and figuratively. Socks hadn't been joking about what he was packing. I stroked his scales, fully planning on doing the same to Brennan, and there wasn't a chance in hell he was ever seeing Rhys again.

"Weak, but better."

"Glad to hear it." His weight settled beside me. "Little dude misses you. He's not a big fan of formula. You got a sec for him?"

"Where's the All-Father?"

"Samael? He hates that you don't use his name, you know."

Not happening. I shrugged like it was no big, and he chewed his lip.

"It's easier if I watch the kid."

My brow creased. There was still a piece I was missing there…

I took Rhys, his smile lighting up his whole face, softening the last bits of Lilith until the old me faded into the background again. Kyle watched me nurse him, a finger trailing down my arm, soft as a butterfly's kiss.

"How did you find me?"

"Chocolate cream pie," he murmured. "Remember when I said Cirro's had the best, and you told me some place you stopped on your way from Vegas to Vel was way better? After looking everywhere else, it was the only place I could think of you might've landed, but I couldn't remember the name. You know how many towns have diners between the two? War had his dogs on it, and we still weren't even halfway through them when Mab sent him a dream."

I glanced at the pixie.

She was perched on the bedpost, looking smug. "I sent it to all the Riders, but he was the only one who showed."

I frowned, but Jonas and Stewie were probably pissed I'd kicked them out, and Pestilence and I had never really hit it off. That whole bug thing was a deal-breaker. "Thank you."

She fluffed her dark brunette bob. "I'm in your service. It's not like I had a choice."

The pixie was full of shit, and we both knew it.

Kyle brushed a knuckle over Rhys's temple and sighed, sitting back. "Anyways, I showed for our day, and the estate was creepy quiet, like someone died. They said you left. Gaia didn't know what'd happened, the imps were ape shit—"

"Was he there?"

Kyle mussed his hair. "Nah. Nobody's seen him or those other three pug-uglies for like a week and a half. The lesser Fire elementals are trippin' out with nobody at the helm and blame Water. Aegaeus says he doesn't have anything to do with it, and the goddamned Gwinth is releasing those freaks of his. Thinks you bugged out with the dae. Normals are losing their shit, and it's all Cleansing the sequel, but this time the lesser fae are on the list."

"War's the only Rider here?"

"Yeah, and he's not fessin' up to where the others

are. That shithead must've made him swear on his mother's grave or something. I can't get him to tell me anything."

Where the hell could they all be? I couldn't understand how everything had fallen apart so fast. Like, seriously, no one blinked twice the last time I—

No. It wasn't that I had disappeared; it was that Brennan had. But there's no way he would have just walked away, was there? He'd never said—you know what, it didn't matter. It was my fault for handing him the keys to the kingdom, and now I had to figure out how to get them back. Man, that pissed me off.

Kyle's voice was soft. "I saw the pics. I didn't think the dude had it in him."

"Me neither." My voice cracked. And when I'd first spoken his name and seen into his soul, he hadn't. God, I knew I was gonna fuck this up, drive him away…

Yeah, I was crying again. I sobbed against Kyle's neck. He stroked my hair. It felt so different from when Brennan did it. Right, but wrong. Ugh, I was a mess. I didn't even know why I was crying anymore. Everything was all mashed-up from Adam onward, the only constant that I got played and was stupid enough to do it twice.

Kyle held me until I was a snuffling mess, then put Rhys in another one of those porto-cribs and handed me a box of tissues. "I—We're real sorry for all that with Aegaeus, Snow. Me and Samael. If we'd known he was gonna threaten your kid…dude's whacked. Samael's rip shit over it and says he owes you big. I mean, Aegaeus can be a douche, but—doesn't matter. Shithead's ass is grass if ever pokes his nose above sea level."

I shrugged, not really mad at Kyle for any of it, but knowing the All Father was part of him…If I wasn't feeling so freaking needy, I wouldn't hang out with either of them.

He sighed. "I'm gonna get you some of that udon you like, 'kay? You need to eat before you blow away." His phone pinged, and he glanced at it, a frown marring his brow.

"Does anyone else know I'm shacking up at your temple?"

He scratched the back of his neck, then texted a quick message. "You want me to call someone?"

It wasn't an answer, and I didn't push for one. "No. I don't want…I don't want anyone else to know."

His jaw tightened, eyes creeping toward green as he shoved his phone in his back pocket. "Someone already does and is going down for it," he said, his voice trending to the All Father's. "Get some rest, I'll be back."

Great. I stared up at the ceiling for a long time, my eyes tracing the grain of the big wooden beams. Outside, a massive storm had blown in, sleet lashing against the windows. A week and a half and Brennan hadn't looked for me, or Rhys. Me I could understand, but how could he not care about his son? All I felt was numb when I didn't want to incinerate something. Fear at the prospect of whoever the Gwinth released finding me was a very distant thing, and if they did, I don't think they'd like it very much.

I slept a dark and dreamless sleep.

The storm raged all night and into the next day. When I woke, a sprite, not Bunny, offered me udon, with shredded chicken and extra snow peas, just the way I liked it. All it did was remind me I was still pissed at the All Father and Kyle by proxy. The soup won him a temporary reprieve, but we were gonna have words. I managed the plain broth and a couple shreds of meat before my stomach threatened to rebel.

Once I was sure I wasn't gonna hurl, I brought Rhys into bed with me and propped myself up on the pillows with him against my knees to play, guilty I'd been such a shitty mom for what equated to the better part of his life. Man, he'd gotten big. He started flopping himself forward for me to set back, tickling his tummy. I had to smile at the way he laughed and clapped his hands like it was the best game ever. Anyways, around the thirtieth time, he farted loud enough to scare himself. I just about died laughing at the look on his face. My smile felt weird. Good, but like it didn't belong to me.

And it didn't last when the All Father came in wearing blackened and bloodstained armor. His face was all bruised, and he walked with a limp. He picked up my bag and came to the bedside.

"We've a problem. The Gwinth isn't releasing the huntsmen—they're escaping."

My jaw dropped, and I stared at him. "What?"

"He's downstairs with Gaia and everyone from the estate. Will you come?"

I got dressed. He poofed us into a long hall, lined with trestle tables. At the far end, a massive hearth took up the wall, whole sections of trees crackling. War stood with a hand on the mantel staring into it, several dogs at his feet. Gaia and the Gwinth sat on benches piled with sheepskins, drinking from steaming mugs.

I clutched the All Father's arm, my knees weak. All of me weak.

"What have you gone and done to yourself?" Gaia's brow crumpled, looking between us. "I thought you said you were feeding her!"

"I can't undo ten days of fasting in one," the All Father growled.

"Like hell you can't. Get me a bowl of something!" She snatched Rhys and gave me a dirty look.

"Where were you?"

She frowned. "The normals subpoenaed me. I had to give testimony about registering my people, and then meet with the lesser queens. By the time I was finished with them, you were gone. We can discuss it later. Sit your ass down, and put something your belly."

Karen came in, and I ended up on a makeshift pallet of skins with another bowl of udon. Gaia did something to it, and it was, I don't know, like vitaminized or something. I could feel my strength returning as I ate, which the others were trying very hard not to watch me do. A quick glance in the mirror before we'd come down had been enough to see I definitely wasn't at my best, but what can I say? Even half dead, I'm riveting.

While I ate, the others talked. Socks slithered out from somewhere and nuzzled into my neck.

"...two score. What's left of the host has beaten them back, but this storm won't keep them off her trail for long," the Gwinth was saying. I was glad he looked like he'd taken a worse beating than the All Father. What had gone down while I'd checked out? "The most powerful of them have broken my hold, and with every passing hour I lose more. The geas needs to be passed on—"

"You need to keep your damned dick in your pants, before I remove it and save you the temptation of waving it around," Gaia snapped.

"If she had just acquiesced at the beginning of this, it wouldn't be an issue!"

"Don't you take that tone with me. Acquiesced." Her head snaked back and forth with each syllable. "I didn't know cavemen used such big words. What century we living in? Acqui-freaking-esced. More like you should've been on the other side of the veil, minding your business. What was that? None of this would have been an issue if you had? Now how about that? Poor planning on your part does not constitute an emergency on mine or anyone else's."

The Gwinth grumbled something and looked away. I grinned around my udon. Seeing Gaia lose her zen always put me in a good mood, and she was in rare form.

"Except when it releases a plethora of psychopaths for us to deal with." The All Father ran a hand down his face and turned to War. "You've no idea where Brennan or the other Riders are? Their help would turn the tide and then some. He's the only one the damned normals will listen to." The big dae acted like he hadn't heard him, and the All Father's knuckles popped, turning to the Gwinth. "What about you?"

"No," he said, his words bitter. "My power's fading. After Brennan checked out of the Venetian, I lost all sense of him. I thought Envy was hiding him with whatever's been keeping me and the rest of the wild hunt from getting a location on her. That's the only reason the fugitives haven't stormed this place, but they're not stupid. They'll follow you from the estate and come here."

My chopsticks froze midair. "Your escapees are camped out at the estate?"

The All Father nodded, glaring at the Gwinth. "Gaia sent me a text after they had it surrounded. One of them can throw up a shield and trapped everyone inside before they could evacuate. They're watching that flat of the dae's as well."

I poked at my soup. It must've been bad if she texted him. That was like me asking Morgana for help—What about Gaia taking them out? I told you, Earth moves slow. She's amazing at defense, but not so hot on the offense. Yeah, a bunch of sentinels would've ripped some fugitives up, but unless they were camping out under the estate, no dice, and any lesser fae she called in would've been lunch for the host.

You know I'm being literal.

Socks hissed.

"Mm-hmm." Gaia's lips pinched down. "He's right. Maybe you shouldn't have gone dangling her in front of them like a cookie then."

Was everyone talking to my snake now?

The All Father grunted his agreement. "What about the woman? Is he still with her?"

"Not that I've been able to tell." The Gwinth shrugged. "As far as who she is, Stephie Morte heads up a super PAC based in Washington. It's probably where they met. She's been pushing for this biometric legislation. Despite those photos, they've been adversaries on the Senate floor. Perhaps they found some mutually agreeable terms." He smirked, and I felt like I was gonna puke. "She checked out right after him and retired to a manor in upstate New York."

"Mmm," Gaia said, sounding about as pleased as I felt. Her eyes drilled into the All Father. "She was there when I gave testimony and stank like sylph. You need to get a handle on your people. She sat on the committee grilling me, and the questions she was asking—It's like the woman's trying to incite the normals against us."

The All Father's head snapped up. "There's another fae lady on this side of the veil? Then why…"

We all looked at the Gwinth. Well, everyone but me. What? I was supposed to be eating my soup…and you know, the whole curse thing.

"Trust me, Envy wasn't my first choice. I prefer blondes."

Yeah, my udon was airborne. He dodged, and it splattered against the wall.

"So you ruined my freaking life as a consolation prize? You son of a bitch!"

Gaia's hand clamped down on my shoulder, and I sat there seething. What? I don't care if it was my fault; he didn't have to be such a—

Wait a minute. Stephie Morte. Ms. Morte. You gotta be freaking…I went limp beneath Gaia's hand.

She glanced at me. "You know something about her?"

"I heard overheard Brennan on the phone…I think she was trying to blackmail him." War probably knew, but his stupid mouth stayed shut. My stomach churned. Was Brennan a sleazy cheating prick, or was he working some other angle? God, it was probably both.

The Gwinth broke the uncomfortable silence that had descended. "While fascinating, none of this is pertinent. Kennet is the only thing keeping what's left of the host together, mainly because they think I'm currently impregnating you." I scowled at him, and he shrugged. "If they don't feel the geas passed on by the next sunrise, I've no doubt they'll turn on him."

My head snapped up. "Wait, you pass the geas on at conception? Then why the hell—"

"Because a child in utero can't very well give

orders, can it? All the other Gwinths were female and able to continue to access the geas through a bond developed during gestation. Thanks to your damned infertility curse, I was the only option this time around and have no such luxury. I was waiting for my most suitable female offspring to become, but normals got to her before I did. That's why I was on this side of the veil when you sealed it."

Oh. That was actually a pretty good reason. Whoops. "But you're a shape-shifter. Can't you just lose the wang and have Kyle knock you up?" I mean, aside from the whole curse thing.

The All Father snorted.

"Gender is more than an outward physicality," Gaia said from behind me. "It's—"

"I know, I know, that whole form-and-spirit thing." I mean, she would know, but I still rolled my eyes.

Her mouth pinched down again. "No, I was going to say if you take a cock from rooster, you're still not getting any eggs." Something about the pained way she said it…her expression told me to leave it the hell alone, so I glowered at the Gwinth.

"I'm still not banging you."

"Then you're going to have two hundred and sixteen psychotic fae outside those temple walls at sunrise. I very much doubt they'll give either of you the choice." Asshole grinned at Gaia and me like that was just dandy with him.

Socks hissed. Huh. Would it work like that? "The geas…how did you plan on passing it on to your offspring?"

"Why? Having a change of heart? I'd be happy to demonstrate." He licked his lips, and I rolled my eyes.

God, he was a pig.

"Just answer the question."

"I'd will the part of me attuned to the host into her, via a kiss. The geas is keyed to latch onto my DNA, but the pull to be with a female of my line would be stronger than its desire to remain with me."

I could totally relate and wasn't the only one who snickered, but the sucky kissing part aside, it sounded a lot like keying a fae-band…which meant it could probably be removed the same way, and that didn't require mouth to mouth.

"What if I could hold it for you?"

His eyebrow quirked. "Hold it for me?"

"No, not—God, I hate you." Yeah, I didn't care about buying time anymore. "I'm assuming it would work like elemental energy. I can take it in and store it, then send it where I want…Like into your heir once the veil opens." If we could get it open. Stupid Aegaeus.

His face went very still. "You would take control of the wild hunt?"

"Until I can pawn them off on your offspring. I mean, if you bargained for it."

Everyone froze like I'd just casually flipped a bomb into the center of the room.

What? How hard could it be? He'd blown a horn, and they'd snapped to. That, and no matter how nasty his energy was, sucking him off would be worth it. Eww, no, I totally didn't mean it like that, but look, if I had control of the host, the Gwinth would be off my case, and I could sic them on whatever prey I had in mind. He might not be able to sense Brennan, but I could very faintly through his fae-band. Well, yeah, I'd taken mine off, but until I released him, he was still bound to me. All I'd need to do was point them in the right direction, then sit back with a tub of popcorn and a six-pack.

How was that not a win-win?

The Gwinth wet his lips. "What do you desire?"

Here came the tricky part. "For all intents and purposes, you'll continue to act as Gwinth, but you'll take orders from me. The first of which is all the raping and tearing apart of female hostees stops."

He snorted. "Orders from you? The only ones I've seen you give are for coffee."

"I only involve myself with critical matters." What? Getting the correct whipped cream to caramel ratio on a frap was super important. "And as Monica pointed out the other day, despite being a prick, Brennan was a gifted administrator, and I believe strongly in delegation of duty." I also believed he was a dead man when the hunt dragged him from whatever hole he'd crawled into with that slut.

"Riiight," the Gwinth drawled. "And I'm assuming once the host is under control, the second will be tracking down Brennan?"

"You would be wrong." Unfortunately, it was gonna have to be business before pleasure. All this shit the lesser dae were stirring up with Water needed to stop. I batted my lashes, though it was probably a lot less effective than usual in my present bedraggled state. "Are we agreed or not?"

"You would have me as your captain?"

"If that's what you call the guy who does all the work."

His lips pursed, and then he sighed. "Agreed."

I patted the floor beside me. "Sit."

He growled but obeyed. I could get used to having a

trained Gwinth…Except I had to touch him to do this. I blew out my cheeks and slapped a hand onto his wrist.

Do you remember that whole spiel I went into about doing things on the fly and those more experienced laughing a lot and wondering why you're not dead? Yeah. That one. You'd think I'd have the benefit of experience being a primordial and all, but nope. Apparently wisdom did not transfer with the body swap. Trying to go all succubus on the Gwinth was not wise for a few reasons. Allow me to list them in ascending order of stupidity.

Reason four. He was a shape-shifter. That meant that instead of shitty food-truck tacos or schnitzel, I got a mashed-up smorgasbord of flavors that did not sit well on a stomach that had pretty much nothing in it for the past week. Pickles and ice cream, psh. Try mayonnaise and coffee with anchovy chunks. Yeah, super gross and I'm not even talking about the texture.

Reason three. He was a cannibal. I'd had zero desire to know what nixie or another of the lesser fae tasted like and was pretty sure my palate had been expanded way out of my comfort zone, further exacerbating the state brought on by reason four.

Reason two. He was a massively skeevey dick, and all that nasty karmic wang-fu melding with what I had going on was way more disgusting and intimate than if I had just closed my eyes and bent over. Yeah. Almost regretting that call.

And the number one reason? The geas. So, like all of two seconds ago I had thought, how hard could it be? Well, let me tell you, crazy fucking hard. Like, there was a reason Gwinths burned out after a couple centuries. It wasn't like pulling Amelda's energy out of Brennan's watch; this was like trying to thread a brick through a keyhole. Yeah, not happening. I mean, it should be happening. I just—

Oh shit. Duh.

I didn't have anything of him in me.

Oh no, that I did mean. Water's stupid nepotism clause. He'd even said it, the geas was keyed to latch on to his DNA. His essence wasn't enough. I didn't have his kid or his blood. Damn. Both sounded revolting, but one was easy enough to remedy.

I bit him. Hard.

He screamed and tried to pull his wrist out of my mouth, but the floodgates had opened, and he was stuck fast as I drained him. Power flooded into me with all that nasty shit I listed above, and I started to get that twitchy too-many-twisted-off-baggies feeling, but along with it came some pretty cool door prizes.

Shape-shifting was definitely one of them, and before I went all pogo-stick, I used it.

The leathers I had worn the other day shingled out of me and into place as I stood, dropping him like cell service on the subway. Energy blazed through me, and the geas kicked into high gear, compelling me to use it. I smiled down at the Gwinth all sprawled out, gripping his mangled wrist to his chest, the whites huge around his black pupils.

I toed his calf, and for my next trick—

A fae steed stood where he'd been. He shied back from me when I went to grip the reins and I laughed. "Aw...I thought you wanted me to ride you."

He snorted, and if looks could kill—

Well, that would have defeated the purpose of me taking the stupid geas, now wouldn't it? I mounted him, and a horn of ivory appeared in my hand. I turned to Gaia. "You'll keep Rhys safe until I return?"

She met my eyes with a gaze of iron. "I've already sworn to protect him, with my life if necessary."

Her bargain with Brennan.

Son of a—I didn't have time for this, and even if I did, no way could I sit still long enough for the discussion.

"I want him back." I growled, raising the horn to my lips.

And no, I wasn't sure which one I was talking about right then, either.

I blew the damned thing. It was time to hunt.

1 Day, 5 Hours, 12 Minutes

So I'd said I wanted the Gwinth—well, I guess he was just Connell now, but the stupid title suited him, so whatever, he's the still the Gwinth—to be in charge, but the geas was like this weird compulsion, and that horn blast amplified it. When faced with the reality of the situation, I wasn't sure delegating was actually gonna play out. Like, I could sense the fae that had broken from the main host and let me tell you, their defiance wasn't gonna fly. I had this visceral need to hunt them down and beat the shit out of them.

Yeah. We all know how good I am with impulse control.

The main body of the host wasn't too far away, like just outside the limits of Samael's storm. I poofed to them. They'd heard the horn and were already mounted, and when I charged through, headed toward the estate, they fell into my wake.

So, I should explain a bit more about fae steeds. They don't really poof, but they can, I don't know, fold distance. Like, every stride ate up hundreds of miles instead of a single step, and they were booking ass. The Himalayas to Vel? Three minutes and change.

I know, right? It was way cool.

Anyways, the fugitives must've gotten bored camping out, because they weren't at the estate. It looked like the Gwinth had lost about half of them, and they'd migrated down to the highway looking for entertainment. We came upon a bloodbath where it cut through a narrow canyon. They'd ambushed a line of tour buses, scattering them like a three-year-old's toy cars across the pavement. The midday sun beat down upon the remains of God knew how many poor souls, and psycho fae were intent on rending apart the normals still breathing. More were playing with the ones that had managed to flee ground zero.

A little girl's scream cut above the carnage, echoing from the stone.

Oh, hell no.

Something primal kicked in, and before I knew it, I'd gone all elemental, leaving the Gwinth behind and sweeping through the canyon ahead of the host, trained on where that scream had come from.

"Back off, assholes!"

The majority of the fugitives jerked like a pole had been shoved up their rears, backpedaling from their prey. Serpents of flame shed from my wings, making sure they didn't have any second thoughts.

Most of them didn't, but Crest-kin was another story.

Yeah, that fae with the purple mohawk. I could feel his defiance, and it enraged me. He'd cornered a little girl against the canyon wall. He spun as I alit behind him, his rubbery lips drawing back in a gruesome smile.

Huh. I was pretty tickled to see him, too.

He reached for me, and I let him reel me in close, his dank, nasty breath on my face and his hand at my belt. Mine incinerated a hole through his chest, boiling his insides. A heartbeat later—mine, not his—and he was nothing but steam and memory. Gaia may rock at defense, hah, but there was a reason war was dae business. Take that, fish.

The girl in the cave crossed herself, murmuring something about the Great Lady. What—? I glanced back at a bus. You gotta be—It was a freaking pilgrimage charter to where Our Lady of the Blessed Inferno had once stood.

Goddamn it.

She could get herself out. I stomped back to the host, ignoring the cowering fanatics genuflecting. Of course they had cell phones recording. I couldn't catch a break with these assholes. I was pretty sure saving their asses didn't constitute as provoking Aegaeus, but I wasn't gonna bet on it being good PR. Seriously, normals could put a bad spin on Santa Claus.

The rest of the host was on clean-up crew corralling the fugitives. Along with the newly strengthened geas compelling them to mind their freaking manners, my serpents had put the fear of—well, me, I guess, into them. It probably helped that they'd all seen me vaporize the biggest bully on the block and were on their knees waiting for me.

Not gonna lie, that made me smile.

I stood in front of them with my hands on my hips and pulled a Calista. "Well? What've you got to say for yourselves?" Yep, I was feelin' sassy.

They all glanced at each other like they needed to get their stories straight. Seriously? I sent a blast of plasma at the one I'd seen gnawing on a femur, spattering the rest of them with what didn't incinerate.

"You wanna try that again?"

"Uh…s-sorry?" lisped a dopey frog thing with fangs.

"Sorry? You think sorry is gonna reassemble these people?" Yep, fried him too.

The rest of them were downright groveling at this point. Don't get it twisted. Yeah, I was super badass, but that geas, man. I could feel it literally crushing any spark of resistance to my will. It was kind of sickening. True, these guys were seriously the worst, but I wasn't sure if they deserved getting shackled with this in perpetuity for running amok a time or eighty.

It was as bad as being collared. No wonder they'd split when they'd had the chance. The ones I'd fried had gotten off easy.

Whatever, not my problem, right? We had shit to do, and it wasn't like they'd found Jesus while they were loose. They probably would've eaten him if they had.

The Gwinth ambled over and lipped at my hair. I smacked his nose and changed him back, abruptly very tired. I've said it before, and I'll say it again, divine retribution is hard work. The horn materialized in my hand, and I held it out to him.

"Take the host and put down any conflicts between Fire and Water. I'll send out an emissary to them and the normals, but they need to know I can back it up. I want eyes on that bitch in New York and where she lives texted to me. She steps a toe out of that manor, or if there's any sign of Brennan, I want to know it in the next breath. I'm taking Kennet with me. Where is he?"

"Over by the survivors..." The Gwinth's eyebrow rose.

I knew what he was thinking and rolled my eyes. "Shut up and get it done. And stop eating fae while you're at it. God, go find a Micky D's or something. The imps will set up a corporate account. I'll be at the temple."

What you, too? Look, just because I know how to do something doesn't mean I want to do it. In fact, a lot of times that's exactly why I don't do it. Case in point, my stint as the Queen of Sheba. Yeah, that was me, get over it. The one freaking time I didn't shave—What kind of an asshole installs mirrors on his floor? Seriously, who the hell does that?

Whatever, what I'm trying to say is taking initiative will bite you in the ass every time, and the bigger the project, the more trouble it is. Don't believe me? I'll give you an example. I don't know, say, redecorating a bathroom. You're thinking paint and cute curtains, maybe you'll go all shabby chic and up-cycle a vanity to look like that chippy vintage crap. DIY's so fun, right?

Then you find the black mold behind the sink. The plumbing leaked, subfloor needs to be replaced, it ruined a ceiling in the closet downstairs, and oh, by the way, none of your wiring's to code.

Screw that and hand me my truffles.

God, I needed a nap. Kennet was by the fanatics, and they all prostrated themselves when they saw me coming. No, not Kennet, but the rest of them did. I might've kicked sand at them as I passed. What? We were in a canyon; it was lousy with the stuff.

He didn't want to look at me, and my stomach clenched. He knew something. That comment about Brennan picking up the phone suddenly made a lot more sense. I tried to keep my voice steady and was only marginally successful.

"The Gwinth has this handled. You're coming with me."

Kennet sighed, rubbing the back of his neck. "Aye.

Figured as much."

I didn't cry. Stupid sandy canyon.

We poofed, but not back to the temple like I said. I didn't want him within a thousand miles of Rhys. I poofed to the cafe in Vel.

What? If I wasn't getting that nap anytime soon, a triple shot of espresso was next on the list.

I just about shit at my reflection at the door.

Taking on the geas had given my eyes that same gold the Gwinth's had had, but instead of a flat gleam, sparks of the stuff scintillated over the green. I stared at it. Damn. Talk about bad ass.

Kennet cleared his throat, and I shot him a dirty look, going in. I ordered my frap and a brownie; he got a black coffee. We went out onto the patio, and people scattered. I guess seeing goth Emma Peel with eyes of gold fire and Braveheart will do that. Yeah, he was in a kilt again, and those calves of his, man…Anyways, normals bailing was fine by me, I didn't need an audience, but I did need the caffeine. We sat, and I slurped, picking at my brownie.

"What do you know about Stephie Morte?"

Kennet played with the lid on his coffee, pressing those stupid buttons in. When he figured out none of them were triggering an eject mechanism, he sighed. "Right. Before I get t'that…I'm assuming Brennan told ye a bit about me?"

I pinged a walnut across the table. When the hell had they started putting those in? You'd think the allergy brigade would be all over that. "You were a Welsh chieftain. Some kind of a lord."

"Aye, but it weren't always so…" He caught my eye roll. "Won't bore ye with the details. Suffice t'say, there weren't much opportunity for advancement where I started from. When I was presented with one, I didn't think much of the consequences."

"You made a bargain." God, what was with these guys? Didn't they know any better—

"More like a sale." He took a sip of coffee, his lips hissing back at the heat.

I blinked, a lot. "Wait, you mean—"

"I ain't confirmin' nor denyin' a thing."

Holy shit, he'd sold his soul. That'd been outlawed way early on. Like, the original Thou Shalt Not before all those tablets on the mount, and the only one fae took seriously. Mainly because it resulted in spontaneous combustion. That burning bush? More like the first PR spin. Everyone toed the line after that.

Well, everyone except Her.

Hmm? Nope, you're not missing anything. None of us like to bring up God's other half. Their relationship was complicated, and what little of Her I remembered made Joan Crawford look like Mary Poppins. She pretty much viewed His creation as an elaborate model-train setup out in the garage that made Her park in the driveway. The dinosaurs dying out? Totally Her throwing a dust cloth over the whole damned thing. By the time He noticed, hello ice age. Yep, I shit you not. After that, She got really pissy about Him constantly fiddling with it, but They'd come to a detente somewhere post-Exodus; as long as He kept up with his honey-do list, She didn't mess with it.

He must've forgotten to wax Her car.

Kennet was staring at me, and I snapped my jaw shut. He grunted and took another sip of coffee. "Lands were the least of it. I gained a certain, ah, influence, over currency of a similar nature. Amelda sought me out, hoping those abilities would transfer, and they did, in spades."

Okay, hold up. I pinched my temples. So he was telling me he sold his soul for wealth and power. I was on board with that cliché, except said power was manipulating other people's souls, which was like, super bad mojo, and explained Kennet's standing in the hunt. If he could mess with souls, it was no wonder all those nasties gave him a wide berth.

And it jived that Brennan's mother would want a piece of that pie, because it also meant that Brennan's shadows weren't really shadows—they were shades. Like, the souls of the dead…which now made total sense why he borrowed them from the Underworld, and the whole sentience thing they had going on.

And he'd slicked them on me like white on rice. Eww—

My stomach plummeted. What did that mean Rhys could do? That black hell-flame…

Oh yeah, if I hadn't wanted Brennan dead before this, you better believe I did now. How could he not tell me? I was gonna kill him. Bring him back and kill him again. Maybe twice. I stabbed the straw into my frap. "Go on…"

"He's told ye about his stigmata comin' in?"

"He said he called shadow, and it almost took him with it." What did this have to do with anything? Man, Kennet liked to ramble…

"Aye. I found him after, in the great hall, wrapped in naught but his wings and blue with cold. All I could get out of him was that there'd been a lady, and she'd said he didn't belong there yet. Suffice t'say that Amelda wasn't the only one keen on getting her claws into him." Kennet took a sip of coffee and stared into his cup.

"Well, who was she?" Christ, you'd think he was Gaia making me wait so long.

"Persephone, concubine of the last ruler of Hell. Nasty bitch. She's been running the show down there since she offed Hades and goes by Stephie now. Word has it she's been dabbling in normal politics for the past decade or so and is some muckety-muck in Washington."

I almost laughed. What had I said about things I'd ignored waiting for the worst possible moment to bite me in the ass? Oh yeah, that.

And in case you're unfamiliar, around 40 BC give or take, a bunch of fae had set themselves up as gods north of the Mediterranean. Yeah, it was pretty common practice for a while. Anyways, rumor had it one of their daughters had been nabbed and taken to the Underworld, then gotten tricked into taking a gift that landed her on her back down there six months out of the year in perpetuity. Right? She totally got the shaft, like literally, and it wasn't even a good gift. Seriously, we're talking pomegranate seeds. No wonder she killed him, but man, she had to be dumber than a rock to fall for that in the first place.

The revelation didn't improve my mood. Why the hell wouldn't Brennan have told me about her when I'd asked about his shadows, or after the "you need to tell me things" fight? God, I was so stupid. Of course he wouldn't have said anything. Especially if he'd been screwing around behind my back the whole time. There was no way he could be that stupid otherwise.

All right, there was a little piece of me that hoped he

was, but that just pissed me off more. And if it was part and parcel of one of his goddamned bargains—

"You think he's with her now?"

"Can't ye sense him at all?"

"I can't pick up his scent or the Riders'." What? Technically it was true. There wasn't any trace of them on the wind, and I was getting wafts of Rhys's diaper when I focused on him. God, that was foul. Radioactive bananas must be back on the menu.

"Ye know that's not what I meant."

The pained expression on Kennet's face cut through the annoyance on mine. I sighed. Yeah, he meant through the fae-band. You'll think I'm stupid, but I'd been avoiding looking at that too closely. I was terrified of what I'd feel from him if I tried.

Okay, fine, I was chickenshit, but the last thing I needed was to poke my nose in and find him in the middle of banging—Whatever, if he was, then I'd know for sure, right? I reached for him through the damned thing—

And just about died, my insides icing up. I sucked in air and coughed out a frigid burst that rimed my lips. Kennet was at my side, steadying me until I could call flame. I shivered against him, downing his coffee. God, I couldn't get warm...

"Suspect that answers that question," he muttered.

It did. One of them anyways. Brennan was in the Underworld, but the Gwinth had said she was at her manor in upstate New York. Why wasn't he?

Kennet went inside to get me another coffee. Well, that and to escape me grinding my teeth. I mean, the blast of cold was better than feeling him in the middle of—My cell pinged, and I glanced at the screen.

It was a pic of a stately Victorian manor behind an iron gate.

Her manor.

Despite what you might think, I didn't poof right over. No, impulse control had nothing to do with it. I told you, I was exhausted, and that few seconds in deep freeze had killed what little energy I had.

That and I wasn't gonna go see this bitch with spatters of fae on my boots. True, it'd be one hell of an entrance, but as much as I hated to admit it, this was going to take diplomacy if I wanted answers.

Yeah, I knew what that word meant. Shut up.

Speaking of which, I shot a quick text to Karen for her to pass on that I was captaining this shit show to the imps in legal. Yes, I was still pissed at her for epically betraying me by keeping Brennan's whereabouts mum, but she was on the payroll, and I didn't have anyone else's number. Of course she had a cell phone. How else do you think I let her know when I ran out of nachos? I mean, she's a super imp, but she's not psychic.

Kennet came back, and I downed the coffee. Mmm. Macchiato. Good call. He stood there like he had something to say. I didn't want to hear it and kept texting. He didn't take the hint.

"For what it's worth, I don't think the boy's been unfaithful t'ye intentionally."

Because tripping and landing with your dick in someone was totally plausible. No wonder chastity belts had been a thing. I scowled at him. "Is that right?"

" 'Tis. I think he stuck his neck out hopin' t'pull yers out of the noose, and his got roped instead."

Not "there's no way he fucked some bimbo" or "he'd never do something like that." His own father didn't question it'd happened, and sorry, not sorry, whatever squirrel's nest of logic had convinced him cheating on me was in my best interest—

Yeah, didn't want to hear that either. Line crossed, plain and simple. I stood. "That it?"

"No. Assuming the geas yerself was bloody stupid. Ye ain't gonna be able t'walk away, lass. Soon as Connell blows that horn, ye'll be back in the thick of things. I suggest ye take that into account the next time yer holdin' the wee lad. Clean up's one thing, but the hunt can't ride without the Gwinth at its head, and by assumin' the geas, yer it."

Goddamn it. Working third shift was not what I'd envisioned. "It'll poof me there?"

"Aye."

"Then tell the asshole to text me first. I know he's got a phone." Kennet didn't look happy, but nodded. I didn't care. "Go help the Gw—Connell with whatever he needs. I've got work to do." Ugh, that word tasted terrible, and I'd just inadvertently signed up for a salary position. I grabbed the rest of my frap and poofed to the temple.

Kyle was in the hot tub, and that chill I'd been fighting suddenly seemed way worse. His face lit up when he saw me and so did my mood, even though I was supposed to be mad at him and his symbiote.

"Hey, babe, heard you kicked some ass. Wanna join? Plenty of room for two…" He waggled his eyebrows, and I snorted. There was, barely.

I set down my drink. "Where's Rhys?"

"Zonked." He jerked his head toward the porto-crib, flipping his damp hair out of his eyes. "Gaia and Mab have been fighting over who's playing with him since you left. Poor kid's out cold."

"Oh." Hopefully they felt the same way about changing his diapers. I put a hand to the side of my achy breast and winced, but there was no way I was firing up the moo machine anywhere near Kyle. I'd never hear the end of it.

"Sore?" He wet his lips. "Bet a good soak would help."

He was probably right…Well duh, he had an ulterior motive, but that didn't mean I had to entertain it. I told you, divine retribution is hard work. My boobs weren't the only things that were feeling it. I raised an eyebrow. "What've you got on in there?"

He just grinned at me. Asshole.

I rolled my eyes. "Turn around."

"For real? Like I haven't seen—"

"Yes! Ugh…just do it."

He laughed and put his back to me, the muscles beneath his stigmata rippling as he folded his arms on the side of the tub. God, he looked good wet.

Shut up.

I put my hair up, stripped down, and eased into the water. Holy crap that was nice—And if you must know, I kept my panties and bra on. Not that it mattered, because he wasn't getting anywhere near me. I wasn't in the mood.

"You set?" He was totally laughing at me, but I was too busy turning to mush to care.

"Mmm."

He turned and settled against the opposite side.

"Keep your hands where I can see them."

"Then I can't do this…" My foot was in his hand, and his thumbs were on my instep.

Oh, sweet baby Jesus—

So, I don't know if I mentioned it before, but Kyle actually had like a career before everything went down. Yeah, seriously. He'd used the cash from his singing gigs to go to night school and was a licensed massage therapist. Why? Because he was a total gigolo and his clientele had consisted of every rich widow and lonely housewife in Vel. They'd literally fought over appointments with him.

With good reason. I totally melted. Like eyes rolling up into the back of my head, slipping down in the water to my chin, putty in his hands. What can I say? I'm a sucker for a foot massage. Unfortunately, he wasn't smart enough to keep his mouth shut.

"You find him?"

Instant tension. Damn it. "Kind of." I raised up enough to rest my elbows on the lip of the tub and dangle my fingers in the water. "I think he's in the Underworld."

"You're kidding—the Underworld?"

"Last I knew there's just the one."

"Shit. So what're you gonna do?"

A sprite, not Bunny, delivered us goblets of mead, and I sipped at mine. "Pay that bitch Stephie a visit. The host texted me a pic of her place." And I wanted a goddamned explanation. Brennan was a fucking idiot, but he wasn't stupid. Everything he did was calculated to result in a very specific outcome, and as much as I hated to admit it, Kennet had probably been right about his motive.

It burned my ass, but I wanted to know what that freaking squirrel brain of his had been trying to build. I was pretty sure it wasn't a fire escape for a bird cage. Why? Because that would've been pointless. Birds can fly, duh.

Anywho—

Kyle hit something just right behind my ankle, and I gasped. His eyes met mine through that fall of damp blond curls. "Like that?"

I bit my lip and nodded.

He shifted his grip, and my toes brushed against him. "Me, too." I didn't pull away, and it wasn't his thumbs against my instep anymore.

"Kyle, I—" My stupid eyes teared up.

He sighed, letting my foot go. "Shh…Hey, it's okay. I'm sorry. Shit, Snow, I didn't mean…" He pulled me onto his lap, and I sobbed miserably against his neck. God, I was pathetic and I'd known better. It had all been one big mind-fuck. "It's not your fault he turned out to be a dick."

I pushed back to look at him, and yes, I was totally trying to ignore his not inconsequential interest and finding it way too interesting. "What makes you think I think it's my fault?"

He smiled, wiping the moisture from my cheek. "Because I know you."

I sniffled, my gaze dropping from his. He was wearing one of those dumb cowrie shell necklaces, and I fiddled with it. Stupid thing looked good on him. My vision doubled, and it was a bronze torque. I wondered where that had ended up…

He tucked a tendril of damp hair behind my ear, his fingers sliding down the side of my throat. My eyes closed, head tilting with a whispered exhalation of breath. Kyle shifted my thighs to either side of his. He inhaled where his fingers had just traveled, his stubble prickling my skin, and my heart beating very fast.

"It's so weird," he murmured against my throat. "I remember, Vy. Like the memories are mine. Everything with Lilith. Being with her, how she felt..." I let out a soft cry as he shifted his hips, kissing along my jaw. "How she tasted...and then us. So close but never quite..."

"I wanted to."

"I know. Me too." His nose brushed against mine. "Do you now?"

God, help me, but I did, and there was no goddamned reason why I shouldn't. Kyle had never been anything but totally honest about who he was or what we were together. Why shouldn't I have a good time? The fact that I couldn't answer him right away pissed me off. What loyalty did I have to that cheating asshole?

Zip, zilch, nada.

I still felt like I was doing something wrong.

Ugh! Fuck him!

I kissed Kyle, feeling his smile as I did. His hands smoothed down my back to knead my rear, fingertips skating between my cheeks. I gasped, and his tongue was in my mouth. The length of him against me, rasping across my panties.

Yeah, yeah, shut up.

My fingers tangled in his locks, and his lips dropped to my throat, then my breast to suckle through the thin lace of my bra. He nipped at me, and I moaned, running my hand through his curls, pressing him close.

"Damn, Snow, I've missed you..." He kissed me again, his tongue dancing with mine, mead and cherry candy—

Not cognac and tobacco.

My eyes welled up. "I can't. I'm sorry, Kyle. I

can't."

He pulled back, his breath coming fast. "Nah, that's cool, babe. My bad. I get it." He bit at his lips, then dragged a hand over them. "Shit. You gotta give me a few."

Poof.

I leaned back in the hot tub and closed my eyes. What the hell was I doing? Christ, what the hell was I not doing? This shouldn't be so goddamned—

Whatever. I got out and went to take shower. A cold one. Like my life wasn't complicated enough. The last thing I needed was to rebound with Vel City's favorite boy-toy who was currently housing my estranged lover and wanna-be husband of like a thousand years after my baby-daddy cheated on me. God, I belonged on a daytime talk show. I blasted the hot water and scrubbed my skin so hard it turned pink, wanting to blow something up—preferably with all of them in it.

The hot water ran out before I was done. Stupid temple. Whatever, I could hear Rhys crying in the other room, and my boobs started leaking. God, that was gross. I threw on a robe that looked like it belonged to a very expensive hooker, probably Bunny, and grabbed Kyle's towel to stem the flow. He wasn't in the bedroom, but Mab was, hovering with a bottle. I swatted her out of the way. She looked me up and down, and her lip curled.

"I didn't pick it." Stupid robe barely covered my rear, and sheer petal pink silk was definitely not my jam.

Mab sniffed like I was lying. Whatever. "It's about time you showed up. Motherhood is a full-time responsibility—"

"I hadn't noticed." Rhys just about inhaled my nipple, and I gasped. Guess he wasn't a fan of formula. I closed my eyes as the pixie nattered at me. Why had I signed up for this again? The pixie, not the kid. I flipped my phone over. Holy crap, my stupid ringer was off, and I'd missed a shit ton of messages.

Most were from the imps in legal. Long story short, the normals were refusing to deal with anyone but Brennan. Psh. Guess they'd be holding their hands on their asses then. So would the two mail-order wannabes with different names and the same picture, and the dude trying to sell me the African secret to penis enlargement. Seriously, does that even work? The phishing, not the secret. Think I can confidently say that's a scam. Man, I get that there's plenty of lonely guys out there, but come on…Whatever, swipe right—

I almost dropped the phone.

Morgana had texted me. —*I don't want 2 talk, I want 2 bargain. Help me, all debts cleared.*—

What the hell?…My thumb hovered. She had to be desperate to offer up the two favors Brennan owed her. What would make her—screw it. I could always tell her to shove it after—what? No, it wasn't that I wanted to get him off the hook. I wanted to see what had her all hot and bothered.

—*What do u desire?*—

A picture of a shitty beach popped right up.

—*Tell u tomorrow 7pm EST alone.*—

I frowned at the clock trying to do the math…There was like a twelve hour difference with me ahead which meant that bitch was getting me up at the ass-crack of dawn. WTF? Ugh. It was probably stupid, but… —*See u then. Coffee?*— Quiet, just go with me for a sec.

—*So u can spit in it?*— Those stupid dots bounced in their bubble. —*Tall iced soy chai tea latte xtra cinnamon coconut whip.—*

Barf. *—U got it.—*

I read through the convo twice, gnawing on my manicure. It was bitchy enough to be Morgana, but had it been? No way Aegaeus would drink something prissy like that, but I didn't trust him as far as I could throw him, which was to say not at all. Whether I was a primordial or not, the dude was stacked.

Well, duh. Of course that was why I asked her what she wanted. You think I'm gunning to start up a take-out service? Between the running the wild hunt and picking up Brennan's slack, it was already like I was trying to put myself through some bullshit ivy-league college.

I was tapping the phone on the arm of the chair, lamenting, when the door opened. Kyle came in with a towel wrapped round his waist, shooting me a sheepish grin from under his curls. Somebody had gotten some.

"Hey, babe—"

"Bunny?"

Cue deer in the headlights. "Uh…"

I rolled my eyes. Typical. "What does Morgana order at the cafe?"

He blinked, then shrugged, flopping down in the chair next to mine. Of course he didn't bother to put on clothes, and yeah, he totally man-spread. It was kind of Kyle's thing. "I dunno, some soy crap. Pad Thai cool for dinner? I got dessert covered."

"Sure. Iced tall soy chai tea latte with extra cinnamon and coconut whip sound familiar?"

"I dunno. Yeah, I guess. Why?"

"She just texted me and wants to meet."

His eyebrows shot up to his hairline. "No way."

"Way." I tossed him my phone.

He scrolled through the messages, that freaking towel slipping. "Huh. Sounds like her. You gonna do it?"

That was the question, wasn't it? I buzzed my lips, shifting Rhys to burp him. "What's it like when you're not driving?"

Kyle shrugged. "Depends. Sometimes it's like standing over Samael's shoulder, but it's gotta be super dope to keep my attention. He's always with me when you're in the room." He wet his lips and adjusted his crotch. "Damn, Snow, you gotta know Bunny's just—"

"I don't care." What? I didn't. Kyle was…Kyle. "What about the rest of the time?" I tried to pull down the robe's hem, and the stupid thing gaped to my navel. He grinned, and I felt myself flush. Forget him, I needed to find some clothes.

"Mostly like I'm asleep but not. You know, like right before you wake up, when you're not sure stuff is real? Kinda like that. In and out." He licked his lips again and made an obscene hand gesture I ignored. God, I can't believe I almost slept with him.

Yeah, I was still thinking about it. Shut up.

"Can you keep stuff from him?"

"Never tried."

"Could you?" It was a long shot, but I wondered how much Aegaeus and Morgana actually talked. Neither one of them were especially cuddly, and both had been rip shit that they'd had to share a body. If they were on the outs with each other…

"What like now?" I rolled my eyes, and he laughed, then was quiet for a moment. "Yeah, okay. We're game. Shoot."

"Seriously, just like that?"

"I dunno, tell me something and we'll find out."

I bit back a smile. "Don't let him know that I was the one that infected that courtesan in Haram." If the All Father was able to find that out, I'd know tout de suite, trust me. He hadn't appreciated contracting the first case of VD, and I'd convinced him Gaia had cooked it up.

Well, yeah, it'd been a curse, and he'd totally deserved it. Nothing like oozing pustules to make one lament the error of their ways, and not for nothing, but the look on his face when I told him his dick might fall off had been priceless.

Kyle's eyes went fuzzy. "Yeah, nothing...but he's trying...I don't know how long..." He grimaced, and it was way weird watching the internal struggle play out on his—

"You fucking bitch, I knew it was you!"

I laughed. Sorry, couldn't help it. It was definitely the All Father that lunged for me, and I sprang up shrieking. "Hey! Stay back, baby!"

"You'll have to put the little bastard down sometime, and then you're—damn it."

Yeah. Hearing the kid called that was like a gut punch, and I lost it.

The All Father sighed and pulled me into his arms. He smelled wrong, and that made everything worse. I didn't want him, I wanted stupid Brennan. Why did—

My phone pinged, and half a second later, my stomach gave this weird lurch.

I thrust Rhys at Samael. "Take—"

Poof.

I was standing in the center of a crowd of psychopaths, ankle deep in mud, wearing a slutty little robe and holding my arms out to Connell. I clenched the stupid silk shut, and he smirked, sauntering over with the horn. Behind him, Kennet crossed himself, muttering a quick prayer.

"You forgot the heels, but this is very nice." Connell pressed up against me, and before I could knee him in the nuts, his breath was hot on my ear. "Your power wanes, and they feel it slip away. I suggest you play along unless you fancy servicing all of them. You need to bite me again, now."

Then his mouth was on mine, and his tongue in my mouth. Ugh! I struggled against him, and the asshole chuckled. I chomped down on his lip.

He gasped, clutching at me, and the surge of energy that came with his blood was no joke. I pushed away, panting and going all splintery to get out of that damned robe and shift into my leathers. The host's desire to hunt burned. Shit, how long had it been since I took the geas? Four, five hours? There was no way I was gonna be able to keep this up.

Connell brushed a stray lock from my cheek. "You feel it? That burn to flush out prey? The ache it brings?"

His hands were on me again, and in that moment, I was totally cool with it. Yeah, there was something really wrong with me, but God, the rush—My eyes fluttered, and I could hear the smile in his voice, his lips warm in the hollow beneath my ear. "Cast out your senses and find your mark…"

The horn was in my hand, and I blew it. "Mount up!"

Beside me, Connell's form shivered, and the fae steed stood in his place. I poofed onto his back, and we rode.

I wish I could adequately explain the thrill of the hunt. The exquisite terror of it. It was nothing like riding down the fugitives. The chase was a thing born of adrenaline and desperation spiking in the wind. Our prey was crafty, leading us through valleys and across mountain ranges, a banshee, creature of Air with a penchant for stealing her victims' breath.

Twice it tried to circle and attack the host, men injured, one falling to her cries. He was not mourned but revered for having earned his final release. The host moved on, cornering the creature in a gully between rolling hills of moonlit green.

Connell's sides heaved, dancing back. Around us, the host awaited my choice of who would advance. I felt what they wanted, their violence and lust coursing through my veins. She was their prize to do with what they willed and had earned her fate—

Yeah, but…Nobody deserves that fate.

"She's mine." The host grumbled around me, their dissatisfaction chipping away at my hold on them. I sent out my will, lashing them into submission, and Connell was at my side.

"It's the Gwinth's prerogative to claim prey, especially that of her first hunt!" The host settled but wasn't happy. "You better make this good," he murmured in my ear. A weight slapped into my palm. "They want blood and will have it, one way or another."

I curled my fingers around a dagger of ivory bone, glancing at him. His face was stone. Shit. How was I gonna work this?

The banshee crouched in the shadows, the wispy tendrils of her gown moving of their own accord. Her skin was alabaster, and her eyes great sucking pits of blackness. My boots crunched on the sandy wash of the gully as I approached. Her pale lips split into a jagged crimson maw, and she hissed at me.

Oh, please. I totally did it bett—the bitch lunged. She hit me hard in the gut, and I went backward, the air knocked out of me. Crap! The knife clattered away, and she went for it. Not a fucking chance—I snagged her ankle, and her arms pinwheeled as she fell. Her chin clipped a rock, and she screamed, spinning at me too quickly to fend off, her hands latching around my throat. Mine were over my ears, trying to stop the searing agony from her cry. It was like she'd boiled my brain—that crimson maw descended to mine, and I couldn't breathe—her tongue jammed down my throat, pulling the air from my lungs.

Oh, you wanna play, bitch? Let's play.

Her essence was mine.

For the record, it's a really bad idea to get into a sucking contest with a succubus. Yeah, you'd think the name would've given her a clue. Her body jerked, and those streamers of her gown started thrashing, the edges like razors, trying to get away.

Too bad, so sad.

Look, it's not like I enjoyed it. Like at all. Let's set aside the fact that a breath mint wasn't gonna cut through the halitosis she had going on and focus on the pure evil I was sucking down. The host wasn't hunting her for a normal or two, it was thousands, and the majority of them were minors. The acts of depravity…Yeah, wasn't gonna linger on that, thanks but no thanks. Suffice to say, the host had been right wanting to tear her apart mid-sexcapades. She totally deserved whatever they had been ready to dish.

But then again, having your essence sucked out wasn't real pleasant. Somehow I'd ended up on top with all her thrashing, and now she was completely limp beneath me. Her heart slowed, and with every juddering pump, I subsumed what made her, her.

Let me explain. Freebasing on someone's adrenochrome is an entirely different thing from sucking them dry. Think about a black and tan. Yeah, as in beer, not the Irish Constabulary—how would they be relevant here? Anyways. You've got three layers. There's the foam at the top, that's like all your surface thoughts and pretty much reads "Oh, shit, a succubus is eating my soul!" The second layer is the dark, all that nasty I'd been slurping from my father onward that made me hella wired. Right, that was the adrenochrome bit; it had memories going further back and the abilities, like shape-shifting.

The last layer was light.

Yeah, that's what the All Father had offered up to me back in the motel, the jerk. Whatever, I don't care who you are, nature vs. nurture, blah, blah, blah, no one's born bad. I mean, that's not to say you can't have some seriously fucked-up tendencies, case in point with the bitch I was currently lip-locked to. Banshees fed on a normal's breath, and fear tasted like red velvet cake. Ask me how I know. Anyways, her sweet tooth had led her down the slippery slope, and boom, welcome to the dark side.

But she hadn't started that way.

I drained her down to that last, pure elemental spark and let her go. Her heart stilled, and I ended the kiss, spitting out her too long tongue and wiping a hand across my mouth. Ugh, where was a bottle of mouthwash when you needed it? Those black eyes had filmed over, and her skin was shrunken and tight. Oh yeah, serious mummy action. I stared down at her, Lilith's memories cresting up from my subconscious.

History would tell you all succubi are soul-eating daemons, but that's not true. We're more like karmic vacuums, and I had enough of my own without banshee baggage in the hallways. I put a shaky hand on my temple, moving it all into a back room of my brain, then put it in one of those space-saver bags, and shoved it under the bed.

Look, you're not getting a better description than that. I don't even know how I did what I did. Long story short, I condensed all of it and jammed it somewhere until I could deal with it. Now wasn't the time to go all pogo-stick, and there wasn't anyone's breath I felt the need to chow on.

Boots were in front of me, and Connell held out that knife. "Finish it."

"For real?" I took the stupid thing. Whatever. She wasn't there anymore, but I wasn't real big on desecrating corpses. I held his gaze and buried the blade in her withered chest, wishing it was his.

"Nicely done." He toed the husk, then held out a hand to help me stand.

I ignored it. The way he was looking at me, I needed another shower, and with the hunt over, I was running on fumes. Yeah, even after draining the banshee. I told you, I'd balled it all up to deal with later. I started out of the gully and stumbled. He caught my elbow, his other arm around my waist. I was too tired to tell him to fuck off.

"We done here?" I asked, flicking a braid over my shoulder.

"For tonight, though I'd suggest you kiss me goodbye, else I'll have to visit sooner than not…unless you'd prefer a different bodily fluid?"

Ugh. I went to slug him, and he caught my fist, laughing, and catching me up against him. "I'll take that as a maybe."

God, he was an arrogant asshole. "You can take it any way you want, but it's not happ—"

Yeah, he kissed me, I bit him on principle, and a surge of power went through me as the geas re-upped. I felt a distant sense of panic, and it took me a moment to realize I was kissing him back. It took a lot longer to make myself care. What the hell?

I kneed him in the nuts, and he dropped.

"The fuck was that?" I spat and wiped an arm across my face. When had he unzipped my jacket? My red lacy bra was on full display, and the host was around us, murmuring in group of twos and threes. I didn't like the way they were looking at me. Like, at all.

A hand circled my bicep, and I jumped. Shit, it was Kennet.

"Let's get a coffee."

Poof.

He sat me out on the cafe's patio in Vel and went inside to order. The sun wasn't even up, and he had to threaten the pimple-faced normal behind the register to open fifteen minutes early. I watched him pull the kid halfway across the counter and was pretty sure he pissed himself.

Me? I'd started shaking. Why had I let him touch me like that? I couldn't get my fingers to zip up that damned jacket...

"Here, lass. Let me." Kennet set the coffees down and kneeled, raising my zipper up as neat as you please. He stayed there, looking up at me with knit brows. "Are ye okay?"

I grabbed my coffee, stupidly glad it had a lid. "Yeah, just tits."

Kennet took my hands between his, and I couldn't hide the tremble. "It's the geas. The Gwinth...Connell said he told you he's the first male t'hold the position. Traditionally, part of her role is t'sate the host by sleepin' with one of their own. You made him your captain—" There was that word again, traditional. God, I hated it. He shook his head and looked away. "The compulsion t'bed him's only going t'get worse."

"He knew."

"Aye."

That son of a bitch. He'd loopholed me again. "How do I stop it?"

"Ye don't, save for passing it t'an heir of his blood."

I took a shaky sip of coffee. Morgana would help me. It was Water's stupid clause. She had to. Forget about Brennan's debt to her, I needed to bail my own ass out. I looked at the big clock across the park. Fourteen more hours. That was what? Three, four more times I had to take the Gwinth's blood? As long as I did it with Socks playing boa, I could probably pull it off.

I had to. The alternative made me want to hurl.

0 Days, 18 Hours, 29 Minutes

I stood at the sink gargling my second bottle of mouthwash, tempted to ask Karen to find me some lye to burn the feel of Connell from my lips. Ugh. The rest of me felt like it'd been dragged behind a chariot and left to die in the bracken. You're just gonna have to trust me on that. Being Lilith hadn't been all roses.

Being Envy wasn't either, but whatever. I was too tired to lament my poor life choices. I fell into bed and was blissfully comatose for all of an hour and a half. My phone losing its shit woke me up.

I dragged it out from under a pillow and blinked at the screen. Legal. The normals were still pitching a fit, even with the lesser fae minding their P's and Q's. I propped up on an elbow. Were they serious? Freaking Congress had passed a joint resolution to look into Brennan's disappearance and were trying to subpoena me. How the hell had they pushed that through so fast? It'd taken them months to work up that stupid biometrics bill.

I fell back against the pillows. Things were so much easier before due process and democracy. It hadn't panned out in Greece. You'd think normals would've gotten a clue, and there was a lot to be said for beheading people. Problem? Solved. I scrubbed at my face. Whatever. Rhys was meeping, and I had to get up anyway.

I settled back with the kid, wondering where Samael was. Kyle never got up before JD's opened, and his side of the bed had been cold when I climbed in after the hunt. I texted legal to tell the normals to sit on something and spin, then Karen to bring me a coffee. I should look into getting an IV drip of the stuff the way I was downing it lately.

The door opened about half a second after a knock, and Mab zipped in with Gaia right behind her. She was pissed. Like, beyond anything I'd ever seen from her, and trust me, I'd been on the receiving end of it a lot.

"I don't care if that fool tracked you down, if you slept with him, I'm washing my hands of you. How you stand him is beyond me. Of all the air-headed…"

Ah. That made sense. I told you, Gaia and the All Father were opposing forces. It didn't make for great roommates. I interrupted her tirade. "I didn't." Barely. She cocked an eyebrow like she knew it. Whatever. "You gonna head back to your cistern?" What, it sounded better than hole in the ground.

"We're heading back to my abode, yes. That idiot just gave testimony that has the normals up in arms."

Oh. That's where the All Father was. And him saying something stupid was kind of a given, especially if Kyle was driving. I mean, he was pretty much clueless. The All Father wasn't, but when he got all verbose, his mouth outran his brain by a mile.

"Wait, we?"

"The hearings have turned into an inquisition, Spanish-style, and they're calling for blood—yours."

Was she freaking—"What did I do now?"

"He let it slip that you found out Brennan was having an affair and wanted to kill him. The FBI is now handling this as a murder investigation. The viral video of you incinerating swamp-thing in that canyon didn't help."

Told you they'd spin that, but it wasn't what had my attention. I blinked at her. Everyone knew he cheated on me...and they thought I killed him for it? Anxiety choked me, and I broke out in a cold sweat. But he wasn't, I didn't—she put a hand on my ankle, grounding me, and the room stopped telescoping out.

"I can't protect the boy if you don't come with me...Envy, they want to take Rhys into protective custody. I can keep him safe, but you need to find your dae."

Yeah...you can imagine how I reacted to that. Gaia wasn't having it. She did something, and the blast of rage I sent out was absorbed before it'd gotten past the foot of the bed.

She raised an eyebrow and tossed me a baggie. "You also need to stay calm."

Calm? I was rip shit! They wanted to take away my kid—

No.

She was right. The last thing I needed to do was finish what I'd started in the South Seas. I downed the pills dry, glaring at her. She couldn't hold my gaze...

"You know something. Spill it."

She sighed and the mattress sank a good six inches as she settled onto the bed. I swapped Rhys and got comfortable again. I could tell this was going to take a while.

It did.

Five minutes later..."What do you remember about the Underworld?"

This again. "They've got crappy B and Bs. I don't know, nothing. It's not anyplace I've ever felt the need to go on vacation."

Gaia took a breath like she was trying not to throttle me. "No, but we've all heard tales."

Well, those were always oh so accurate. Whatever, I'd humor her. I batted Mab away. "It's the realm where the souls of the dead go."

"And its geography?" she asked, way too casually.

My eyes narrowed. "I dunno, a bunch of circles, a freaky dog, and a handful of rivers. How is this relev—oh…Shit…" The blood drained from my face, and I felt faint. The Lethe was one of those rivers. The same Lethe that came out beside the mesa in Fae. Gaia's eyebrow quirked. "What did Brennan promise you in exchange for protecting Rhys?"

"An item that had passed from this world into the next. It's of no consequence to anyone but me, but seeing how he planned on going right by it, twice…" She shrugged, then gave me that pinched-lip look. "Any promises I may have made in exchange seemed a small thing. I should've known better."

He was going by it twice…to Fae and back…for what? My stomach dropped.

No, not a what. I was betting it was a who, as in the Gwinth's freaking heir, and I was positive Brennan had been in Vegas to cut a deal with Stephie Morte, aka Persephone, for passage through the Underworld. If anyone knew what had happened to Brennan, it was her.

Gaia stood, holding her arms out for Rhys. "Mab and I'll get the two of you packed up. You need to speak to that woman."

"No…" I chewed my lip, more than happy to pass

him over. What? The kid stank. Goat milk might be a substitute, but it didn't wear well. "Not yet. I need to talk to War."

He was out in the temple gardens, and I found the dogs first, or rather they found me and took me to him. He was smoking a cigar at the side of an idyllic brook, almost hidden by the verdant greenery. I cut straight to the chase.

"I know Brennan went to Fae to get the Gwinth's heir. Now start talking."

He sighed and ran a hand through his spiky black hair. It looked like pipe cleaners had been jammed into his skull, then chopped off with a weed whacker. The points of his ears drooped. "Who told you?"

"I figured it out." He shot me a look, and I wanted to slap him. "Why does everyone think I'm an idiot?" Okay, rhetorical question. I hadn't exactly spent this incarnation applying myself to anything aside from catching a buzz, but it was still insulting.

"I don't think you're an idiot, just not interested in anything other than yourself."

Ouch. "Listen, War—"

"Name's Dan."

Yeah, that was kind of case in point. I mean, I had known the guy for almost a year. "Okay, Dan, I need you to tell me what happened."

He chewed on his stogie. "It's like you said. Should've been a quick in and out, but that bitch—"

"Persephone."

His mouth curdled, and he flicked his ash. "Yeah."

I sat down on the bank opposite from him, and the brindled dog from the other night cozied up to me. I scritched behind its ear.

"She likes you."

"Why don't you like her?" Both of us knew I wasn't talking about the bitch next to me.

"She saved Brennan when he was a kid. Sang to his fiend or some shit when it first took over." He rolled the cigar between his thick fingers, staring at it. "Told me once she never asked for anything in return, that he owed her. She's made up for it and then some since. Half the shit we've gotten into's on her."

Yeah, I was pretty lost for all my outrage at being called an idiot.

Dan must've noticed. He started ticking off fingers. "Leningrad, Stalingrad, Bagdad, Berlin, Gurganj, shit I got a list as long as my arm. Hell's numbers dip, she whistles, Brennan rounds us up, and normals go down like we're threshing wheat."

Mmm…that didn't help. I mean, they were the Riders of the Apocalypse…

Dan looked frustrated that I wasn't getting it. "Look, I ain't saying me and the guys don't like what we do, but none of it should have gone down the way it did. Say what you will about Amelda, but his mother stopped that shit cold by banding him, and now…" Dan looked at me and shook his head. "He said he was done with the cunt."

"Is he…" God, I couldn't say it.

Dan knew what I meant though. "Then, yeah. Now…I dunno. He and Persephone got into it back before he was banded, and he wasn't exactly welcome down there unless he showed up on hands and knees. Man was adamant that wasn't happening. I don't know what he promised her to pass through, but she was pissed he kept ghosting her after you released his fiend. She wanted him back, and that woman don't take no for an answer."

Wasn't what I wanted to hear. I wiped at my cheek. Stupid pollen. "Tell me."

He cracked his neck, looking into the garden's canopy. "Not much to say. Sometime in April she called him. S'usually when she pokes her head up. Wanted to know what went down with the veil. He gave her the skinny but didn't meet with her. Then all this Gwinth shit...She called again. Whatever she said...he caved."

"And met her in Vegas."

"Yeah. Wanted us to go with. She wasn't real happy about that. Acted like she was, but you could tell she wanted to get him alone. He didn't seem keen. Anyway, she hired a bunch of—never mind." The tips of his ears flushed red. "We lost track of him."

I ran my fingers through the silk behind the dog's ear, not wanting to see the pity I heard in his voice. "Then what?"

"Jonas got a note, telling us to go back and keep tabs on you. It said they'd reached an agreement, and he'd hook up with us in a couple days when it was his turn on the rota." Dan blew out a long plume of smoke, and it hung over the water between us, shafts of sunlight splintering it away. "None of us were cool with leaving him, and then when you split—I saw the shit pics Connell gave you. Can't blame you for leaving, or kicking our asses to the curb. Jonas was fucking pissed; he hates her. Him, Stewie, and Frank went to beat the shit out of him and haul his ass back."

Frank? Oh. That had to be Pestilence.

Dan rolled the cigar between his fingers again, his mouth all screwed up. "That bitch laughed at them. Brennan was already gone."

I felt sick. "He never got the envelope?"

The big dae shook his head. "No. It's back at the estate."

I ran a trembling hand over my face. Then Brennan didn't know why I'd taken off his fae-band...The dog whined and thumped its tail, looking up at me. I ran a hand down its back. "The others went after him?" Jonas would tell him what had happened—if he didn't hear it on the six o'clock news first. I was sure the press was having a field day with that little tidbit.

"Yeah. Brennan told us what he'd planned on doing, man's out of his goddamned mind. Lethe this time of year's no joke." Dan grinned, showing rows of pointed teeth, but it didn't last. "One of us had to stay here with you. Seeing how you ain't real keen on Frank, I volunteered."

"He's okay; the bugs just freak me out."

Dan grunted. "They come with the job, like the dogs."

I made whirls in the dog's short brindled fur. The brook was very loud between us. Chirping of birds. Wind chimes. All Mother Earth zen. It was seriously annoying.

"He still banded? You can feel him through it, right?"

My head jerked up. The expression on Dan's face...man. Forget about my missing baby-daddy—he was missing his four besties. I'd known Brennan for a hot minute; he'd been with the other Riders for centuries. God, I was a selfish bitch.

"Yeah, but I think he's in trouble." I told Dan about the cold.

He grunted, squinting through the trees at the temple. "So what are you gonna do?"

I chewed my lip, hearing what he was really asking. I didn't have an answer. I mean, I wanted answers from Brennan, but I didn't want to see him, and if I couldn't find him and haul his ass back from wherever he was, the normals were gonna lock me up and try to snag my kid. Not for nothing, but I would torch the planet before that happened. Wasn't an option I was real keen on, but neither were the others, and the fact that I had no idea how to get into the Underworld short of slicing my wrists didn't help...

But I bet I knew someone who did.

"Gaia and Mab are packing up Rhys. We're bunking with her until I figure it out. You coming?"

It was an olive branch, and he knew it. By the look on his face, he hadn't expected it, and he latched on like a drowning man.

"Yeah—"

A twig snapped behind me, and my stomach plummeted. At who it was and the flush of heat that went through me. Dan was at my side before I could blink, the dogs surrounding us with hackles raised.

Connell laughed. "Daniel. Nice to see you, too. There's no cause for alarm. I came to escort Envy to brunch."

Like hell he had. Connell held out a hand, and I resisted the urge to spit on it, wondering how much of that he'd heard. Too much, probably. "I'm not going anywhere with you. You knew that damned geas was gonna roofie me, and you didn't say anything!"

He shrugged. "Why would I? I still need an heir, and this arrangement rather ups the odds I'll get one." The dog at my side growled, and Connell chuckled. "Shall we?"

I stomped past him back to the temple. "I'm not kissing you. You can bleed into a freaking cup," I muttered when we got to the wide stone steps.

"As you wish," he said all *Princess Bride*.

I glared at him over my shoulder, pushing through the big doors.

Kyle was at one of the trestle tables with Monica, chowing down takeout from JD's in a suit. Guess he'd gotten tired of organic whatever. I snagged a waffle fry, and he pushed the bag at me. "All you, Snow."

"Spilling Brennan cheated on me in front of Congress must've given you an appetite. You wave the pics at them or just run your mouth?"

He flushed. "Samael didn't say anything about those, just that you'd witnessed his infidelity or some shit. That bitch, Stephie, goaded him into it. Man was trying to defend your honor after she played a clip of you sucking face with the Gwinth."

How the hell…"When did they get that?"

"I dunno. You were at some lake."

Great. So now I was wearing the scarlet letter and had wronged Fae's golden boy. The normals had to be eating that shit up. Did I have a sign on my freaking forehead that read speed bump? How many times could one person get thrown under the goddamned bus?

"Sorry, Snow. Normals suck, and they're freaking rabid. Congress has got a major hard-on for the dae, and that Morte bitch keeps strokin' it. She's got 'em convinced you did something to him, and now they're all inquest."

"Something? You mean like kill him? They want to take Rhys, Kyle!"

He winced. "Yeah…Monica's working with the

imps trying to bury the court order, but Morte's got it out for you, and it's like they think he's our President or some shit."

"I told you your lack of public engagement would negatively impact Air's political clout," Monica said around a mouthful of sad-looking I-don't-know-what. When the hell did JD's put gluten-free anything on the menu? "Not issuing a formal statement of separatism from the other elements when the dae began to speak for us was construed by normals as Air's consent to be under Fire's purview."

"Psh. As if." Kyle snorted.

Monica waggled a fry at him. "While in this realm, we have to obey their laws, unless it's your intent to subjugate the entire human race and enact your own?" He asked it like he was taking a poll about hotdogs or burgers at a cookout. Yeah, fae weren't real sympathetic to the whole needs of the many outweighing the needs of the few. They were all might makes right and you get what you get and you don't get upset. Good thing for normals they were also lazy as hell.

Kyle shook his head. "Too much work." See? Not a moral issue, it was totally a convenience thing. "Issue one of those separate whatevers now; this monkey suit is killing me."

He tugged at the knot of his tie. Monkey suit or not, you have to know he looked amazing in it. Kyle glanced up at me like he'd caught the thought and grinned. It cut off quick as Connell slid onto the bench beside me. Somewhere between here and the door he'd gotten hold of a shot glass and pulled out that bone dagger. Eww.

"Gross, don't use that. It has banshee all over it." Not to mention whatever else he'd used it for.

Dan slapped down a pocket knife and sat across the table from him. Connell rolled his eyes, but flicked it open, sliced his palm, and I froze.

The scent of his blood was heady and sweet. It surrounded me and caught me up. His hand was in mine, then the slice at my lips, my tongue laving across it, delving. He groaned and heat seared through me—I wanted. The bench clattered over, and there was the rip of cloth. Defined pecs beneath my palms, my mouth…

Shouting. I pulled back, my brow furrowed. Connell rose beneath me, his hips pressing between my thighs. He kissed me, deep, and none of it mattered. My nails bit into his shoulders, his scalp—

Something clamped onto my ankle, blooming agony. I screamed, scrambling away. One of War's freaking dogs had bit me! What the—

Connell was on the floor, panting, eyes full of heat and his shirt torn from his chest. His pants were half undone.

Mine were, too.

Oh, God.

The dog whimpered, army-crawling toward me. I sobbed, throwing myself around its neck. A take-out wrapper whipped by me on an angry current of air. Kyle, Monica, Dan…they'd seen the whole thing.

"I suggest you leave." Not Kyle. The All Father's voice was tight with fury.

Connell ran a hand over his smirk. "Until next time."

Poof.

"I think your plans to leave the temple unwise," the All Father said, my ears popping with the change in air pressure as he tried to get a handle on himself. His eyes were that green-grey that meant run like hell. Outside, branches were snapping like dry spaghetti when the chef was pissed. Hail the size of meatballs pinged off the stone walk.

Yeah, I was hungry.

"I'm going with her, and Callie ain't leaving her side," Dan said. Callie? Oh, the dog.

The All Father's eyes darkened. Crap. "It's unwise."

"It's her choice."

I stroked the dog's fur, nose buried in her musky ruff listening to them fight about me like I wasn't there. My ankle throbbed, and I didn't care. I deserved it. Damned unintended consequences…I snuffled and wiped my eyes. The hail got bigger. Anybody but a fiend would've been cowering under the table. Dan was getting in the All Father's face. I appreciated it, but my hair had started to rise. The All Father was gonna zap his ass.

"God, will you two shut up? I'm right here, and if you fry him, I'm gonna be pissed!"

They both turned to look at me like they'd forgotten I was in the room. Lightning flashed and grounded outside hard enough to shake the temple. The room filled with the reek of ozone.

Men. I rolled my eyes. "I'm going to Gaia's. She doesn't like Connell any more than you two, and her cistern's a freaking bunker. Rhys will be safe, and as soon as I find Socks, he's gonna be my favorite accessory until I get rid of this stupid geas."

The All Father gritted his teeth, knuckles popping. "And how, pray tell, do you intend on doing that?"

Dan looked just as curious, and I sighed, getting to my feet and pulling my hoodie around me.

Yeah, not a clue. Callie's head bumped my thigh, and I scritched it, digging out my phone. I scrolled to the text with Persephone's address. "I dunno. I've got a date with Lady Death, first."

I couldn't put it off any longer. I pulled on the Gwinth's power and went all corporate. Well, my version of corporate. Dark green pencil skirt and fitted jacket with a subtle pattern of scales over a crisp white button-down. Hair in a French twist and scarlet lipstick. The fuck-me heels were a given. A quick burst of elemental energy took care of the dog bite.

"Cool trick," Dan said, impressed.

I smoothed my skirt, feeling way too adult, but a Ramones tee and trainers weren't gonna cut it. "Where's Mab?"

The All Father snorted. "Mab? If you're taking anyone, it should be—"

"Someone that can snoop around?"

"Yes. I was going to suggest Monica accompany you."

The jinn rubbed his hands together. Okay…Dopey-looking lawyer or not, I had to admit he was more than suited for the role. He wouldn't bitch the whole time, either. "All right, fine."

His form shimmered, and a slim chain of silver settled around my ankle. Yeah, super creepy, but at least I'd know where he was.

The All Father came over and kissed my cheek. "Be wise. I know you won't be careful. Text me after."

I snorted, but he wasn't wrong. My palms were damp, and I felt like I was gonna puke.

Poof.

So, upstate New York is beautiful in the spring. The leaves had unfurled with that first burst of green, and the air smelled like growing things. My breath caught. I stood outside of the wrought iron gates telling my pulse to calm the fuck down. Hmm? Oh, the gates were open. I was just chickenshit, remember? The third movement of *Moonlight Sonata* was coming from inside.

Goddamn him.

My heels clicked in time to the music down the flagstone walk and up the wide steps to the veranda of the gingerbread Victorian manor. Seriously, that's what they call it. I think because of all that intricate trim. Look, I don't know why either; the one and only gingerbread I'd attempted had looked more like a gum-drop bedazzled hovel.

Notes pounded from the keys, and the door was right in front of me, its polished brass knocker shaped like a cat. I lifted its tail and slammed it down.

Probably more times than I had to.

The piano cut off, and I took a breath, flicking an errant lock from my eyes. Footsteps inside. Murmur of voices, two females.

My heart pounded.

A bolt turned, and the door cracked open. An older normal, mid-sixties maybe, peeked out at me. She looked like a Betty. "Can I help you?"

"Envy Malten, here to see Persephone Morte."

Betty's cornflower eyes widened, and I'll be damned if it wasn't in anticipation. She looked me up and down with a sly smile on her lips and held the door wide. I felt Monica dematerialize from my ankle. "Won't you please come in? She's been expecting you."

I'll just bet she has. I sashayed past her into a pristine entryway. Like, whoever she had cleaning for her one-upped the imps with dust removal. The place gleamed, all honeyed wood and floral crap. It even smelled like lilac.

My heart leapt. Not a whiff of tobacco.

Betty closed the door and waved for me to follow her down the hall. She led me to a room with a grand piano on a dais. A row of low couches and occasional tables surrounded it. There was nothing on the walls, and the floor was gleaming oak. Persephone stood by one of the windows, a baby blue pants suit hiding the curves the cream satin gown in the pictures hadn't.

"I'll fetch tea," Betty said, leaving us. Persephone didn't move. I took a seat. What? My feet were killing me. She turned as I settled, her posture going rigid. I could guess why, given the ashtray at my elbow. Suck it, bitch.

"I heard you were expecting me. If that's the case, I'm assuming you've had plenty of time to think about what you're going to say." I crossed my legs and sat back, bobbing a foot. "Lay it on me."

Her wheaten eyebrow rose. Gaia was right; she had to be a sylph. The way her steps glided across the floor as she came to sit at the other end of the couch confirmed it. I kept waiting for a data dump from Lilith but got crickets instead. This time she wasn't keeping anything from me; she'd just never crossed paths with this bitch. I guess that made sense, seeing how Persephone spent half her time in the Underworld. She flicked off her heels and tucked her stocking feet up under her. Her pedicure was on point.

"I have, but it's funny how all of that goes out the window in the moment." She offered me her slim white hand. "Let's start here, Persephone Morte, but please, call me Stephie, everyone does."

Yeah, not happening, and she damn well knew who

I was. I just looked at her, and she smiled again, drawing her hand back. Her eyes went to the piano. It was beautiful, and you could tell it was crazy old. Probably worth more than the entire house. "Did you know I was the one who taught him to play?"

Did I care? "Nope."

"Mmm." For whatever reason, she seemed pleased as punch about that. "It will be interesting to see if his son inherits his talent."

As in, she fully expected to find out personally. Oh yeah, she was trying to piss me off, and trust me, it was working. I might've sent a trickle of flame to warp the piano's harp. Try playing a sonata now, bitch.

Betty came back with tea and poured us each a cup. I ignored mine, and Persephone smirked around the rim of hers.

"Where is he?"

"Right to the point."

"Forgive me if I don't feel the need to exchange pleasantries."

"I doubt there can be many of those between us, but I'd expected you to want the details of our relationship." Her eyes dropped to my naked ring finger. I fought the urge to hide it, and a smile ghosted over her lips. She made a weird come-hither gesture, and the shadows Brennan had coated me with flowed into her hand. "I know all about yours."

Bitch. I snorted like I didn't care and wasn't totally freaked out. "What? Like if you're fucking him? Lady, at this point I couldn't give two shits if you had him upstairs tied to your bed." Not a lie, I'd voided my bowels earlier, and quiet, she didn't know I wasn't full of crap. Okay, maybe she did. Whatever. "But unless a full-scale war between us and the normals is your intent, I suggest you pony up his whereabouts."

She pursed her lips, placing her cup back on the saucer, and aligning the design. Pink roses and ribbons or some shit. "I don't believe you."

"Which part, about the war, or me not caring if you're fucking him?"

"I've never fucked Beebee. I leave that to cheap sluts like you."

I laughed. Yeah. Couldn't help it. Come on, Lady Death with a death wish? Classic. And Beebee? Come freaking on.

She didn't seem particularly thrilled that dart hadn't hit, so she threw another. "He's told me all about you, in particular your tiresome lack of mental stability. Did it take you this long to be able to wash yourself, or did you have someone else do it after they hauled you out of that flea-infested motel? It's no wonder you drove him away. I suspect I should thank you for that." She smiled, tonguing a canine.

Aww, the kitten had claws. I smiled back, envisioning tearing her tongue out and making her eat it. "You're welcome. Tell you what, answer the question, and we'll call it even. Where is he?"

What? I wasn't gonna beat the shit out of her until she told me what I wanted to know. That and I had zero doubt this was being photo-documented for her next session with Congress. She inspected her manicure. The gel of her lousy French tip needed filling.

"If he wanted you to know, he would've told you."

God, this was like every meal I'd ever eaten with Calista. Barb, barb, barb, you're pathetic, barb, barb, kill yourself, barb, barb, barb, everything's your fault. I rolled my eyes, pretty much immune to it. Time to throw one of my own.

"And if he wanted you, you wouldn't have had to blackmail him into meeting with you."

Her eyes narrowed. Score. Vy-1 Calista-wannabe-0

"Didn't those pictures get it through your thick skull, or are you delusional on top of everything else? God, you'd think having the evidence delivered to you…"

She kept going, but I was stuck on what had already come out of her mouth. She knew about the photos. Don't get it twisted, I didn't put it past her to have set Brennan up, but if the Gwinth was the delivery boy…

"…take you back after you've been whoring for the hunt. Don't think I don't know what those gold eyes mean."

Excuse me? My head jerked up, and she laughed.

"Do you have Connell wear Beebee's form when he's fucking you? He'll do it if you ask, and it's the closest you'll ever get to Brennan again. You think you're special because he knocked you up? You were a convenient hole with enough political sway to make it worth his while."

Yep, it was time to go. I stood. Hmm? Why was she still breathing? Honestly, I hadn't been really listening. Call it a defense mechanism or whatever, but this kind of abuse had been heaped in with my breakfast cereal for nineteen plus years. There was nothing she could say to me that Calista hadn't said better. Worse. Whatever, you know what I mean. Anyways, I had her number and wasn't going to feed into it.

Oh, trust me. She'd still pay for it.

I smoothed my skirt and smiled at her. "Thanks for

tea, it was lovely. I'll see myself out."

Betty scooted away from the door as I went through it. Like I hadn't known she'd be listening. Monica the ankle bracelet reformed as I closed the door behind me and poofed to the estate.

Yeah, the estate. A monsoon must've come through because there were puddles and mud-spattered plastic everywhere. A steel frame had been erected, and a low wall of field stone was taking shape around its base. Monica slid from my ankle and re-lawyer-ized at my side. I made my way to Brennan's office.

"You find anything?"

"A lot of photos of you, but the place was pretty clean incrimination-wise. You should see her collection of vibrators—"

"I'll pass." And that was why I didn't need a jinn snooping around.

The envelope was in the center of Brennan's desk, and I shook it out. Pictures, but no ring. I felt a pang, opening the envelope to peer inside. Stupid, I know. Would Jonas have taken it?

"She had copies of these," Monica said, flipping through them. "There were others, but they weren't as suggestive."

Didn't surprise me. I'd had the feeling she'd set him up, but to what extent...I sat in Brennan's chair, tears pricking my eyes at the waft of tobacco. I blinked them away. Who would've thought I'd ever miss that disgusting habit? I picked up the photos, slowly flicking through them. Monica went to the mini bar and poured us both a cognac. I sipped on it, but it didn't do a lot to make me feel any better.

"What are you looking for?"

"I don't know. Connell swore on the Midsummer's moon they weren't doctored, but—"

Wait a minute.

I flipped through them again, stopping at the one of them at the blackjack table, smoke curling up from the cigarette in the ashtray at Brennan's elbow. Another smoldered beside him at the pool, and on the rail of the balcony. My pulse jumped, and I ripped open the drawer with the album of pictures Peter had taken of us.

There was a glaring difference between the two sets. In Peter's, once Brennan lit a cigarette, it didn't leave his lips.

...Do you have him wear Beebee's form when he's fucking you? He'll do it if you ask...

God, I was an idiot.

Connell had smelled like lilac the morning of our "interlude," and remember that Bacchanal fog he'd given me? One of the main ingredients was water from the Lethe, which had a super-short shelf-life, so short I'd already chucked it. No way he'd been holding onto it in his bedside table drawer for a year, and the only place to get more of it was from the river itself.

Which started in the Underworld.

That shape-shifting son of a bitch. He'd totally fae'd me, and she'd helped him do it.

0 Days, 4 Hours, 22 Minutes

I ditched Monica and poofed to the hunt.

They were set up in the parking lot of a shitty motel chowing Micky D's, "Margaritaville" blaring over the speakers. Connell's eyes lit up when he saw me, that gap-toothed grin all smug. Asshole was about to find out what'd happened to that last shaker of salt.

"Missing me? You must be, and those heels are divine. What do you say we go somewhere where you can throw them over my shoulders." He held up a key and jingled it.

I cocked a hip. "Lead the way."

His eyes widened, then narrowed. Didn't expect that, did you shithead? Hmm? You either? Look, I needed to be sure, and there was only one way I could be. Pictures, aphrodisiacs, and a faint thread of some bitch's nasty-ass perfume weren't gonna cut it.

I needed a demo, and I was getting one.

I sauntered to him, running my hand up the back of his neck and giving him my best spank-me-daddy look. His throat bobbed, and he tripped up the stairs in his rush to get to his room.

Yeah, seriously. Did you think I was kidding about tongues lolling when I put a little shimmy in my step? It wasn't a euphemism. Who do you think instigated the Original Sin? When I turned up the heat, you better believe things got hot.

I took my time, prowling after him. The rest of the host didn't move a muscle, watching me sashay mine. Connell fumbled at the door, dropped the key, and then fumbled again, finally throwing it open with a wide grin. I walked past him into the nasty little room, unbuttoning my jacket and sliding it from my shoulders. His hands were on me...

"No...We do this my way."

"Your way?" His voice was thick with anticipation and a healthy dose of suspicion.

I'll give credit where credit's due, he wasn't stupid, but he was a guy. I sucked on my lower lip, looking up at him through my lashes and easing off his coat all breathy.

"Is it true you can be anything you want?" My fingers traced the bulge in his pants and his Adam's apple bobbed. So long, suspicion.

"I—yes."

"How do you do it? Make it convincing? I wouldn't know you from a true raven." He reached for me again, and I stepped away. "I want to do it."

Connell's brow furrowed, and I undid a button on my blouse, then moved to the next, turning away from him. His breath caught when my shirt fell away, and I tossed it onto the bed. His tee landed on top of it, and then his pants. Somebody was eager. I arched my back and pulled the clip from my hair, rippling it down my spine.

"I mimic through observation," he murmured, running his hands over my hips and finding the zipper to my skirt. My libido jumped when his skin touched mine, but it wasn't anything I couldn't handle. As long as he didn't bleed.

Yeah, wasn't gonna think about that possibility, but you know how I like playing with fire.

My skirt pooled around my ankles, and his hands tightened on my hips, pressing himself between my cheeks. He groaned, fingers playing with the straps of my garter. I turned, running my hands over his pecs. Damn, this body was wasted on the prick.

"People too?" I gazed into his eyes all winsome.

He fondled a nipple through my bra, and I gasped. "That requires more intel to be convincing."

I dropped my gaze, letting myself tear up. "Brennan's not coming back. He's not coming back, and the normals think I—they're going to take my son if he doesn't. Could you…?"

Connell's eyebrow cocked. "You want me to be him? To take his place?"

I bit my lip. "Would you show me?"

His form misted, and Brennan stood before me. A perfect copy. I stepped back, then slowly circled him. His stigmata, the way his hair fell…my chest ached standing there in front of him again. I raised my face to his, sliding off his eyepatch.

A sunken pit was beneath it, and my breath caught. It'd never looked like that.

Which that bitch would've known if they'd been fucking.

Connell smiled Brennan's crooked smile, his cheek dimpling when he bent to kiss me. I swallowed a sob and let my anger bloom. He kissed the way Brennan did, and the only way he'd know that was if that bitch had coached him.

She'd coached him on all of it.

You better believe I drained that fucker, packing

away all his nastiness with the banshee's. Talk about a matched set.

Connell thrashed, but by the time he realized what was happening, it was too late, and when the beat of his foul heart had all but stilled, I let him drop to the floor. His form had changed. It was grey and misshapen. Eyes like an insect. Fingers longer than they should be with an extra joint. He raised them, beseeching.

I ignored him, rooting around his room until I found that bone dagger. I tested its edge with my thumb, standing over him. "I know you and that bitch set Brennan up. Where is he?"

"Where he belongs. Please—"

I kneeled over him and traced his throat with the dagger's tip as I kissed him again, drawing out more of his essence. "Where is he?"

"T-treachery…the Ninth Circle of Hell. She wanted to teach him a lesson…"

"She won't kill him?"

"No." He spat. "She needs him, as you need me—"

A phone rang, playing the theme song to *The Graduate.* His eyes flicked to his jacket. Huh. Wonder who Mrs. Robinson could be. I slammed the blade into his chest and then answered it, watching the light in his eyes fade.

"Connell's phone."

I could hear her breathing. I licked a finger of blood off the knife. Yeah, it was gross, but power still rushed through me, despite the fact that he was dead at my feet. I'd figured as much. See, the thing about a curse or geas is that they're not real nuanced. For me to keep hold of the host, I needed something of his body in me. He didn't need to be alive for me to accomplish that.

By the catch in her voice, Stephie must've had a similar epiphany. "What have you done?"

"Oh hi, Stephie! I'll tell if you do."

"You little bit—"

I laughed and hung up. Whatever. I got dressed, then dragged Connell's corpse to the motel railing and pitched it over the side. It hit the pavement with a satisfying thump. The host's eyes went from it to me.

"Kennet's in charge. Make me some jerky. Extra spicy. I want a to-go bag, stat." They were looking at me the same way you are, then hopped to it.

What? Yeah, I'd just murdered the dude and ordered him made into a trail snack. Like the host was gonna complain, and aside from smoking a portion of the bastard with delicious spices, I could give two shits about whatever else they did with his corpse. Deal with it. Long story short, Lilith was pre-Mesopotamian born and raised. She, and by that I mean me, stood by the concept of an eye for an eye. Honestly, he probably should've suffered more. Look, the ancient world was big on corporal punishment, and the fae haven't evolved much past the dark ages judicial-wise.

Whatever. I was done being yanked around and, quite frankly, rip shit I'd gotten played so hard. Not to mention I'd flipped out on Brennan when all he'd been trying to do was save my ass. Granted, all of this could have been avoided if his communication skills weren't for shit, but considering that bitch had him cooling his jets in the Ninth Circle of Hell, I was inclined to give him a pass.

Did I believe Connell? Absolutely. I mean, she could've lied to him about where Brennan was and needing him, but I didn't think so, and I could taste that he believed it was the truth. Hmm? Oh, vanilla pudding. The fancy kind with those specks.

Anywho, I went to go find Kennet and give him the skinny. He was as pissed as I was and a lot less surprised. What the hell is it with men not opening their damned mouths? Everything was a freaking state secret.

"So what are ye planning t'do now?" He waved to the bar for two more beers.

I hated that question. Like, seriously, you'd think by now people would've figured out that I'm a seat-of-my-pants-type girl. I shrugged and checked the time on my phone. I had to meet Morgana in a half hour.

Rodrigo, that troll that'd been behind the bar, came over holding a takeout bag with a big yellow happy face on it and our drinks. "Jerky's gonna take a while to do right. I made you up some Cajun fae tips, well done, heavy on the heat. They travel pretty good."

"What's the other one?" I cracked the bottle and took a sip.

His ruddy face flushed. "Death by chocolate."

"Seriously?" I snagged the spoon out of the bag and popped the container open. It was literal Heaven on my tongue. "Holy crap, I could take a bath in this. You use that coffee booze?"

"It's a secret." He winked at me. "I'll share it as soon as you get in that tub."

I laughed, and he went back to his trailer. "What's he in for?"

"Poisoning the tristate area back in '65."

I choked a little, and Kennet chuckled. Screw it, if I got to pick, this was the way to go.

"They're not all bad. Don't get me wrong, most are a bit off, but who isn't?"

He had a point. "So, Mr. Soul Control, tell me about Hell."

"What did ye want t'know?"

"Let's start with how I get in."

Kennet ran a hand over his goatee. "Could be I know a way…one a might faster than workin' through all them torments."

My eyebrow quirked as he made me wait for it. "Do tell."

"Not without a bargain. I want t'go with ye and wouldn't be surprised if the rest of the host feels the same. Takin' a few of 'em wouldn't be a bad idea."

Men and their freaking bargains. I licked the back of the spoon. "Why would they want to do that?"

He rolled his eyes. "They were pissed about the banshee, but Connell was a shitty Gwinth. Isn't natural having a man in charge. Takin' him out made up for it and then some. Ye've got their respect. Suggest ye use it." He grinned that crooked smile, his cheek dimpling, and my heart ached seeing it. "Besides, not one of 'em would turn down the chance t'storm the gates of Hell. What a tale that'll be!"

I laughed. God, he was bat-shit. I tossed my spoon into the empty container. Man, that'd been good. "Fine, pick out your posse."

He literally rubbed his hands together and cackled. "Right then, there's some things ye need t'know. First off, none of yer powers will work there."

Ouch. That was gonna suck.

"And second, that *Inferno* shite of Dante's was pure poetic license." He tapped the side of his nose. "Certain people of importance heard he'd been runnin' his mouth and made him write it as a retraction."

Wait, what? "There's no circles?"

"Those are for true, but as t'the rest...." He shrugged. "We should be able t'bypass most of it by going through the hub. Dress warm. That blighted city's colder than a witch's—"

"Hell's a city?" Yeah, I was blinking a lot. Look, in case you haven't noticed, I'm not very big on the why's and wherefores of anything that doesn't personally affect me. Death had never been one of those things. Hmm? Exactly. I'm a narcissistic bitch and a total idiot. Thanks for reminding me.

"Ninth Circle is." He chugged his beer and slammed the bottle on the table. "Ye ready then?"

"What, now? No...I've got to meet with someone first and make sure Rhys is settled. Hunt rides at sundown?"

"Aye. But they're due a night off. I'll find some likely lads meantime, and we'll be waiting for ye."

I stood, wiping my sweaty palms on my skirt. "Yeah. See you then."

Holy crap, I was going to Hell.

Shut up. I meant on purpose.

Poof.

Gaia's abode smelled like brownies and pot. She was in her beanbag toking up, Callie at her feet. The furniture had been pushed back, and Rhys was propped up against a bunch of pillows trying to grab Mab as she zipped around, just out of his reach. Dan was channel surfing.

Yup, totally homey.

"Pretty sure normals frown on illicit drug use around minors," I said, picking up Rhys.

Gaia blew a smoke ring. "Marijuana's not illicit, and

none of us are normal. You decide what you're going to do?"

Woman had a point, but I rolled my eyes at the question of the day and puffed out my cheeks for Rhys to whack. He giggled, smacking my face. "Meet Morgana, then take Kennet and his posse to go get somebody's daddy. You see Socks anywhere?"

"He's in the guest room curled up around a heating pad. The temple put him into torpor."

Mmm. It had been cold, and having to move belly over stone probably didn't help. I plopped onto the couch, Rhys nuzzling at my breast. Time to make the donuts.

Gaia eyed the to-go container. "Anything good in there?"

"Nope, just Connell."

She started coughing. "You didn't."

I shrugged. "Shit happens."

"Mmm. Especially when you're in the room. That woman keeping him company?"

"You mean Stephie, the literal ex from Hell? No." I shifted Rhys. Man, he got bigger every time I saw him. I blinked back tears, I'd missed so much the past few weeks—damn it. I couldn't think about that right now, and his father had missed more. "I was thinking Brennan would want the honor of dealing with her."

Her eyebrow rose, and I could already hear the questions, but she only asked one. "Think that's wise?"

Probably not but…Okay, fine, I'll say it to you, though I just ignored her. If he offed Stephie, I'd know there wasn't anything between them. Like, it was over. If he couldn't…I don't know what I'd do, but when do I ever? I'd cross the Rubicon when I came to it.

Meanwhile, the Alps were gonna be a bitch, and I was fresh out of elephants. I pulled out my phone and shot a quick text to the All Father, letting him know I was still alive.

What? No way was I gonna let him know what I was doing. A big part of why I'd never caved to "being his" was he had this annoying tendency to tell me what I could and couldn't do. Well, duh, I didn't listen, but dealing with his ego was a serious buzzkill. If he knew I was going after Brennan...Yeah, no thanks.

"It was Connell in those pictures. He and Stephie framed Brennan. I'm pretty sure she set him up to get trapped in the Underworld, but I don't know why. Connell said she needed him for something."

"It ain't so much her, as Her," Dan said, chucking down the remote. He ran a hand over his bristly jaw and sighed at my terrified confusion.

Yeah, terrified. Why? Because there was only one She with a capital S. God's other half. Lady of the Underworld, Goddess of the Dead, et cetera, et cetera. Hmm? You thought a dude was the Big Bad? You'd be wrong, but that bridge is still for sale.

Hellooo...Hell hath no fury and all that. I mean come on, men can be dicks, but if you seriously think one can top a female in the torment department, you should spend some time in a middle-school girl's locker room. Heads-up, She's the preppy blonde already sporting a C-cup.

And She'd stolen my freaking boyfriend. I ran a hand over my face. "What does She want with Brennan?"

Dan shook his head like I was an idiot. "You don't get it. What he is, what we are...Being a Rider of the

Apocalypse isn't just some bullshit honorific, it's a job, and he hasn't been doing his." He stood and grabbed a beer out of the fridge.

"I thought Stewie—"

"Stewie isn't Brennan. He can lay it down enough to get shit done, but there's a reason Brennan's the boss. I ain't gonna get into it, but you got no idea what that man's capable of, and him comin' off the bench to play politician, trying to stop Her agenda from happening's been pissing Her off something fierce. We're supposed to be neutral."

And She was supposed to stay out of creation entirely. Crap. So much for that. But then Brennan had said he didn't give a rat's ass about politics because he couldn't, not because he wasn't good at it or didn't want to…and my lazy ass had pushed him into it.

"Give me one of those," I muttered, pointing at Dan's beer. He tossed one over. "I thought where the Riders went the Apocalypse followed." As in they were the ones that stirred shit up.

He rolled his eyes and took a pull of his beer. "She don't like the Big Man messing with things, and She ain't supposed to. The Riders were a compromise. His creation goes off the rails, we put the fear of God back into whoever's fucking things up, and She gets to play with the spoils. Brennan's been taking away Her toys."

I went numb. That was bad. Like really bad. Was he out of his freaking—yes. Yes, he was. Man was a fiend. I told you, they were all out of their goddamned minds. I pinched the bridge of my nose.

"So let me get this straight. Brennan's been slacking on the death-dealing front. She sends Stephie to convince him otherwise. He tells her to piss off. Stephie starts pushing the biometrics crap to force his hand, and when that didn't work, they roped me into it."

"Basically," Dan said, taking a swig off his bottle. "Connell should've been able to hold the geas for another century. You and the kid are Brennan's Achille's heel, and She's hell bent on getting him back under Her thumb."

You gotta know my head was throbbing at this point. "And none of you thought that it might be a good idea to clue me in on any of this?"

Dan squirmed, fiddling with his beer. "Jonas and him got into it over that a bunch, but—"

"Bros before hos?" The tips of his ears turned bright red. Asshole. "Do me a favor, next time he gets the bright idea to keep something like this from me, give me a heads-up so I can kick him in the nuts." Dan gave a sheepish nod, and I shook my head, exchanging a "freaking men" glance with Gaia.

"You're going to be late," she said eyeing the clock.

Crap, she was right. "My stuff here?"

Gaia waved at a tunnel leading out of the room. I handed her the kid and went to go find some jeans.

The guest room hadn't existed when Berk owned the place. I guess you could call it cozy, but it was basically a hole in the ground tricked out with batik sheets covering the walls and a futon. Socks was in the middle of it on that heating pad she'd mentioned, looking miserable. I stroked his scales, poor guy.

My stuff had been jammed into a gym bag, and I frowned. Karen and the other imps hadn't been real friendly since I'd come back from my mental break. I wasn't sure if they were pissed at me for buying into those pics, or because I'd roomed with the All Father while we were at the temple. God, nothing had happened—I mean, nothing serious. Okay fine, I made out with the guy. Excuse me for thinking Brennan had abandoned me. It wasn't like he didn't have just cause. I shoved my legs into my jeans, irritated that I was gonna have to explain myself to them. I wasn't telling him shit if I could help it.

Yeah, okay, I was more irritated that I'd fallen for the whole thing. If Brennan didn't kill that bitch, you better believe I would. Frowning, I dumped the bag out. Damn it, they'd only packed my tee that said "Pretend I'm a Carrot." What? I got lazy at Halloween, okay? I pulled the day-glow orange shirt over my head, grabbed a teal flannel, and my camo trainers, feeling all clash-y grunge, and poofed to pick up coffee.

Well, coffee and Morgana's foo-foo whats-it. No, fraps aren't foo-foo. They're for discerning connoisseurs. Anyways, I snagged a tray and poofed again to that sad-looking beach.

It was even sadder in person. The smell hit me like an arcade monkey had chucked a barrel. It was low tide, and garbage was strewn around the high waterline. To the north was a massive clanking power plant adding the stink of progress to the mix. Beyond that, buildings on top of buildings and the hum of too much humanity in one place. An oil tanker was docked out on the horizon, and the cold grey water screamed Atlantic…Wait a minute…anywhere in the world only a poof away, and she'd wanted to meet in New Jersey?

Man, there was something wrong with that girl. I scanned the beach again, then dug out my phone. It was seven, and she was nowhere—hold up. Closer to the waterline a bunch of cliffs jutted out, and it looked like there was a sea cave. Great. If I'd known I was going spelunking, I would've worn boots.

I picked across the beach and squeezed in sideways. You better believe that if I had to drop a coffee, it was gonna be hers. The floor dipped down, tide pools caught between the outcroppings of stone. This place must be totally submerged when the tides changed. A weird glow flickered beyond them.

I headed that way, the walls coated with some kind of a bioluminescent slime amidst the hanging curtains of green. Hmm? How would I know if it was seaweed or algae? I just know it stank. Some of the pools had rotting fish in them, and crabs were feasting. All of it seemed like a good omen.

Why yes, I did feel like I was doing something incredibly stupid, thanks for asking.

Anywho, the cave jagged, and beyond it was a large subterranean room. At the center was a pool. The stone was all slicked down with more of that glowing crap, and it was clammy. Hah. No, seriously, it was like I could see my breath, nasty wet cold. I stopped at the halfway point between the pool and the way out and set down the tray, wishing I'd snagged a macchiato—

The pool rippled, and Morgana pushed up from its depths.

Oh yeah, she was definitely herself. Beard, man hands, all of that was gone. So were the dangly bits. Trust me, I know. She was stark naked. The gills on the sides of her throat closed up, and she took a deep breath, her chest expanding.

That part of her anatomy still wasn't particularly impressive.

She walked over to an alcove and threw on a robe,

then started toweling off her hair like I didn't exist.

I didn't have time for this crap. "Hey, Morgana. You look good."

She snorted, turning and thrusting out one of those bony hips. "No thanks to you. You get my chai?" I waved at the tray, and she minced over to snag it. "You didn't spit in it, did you?"

"Nope." She took a sip. "Just peed."

"Liar, it doesn't taste like whiskey."

I snorted, and she actually cracked a smile. "So what's up?"

Her face went classic Morgana sour. "I need you to kill Aegaeus."

I stared at her, my jaw on the floor. What the hell do you even say to that? I mean, I wanted to after all that shit at dinner, but…"Why are you asking me? Why not Kyle or Berk?" Gaia. That stupid lump rose in my throat. I wasn't sure there was much left of Berk.

She rolled her eyes. "Because Kyle's an idiot and the All Father's too honorable. Berk wouldn't hurt a fly, and Gaia would say I was messing with the natural order of things."

Translation; I had no morals and didn't give a crap what I screwed up. She wasn't wrong, but that didn't mean what she was asking me to do was right. I rubbed my forehead, and her stupid foot started tapping.

"Look, I know you can. Do it the same way you drained those elementals at the mesa. Just suck him out of me."

"Morgana, elementals are one thing, but swallowing the droplet blew me to pieces, and that was before Aegaeus could use his powers. There's no way—"

"There is. I can hold his power if it's my time of the

month and he's sleeping. You don't understand, he's…he's crazy. Like certifiably talking-to-people-that-aren't-there insane. He's been letting Water run rampant on purpose to egg the normals on…H-he told them where the lesser faes' safe houses were."

My stomach dropped. "The halflings?" She looked away and I teared up. Damn it. "Morgana, I can't…look, I tried to send the normals an envoy after everything went to hell, but they'll only talk to Brennan. They think I killed him and started an inquest. If I try to kill Aegaeus and it doesn't work…They already want to take my kid…"

Morgana fiddled with her lid. "I know. There's this woman, I swear she's fae for all she acts like a normal. Her and Aegaeus are behind all the biometric stuff—"

"Stephie Morte?"

"Yeah, you know her?"

I sat down on a scummy rock and slurped my frap. "We've met."

"Look, I'll trade you both the favors that dae of yours owes me—"

"It's not about that." Seriously, it wasn't, but what it was…I couldn't quite put my finger on it and Lilith wasn't talking. "I have to think about it."

"What do you mean you have to think about it? He's a traitor to our kind and needs to die! Who cares what the normals want to do; it's not like they can."

Maybe not, but it wouldn't be pretty. I stabbed at my frap. "You don't understand, I'm not disagreeing with you, but all that elemental energy, his essence, it has to go somewhere, fast. I won't be able to hold it, and I don't know what will happen if I just let it go. Look, I'll text you as soon as I figure something out, okay?"

Morgana's shoulders slumped. "Okay, but it has to be soon. Right now is the peak of my cycle and he's out cold, but in another few days he'll become restless. We'll have to wait another month, and if he catches a stray thought while I dream…I don't know what he'll do." She shivered. "Right after we became…it was bad…"

God, she had that hollow look in her eyes that battered women get, and the asshole was in her head. "If I can do it, I will."

She sniffed. "I'll believe it when I see it." Her face crumpled, and she threw off her robe, diving back into the pool in one smooth motion. Whelp, that had definitely been her. I poofed back to Gaia's.

She was snoring in her bean bag with crumbs all over her kaftan. Dan was watching some black and white monster flick with Mab on his shoulder.

"Rhys sleeping?"

The pixie nodded and shushed me. Whatever. I grabbed a beer and tried to process what the hell was going on. It was pretty simple, actually. She, as in the Big Bad, wanted souls to play with, hence a war between normals and fae, and was pulling out all the stops to get it. I wondered what She had on Aegaeus. None of us would willingly work with Her…or wouldn't have. Maybe he really had lost his shit, but did he deserve to die for it? Ugh. The better question was if a true death was even possible for a primordial. I frowned at Gaia, wondering if her meditation on the subject had been fruitful or if that was just code for a nap.

I snagged a piece of Connell out of the takeout box and popped it into my mouth. Holy crap, that was spicy—I slammed my beer, getting the same rush of power I'd gotten before, and all hot and bothered. Damn it. I went into the guest room picking Gwinth out of my teeth, hoping I could catch a few z's before this next bit of fuckery I was about to engage in.

Rhys was in his porto-crib out cold, and I lay down on the futon. It wasn't long before I was out, too.

I dreamed.

It was part of that missing piece, the void in my memories. It fell somewhere around the time I was hoofing it back to the garden. Remember those angels that had tried to convince me to do just that? Yeah, the whole beginning-of-fae thing. God got pissed and doubled down, offing our kids.

Anyway, when that happened, each of the angels took their remaining children and scattered. Before you get too down on them, I told them to do it, hoping they would be spared. They were, but He didn't let the angels off easy. He exiled them from Heaven, cursing them to roam the Earth until the End of Days, which was basically like making them peel potatoes for eternity.

Cue His whole taking-personal-responsibility kick. Beyond exile—since they'd been so hot to donate genetic material—He laid down that they were damned well gonna cultivate it. The two that took the names Samael and Aegaeus got to keep their dangly bits, but the last of them He transformed into a female, and Gaia was born. God's big on symmetry. All that yin-yang crap she's always harping on she gets from Him.

Anyways, They were pissed. Which I could totally understand; I mean, I'd gotten them kicked out of Heaven, and Gaia wasn't super keen on having to pee sitting down. That whole cultivating your offspring edict? Yeah, not so much. Remember free will? They exercised it. Me? I was lying low after Socks slipped Eve that apple, and Adam was all WTF over God evicting the two of them, too. Let me just say, shitty mood didn't even come close to describing His frame of mind.

Man, His other half had to be laughing Her ass off.

So what do You do when You're an omnipotent being and a creation that took You six days of mind-numbing labor and an infinite amount of cosmic materials goes awry?

Well, You're not gonna scrap it and admit that You fucked up.

He did what any guy would do. Uninstall the program, and reboot the hard drive. Problem solved. Aegaeus, Samael, and Gaia woke up one morning with no memory of Heaven or ever having been celestial beings. In place of it, they were each tied to an element. Me? I got called to the principal's office. See, I wasn't modeled on Him; I was modeled on Her. This was an issue, inasmuch that He hadn't the faintest clue how Her mind worked, which meant He couldn't change mine.

Yeah, He didn't make that mistake again. They literally broke the mold after me.

Anyways, She pitched a fit when He suggested hitting my delete button. Something about me being the only redeeming quality in all His creation. You can imagine how that went over, and sitting in the hall listening to Them go at it behind closed doors was probably when I first started pissing myself. When He called me back in, I got hit with the same punishment as the other three, with the added caveat of no more kids or else, keep your mouth shut, and have a nice life. Oh, and here's some fire. I hope you burn.

Please, I think we all know He's got a vindictive streak.

Whatever, the reset worked. Fae actually became, I dunno, fae, and if nothing else, I kept my mouth shut, as for the rest—

Rhys was squalling.

I rubbed my gummy eyes and picked him up, swearing. Kid had blown out his diaper and crap was all the way up his back. God, that was disgusting! He'd gotten it in his hair—Ugh, my hair!—Forget wet wipes, I needed a damned garden hose. I incinerated his onesie and took him into the shower with me. When we got out, there was a text waiting for me from Kennet. Shit, I'd slept way longer than I'd planned. I shot him one back and shingled into my leathers. Not gonna lie, that was handy.

Gaia was making pasta, and the other two were playing pachisi. They all looked up when I came into the room.

She raised an eyebrow. "You going?"

I kissed Rhys's chubby cheek and handed him to her. "Yeah. You got him?"

"Girl, you know it."

I laughed and snagged two of those stupid pills and an empty baggie from the counter, turning to Dan. "Keep the kid safe." He gave me a grunt that made me feel way better than it probably should've from a guy with all his game pieces blockaded by a pixie.

Mab zipped to my shoulder. "I'm going with you."

"Seriously?"

"Yes, Seriously. I rode with the hunt for centuries, and I'm in your service. I'm going." She crossed her arms over her chest and stuck out her jaw. I shrugged.

"Okay." Far be it from me to tell anyone what they can and can't do. I gave Rhys one more kiss, breathing him in. "New-baby smell, new-baby smell…"

Gaia cocked her eyebrow.

"What? You told me I needed a mantra."

She smirked at me. "Whatever works."

Yeah. Hopefully this would. I filled up the baggie with some Connell-to-go and popped another piece into my mouth.

Poof.

0 Days, 0 Hours, 35 Minutes

So timing has never really been my thing. The surge of power from my impromptu snack hit me when I poofed into the parking lot of that shitty hotel the host had holed up in. Kennet was front and center, his head-to-toe denim ensemble resplendent in the flickering glow of the parking lot lights. Forget his calves, his glutes had them way beat. Man should wear a Canadian tux more often.

Yeah, that stupid compulsion to get it on with someone from the hunt was still in effect. His eyes got real big, and he tried to take a step back, but the jean jacket he'd traded the kilt for made a great hand hold.

Yep. I totally kissed him. With tongue.

Lots of tongue.

In my defense, I snapped out of it pretty quick, but not before he'd leaned into it and copped one hell of a feel. Damn it. I turned bright red and flicked a hand at Mab snickering against my neck.

"Sorry, lass, but there isn't a man alive who wouldn't have enjoyed that while it lasted."

Well, duh, but that didn't make it any better. He was practically my father-in-law. He grinned like he knew it and didn't care. Two other fae came to stand behind him. Some sour fishy-looking dude named Sal, and Vinny was straight-up the biggest dae I'd ever seen outside of the Riders.

Introductions finished, Kennet turned back to me. "Ye ready for this?"

"As ready as I'm gonna be. We're going to the hub?"

"Aye. Should be able t'get right t'the Ninth Circle through it. After that, ye'll have t'track him down by his band."

Whoa there, cowboy. "That'll work, but my powers won't?"

"S'right. Power's self-contained, like the Gwinth's geas, though ye'll be stuck in whatever form ye enter in. Whoever said death's the great equalizer was on the money. Powers, curses, they all draw from yer element and can't pass into the Realm of the Dead. A fae's shade isn't any different from a normal's till they work off whatever karma's staining their spark and get recycled back t'their element."

Yep. Blinking. How did he know so much about this stuff?

"The wee lass needs t'stay out of sight, and ye boys are gonna have t'put on normal-wear."

They grimaced, but after a moment Vinny's bulk condensed by half, and he lost the tusks. Sal's gills disappeared. Yep, now they both looked like a couple of regular thugs.

Kennet rubbed his hands together, way too excited. "Right then, we're off."

Poof.

We materialized in a parking lot in front of, I shit you not—

"The hub to hell is in a cheap-ass Vegas superstore?"

For reals. It was Wal-Corp west of the strip, just past

Chinatown. Calista used to send me here to pick up her stupid vape pods. What? It was the only place that carried the scout cookie variety, and anything that chilled her out, I was all for.

"It ain't in Bloomingdell's, sweetheart," Sal said all smirky. Vinny sniggered. Jerks.

"Aye, and they don't call it Sin City for naught." Kennet shot me a grin over his shoulder, and they started walking. I might've shot the bird at Sal before I followed.

Okay, I totally did.

The automatic doors slid open, and we went right in, the funk of desperation and past-its-prime deli meat greeting us along with Herman, the normal in the blue vest manning the door. We were well acquainted. Looked like he got new tennis balls for his walker. Someone was moving up in the world, albeit super slow. I waved.

He fumbled for his walkie-talkie. "You! Stay out of aisle nine, and I'm calling security to frisk you before you leave, missy!"

What? I said we were well acquainted, not friends.

I rolled my eyes at the guys' snickers. Whatever. Like they'd never gotten snagged for pinching a bottle of nail polish or seven—never mind. You know what I mean. Jerks. We followed Kennet down the aisles of haphazard merchandise, my eyes lingering on the pile of flannels shoved onto one of the shelves. My steps slowed. Hey, that looked just like my favorite green waffle-sleeved hoodie that'd gotten fried with the Priory—

"Ye comin', lass?"

The guys had stopped, snickering again. Goddamn it, that was freaking annoying. I stomped past them.

Whatever. I'd come back. Yeah, I'd shop here, you got a problem with that? No way can you beat those prices, or their lax security. Tarjay had way more cameras.

"It's the wrong green for your eyes," Mab shrilled in my ear. "Too olive."

"Okay, Karen," I grumbled, missing the imp. And I liked olive. Screw my eyes.

Kennet led us to the frozen food section and perused the cases with a frown. Guess he wasn't a TV dinner kind of guy. Wasn't really my jam either, not now anyways. I'd OD'd on orange chicken in high school. The Priory's food had sucked, and it was way worse at Vel Parochial, one of their many misguided attempts to indoctrinate the community. Whatever, it went belly up right before I graduated.

What? No, the flaming streaker incident didn't have anything to do with—okay, maybe it did, but it totally wasn't my fault. How did you even hear about that?

Look, it doesn't matter. Focus. Kennet had stopped and was checking out the hot wings and taquitos. I went up alongside him.

"Hungry?"

"I've a cravin' for somewhat, but bar food ain't it." He opened the door, and a too icy cloud rolled out onto the floor, dry-ice style. "She'll know the moment we pass through, if She don't already. Be on yer guard." He grinned like a maniac and stepped through. My jaw dropped as he disappeared. No shit…The guys followed, and I hopped in front of Sal. No way was I gonna bring up the rear.

A horrible ripping sensation went through me, and we were in a bombed-out alley, the ground heaving beneath my feet. Nausea surged up my throat, and then the cold hit. Like, holy shit cold. The inside of my nostrils froze, and it felt like I was inhaling shards every time I drew a breath. Mab dove into the collar of my jacket and wriggled down to huddle in my cleavage. I was too busy wrapping my arms around myself trying not to puke to swat at her. I instinctively called fire—

And it came. Huh, what do you know about that?

The ground beneath us trembled again. Vinny and Sal were looking around like that wasn't supposed to happen. Them muttering amongst themselves didn't give me warm fuzzies, but I wasn't warm anything. Man, it was cold.

Kennet was at the crumbling mouth of the alley. He peered around a jagged corner and hotfooted it back, his brow creased. "I dunno what that was about. Can ye—" He stopped dead to stare at me. "Yer not cold?"

"Nope." I mean, I wasn't comfortable, but I wasn't gonna get frostbite. I flicked a braid over my shoulder. "Fire came when I called it." So there.

The others' brows wrinkled in concentration. A flame bloomed in Vinny's palm—

And black hell-flame rose up to eat it, the ground shaking again. He screamed—

Nope. He was a pile of ash.

New mantra. No open flames, no open flames.

Sal abruptly looked very glad he hadn't been able to access his power. Kennet chewed at his lip, watching what was left of the dae blow away. "Don't suggest ye do that."

Ya think?

The stupid alley started closing in on me, and I wanted out. Like, I had the worst feeling I wasn't supposed to be here. I reached for the wall we'd come through and hit solid brick. What the hell?

"How are we getting back?"

"Not that way," Sal said.

Well, duh. "Thanks for the update, Captain Obvious."

The asshole saluted me. God, we would get stuck with him.

Kennet scratched his jaw. "We get back with my boy or not at all. He'll be able t'get us topside through shadow."

I shot him a look. Would've been nice to know I was buying a one-way ticket to Hell before I'd left my kid with a babysitter. "They just leave it open like that for anyone to wander in?"

"Yes and no…" Kennet's voice dropped off as he scanned the broken tops of the surrounding buildings. They looked like they'd been tenements at one point, but I'd be surprised if anyone was living there now. I mean, beyond the fact everyone here was dead.

Yeah, I was trying not to think about that, but it was hard. Like, everything was creepy quiet except for the wind howling through. It carried flakes of ash with it, and drifts of the stuff were everywhere. My hair must've looked like a walking dandruff-shampoo commercial. Stupid fishy Sal was definitely a poster boy. He riffled his and—boom—it was snowing.

Kennet's attention came back to me. "Normals can't pass. Nor can fae unless they've been touched by death. All in the hunt have, and I suspected ye'd qualify as well. Can ye sense him, lass?"

But I hadn't been touched by death. Maybe he meant in a metaphorical/Biblical sense. I'd been touched by Brennan plenty. And now I had to find him. Sal tapped his wrist like he was wearing a watch. I glowered at him and swallowed the lump in my throat, not looking forward to getting hit with that burst of arctic again, but there wasn't anything for it. I rubbed my hands and blew on them, then shoved them back under my armpits. It was like the cold had dipped just for me, and the others were turning blue. Crap, I needed to get this over with. If finding Brennan didn't kill me, the cold was going to take out everyone else. I concentrated on him, and my eyes flew open.

"He's close." And that debilitating arctic blast hadn't been there, but I would've almost preferred it. The mash-up of anger and despondence I was feeling from him…"We need to hurry."

Kennet stepped back. "Lead the way."

So, what can I say about the Ninth Circle of Hell? Well, it's a whole lot of grey. Like zero color. Zip, zilch, nada. Other than that, it's pretty much how you'd expect a metropolis to look after it'd been hit by a nuclear bomb umpteen times. Clouds roiled above, and there wasn't any sound, other than us picking through the streets.

Don't get me wrong, the guys were on the prowl, but this place…whole 'nother level. It was freaky. When the wind dropped off, a funky murk came up from the ground making our footing dicey. The stuff puffed up beneath our boots and hung at knee level before it was whipped away again. Shells of buildings lined the pitted streets, and those were choked with debris and drifts of ash. Odd fires burned sporadically throughout the ruins with black hell-flame.

Oh yeah. Rhys was definitely pulling his power from here. Trust me, I wasn't thrilled. About that or the awful feeling of being watched. Things moved at the corner of my eyes, but weren't there when I looked. After a while, I stopped trying to catch a glimpse of whatever was there, afraid of what I'd see. Impending doom pricked between my shoulder blades and sped my steps.

"Easy, lass. Ye don't want t'run. That'll draw them out like naught else." Kennet's voice was tight, and his hand had drifted beneath his jacket. Sal had pulled out some serious bladeage.

I didn't even have a nail file. "How much farther?"

It felt like we'd been walking forever, but Kennet said time moved slower in Hell. You know, same as the DMV. I think the standard conversion is an hour forty-five for every seven minutes. What? It's a legit phenomenon. Look it up.

Anywho, we'd come to one of those stupid rotary things in the road, and I stopped, concentrating on Brennan's band. I couldn't understand it, we should be right on top of him—

Crap. We were right on top of him.

"Which way, lass?" They'd flanked me, looking out into the murk.

"I think he's below us."

Kennet grunted. "Well, that's gonna be a problem. Envy, yer with me. Sal, try t'find the way in. Half a Twain count, then regroup."

"Twain count?"

"Six hundred Mississippis is ten minutes. I'm givin' him five," he murmured, peering past the rotary, then moving in that direction like he'd seen something.

I picked through the rubble after him. Was there something there? Shit, there was, a body in the road. Yeah, I meant *in* the freaking road. Part of it at least. My breath caught. It was the wrong shape to be Brennan, but no less familiar.

Stewie was splayed out in a trench, half buried by shattered stone. The faintest haze of breath came from his slack jaw. Kennet moved some of the rubble, and I wiped the grime from his frozen skin. I'd say he looked like death, but I called him the Crypt Keeper for a reason. Still, he didn't look good, even for him, and none of his wounds had healed...Crap, did that fall under powers?

Kennet sat back on his heels and sighed. "Shite. It's too late, lass. Leave him be." He stood, and I glared up at him.

"What? No. I'm not leaving him here to die." Not when I was packin' two faes worth of adrenochrome and could use it. Kennet went to say something, and I ignored him, lip-locking Stewie and slowly breathing some of that stored-up essence into him. What? Like I hadn't been kissing everyone else.

The ground rumbled, and it took way too long to jumpstart him, but once it caught, he took up what I was offering way faster than I'd expected. His wounds began to knit together, and then he coughed his brains out, shivering violently.

Kennet gripped his shoulders, steadying him. "What happened?"

"Kennet?" Stewie scrubbed at his face, blinking like he couldn't trust what he was seeing. I waved, and his face went grim. Well, you know what I mean. Grimmer. "Shit, Envy. You can't be here."

"And yet, here I am."

"No, you don't understand...She's got him, and he's not Brennan anymore."

All of a sudden I was rocking that monochrome look again. "You mean, like, *Her*, Her?" He nodded. Crap,

She really—"She's here? But She's not supposed to interfere." And personally dropping into creation definitely qualified, like above and beyond. For fuck's sake, God had only done voice-overs.

Stewie snorted. "Since when does She follow the rules? Brennan seriously pissed—"

"I know. Dan told me."

"He did?"

Forget about Her, his tone was pissing me off.

I stood, dusting off my leathers. "Yeah. Right after I figured out that it was Connell in those pictures and that bitch Stephie had set up the whole thing to incite a massive war to make Her happy. Thanks for not cluing me in—it was awesome getting jerked around, and I'd been due a nervous breakdown."

"Really? It wasn't him?" His relief almost made up for him being a dick, until he laughed. "Man, Jonas was gonna beat his ass…"

"Whatever. What do you mean he's not him anymore? Where are the other Riders?"

Stewie's mouth screwed up, and he looked away. "Brennan called shadow on us. The freaking Legion of the Dead, and I couldn't wrestle control away from him. The fiend is taking over. Last thing I remember, Frank and Jonas were in chains at Her side, and then She ordered the shades to leave me here." His gaze found me again. "You can't help him. If he turned on us…"

Yeah, yeah, bros before hos. My stomach cramped. Maybe not, but I had to try. He was here because of me. I owed him that much.

Fine, and I loved him. Shut up.

"She wanted us t'find ye," Kennet muttered, scanning the surrounding buildings. "That can't be good, but explains why none of them shades out there have made a play for us. Ye know how t'get below?"

Stewie nodded and clambered to his feet, wobbling. "Two streets over, there's a portal that drops into the undercroft. That's where they'll be."

"Then let's go." Kennet gave a weird whistle and helped Stewie back to the rotary. My eyebrow rose. Not for nothing, but I after all the adrenochrome he'd sucked up, I was pretty sure he was milking the whole weakness thing so he could get up close and personal with Kennet.

I caught Stewie's eye, and he totally blushed. Hah! I knew it! That sly devil.

"Down there, past those buildings," he said, waving at another side street. At the end, dim lights flickered. Sal caught up with us, and we headed toward it. I glanced at Stewie again.

"So what's the deal with the Legion of the Dead?"

"You'd think the name was self-explanatory," Sal muttered.

I glared at him, and Kennet cleared his throat. " 'Tis, t'a point. Think Envy's more curious about what Brennan's got t'do with 'em."

"Yeah." I stuck my tongue out at Sal, and he psh'd me. Jerk.

"He's Death." Stewie sighed. "They're his to command. Every soul in the Nine Circles. I could only compel Limbo, but I was never really a Rider, just filler."

I had a bad feeling he wasn't talking about the dancing under a stick kind of limbo. More like the incredibly boring, super-tedious, gouge-your-eyes-out-with-a-spoon kind of Limbo, which was one step up from Purgatory and Hell's waiting room. Personally, I didn't think that was anything to sneeze at, but Brennan could control all of them?

...You got no idea what that man's capable of...

Why wouldn't he—

Whatever, I added it to my growing list of WTF. Stewie looked super bummed about not really being Death. I wanted to say something to make him feel better, but whatever I did would probably make him feel worse, so I kept my mouth shut.

I know, would you look at me all adult-y. Well, that and stupid Sal was just waiting to rib me again. Trust me, I could tell.

The side street hit a main thoroughfare and across the rubble-filled way, twin torches of hell-flame flanked a gaping maw in the side of a building. The hair on the back of my neck rose just looking at it.

"He's through there?"

Stewie nodded, and Kennet stepped into shadow with him and was gone.

Crap. We followed, and I staggered at the heat that hit me once I was through. Like, it was hot enough for my frozen fingers to sting, and I started sweating. Did they make summer weight leather? I unzipped a good four inches of jacket and looked around. Mab peeked out, but for once kept her mouth shut. We were in the vestibule of a huge amphitheater, carved from pristine white marble. A cage of filigreed gold dominated its center, and the rest of the cavern was filled with screaming shades dressed like Roman senators and their wives.

I should explain. When I say screaming, I don't mean like, "oh, I'm being tormented and repent my evil ways." It was more like a bloodthirsty "fuck yeah, I'm gonna see someone's head get ripped off" screaming.

For real, the Underworld had an MMA ring.

For those of you not versed, MMA, or Mixed Martial Arts, as it's more formally known, is essentially a no-holds-barred pit match where two opponents in boxer briefs try to literally rip each other's heads off. Short of that, they deal as much damage possible to each other before losing consciousness. Seriously. It's super hot and makes boxers look like pussies.

And Jonas was one of the guys in the ring.

Judging by the amount of blood coating him and the lanky guy he was trying to kill, we'd come in near the end of the bout. Both of them were beat to shit. One of Jonas's tusks dangled by a thread. He reached up and ripped it the rest of the way off, then gripped it like a weapon, his footing slipping through the morass of gore beneath their feet. Oozing lines of red striated across older wounds, crusty with yellow pus and rimmed with green.

He wasn't healing either? I glanced at Stewie. His wounds were gone. Had it been the essence I'd given him, or just me showing up? For Jonas's sake, I hope it was the latter. He took a nasty claw swipe to the gut, and I swallowed the lump in my throat.

"I don't think we're in Kansas anymore."

"We never were in Kansas. Vegas is in Nevada, and that motel—"

"Will you shut up!" I spun to glare at Sal. "God! It was a figure of speech, asshat. You know, you didn't have to come."

"Nope, but I did, and the Kansas thing was trite, like most of what comes out of your mouth." He smirked like he'd just one-upped me. Ugh. Him and freaking Morgana should get married and have a hundred annoying fishy babies.

"You got a girlfriend? I know just the undine."

"Like I'd take dating advice from you." He snorted and cocked a hip, his arms crossed over his chest. Oh yeah. They were freaking soul mates. That settled, now I just needed to figure out how to evict Aegaeus from her body, and we'd be golden. I rubbed a temple, getting ahead of myself. One massive clusterfuck at a time, Envy. Pace yourself.

So, back to the marble cavern thingy we were in. Let me just point out I wasn't real keen being underground with all the rumbling that was going on, but aside from Kennet and Sal, everyone else seemed cool with it. Those shades in togas alternately lounged or stood on the wide stone steps, eating and drinking from low tables scattered about. The ones that weren't into the entertainment were having animated discussions about crap nobody actually cared about.

Seriously, to be or not to be isn't a freaking question. You are or you're not, and they were dead. Which did beg the question why they needed all that food. My stomach gurgled. Fruit, bread, and cheeses. Olives, whole roast birds, and freaking casks of wine—

"Wouldn't partake of the feast, lest ye fancy staying," Kennet said above the clamor, his eyes glued to the other side of the room.

So, remember I did this whole you-gotta-be-kidding thing about the hub to Hell being in a crappy superstore? Yeah, that. I take it back. Totally plausible. So was the fact that Kennet had locked eyes with freaking Calista on the other side of the room.

It was also no surprise that death became my mother. She was wearing a white stola with two wide purple bands at the hem. Hmm? Oh, same deal the Statue of Liberty has on, and the bands denote royalty. Because of course. Yeah, she looked good, but when did she not? Bitch. Whatever. That wasn't what had my hackles up.

She was reclined on my goddamned throne, and Brennan was in chains on the floor beside her. Shadow writhed around him, and he was all bulked up, horns spouting from his temples and curving to his chest. He was shirtless, rocking some badass military cargo pants and boots, and let me tell you—

Calista met my eyes and started petting him like a dog.

Oh, hell no.

Kennet grabbed my arm before I'd realized I'd lunged forward. "Ye know who that is, don't ye lass?"

"Yeah, my bitch mother."

He grunted. "Might be her form, but that's not Who's lookin' out her eyes."

I didn't give a flying fuck. I shook off his grip and marched across the room, hell bent on kicking Mommy Dearest's ass. Her smile widened, and she bent to whisper something in Brennan's ear. His head wavered like he was drunk as he lifted it, and the hatred in his eye when it landed on me stopped me dead in my tracks. Well, that and the full beard shadowing his hollowed cheeks. It was like six months of growth.

"You!"

His voice boomed over the clamor, and the noise level in the room dropped as shades turned to the new source of entertainment.

"Come to torment me again?" He looked me up and down and scratched at his jaw. Talk about Hell, that beard had to be making him nuts. More shadows trickled across the floor to writhe around him. "Leather's a new look. Let me guess, she wears it for the sylph before she fucks him. Not a chance you've gotten your spawn on her, for all you've made her eyes gold. She'd kill you first."

He thought I was Connell. My jaw dropped, and pain rippled over his face.

"I-I'm not—"

Someone in the cage went down hard. I glanced over. The gaunt man was on the ground, not moving, and Jonas was staring at his hands. The wounds that had sliced across him were half healed. He looked up at me, eyes wide, and I gave a little shrug. Guess it was me.

Brennan's bitter laugh snapped my head back to him. "Right. You're not."

I stepped closer, the marble beneath my feet trembling. Or maybe that was me, too. Shades returned to their seats to watch whatever was about to go down. God, I knew people. Serena and Mica, Horatio with Amelda and the Dowager beside him. Sister Reticence was frowning at me, and the rest of the nuns I'd fried in the Priory were in the front row, smiling and elbowing each other, like this was some big joke.

God, it was. On me and Brennan. How many times had Connell worn my form to taunt him? My eyes got hot, and I dashed at them, trying to hold my head high for all I was a freaking mess. This was way too much like being on stage.

"Gotten down all her little tells, haven't you?" Brennan's voice caught.

"Brennan, please, it is me. I sucked out the Gwinth's power—"

"Lies!" He lunged at me, and I screamed all shrill

and girly, cowering back. The chains brought him up just short of wringing my neck. They clanked and squealed as he strained against them. His skin bubbled with shadow, and the temperature in the room dropped. He fell back to crouch on the iced steps, glaring at me with gritted teeth, his breath coming fast.

Mine was, too. He'd seriously just tried to kill me.

Stewie had been right about the fiend taking over, but if he was Hers, why would She have him chained? I had to believe some part of Brennan was still in there...

Unfortunately, I was pretty sure that was the part that wanted Connell dead, which, as far as he was concerned, meant me.

I wrapped my arms around myself, face streaked with tears. That son of a bitch. Who knew how long Connell had been studying me, or what Stephie had heard through shadow. It all would've been twisted into one big mind fuck. I'd just gotten those pics and lost my shit. What had they shown him? I could feel how slippery Brennan's sanity was through the fae-band. He wasn't going to believe I was me. They'd made damned sure of that, and once he killed me, I had no doubt that bitch behind him would clue him in, and he'd break.

He saw me looking at his fae-band and growled, pulling a Gollum and hiding his hand from my sight. God, he'd gone feral...I dropped to my knees. Out of options.

Go elemental, get eaten by black hell-flame.

Say his name? No way could I get close enough to whisper it, and I wasn't gonna spill it to the entire room. Yeah, I could compel him, but I'd given him my word I wouldn't. If I broke it, the stigmata would be flayed from my back, and if I released him, his psycho ex Serena was right there in the front row, waiting to control him with his true name.

No matter how I sliced it, I kept coming up dead.

Brennan's chains clanked again as he shifted in his crouch, glowering at me.

I raised my face to look over his shoulder. At Her. Kennet was right. Calista was a vindictive bitch and cunning as hell, but I was used to her looking at me like I was something on the bottom of her shoe. This version pursed her cherry-pop smile like she was eating something delicious instead of being disgusted. But victory usually was, and I'd delivered it to Her myself. When I'd fallen to my knees, that last bit of my mother had peeled away. Her eyes glittered as they met mine. I had a bad feeling that She might be super pissed at Brennan, but She wanted something from me.

Why did I think that? Lilith was modeled after Her, remember? Which is how She'd known how to play me so hard…But I wasn't Lilith, and wasn't all Envy anymore, either. Maybe I could still piss in Her cornflakes even if She had totally screwed me over.

I went to open my mouth, and She snapped Her fingers, totally anticipating what I was going to say. Everyone in the room froze, save for the two of us.

Crap. I said it anyways.

"I would bargain."

Yeah, I know. Stupid. But fae can't resist making a deal, and I was betting that stellar character trait came from Her.

I was rewarded with Her smile stretching to Her ears. "With what? You're in an untenable position and have nothing I desire." She was full of shit. How did I know? Her thumb and forefinger were rubbing together.

Hello, tell. See, I'd been right about Her wanting something.

"No...but I desire to live, and You prefer to play with other people's coin." Lilith sure as hell had. It'd been way more fun setting up other people to take the fall for her shenanigans. Yeah, that whole VD thing's a prime example.

She laughed. "Perhaps. Let's hear it then. What bargain do you propose?"

"An hour with Brennan, alone." I licked my lips, trying not to see the frozen malevolence in his eye. "If I can convince him to return with me topside, You leave the realms and quit meddling in His creation, abiding by Your original covenant with Him."

Surprised rage flashed across Her face and was gone. "High stakes for Me, less so for you." She tapped Calista's veneers with a crimson nail. "I'll give you five minutes to get him to profess his undying love for you, and when you fail—"

"Thirty-minutes."

"—your soul belongs to Me."

Was She for real? Yeah, that Thou-Shalt-Not thing, the big one about selling your soul. I said as much, and She laughed, because of course She did.

"I wouldn't think you'd be afraid of flames."

I was of those black ones. "It's not so much the flames as pissing Him off."

She moued at me like I was an—ugh, whatever. "The primordials have never been subject to that clause. You really have to start reviewing your own contracts."

Hold the freaking phone. Say what? Why wouldn't we be—

Oh.

Yeah, I'd had one of those epiphany things. Let me walk you through it. So, when a fae dies, they return to their element after their karma's all settled. The primordials are the embodiment of the elements. Remember at the beginning of all this when I said I had more power than I knew what to do with, and that it trickled down to all the lesser dae? Our powers sustain those below us, which is why they trapped us in those stupid anathemas instead of killing us way back when.

I still didn't know what would happen to the four of us if these forms died, but if She owned my soul, it stood to reason that She'd hold sway over all of Fire.

Crap. By not making us part of the contract, God had given Her an option to buy into creation, and She wasn't just content to watch. She wanted to play with the plot lines. Worse, that feeling I'd had that I shouldn't be here? Yeah, I really shouldn't be here. Gaia was gonna have a fit about me messing with that natural-balance crap.

"Suss it all out, Lovely?"

My eyes snapped to Hers. Bitch.

She laughed again. That it was Calista's made it worse. "Are we agreed?"

That lump was in my throat. She had me over that damned barrel. I'd been betting on luring Brennan back with the promise of seeing Rhys…his crooked smile and that chubby dimpled cheek flashed in front of me. My stomach plummeted with the certainty that I was never going to see any of it again. Crap. I couldn't think about that. Come on, Envy, what would convince Brennan I was me in five freaking—

Shit. The only thing I could think of was something neither Lilith or Envy would ever do. Would it work? Ugh, it had to. Otherwise, I was up shit's creek and forget not having a paddle—you know what being in a boat does to me.

Time for a Hail Mary.

I swallowed my fear, trying not to piss myself. Stupid fraps. "Okay. Agreed. I get five minutes with Brennan to get him to say he loves me. If he does, You quit the realms immediately, abiding by Your original covenant with Him, and primordial souls become part of that soul-selling Thou Shalt Not."

She tapped that nail against Calista's veneers again and waved a hand. A massive stopwatch materialized behind Her, and I was in that cage with Brennan unfettered. "Agreed. Time starts…Now."

He lunged at me. I fell back beneath his weight and skidded a good ten feet across the nasty sand. His hands were around my throat, and my head slammed against the cage. Everything started to go grey…

Mab zipped out of my jacket. She hit Brennan square between the eyes, and a cloud of dust burst over him like a five-pound bag of flour had exploded. He fell back trying to get the stuff off him. I sucked in a gasping breath. God, I'd forgotten how fast the fiend was—

"Stop it, you stupid asshole! Don't you recognize the mother of your child?"

Mab went for his eye, and he jerked away again, swiping at her as she dive-bombed him and continued her diatribe. "You're pathetic! Falling for their bullshit—she didn't screw the All Father. I would know, since I've been picking up the slack, watching that darling boy of yours while Envy goes catatonic! You know what she did for you? She ate the Gwinth!"

I struggled onto my hands and knees, coughing and caught that freaking clock. A minute was already gone?

Crap. I was gonna puke, and it wasn't just from the concussion. I hadn't specified the standard of time. The crowd around us screamed for my blood, and She lounged back on my freaking throne smug as shit inspecting Calista's manicure.

I pushed back onto my heels, grabbing the side of the cage to steady myself and closed my eyes, and with nothing left to lose, I opened my mouth.

Yeah. I sang like my freaking life depended on it, because, duh.

"Candy..." The notes tore through my throat, rasping all smokey. It seriously sucked, but I couldn't think of anything else that would prove to him I was me. Sitting at that piano with him, the look on his face as his fingers ran through the notes. His smile, knowing how totally full of shit I was when I told him I didn't know the song because just the thought of singing made me want scrub all my skin off. I drew in a deep breath to belt out the next verse, deep and soulful—

The fiend let out a roar that shook the room, and I fell to my knees again, the air moving in front of me, and the horrible sense that he was inches away, about to strike. I scrunched my eyelids tighter.

"Shut. Up." The fiend's breath glazed ice over my cheek, its voice resonating through my bones with the crackling skitter of dead leaves on stone. A hand gripped under my chin, and razor-sharp claws sliced slow along my jaw, too sharp to hurt. Blood slicked down my throat and spattered onto my jacket, my death way too close.

I sobbed out the notes, not wanting to see him hate me, clinging to the memory of him holding Rhys that first morning, the look on his face when I said I wanted to be his wife. Goddamn it, I couldn't stop—

"*Shut. Up!*" He slammed my head back against the cage, light bursting inside my skull with each word, and I totally pissed myself.

The fiend drew in a sharp breath, and then I was in Brennan's arms. "No..." Rough fingers followed the slices at my jaw. "No...Oh God, it is you..."

My eyes cracked, everything grey and out of focus. "Tell me you love me—"

"Shit. What did I—" He was crying. "I do. I do love you. I-I'm so sorry..." His hands were on my face, coppery and slick.

Then he kissed me like it was goodbye.

0 Days, 0 Hours, 9 Minutes (Topside)
0 Days, 13 Hours, 5 Minutes (Hell)

As I'm sure you can imagine, She was not pleased.

It didn't help when an omnipotent voice gleefully boomed through the room. "Hah! Better start making Me that sandwich, Woman!"

Yep. The stakes for a quarter of fae's souls was a freaking sandwich. It better have been something good, like a *pan bagnat*. Hmm? Oh, fancy tuna salad on a baguette. PB&J would just be insulting; I don't care if She did cut the crusts off.

Anywho, under normal circumstances, I would've totally gotten off on sticking it to His other half, but trust me, there wasn't anything normal about what was going down. Sorry if this gets confusing, but there was a lot, and I hadn't been kidding about that concussion. Blood loss wasn't doing me any favors, either. Every time I blinked, Brennan fuzzed into conjoined twins that slowly sucked back together.

Yep, I barfed. Was a great complement to my piss-soaked pants. Man, that smell was never coming out of the leather. He didn't seem to mind, but I've said it before, and I'll say it again, love's gotta be a mental illness.

Anyways, She let out this furious screech and was gone.

Trust me, it wasn't a total win, and it was far from

over.

That marble colosseum? Poof. The cage and everything else disappeared, and we were in a vast subterranean cavern. Black hell-flame burst up from the floor casting a weird grey light, and it was chased by regular old fire lapping at the darkness.

Brennan's jaw dropped, and every shade in the room lost it. Seriously, their forms, their minds…They all became those shambling shadows, lumbering away from the warm yellow glow as fast as they could to converge on anything in the room that was living. Yeah, the dead aren't real keen on stuff that has a heartbeat.

I didn't know it at the time, but aside from us, that included Kennet and Sal, the missing Riders, and the Gwinth's heir. Don't worry, I'll come back to her. Apparently while I'd been drawing everyone's attention by getting the shit kicked out of me, Stewie had helped Kennet and Sal track down Frank. The Gwinth's heir was in the cell with him, and Jonas had been poofed into another when She cleared out the cage for my smackdown.

So, how do you fight a shade? Well, you don't. I mean, they don't have any substance, which makes them pretty much impossible to hurt, unless you've got something going on other than a blade. Kennet and Sal did, and let me tell you, holy Chuck Norris, that fish could kick ass, and Kennet was a wild man. Their weapons were some crazy multi-tool ninja shit spelled for any-and-every prey they might come across with the hunt.

The shades were not expecting to be that prey, and a pitched battle on the other side of the cavern ensued. Don't get it twisted—it's not like they could kill something already dead, but they could slice it up until it played that way. Hmm? Why didn't they come for us? Because Brennan had let out a growl when they started to advance, and if I hadn't already pissed myself, I would've then. The shades took the hint and kept a wide berth.

Well, yeah, I suppose he could've banished them from the cave, but cut him some slack. He had a lot on his mind. You know, the whole return-to-sanity thing, only to discover he'd most likely murdered me. I mean, I was bleeding out in his arms.

Right, I should probably do something about that. Hello, banshee adrenochrome…

Not gonna lie, that shit was coming in handy, but my control wasn't particularly nuanced. Shocker, I know. I may have broken into it a little too quick.

Yeah, think of one of those vacuum-sealed foam mattresses from the internet. It looks like a rolled-up yoga mat, but then you go to open it and all of a sudden you're flat on your back under a foot and a half of California king wondering what the hell just happened.

What can I say; that's a common position for me.

There was this godawful rumble, and a 5.0 ensued, shit falling from the ceiling and cracks crazing across the cavern floor. And that little bit of fire that'd been lapping at those black hell-flames? Not so little anymore. It burst up from below into freaking pillars of fire, consuming the stuff the same way it'd eaten Vinny. Me? Twisted-off baggies didn't even come close to what I had going on. I went rigid, like I'd been hit with a jacked-up defibrillator. My concussion and all the rest of it went poof, and the cavern snapped into focus. I sucked in a huge breath, rocketing up to sit.

Holy crap, that was a rush—

"My God, Lovely…" Brennan pulled me to his chest, weeping. Yeah, I like them strong and sensitive, got a problem with that? "You sang for me, and I didn't…I'm so sorry I didn't believe it was you."

"Wait. That wasn't what convinced you?"

"No, it was when you pissed yourself."

Okay, forget what I just said. I pushed away, smacking him. "Seriously?"

He grinned, and that dimple was a mile deep at the crooked end of it.

"God, you're a jerk!" And I was disgusting. I stood, shingling myself clean like I'd seen Connell do when we'd goo'd him—

The floor tilted with another rumble, and I fell against Brennan.

"How did you do that?" His face was ashen.

"I told you, I sucked out the Gwinth's powers. Shape-shifting was one of them. Cool, huh?"

"No, powers don't work in Hell." He looked around and swore. "Nor is true flame supposed to burn. Something's very badly awry. We need to get you topside."

I wasn't gonna argue, or explain. This place sucked. "Where's Mab?"

"The pixie?" He grimaced. "I'm not sure. I think I batted her somewhere that way…Damn it. I need to deal with the shades. She's pulling more of them from the Legion." Kennet and the rest of the guys were holding their own, but there were only five of them, plus the Gwinth's heir, and shades kept coming.

"She? But I—"

"No, not *Her*, her. Persephone." He said it with a

growl and left to deal with them. I went off in the vague direction he'd waved in. My Gwinthy senses kicked in, and I tracked down Mab in one of those freaking crevices, crumpled against an outcropping of stone. She'd hit hard, and one of her wings was smashed. I sent a puff of essence at her, hoping it would kick start her the same way it had with Stewie.

Cue more earthquakes. Oh yeah, they were definitely related to me using my power. Kennet had seriously miscalculated. I don't think he'd taken into account that I was a primordial. I was pretty sure that the whole reason Vinny had been able to call flame was because unlike Sal, who'd left Water behind, the source of his power had come with, and me being here was screwing with something hardcore.

Like, Hell's nostrils were totally flaring. Whoops.

Anywho—no dice on Mab's wing, but I wasn't going to push my luck and have the ceiling fall in. The fact that I was lucky enough for her mouth to work just fine would have to do.

"Ugh! Blow your vomit breath on someone else!" She gagged. "God, that's disgusting, have you put anything in your stomach other than beer and Gwinth?"

I sighed and held out my palm for her to climb onto. Why I even bothered…"You coming, or can I leave you here?"

"Your boyfriend's an asshole. Just look at what he did to my wing! You'd think with one eye his depth perception would've suffered more."

Yeah, I rolled mine, which is how I caught sight of Stephie creeping through the shadows in a chichi grey pants suit. She gripped Connell's bone dagger, her eyes on Brennan's back as he tried to deal with the shades inundating the others. He looked super pissed that they weren't snapping to. Like, as soon as he got one wave of them sorted, another came.

You gotta know, whatever she was planning wasn't gonna happen.

"Stay here." I set Mab onto a rock, then poofed behind that sneaky bitch and tackled her ass. Yeah, the cavern shook, but it was totally worth it. She faceplanted hard, the knife clattering out of her hand.

"You fucking—"

My fist smashed her mouth before another lie could come out of it.

"Agh, whore!"

Another tremor rocked the room, and I fell off her, then scrabbled back. "Me? You're the one trying to steal my boyfriend!" I decked her, and she clawed at my face. Yeah, she totally fought like a girl, by which I mean dirty as hell. Forget about fists, she was all about the hair pulling and biting. Fine by me. I spat at her and got my hands around her throat.

She raked her nails down my face. "He was my boyfriend first!"

"Only because you groomed him, you perv!"

"She promised me him! We had a bargain!"

We rolled around, the guys widening their circle for us, just freaking ticked by the show if I had to gauge by the comments. Well, of course they watched, they were guys, and hellooo, cat fight.

Whatever, I was on top again, slamming her head against the floor as I choked her. She was turning a really satisfying purple, it totally went with the pants suit. "I don't give a shit what She fucking promised you, he's mine!"

Her temple smacked a rock, and her eyes rolled up, head lolling. I pushed off her and kicked her a bunch. What? Like she didn't deserve—hands were on me, and I spun.

"That's enough, Lovely."

"Like hell—umphf—it is." Brennan's arms went around me, preempting another kick. I glared over my shoulder at him, breathing hard. He kissed my temple and handed me Mab. She gave me a thumbs-up, looking impressed. I tipped her back onto my cleavage.

Brennan raised an eyebrow as she settled between my boobs like they were beanbag chairs. "Don't worry. I've something far more painful planned for Ms. Morte."

And this was why I loved him.

So, I guess me beating Stephie's ass had broken her control over the shades, and Brennan took over, clearing the rest of them out. I don't know, something about Hell's hierarchy and her outranking him. Whatever, Jonas threw her over his shoulder and grinned at me.

"Nice job, Miss Kitty. Sure you ain't got some fiend in you?" His grin widened at my glare, and he adjusted himself. "Lemme know if you want some."

Eww.

"Psh, that was nothing," Sal scoffed. "You should've seen her sucking off the banshee we rode down. That was hot enough for me to think about doing her."

And double eww. I snorted, turning to the Gwinth's heir. I knew Brennan had gone to find her—Hmm? Oh, I had no doubt that's who it was. She looked just like Connell, with that same gap-toothed grin, but was way petite. Five foot, tops.

She was also clearly pregnant. I raised an eyebrow.

"How…"

"It's as I said, lass. Curses don't keep in Hell." Kennet smirked at Frank, and the big dae scratched the back of his neck with a stupid grin.

Whoa, she was banging Pestilence? Huh. I guess there really was somebody for everyone. Though after seeing Connell's true form, it was no wonder bugs weren't a dealbreaker.

She held out a hand for me to shake, and a charge passed between us, the geas straining toward her. "You must be Envy." Wow. Her voice was all smoke and molasses, I wondered if she sang jazz. "I'm Neara. I think you have something of mine."

No time like the present, and it clearly wanted out. I shot a glare at stupid Sal, still flapping his dumb lips. He was such a liar. I'd been way too busy killing the banshee to cop a feel.

"Yeah, pucker up."

She moved closer and put her hands on my waist. I gotta tell you, it was totally bizarre kissing someone shorter than me. Like, I could totally see how guys got off on being bigger than who they were making out with.

I mean, not that I did. Much.

Anywho…I willed the geas into her, happy to be rid of the damned thing, and it was pleased as punch to say sayonara to me. I ended the kiss, and Neara pulled back, putting a hand to her lips all flustered. She looked up at me through thick black lashes, the gold of her eyes scintillating. Man, I had to have been smokin' with that going on. I mean, more than I usually am.

"We should get together sometime," she said, wetting her lips.

Jonas shifted his crotch again. "If you do, I want in."

I snorted, and another tremor went through the room. Hmm? No, pretty sure that one was just coincidence. At least I didn't think I'd done anything.

Brennan put an arm around me, eyeing the cavern. "As enjoyable as that was to watch, we need to go." The vestibule wasn't far, but when we got there he swore. Where the portal had been was a solid wall. He scratched at his beard. "Well, that's bloody inconvenient."

"I could poof us—"

"No. I don't think it's wise for you to use your powers. I'll take us home through shadow from here. Link hands." We did, and he stepped into the darkness, but didn't fade like usual. His mouth twisted, and sweat broke out on his forehead. There was a weird grinding sensation, and then we were on the street.

Like the street above in Hell. Brennan stumbled and sat on the curb, his head drooping.

I put a hand on his shoulder. "What happened?

"I don't know, but it isn't good…It feels like shadow's sprung a leak, and it's taking my power with it. It's not stable enough to travel topside. We're going to have to ride the circles." He looked up at Jonas, and the big dae gave a nod, putting his fingers in his mouth. An earsplitting whistle sliced through the air, followed by the sound of hooves clattering through the streets.

Four horses resolved out of the swirling ash. One white, one pale, one red, and one black.

Holy crap.

Look, I'm not talking Kentucky Derby horse. These were thoroughbreds the size of Clydesdales, saddled in black leather that ate the dim light. The pale one ambled up to lip at Brennan's ear like it was worried. I say pale because I can't really tell you what color it was. Nothing was quite right, like ashy, but almost a green, kind of a weird curdled yellowish, I dunno. It sounds horrible, and it was, but in a really awesome way. Like I wondered if the Dumper's paint department had something close I could do the stupid blue room over in.

Whatever, Brennan rested his head against the horse's muzzle, rubbing a hand along its jaw, and I felt a pang, missing Socks. Well, yeah, I felt a pang for Brennan too. Moving us through shadow had seriously messed with him.

Jonas tossed Stephie over the white horse's back like a sack of laundry, and Frank lifted Neara up onto the black one. "Stewie, you got Kennet on War's ride. Who's taking the fish?"

Yeah, nobody jumped at the opportunity.

"Och, stick Sal with us. Weight wise makes the most sense," Kennet muttered, pulling himself onto the red horse. I bit back a smile when Stewie got on behind him. Trust me, so did he.

Brennan stood and laced his fingers together for my foot. "Up you go, Lovely."

Up I went, and let me tell you, this was no petting-zoo reject. I can't even explain how it felt to be up on that thing, other than surreal. Brennan settled behind me, the saddle morphing to fit us both. Yeah, it was way cool, but the exhaustion I was feeling from him was not. He was totally trying to play it off, but I could tell from the way he held himself that it was bad. The ground trembled as he took up the reins, and the horse danced, tossing its head.

"Don't be alarmed when we travel," he said, kissing my temple. "Avita adapts to the terrain. You're perfectly safe." Then he grinned. "I've never taken anyone out on her before."

I opened my mouth to ask what he meant by adapt, but we were off, galloping through the streets. Buildings went by at a blur, and I swear half the time Avita's hooves never touched the ground. Time may move slower in Hell, but on that horse, man, you wouldn't know it. We flew through the city and out onto a blighted plain. The rubble from the streets disappeared, and Avita's form melted, lowering to the ground, and between my thighs, the horse's muscles turned to metal.

I stiffened, and Brennan chuckled, leaning forward and revving the motorcycle. It shot forward, and my eyes streamed as we picked up speed. Holy crap!

He made for a structure in the distance. It was a bridge of twisted iron. Spikes jammed into the sides of a rocky ravine riddled with caves. I looked down as we careened across it, shades seething beneath us in tumultuous waves.

"The Bolgias in the Eighth Circle hold the fraudulent," Brennan said, his smile brushing my ear. "Mostly politicians. Corresponds to the pharmacy's consultation window at the hub."

Psh, that sounded about right. We zipped over ten bridges in total, and it wasn't a straight shot. How he could tell where we were...

There were no landmarks, and the sky was occluded with roiling clouds. Ash still fell, and my eyes watered from the wind. Ahead, a glow was on the horizon. We slowed, and the motorcycle morphed back into a horse. That was so freaking weird. Did they take gas, or eat? Brennan held out a hand, and a thick ebony staff appeared in it.

"Cool trick."

His grin was feral. "Just wait." He did something and a curved blade snicked out from it.

Come on, he had an actual scythe? I laughed. "Is that thing for real?"

"You want to touch it?" He brought it close as we crested a rise. I slid my fingers down the smooth shaft, a tingle shooting up my arm. "Mmm. My, you've been naughty while I've been away. Connell, a banshee...Been dealing a bit of death yourself, haven't you?"

Oh yeah, he was totally turned on by it. I might've scooched back against the evidence. All right, you know I did. "Maybe."

He chuckled low in his throat, his lips at the nape of my neck. "My God, I've missed you. Tell me, did you really eat him?"

"I've got some Cajun fae tips in my pocket if you want a piece."

Avita had been picking her way down into a low valley. Ahead, the ground was sundered and broken, the chasms filled with rivers of crimson, seething and bubbling between the jagged outcroppings of rock. Shades thrashed about, howling in the depths. A dog bayed way too close, and I flinched.

"Perhaps I'll try some later. This is Violence, the Seventh Circle. It can get a bit dicey." And no, he didn't sound upset at the prospect.

I wasn't as excited. "Gun counter?" Ugh, that totally squeaked out when I said it.

"Video game console in aisle twenty-six." He glanced over his shoulder at the others. Jonas had his morning star out, and Frank was packin' a massive crossbow. Sal and Kennet were all geared up, too. Nope.

I was definitely not excited. Brennan clicked the reins. "Right. Here we go."

Avita went from a sedate meander to a full bore gallop in, like, 0.02 seconds. I screamed, then the freaking ground dropped away and we were airborne. Brennan laughed like a maniac, and that damned horse had to have been part goat the way it leapfrogged across those splinters of stone. My teeth chattered as we hit another, and Brennan's scythe flicked out, taking off a shade's head before I'd even known it was there. I mean, granted my eyes had been closed, but it happened super fast. There was the clank and thunk of Jonas's morning star behind us, and something other than a shade screeched.

Another something flew low overhead, and the scythe flicked out again. This time a woman screamed. "Damned harpies," Brennan muttered, looking skyward.

Above us, huge winged creatures spiraled over the fractured land. A twang sounded, and one of the misshapen creatures plummeted, the rest veering off to circle for another pass. Ugh, they were part woman, part bird, and totally hideous.

Other things came at us. I'd describe them and the Rider-induced bloodbath, but I was pretty occupied not freaking out or falling off the damned horse. Gradually the gaps where we had to jump became fewer and stunted trees began to dot the craggy landscape. Whatever the guys had been fighting off was left behind, and Avita slowed to an amble, blowing out through her nose.

"Yes, I think a break is in order." Brennan patted her neck and made for a grove. Twisted and bare of leaves, the trees clung to crumbling bits of earth between the outcroppings, their roots dry and exposed.

He stumbled as he dismounted. I flipped onto my belly and slid off, 'cause I'm super graceful, and went to him. He'd sat down against a boulder, his head back and his eye closed. The others were talking together in low tones, watching the sky. I sat beside him, and he put his arm around me.

"Are you okay?"

His brow knit, and I didn't much like it. "I'm weaker than I should be, and Hell's denizens can sense it. The harpies and the rest of them never would have challenged me otherwise."

I swallowed the lump in my throat, feeling like it was somehow my fault, because let's be honest, it probably was. "So what, are you, like, the boss down here?"

He snorted. "Hardly. More like the muscle." He glanced over at Stephie, still out cold over Jonas's saddlebow, then at Kennet. Something passed between them. Brennan frowned and dug into his pocket. He set his cigarette case aside, and then pulled out my ring.

"Jonas told me what they put you through. I don't blame you for thinking the worst, but I wasn't unfaithful to you, Envy. I hope that you'll take this back."

You know I wanted to grab the stupid thing and shove it onto my finger, but I didn't. He wasn't getting off that easy. "Maybe I wouldn't have if you'd told me about her."

He grimaced. "I've been hating myself for that. I felt your pain, and when you took off your band, the fiend…I lost my grip on it. The echo of everything through shadow after I couldn't—He was the one that found you, wasn't he."

Yes, he meant Kyle/the All Father, and yes, he still

said it all sour.

"He did, and it's a good thing. I was seriously messed up."

Brennan grunted, biting his lips to stop from asking what I knew he was dying to. I pretended not to notice for like a hot minute before taking pity on the poor guy.

"Nothing happened." His eyebrow cocked like I was full of shit. Okay, so maybe I was. "Ugh, fine, we made out, but I couldn't do it."

"No? Why not?"

"I don't know. I was so freaking mad at you, I should've. I just—it felt wrong. Like I was doing something wrong. Happy?" I crossed my arms under my boobs, and Mab almost fell out. Damn, I forgot she was there. Brennan zipped up my jacket, entombing her.

"Very. More so if it means you'd like this back…?" He waggled the ring between his thumb and forefinger, and my stupid eyes got hot.

"Yes."

That eyebrow of his cocked again. "To all of it?"

God, I wanted to punch him and screw his brains out at the same damned time. Why do men have to be so freaking needy? Whatever, I was still mad. "Not until I get the skinny on Mrs. Robinson over there."

Brennan laughed and scratched at his beard. He picked up his cigarette case, and it fell open. So did his jaw. "Bloody hell, they regenerated. It's not just you…All of our powers are bleeding in…" His eyes met mine, and he wasn't happy.

I shrugged. "Sorry?"

He took out a cigarette and tapped it on his knee. Crap.

"I suppose it is what it is, and hopefully that's not

permanent." He dug out his Zippo, frowning at its warm yellow glow when he struck it. Not that it stopped him from lighting up, and I swear to God, by the look on his face, he might've come when he took that first drag.

"God, that's good...It's been months since I've had one of these..."

"Maybe you should quit."

"Not bloody likely."

I rolled my eyes, and he grinned. The sky had darkened, and the clouds churned above like a storm was rolling in. Did Hell have storms? Probably, it had everything else that sucked. On the other side of the grove, Jonas was setting up a few low tents. Looked like we were gonna be here for a while. Brennan exhaled with another satisfied sigh.

"Okay, you got your fix, now spill it."

He shrugged. "You know Stephie sent me back from shadow. She kept tabs on me after, checking in every spring. Taught me to play piano when she discovered I had an ear for music, and our relationship...progressed. When I took the position of Death, she began asking for favors. Small at first. A battle here, civil war there. At first I wasn't opposed, though it wasn't strictly within the guidelines, but the scale of incursions she was asking for steadily increased and she became more, ah, invested in our arrangement."

Jonas waved at us, then pointed to one of the tents and jerked his head at the sky. It'd gotten seriously ominous. Guess they did have storms. Brennan nodded, and Jonas hefted Stephie over his shoulder and ducked into one of them.

Invested. "She wanted a child, didn't she."

He nodded, blowing out a long stream of smoke.

"Along with exclusivity. I wasn't of the mind to give her either. At that point, Serena had struck my fancy. Persephone and I fought, and I told her I was done. I wouldn't be surprised if she was the one who put Serena up to wheedling part of my name from me, probably hoping it would send me crawling back to her. She wasn't pleased when I went to my mother instead."

"I'm assuming they weren't besties?"

"Quite the opposite. Stephie was furious, and once Amelda banded me, leashing the fiend, that was the last I saw of her for centuries. Then this spring she called, wanting to start things up again. She was already entrenched in normal politics and had no qualms about using her connections or her knowledge of Fae to leverage Her agenda. All of which I was assured would go away if I took my place beside her and gave her a child."

"I figured she was banging Connell."

Brennan shrugged. "Probably. In my experience, fae ladies get desperate around the two-millennia mark when they feel their fertility waning, though Persephone's past that by a century or two. She's older than Amelda was, and I was the last child my mother could bring to term."

"And how long ago was that?" Jerk was stupidly elusive about how old he was. I don't know why. I mean, yeah, I was only twenty in this incarnation, but Lilith had everyone beat.

His lips pursed around a smile. "The summer of 1278."

My eyes rolled up. No, not—I was trying to do the math. Seven hundred and forty-three, no, four. Whatever. That was basically the equivalent of late twenties for a fae.

"So, I don't get it. The whole job/politics thing. Dan said you were taking away Her toys and had to be a neutral party—"

"I was being neutral." He flicked his cigarette butt behind some rocks. "What She was doing violated Their original covenant, and She knew it. I'm sure that's why She roped you into it. Bitch knew I'd do anything to keep you and Rhys safe."

"He has your smile."

Brennan's grin was like the sun rising. "Does he?"

I nodded, snuggling against his chest. "I miss him."

"As do I. You have a beautiful voice, Lovely. You should sing to him." My eyes got hot, and he kissed my temple. A drop of rain struck the back of my hand and sizzled. I pulled back, wiping it on my pants.

"Shit, that burns!"

"Only if you're a sodomite." Brennan chuckled, nipping at my ear.

"You would know."

His hand ran across my cheek. "I would at that, and it does sting, doesn't it? We best claim one of those tents." The others were already undercover, and the horses had disappeared.

What Jonas had set up wasn't anything to write home about. He'd left us the smallest one, and we had to crawl in. It was pitched like a triangle and the amenities were limited to a hefty glow stick, a blanket that smelled like horse, and it zipped shut. As soon as we were in, the sky opened up and the slanted sides jumped with sizzling rain.

I rubbed at my hand. That drop had left a welt the size of a penny. "Will it burn through?"

"Shouldn't," he said, stretching out beside me. Poor

guy couldn't even sit up. "These are crafted from shadow. Normally, I'd throw a pall of it over us to keep going…" He grimaced. "Not going to happen."

"So how did they trap you down here?"

His mouth twisted. "The trip out was fine. Lovely, when you sealed off the Neither, you also sealed the fae off from their powers. The realms are in complete disarray trying to figure out how to function without them. Whatever you need to do to get Aegaeus to agree to help, you need to do it fast. Fae is fading. Neara was only too happy to return with me."

Yep. My jaw was on the floor, and I blinked, like, a lot. The bug-zapper spray foam stopped them from accessing their powers? God, what the hell was it with me and unintended consequences? "Morgana wants me to kill Aegaeus."

Oh yeah, it was his turn to look like he'd gotten hit with a net full of fish. What? That shit's heavy. Ask me how I know.

"She wants you to kill him?"

"Kind of. She wants me to suck him out and leave her with all his power."

Brennan's brow knit. "Is that even possible?"

I shrugged. "Probably. I mean, I took the geas and left Connell, but I would have to do something with what I sucked, like pronto. I haven't had much time to figure out the details." And speaking of Connell, I dug out that baggie and flipped it between us.

Brennan smirked and picked it up to sniff. "But you're going to do it."

I shrugged again, watching him dig out a piece. One clusterfuck at a time. "I said I would help but didn't commit." And she was probably gonna be rip shit I hadn't texted her yet. I had a bad feeling Aegaeus was back in charge. "He was helping Stephie and spilled where the safe houses were to the normals. They raided them. Are you really gonna eat that?"

"Absolutely. I haven't had real food in ages. Everything down here is memory and isn't particularly filling." He popped the piece in his mouth, then coughed and grabbed another. "Wow, that's hot. More tender than I'd expected. If Aegaeus has betrayed Fae, then she's right, he needs to die."

"None of us would work with Her intentionally…but what if…" Look, it was seriously wishful thinking, but maybe he'd be over any potential Big-Bad-induced-temporary insanity now that She'd left town. I know, I know, but what Morgana wanted me to do just felt wrong, though if he'd done something stupid like sold Her his soul…Would he have? She'd seemed pretty versed in exactly what was and wasn't covered by the covenant, and temptation was kind of Her thing…Look, I didn't want to talk about it anymore. And yes, Brennan downing the bag of Gwinth was seriously gross, but it wasn't like I could throw stones with that one.

"So what happened on the way back?"

His Zippo flicked and he lit another cigarette, then reached over and unzipped a couple inches of the tent so I wouldn't asphyxiate. Such a gentleman. "God's other half was there, and before I knew what hit me, I was locked up in my rooms beneath the undercroft."

I raised an eyebrow, watching acid rain drip through the gap. "You have rooms?"

"They came with the position. Trust, me I wasn't happy about it, or about waking up to the ghosts of girlfriends past. Every time I closed my eyes, She'd sic a new one on me."

"Did She now?" I took off my jacket and arranged it so Mab would have a little cave, then dumped her in. Stupid pixie gave me this "Really?" look, and I ignored it. What? It'd gotten stuffy in that tent. Brennan's eyes roamed over me, and I smirked, flicking back my braids. Okay fine, I might've taken a deeper breath than was strictly necessary. My bra was totally cute.

He wet his lips, and the cigarette went out the tent flap. "She did."

I slid off his eyepatch and ran my fingers through his hair. "Anything you need to tell me?" His beard was super soft, but I couldn't decide if I liked it.

"I kissed someone."

My eyes narrowed. "Who?"

"Connell, when I thought he was you. I almost killed him."

I laughed. Like, a lot.

Brennan shook his head. "Can't say I'll miss the bastard, but he was one hell of a mimic. Too bad he couldn't get smell down."

"Oh? I smell?"

Brennan pulled me to him, his nose skating up my throat. "Mmm. You do. Like heat coming up off the sand of some exotic beach, and something else that I can never quite put my finger on…" He nipped at me, and then I was beneath him. "Whatever it is, it drives me absolutely mad."

"I really need to brush my teeth—"

"And I really don't care."

He didn't. Mab's cave became hidden in an avalanche of clothing. God, the feel of him against my skin...He kissed across my breasts, stopping to suckle, his hands kneading at my hip. I moaned, arching for him, wanting...

"Are you ready to say yes?" He murmured the question below my ear, his thumb making lazy circles over my panties.

"I never said no." His fingers teased past the side of the fabric, and I moaned.

"That's not what I asked, Lovely."

I rocked onto his fingers, my breath heavy. He chuckled, taking them away, sliding my panties down, his mouth trailing in their wake. His tongue darted out to taste me, and I gasped at the prickle of his beard. My hands buried themselves in his hair. He moaned, lapping gently, then with intensity.

His mouth was on mine again, the length of him sliding across the slick cleft of my legs. I hooked my calf over his hip. "Please..." Oh God, I wanted him. Wanted all of it. My breath caught, and he raised his face from my throat to look at me. Rested on a forearm and brushed my hair back.

"Tell me, Envy, say it. Say you want this. An us."

A tear tracked from the corner of my eye. When have I ever known—

Right then, I did. The house in the freaking suburbs, white picket fence, and even the stupid kids that came with it. They could even have a dumb dog. I wanted all of it, and I wanted it with him.

"I do, and I release you."

The fae-band slid from his finger, and then I said his name.

A groan welled up from the center of his being, and he whispered my name back to me.

I can't even describe what hearing it did to me. When he'd spoken it before, it'd laid me open, exposed who I was. This…this was what I was. Everything. Lilith and me, the new being we'd become, what we could be.

With Brennan. Our son…

An us.

Our bodies moved together, cries lost in the storm. Breath speeding, his mouth on mine, hands sliding across skin, the muscles of his back, nails scoring trails of heat. His lips raised from mine, panting, close. "Let me give you another child."

That sweet pressure was building, passion tipping, his cries twining with my own—

"Yes, oh God, yes—"

Oh yeah. Cue a conversation with the Almighty, and as I descended from those lofty heights, I caught the distinct whiff of pastrami on rye, and the impression that He was ridiculously amused.

Nope. Never a good thing.

0 Days, 0 Hours, 3 Minutes (Topside)
0 Days, 4 Hours, 35 Minutes (Hell)

"Do you think it would screw a kid up to be conceived in Hell?" I spun the fae-band turned wedding ring on my finger, feeling like a piece of me was back. Brennan was spooning behind me, trailing his fingers over my abdomen. And no, he hadn't stopped smiling since we'd done the deed.

Which one? Hmm. Good question. I'll have to get back to you on that.

"I can't imagine why it would but hope we find out." He kissed my shoulder and fumbled for his case.

The storm outside had slackened, and we needed to get moving soon. I missed Rhys, and as epic as that session had been, I'd prefer it on a mattress next time. Rocks and roots sucked. Yeah, I know, I was super prissy.

What? Oh come on, like any of that with Brennan was a huge surprise. I'd been ready to say yes to him weeks ago, and green-lighting the whole kid thing…

Look, it's not like it was gonna happen right away, and I just…It was a bunch of stuff, okay? Everything from the way Rhys looked at me, to how Brennan was with him, even stupid Peter and all his pictures. I wanted that. For me and for my son. A family. Like, a real one. I brushed at my eyes, and Brennan nuzzled behind my ear.

"Having second thoughts?"

"No...I just..." I shook my head. Ugh, why was I so afraid to say it? Yeah. Because I was chickenshit. God freaking damn it. Whatever. It wasn't like he'd leave me. I mean, him speaking my name had given him VIP access to my fucked-up train-wreck inner-self, twice. So fine, yes, I was making excuses again. Why? Because I didn't want to get hurt. Cue the applause, Envy had a breakthrough. Happy? You can send me your damn bill.

He rolled me onto my back so he could see my face. I traced the furrows in his brow. Yep, chickenshit. Whatever. I bit my lip and blurted it out, feeling totally stupid. "Before Rhys, you...nothing meant anything. It was like I was empty." God, that sounded dumb. Calista was right, maybe I should just kill myself.

"And now?"

I shrugged. "Now I'm not."

"Nor am I. We've filled each other up." He smiled, and his dimple was a mile deep when he kissed me.

Somebody smacked the tent flap. "Rain's clear, boss," Jonas said.

Brennan sighed. "Time to go."

"Oh, thank God," Mab's muffled bitching came from our pile of clothes. "Listening to you two grunt and moan was bad enough, the rest of it's enough to make me puke."

Brennan snorted, and I snagged my pants, face burning. "No one asked you to come."

"It's a good thing I did, or lover boy would've pulverized something other than your pelvis."

"Yes, and I'm in your debt, Mistress Pixie."

"I should think so." She sniffed, and I shook her out of my jacket. She landed on the ground in a puff of dust.

"Hey! Watch the wing, and your cleavage better not have slobber all over it." I rolled my eyes. Regardless, she was going in.

"Whatever's there is dry, I can assure you." Brennan grinned, buckling his belt. I glared at him. He left the tent laughing. Jerk.

Everyone was waiting outside, and the horses were back. The sky still roiled grey, but the rain had stopped. Brennan held out a hand to help me up after I had crawled out, that stupid grin still on his face. I went red again, and the Riders snickered. No lie, freaking Jonas fist-bumped him. God, I hate men.

"Is it done?" Brennan asked, lighting a cigarette.

Kennet spat to the side, eyeing Stephie standing beside him all super meek. "Aye. She won't be an issue, will ye, love?" Psh. Trust me, there was no love despite his use of the term, and she shook her head like she was going to cry.

Huh? I didn't—oh, shit. A twist of metal was around her wrist that hadn't been there before. "You banded her?"

"He did," Brennan said, exhaling a plume of smoke. "Formalities were part of the reason we stopped. Neara has released Kennet from the hunt, and he'll be returning to Hell after his affairs are in order to oversee operations. In exchange, Frank will be taking his place as her captain. Shall we?"

Brennan helped me mount, and the rest followed suit. The tent? Oh, Jonas touched it, and it condensed into this little blob of darkness. It was pretty slick. Anyways, Brennan got up behind me again, and we started out of the grove.

And yeah, I was way confused.

"How can Kennet be in charge of Hell? I mean, I know he's got that soul-control thing going on, but if the hunt released him, he's a normal—"

"He's a changeling, actually. His father, Hades, held the position previously. Persephone killed him several centuries ago and assumed his role, no doubt thinking I would step into it at some point. I find her punishment quite fitting."

Yup, I was blinking again, and it wasn't over the whole Hades bit. Let me explain. Every once in a while, a fae is born without stigmata, which means they'll never be able to fully access their powers. They still have the life span and can pass on all the genetic traits that other fae do, but remember the whole might-makes-right thing I mentioned? Yeah, they're basically chum for other fae. Most are offed right after birth. Seriously, it's considered the merciful thing to do. Screwed up, right? Except sometimes, the parents can't. When that happened, they find a normal to take the kid in, and voilà, you have a changeling.

"Jaw, Lovely. Water's not the only element big on nepotism. Kennet's clan has been in charge of Hell since its inception. He's quite capable of doing the job."

Yeah, my jaw wasn't closing, way slow on the uptake, because duh. "He's a Thanatos."

"Mmm."

Crap, that's how he knew so much about Hell. It also meant Brennan was a Thanatos, and so was Rhys. Holy shit. "Why did you affiliate with Malten?" I mean, the rest of Fae went by their matriarchal lines, but Clan Thanatos was the exception. Like, *the* exception.

Oh, sorry. Clan Thanatos isn't one on the five great dae clans, it's The Great Clan, like not just dae, but fae royalty with their own damned realm. Yeah, they owned Hell. There's four like that, Air gets Heaven, Earth gets the Core, and Water's got the Trench. It was a huge deal to be a Thanatos, and super fringe, mainly because it's entirely made up of fiends, and that whole bat-shit crazy thing doesn't make them real popular at parties. Fiends pop up in other dae clans on occasion, but it's usually a one-off. Anyways, traditionally, ugh, yeah, that word again, they stay out of dae affairs because they're busy doing things like ruling Hell or losing their shit.

Brennan shrugged. "Politics. With Kennet's ties to Thanatos obscured by his changeling status, Amelda had claim. If his affiliation had been advertised, both Kennet and I would've garnered more attention than was healthy. Most don't look past the fiend to explain my role as Death, and I can count on one hand the number who are aware I have any claim to the Thanatos name."

"Do the Riders know?"

"I should think so, they're my cousins."

I turned to look at him. "For real? Even Stewie?"

"Yes." He was totally laughing at me again. "He's Kennet's sister's son. The other three are his brother's offspring."

Okay…but…"If Kennet has siblings, why didn't they snuff Stephie when she killed their dad?"

"Because they're fiends, Lovely. Trust me, they weren't pleased to have been usurped and buried the scandal. Most of them can't keep it together long enough to finish a recipe, never mind administer Hell. Persephone was more than capable of doing so after She granted her sway over shadow."

Like She had granted powers to Kennet in exchange for his soul. I sat back against Brennan and stared out at the endless vista of sand we'd been riding through. Hell-flame flickered along its surface, and Avita's gait had changed to a loping camel-y gallop. And yes, it was way too close to being in a boat.

"Is this still the Seventh Circle?"

"It is, but not for much longer. See those two dunes there?"

I shrugged. It was all freaking dunes.

"Just past them is the Sixth. We'll be able to make up time there."

I chewed on my lip. "That's why he sold his soul, wasn't it. To be a true fae?"

"He's never said so, but I suspect that's the case. I'd ask that you keep all of that to yourself, and I'm including you in that, Mistress Pixie."

Shit, I kept forgetting about her. It was no wonder pixies always had dirt on everyone.

"I'll bargain with you for it." Her shrill little voice was smug.

"What do you desire?" Oh yeah, I wanted to smack him.

"Permanent employment, not this fly-by-night year thing she signed me up for."

"You hired her?"

I rolled my eyes. "No, I got her out of hock to the hunt because they were going to eat her, and indentured servitude was the only thing I could think of. Look it's a long story—"

"You owed me for framing me!"

"Like I said, it's a long story." I turned to jab a finger into his chest. "And if you do this, you're the one that's gonna explain it to Karen and Socks. They've met Mab and aren't impressed." Neither was I. Okay, aside from the fact that she was damned good at her job. Not that I'd ever tell her that, and at this exact moment, it was only a marginally attractive selling point.

Brennan cocked an eyebrow. "Wait, Mab…Queen of the Fairies?"

"You've heard of me?"

I snorted, and she pinched me. "Ow! Stop that or I will drop your ass. No, you know what? I'm gonna squish you, and that'll be the end of it." Literally. No way was I listening to her bitching in perpetuity.

"Yeah? Do it, I dare you. My shade will laugh itself sick watching you try to keep track of poofing babies."

My hand froze mid-slap, and I broke out in a cold sweat. "They poof?"

"God, how stupid are you? Any kids you have are gonna be fae, duh."

Brennan chuckled.

Man, I hated him sometimes. "But I thought…" Okay, I'll be honest, I don't know what the hell I'd thought, but that wasn't part of it. It had to be a joke. She was totally full of shit, and I wasn't gonna think about it.

"Will room and board, along with a stipend, suffice?"

I could hear the smile in Brennan's voice, and it seriously pissed me off. How was he amused by this? I tried to remember everywhere I'd taken the little bastard. How many places could he possibly end up?

"What kind of a stipend are we talking about?"

"We can discuss the particulars later. We're just about through the circle. Are we agreed? Permanent employment in exchange for your undying loyalty to Envy, myself, and our offspring, which includes silence on all matters discussed whilst in Hell and anything of a personal nature and/or potentially damaging to the parties just mentioned going forward. Agreed?"

"Agreed." Mab poked me. "You know, he's much better at bargaining than you are."

"Oh my God, shut up," I muttered, not knowing whether to laugh or cry. What had I signed up for? And I said I wanted another kid? I was out of my goddamned mind. Brennan tried to kiss me, and I elbowed him in the gut. Asshole laughed.

Avita rounded the last of the dunes. They ended abruptly at a thick fieldstone wall, topped with a filigreed fence of flaking iron. Beyond it was a cemetery with row upon row of aboveground tombs, New Orleans style. Some were the size of doghouses, and others big enough for a family of four to live in comfortably. I mean, if those black hell-flames weren't pouring out of them. The screams from the shades trapped inside definitely made me think they weren't enjoying a movie night.

"The Sixth Circle's Flaming Tombs of Hersey," Brennan said.

"Customer service counter?"

"Now you're getting the hang of it." Avita's form shrank and hardened, and we were back on the motorcycle. He revved the engine, and we were off at breakneck speed. As we took the first corner, he swore. I glanced back, my stomach sinking. The hell-flame we'd passed had bloomed crimson, lapping at the stone.

Crap. "I didn't do anything!"

"I think you being here is enough, Lovely. We need to expedite this." He put on another burst of speed and rounded a corner, bending me low over the gas tank, his knee brushing the flagstones. I screamed, and that manic laugh burbled from him, his lips split in a feral grin.

"Short cut."

Like hell it was. I swear the jerk was scaring me on purpose. He zipped around another corner, and then another, weaving between the tombs. I lost count and all sense of direction trying not to piss myself. Flames followed in our wake, the cries of the shades frantic.

"Hold on—" He angled toward a fallen slab of marble, and we were airborne.

We were also abruptly wet. What? I was terrified and it was his own damned fault.

The bike hit the ground, and he skidded it to a stop, breathing hard. I turned and slugged him. "Don't you ever do that to me again!"

He laughed and rubbed at his jaw. "Duly noted. That's not particularly comfortable, is it?"

I glared at him, and he laughed again, getting off and brushing at his pants. I looked around and my stomach sank. You gotta be…

Brennan's Zippo snicked. "Fifth Circle, Anger."

It wasn't a freaking circle, it was a goddamned moat. We'd come out by a rickety dock, the pilings rotted and wrapped with slime-covered ropes. Far off on the other shore was its twin, and in between the two, the water surged, shades thrashing about. I slumped, then bolted upright at the howl of dogs. Like, seriously big dogs. Brennan looked in the direction it'd come from, pursing his lips.

"Think he's gonna be a problem?" Jonas asked, rolling his bike up alongside us.

"Everything else has been. You see Phlegyas?"

"Nope, and his boat's gone, too."

Brennan blew out a long stream of smoke. "So are a fair number of shades that should be in these waters." He grimaced and looked back at the other Riders. Those howls were coming closer, and none of them were as enthusiastic as they'd been about the harpies. No way was that a good sign.

Jonas motioned for Stephie to get off the bike, then he pushed it to the water. Where it touched, the wheel flattened and widened out until a boat bobbed in the shallows beside the dock.

Oh God, please, no…

"Off you go, Lovely. You don't want to touch the water. This is the river Styx, and I'd hate to see what would happen when you get truly angry."

Angry? Try horrified. I stood trembling. "Can't we fly over? In Daemon form, plane, hot air balloon?" Christ, anything but a boat…

"Unfortunately, no. That's the only way to get across." Jonas and Stephie were already motoring across the river, with Frank and Neara right behind them. Stupid Sal was waiting on the dock. He saw my grimace and blew me a kiss before jumping into the boat with Kennet and Stewie. Asshole.

"God, I hate him."

"Who, the fish?" Brennan asked, pushing the bike.

"Who else? I'm gonna set him up with Morgana. They'll be perfectly miserable together."

Brennan snorted, easing his bike into the water until a stupid dingy bobbed on the choppy water in its place. I bit my lip trying not to cry. He pulled me close and kissed the top of my head. "Sooner begun, sooner done, yes?"

"I hate you, too."

He grinned. "I know, it's one of the things I love about—shit." His eye had focused on something over my shoulder, and he clutched me tightly when I went to turn.

"Don't. I want you to walk very slowly to the dock and get into the boat."

Nails clicked on the flagstones behind me, and the scythe appeared in his hand, snicking open. He inched to the side, pushing me past him, his gaze locked on what was over my shoulder. A low rumble started, and this time the ground had nothing to do with it.

You know I had to look.

And I was totally sorry I did. If you were expecting me to see that monstrous three-headed dog, Cerberus, you'd be spot on.

If you're not familiar, think something between an Irish wolf hound and a rabid St. Bernard, but like a bajillion times bigger. Claws as thick as my thigh, paws that could crush a VW bus, and the rest of him? Look, he was freaking massive, scary as hell, and his heads were dipped, shoulders bunching with hackles high.

I should've waited to piss myself. He took a creeping step forward, bright red gums raised over his canines. Long stands of saliva dripped from his jaw, and where it hit the flagstones, smoke hissed up. I took a step toward the dock, and one of the heads focused on me. God, its eyes…yellow and horrible, and trust me, it hated.

Brennan flicked away his cigarette and raised his scythe, gripping it in both hands, his form bubbling black shadow. "Don't run, Lovely. Walk slowly. He won't get past me." Crazy bastard walked out to meet the damned thing like he was at a presser.

I swallowed the lump in my throat and took another step. The head that'd been watching me growled, and another's eyes flicked to me. My heart was going gangbusters. Another step, and I was at the first piling.

Out on the water, Jonas had made the far shore. The others were about halfway across. They stared back at us but kept going. I took a deep breath. If they weren't worried, I shouldn't be, right?

My foot touched the dock and from behind me came a furious gnashing. I spun, landing on my butt and skittering backward across the moldering wood. Cerberus had lunged, and Brennan had released the fiend.

Tenebrious, a shadow with form, darker than midnight, licked by black flame. Shadows writhed around him, the flagstones hoary with frost. Wings of carmine and candlelight splayed as he slugged one of the heads, snapping it back. Another came for him, and he swung his scythe. Cerberus howled and jerked back— Well, two-thirds of him did. The other third flew off and splashed into the river.

Brennan fell to a knee, and instead of getting the hell out of Dodge, that freaking monster doubled down, rip shit. It growled, crouching to spring, and my stomach twisted. Why wasn't Brennan getting up? It had to be some ploy…

Cerberus sprang—

Shit, it wasn't.

I screamed, and when I did, the last of what I'd taken from the banshee came pouring out.

Like, all of it, and it went with a shit ton of my own angst. Let me tell you, it was freaky. I could literally see the air ripple back as wave after wave of sound sped outward, bursting through Brennan's shadows. The waves hit that stupid dog square in the chest and tore it asunder. Its rib cage shattered, gore and viscera splattering outward like a 747 had hit it and kept going, dragging the remains after it, and leaving a bloody smear as long and as wide as the line for security at LAX during Christmas break.

The ground quaked, tombs crumbled, and true fire exploded from the Sixth Circle. Shades screamed and then—poof—silence, save for the river's surging waters sending white caps to smash against the shore and the crackle of flame.

I ran to Brennan. He was covered in that weird goo from our powers colliding. The fiend had faded, and he'd dropped to sit, flicking the nasty stuff from his face. The goo looked different here…less like ectoplasm and more, I dunno, ethereal. It soaked into where it'd landed instead of hardening, which was good thing for Brennan. I mean, it had to be better than ending up like a bug in amber, didn't it? Whatever. He didn't seem overly concerned about it, but then shock will do that to a person.

His hand shook as he lit a cigarette. I kneeled beside him, pushing back his hair. He'd gone pale, but aside from that, looked better than he had, despite being covered in ghostly snot.

"Do you know how hard it is to find a three-headed dog?"

Seriously? "You cut off one of its heads."

He shrugged, running a thumb over his palm where the goo had soaked in. "It would've grown another, but there's no coming back from that." He looked from the bloody smear to the ruins of the Sixth Circle and sighed.

We sat in silence while he smoked.

"You okay?" Yeah, I was asking again, and the answer was pretty obvious, but it's one of those things you have to do or you feel like an asshole. Trust me, I was already in that camp.

"I've been better. Shall we?" We stood to leave, but after a step or two, he paused looking down. Took a step back. Forward. Did it again. I raised an eyebrow waiting for him to shake it all about. "That goo…Did it land here?"

I shrugged. "Probably. It was wherever your shadow was when that blast went through it." He grabbed my hand and pulled me to the outskirts of the Sixth Circle. I winced. It wasn't any better up close.

"I want you to do it again. Ah, that tomb there. Let me go first, and then try to match what I'm putting out." He set out a spate of shadow to the ruin, and I followed it with a burst of power. Goo splatted over it like a firehose of snot, and I'll be damned if the freaking thing didn't reform as it sucked the stuff up.

Brennan sagged against me, and I staggered under his weight. "Well, that's promising. Whatever that is seems to be shoring up the damage to the circle."

Too bad we'd need a billion gallons of the stuff to fix the rest of Hell. I snorted, and he sighed, kissing the top of my head and limping to the boat. It was slow going. Even though I could tell he was trying not to lean on me, he did, and the man was freaking heavy.

"Sorry I broke Hell and killed your dog."

He laughed. "My God, Lovely. Hercules could barely capture the damned beast, and you smeared it across the pavement like cake frosting. The clan is going to adore you. Here, let me get in first, and I'll help you down." He clambered into the stupid boat, widening his stance as it bobbed. I was gonna puke just watching him.

"I have to meet them?"

He looked up at me with that freaking dimple in his wan cheek. "Yes, and I'm rather excited about showing off my wife and son."

I rolled my eyes. Because meeting the rest of his family had gone so well. He offered me his hand, and I took the stupid thing, shuddering as I clunked into the watery death trap.

And yeah, the trip across was awful. I puked up everything I'd ever eaten and then dry heaved more. By the time we got to the opposite shore, I was curled up in the bottom of the boat wishing I had let that freaking dog eat him for making me get into the damned dinghy.

It thumped onto dry land, and I moaned.

"Help me with her, Jonas?"

Strong arms lifted me up, and I retched.

"Easy, Miss Kitty, I got you. You good, boss? Don't look real great back there."

"It's not, and I'll be better when we're topside. Settle her into the sidecar. Do we have one of those blankets…"

They kept talking, and I kept feeling miserable. I can't tell you what the Fourth Circle was all about, or the Third, other than wet, cold, and I felt like a drowned rat after it. I huddled in the blanket just wanting to go home and snuggle with Rhys. I mean, I guess we were on our way, but it was taking way too freaking long. Like, you'd think it was a road trip with Gaia. Shut up, I didn't cry. Not much at least.

We slowed again, then came to a stop. The wind had picked up, and I tucked back the loose tendrils of hair tickling my cheeks. Yeah, I was a frickin' mess.

"How you wanna play this one?" Jonas asked. "If it's as empty as the others…"

Brennan sighed and scratched at his beard. I'd decided I didn't like it. A close shave was way sexier on him.

Yeah, I was feeling better.

"The winds will still be an issue." He glanced down at me, his face drawn with exhaustion. "Do you think you can ride with me, Lovely?"

I said I could, and Jonas helped me up onto Avita when she'd gone all horse again.

Brennan kissed the nape of my neck and held me close. "Almost home."

The Second Circle of Hell was Lust. You'd think that would've been my jam, and maybe it would've been if I'd been feeling better. I mean, I didn't feel like I was gonna die anymore, but I had just puked my brains out and another round wasn't too far off every time I moved my head the wrong way. Avita's gait wasn't helping, and I could feel that weird pinched-nerve thing behind my right eye that always signaled a migraine was imminent.

Brennan was just beat to shit. Goo or no goo, calling shadow had taken it out of him, and however long it'd been since then hadn't improved the situation. I leaned back against him, eyes slitted against the wind. It blew in vicious gusts across a landscape of barren stone, whipping ash and anything lighter than a golf ball at us like it had a vendetta. My skin stung, and I was tempted to take off my boots. What? My heels could use some exfoliating; it was sandal season topside.

Anyways, there wasn't a shade in sight. Like none. Probably not ideal, but neither was that whole lust thing. Neara ended up in Frank's lap grinding on him, and thank God she was in skinny jeans. Those things are impossible to get off on solid ground, never mind when they were soaking wet from the last circle and moving at a gallop. His apparently weren't subject to the same restrictions, and some serious X-rated Cirque du Sexcapades went down.

Yeah, let's just say I saw way more of Frank than was cool. Anywho—Kennet, Stewie, and Sal were having problems of their own, in that order. As much as Stewie would have loved to be the happy Pierre, the other two weren't down with it. Must've made for an uncomfortable ride.

Jonas? Jonas hated Stephie, and Stephie hated him. Like, almost falling off the back of the horse hated him. Yeah, I was pretty sure everyone was sick and tired of Hell. Well, maybe not Frank, but he was definitely in the minority.

"Are we there yet?"

Brennan smiled against my ear and pointed. Faint pinpoints of light studded the horizon, and then the darker outline of buildings resolved from the micro-peel we were getting. Seven towers, to be exact.

"Limbo's just up ahead, and the gate to Tainaron's in the lower ward of the city."

We clattered beneath a wide stone arch onto cobblestones not too long afterward. Limbo wasn't bombed out like the Seventh Circle had been. It was more like something out of a penny dreadful. What? I told you I read. Those cheap serials from the 1850s are classics. I mean, who doesn't want to read about Spring-heeled Jack and Sweeney Todd? Whatever. Think creepy Victorian London, all smog-filled streets and skittering rats. They seemed to be the only things hanging around the place.

Yeah, it was probably a problem, but one I didn't feel like dwelling on. I just wanted to go home.

Brennan made for a low tunnel at the back of an

alley. "Don't look back," he murmured in my ear.

I shot him a glare. I hadn't wanted to until he said it. I focused between the stupid horse's ears, fighting temptation. A freaky green glow came from its eyes, lighting our path. We were moving upward through a series of caverns, the echo of our mount's hooves clattering loud on stone. Ever so slowly, the texture of the air shifted and things smelled more alive. Yeah, even in the bowels of a nasty cave. Bats, fungus, bugs. Hey, I didn't say it smelled good, but honestly, after having all that ash and grit up my nose, it didn't smell bad.

Ahead the rock split and beyond it, stars.

I did cry then.

We came out topside on a desolate beach, water sedately lapping at the shore. Brennan took a deep breath and got off Avita. He held his arms out for me, and I slid into them. His grip felt stronger than it had been, like being up here had given him something back. He smiled at me and then turned to the guys.

"Brunch tomorrow at the estate. We have things to discuss." They grunted and poofed away in twos and threes. "Shall we collect our son and go home?"

God, there was nothing I wanted to do more.

0 Days, 0 Hours, 0 Minutes

Dan and Gaia were standing in the kitchen arguing when we poofed into her living room. The clock on the stove blinked behind them. Her eyes narrowed at me with that flat frog look of hers. Great. What did I do now? She sniffed, snagging a steaming pot of pasta from the burner, and went to drain it, all pissy. Whatever. I made for Rhys.

She slammed the empty pot onto the counter. "Tell me you didn't have anything to do with that."

"Huh?" I scooped the little bastard up, and he squealed, all giggles as I pretended to eat his toes.

"Power went out," Dan said plopping back in front of the TV to catch the end of his movie. He glanced at his watch, then at Brennan. "For eleven minutes, 'bout how long she woulda been down there."

I did a double take at the time, then made a beeline for the fridge. Eleven freaking minutes? No, we'd been gone—Whatever, the math wasn't important, but did explain how Brennan's beard had grown in so thick, and yeah, that revelation called for alcohol. And an antacid. Brennan scratched at his jaw, looking grim. I snagged a bottle and cracked the cap.

Gaia was still waiting for an answer.

"Umm…no?" Shut up. Maybe I didn't have anything to do with it. I mean, it's not like she could prove it. Plausible deniability and all that.

She cocked an eyebrow, adding sauce to the noodles. "The abrupt dormancy of my volcanos coinciding with the outage must have been a coincidence then."

Okay, maybe she could. I downed half my beer, sweating. "Stranger things've happened. They online now?"

"Mmm. Same time as the power."

I ignored her glare, eyeing dinner. Hope she'd made extra, I was starving. Oh yeah, it was totally homemade. She didn't trust anything that came in a can...or Brennan, apparently.

"Is our bargain concluded, dae?"

He extracted himself from his thoughts and came over digging into a pocket. "It is." He placed a single seed on the counter, and she snapped it up like it was the Hope Diamond.

"What's that do?" I asked her, cracking another bottle.

"Grow."

I rolled my eyes. No shit, Sherlock. Brennan came over, and his hands trembled as he plucked Rhys from my arms. Little bastard screamed bloody freaking murder. I teared up at Brennan's expression. Like happy and sad all at the same time.

"It's that fuzz on your face," Gaia said, catching it too. "Babies can't differentiate like that."

"Another reason to lose the damned thing then." He crooned a few bars in Cymric, and the wail subsided to a suspicious sniffle. "My God, he's gotten so—ow!"

I laughed and detangled Rhys's sticky little fingers from Brennan's beard. It was harder than you'd think, and the kid thought it was hysterical, flashing that dimple of his. Brennan's thumb ran over it, all teary eyed.

"Can we get on with this?" Mab's voice bitched up from my cleavage. "Not that I don't love being bathed in boob sweat."

Goddamn it, I'd forgotten she was there again. I picked her out and set her on the counter, where she began to regale the other two on everything that'd gone down. Spoiler, she totally saved the day, and we all would have died without her. She got even cockier when Gaia fixed her wing. I snagged another beer. Trust me, I needed it.

Gaia handed me a plate, all pensive. "Do you really think She was influencing Aegaeus?"

"I think it's more plausible than not, considering how weird he's been acting, and if he really did sell Her his soul...I didn't bargain for the ones She had, just to add ours to the covenant. Regardless, I don't think I can do what Morgana's asking me to. I mean, short of sticking him back in a droplet." Yeah, not gonna happen. I didn't care if he really was bat-shit, that was just wrong. But I couldn't not do something either. I just didn't know what. Or how I was gonna break the news to Morgana. God, I felt like an asshole.

"Mmm." Gaia started making up another plate. "All things happen as they should...Well, unless you're involved. What are you going to tell him?" Her eyes were on my ring, and I knew she was talking about the All Father.

Crap. That was another big fat I-don't-know, and an even bigger I-don't-want-to-think-about-it. "Kyle will understand."

Her lips pursed like she wanted to say something about that but didn't. Thank you, Jesus. "I still can't believe you killed Cerberus. Do you know how rare three-headed dogs are?"

"So I've been told, and I didn't do it on purpose."

"Rarely anything you do is."

She had me there. I plopped onto a stool at the counter and started scarfing down pasta. OMG. I'd never tasted anything so frickin' good.

"Meatballs, dae?"

"Extra, if you don't mind." Brennan wrapped up whatever he and Dan had been talking about and joined me at the counter, settling Rhys on his lap. "Now, tell me about these hearings." She ignored his request and served him, then delivered Dan a plate.

He took it, retrieving the remote and flicking from the scrolling movie credits to CNN. "I told you, man—"

We all turned at the screaming. What the hell…

Crap. It was Hell. As in shades were running riot over the planet. My fork clanked onto my plate. The screen flashed from Bombay to Boston and everywhere in between. The dead were returning to their last known residences or wherever else they'd frequented, taking umbrage with the current occupants. Normals were freaking out and being displaced by the hundreds of thousands.

Yep, a zombie apocalypse will do that, and the sidebar about everything fire and/or spark dependent on the planet snuffing out for eleven minutes made me feel like even more of an asshole. Shit. Massive blackouts, planes falling from the sky, medical devices going kaput, and—

You gotta be…Those fucking cult members from the Our Lady of the Blessed Inferno bus tour had released footage of me vaporizing Crest-kin and issued a statement that I had opened the fiery doors of Hell in response to the Senate's inquest. Yeah, they were basically saying bow down or feel my wrath. God, I thought followers were supposed to bring you a fatted calf or some shit, not throw you to the wolves.

I couldn't freaking win.

"On the plus side, I'm imagining that biometrics legislation will fall by the wayside after this." Brennan chuckled around a mouthful.

I glared at him, and he shrugged, handing Rhys a noodle. I snatched it. "You can't give him that. Seriously? That's what you're worried about? I broke Hell, and it spilled into this realm!"

"Look at you all mama bear. He's fine."

I growled and Brennan chuckled again, dangling another noodle over Rhys's nose getting him all saucy.

Hmm? Of course the kid loved it. I rolled my eyes. Whatever. If it killed the little bastard, that was on him.

Brennan smiled. "And everything else will work out as well. I'll call a clan moot. I doubt any of them remained in Fae. With them and your assistance, we should be able to repair Hell with that goo, then Kennet can use the Horn of Solomon to call the shades back."

"Psh." Dan snorted. "If Edna remembers where she put it."

Brennan scratched his jaw again. "I'll get the imps on it. Her manse is due a purge—"

"Good fucking luck with that," Dan said totally not buying it.

Edna? I looked between them and crossed my arms under my boobs. Brennan noticed, and for once, that wasn't the point. "Do I want to know?"

His lips twitched upward. "Edna's our great-aunt

and a bit of a hoarder."

Dan barked out a laugh, muttering something under his breath.

Brennan frowned. "I'm not saying it'll be easy, but it's not unsurmountable. Especially if she's distracted." He dangled another noodle, and Rhys batted at it. The last one was smushed in the kid's ear. Both of them grinned the same crooked grin. God, it was hard to be bitchy when they were so freaking adorable together.

I still tried, attempting to channel my inner Morgana. "And the veil?"

"I'm curious to see how that plays out with Her finger out of the pie…Worst case, I suspect we can evacuate Fae through the Underworld. Again, nothing that's unsurmountable."

Yup, he totally looked like he had a handle on the entire shit show and wasn't even breaking a sweat. Unbelievable. "How do you do that?"

Brennan paused his dangling, and Rhys snagged the stupid noodle, smearing it all over his head and giggling like a fiend. Probably because he was one. "Do what?"

"Make everything so freaking, ugh, I don't know—like, boom, there ya go."

"S'why he's the boss," Dan said, bringing up his plate for a refill. "Man'll have things square by this time next week."

"Normals may take longer, but without Stephie riling them, I don't anticipate it being an issue."

Dan grunted at me like, see?

I rolled my eyes.

He smirked. "There more?" Gaia refilled his plate, and he leaned against the counter, stabbing a meatball. "Man sets his mind to something, it gets done. Though

I'll admit, you took a lot longer to lock down than I'd bet. Jonas made a mint off me, the bastard. So what we looking at, June wedding?"

Brennan nodded, finishing his mouthful. "The caterer I've been eyeing has availability at the end of the month. Midsummer's seems apropos."

"The spring blooms will be gone, and summer's not quite proliferate," Gaia mused, "but I can move things a week or two in either direction, depending on your colors. And whatever you're envisioning putting me in, don't. I'll have something made to coordinate."

"You really expect me to plan a freaking wedding with all of that going on?" I waved at the TV, the screen was showing a close up of refugees pouring out of New York. So much for visiting the Big Apple anytime soon.

"Not at all. I told you I'd handle the details," Brennan said, pushing his plate in front of Rhys and lighting a cigarette sans Zippo, all cucumber calm. "But I would appreciate it if you played along. A fae wedding is just the shiny thing to distract the normals while we sort the rest. Consider it recompense for killing my dog." I scowled, and the asshole smiled, his dimples two miles deep.

So, remember when I'd been considering selling Rhys to the circus? Check that. I was already in the big tent and had signed up to marry the damned ringmaster. I sighed, listening to a matched set of manic giggles as our son manhandled the remains of his dinner. Little bastard was head to toe disgusting and the happiest I'd ever seen him. Both he and Brennan were, and it was weird, but so was I.

You know I couldn't say no.

Yep, this was my circus, and they were definitely

my monkeys. And just like that, things were good.

Well, except for the whole zombie-apocalypse, getting-married thing, but that's another story.

A word about the author…

AK Nevermore writes dark SFF romance and urban fantasy. On the side, she enjoys operating heavy machinery, freebases coffee, and gives up sarcasm for Lent every year. A Jane-of-all-trades, she's a certified chef, restores antiques, and dabbles in beekeeping when she's not reading voraciously or running down the dream in her beat-up camo Chucks.

Unable to ignore the voices in her head, and unwilling to become medicated, she writes about dark worlds, perversely irreverent and profound, and always entertaining. She pays the bills by wielding a wicked hot pink editing pen and writing a regular column on SFF. Very active in the writing community, she volunteers her spare time amongst a handful of industry organizations, teaches creative writing, and on the rare occasion, sleeps.

You can read all about her and Mr. Nevermore hanging out on the East Coast with their kids, a cat, and far too many chickens at aknevermore.com.

Thank you for purchasing
this publication of The Wild Rose Press, Inc.

For questions or more information
contact us at
info@thewildrosepress.com.

The Wild Rose Press, Inc.
www.thewildrosepress.com

Milton Keynes UK
Ingram Content Group UK Ltd.
UKHW022342200824
447185UK00013B/404